Maybe Not
&
Maybe Now

Also by Colleen Hoover

Slammed Series

Slammed

Point of Retreat

This Girl

Hopeless Series

Hopeless

Losing Hope

Finding Cinderella

Finding Perfect

Maybe Someday Series

Maybe Someday

Maybe Not

Maybe Now

It Ends with Us Series

It Ends with Us

It Starts with Us

Stand-alones

Ugly Love

Confess

November 9

Without Merit

All Your Perfects

Too Late

Regretting You

Heart Bones

Layla

Verity

Reminders of Him

Also by Colleen Hoover and Tarryn Fisher

Never Never: The Complete Series

About the Author

Colleen Hoover is the #1 *Sunday Times* bestselling author of more than twenty-three novels, including *It Ends with Us*, *All Your Perfects*, *Ugly Love* and *Verity*. Colleen lives in Texas with her husband and their three boys.

For more information, please visit colleenhoover.com.

Maybe Not & Maybe Now

Colleen Hoover

SIMON & SCHUSTER

London · New York · Amsterdam/Antwerp · Sydney/Melbourne · Toronto · New Delhi

First published as a bind-up edition in Great Britain by Simon & Schuster UK Ltd, 2026

Maybe Not first published in Great Britain by Simon & Schuster UK Ltd, 2023.
Originally published in the United States by Atria Books, an imprint of
Simon & Schuster, LLC, 2014

Maybe Now first published in Great Britain by Simon & Schuster UK Ltd, 2022.
Originally published in the United States by Colleen Hoover, 2018

1 3 5 7 9 10 8 6 4 2

Simon & Schuster UK Ltd, 7th Floor,
199 Bishopsgate, London EC2M 3TY

Simon & Schuster Australia, Sydney
Simon & Schuster India, New Delhi

www.simonandschuster.co.uk
www.simonandschuster.com.au
www.simonandschuster.co.in

The authorised representative in the EEA is Simon & Schuster Netherlands BV,
Herculesplein 96, 3584 AA Utrecht, Netherlands. info@simonandschuster.nl

A CIP catalogue record for this book
is available from the British Library

Paperback ISBN: 978-1-3985-6788-7
eBook ISBN: 978-1-3985-6789-4

Printed and Bound in the UK using 100% Renewable Electricity
at CPI Group (UK) Ltd

FSC www.fsc.org
MIX
Paper | Supporting
responsible forestry
FSC® C013604

To Kendall Smith, one of my very best friends.
You've been by my side since we were kids, and I couldn't do any of this without you.

Maybe Not

Chapter One

I'm convinced that hell has an intercom system and the buzz of my alarm clock is played at full volume on repeat against the screams of all the lost souls.

Which is why I'll never murder anyone, because there's no way I can live with this sound for eternity. I can't even live with it for five seconds.

I reach over and stop the alarm, dreading another day at work. I hate that I have to keep this shitty barista job just to pay for school. At least Ridge lets my sporadic rent checks slide in exchange for my managing his band. It works for now, but *God, I hate mornings.*

I stretch my arms, bring my hands to my eyes, and begin rubbing the sleep out of them. When my fingers meet my eyes, for a split second I think maybe my worst fears have come true and I'm actually burning in hell, because *SHIT! Motherfucker! I'm going to kill him!*

"Ridge!" I scream.

Oh, God. It burns.

I stand up and attempt to open my eyes, but they're stinging too badly for them to be of any use. It's the oldest prank in the book, and I can't believe I fell for it. *Again.*

I can't find my shorts—*God, it hurts so bad*—so I stumble my way to the bathroom in order to wash the pepper juice from my eyes and hands. I find the doorknob and swing the door open, rushing straight to the sink. I'm pretty sure I hear a girl screaming, but that very well could be *me* screaming.

I cup my hands beneath the stream of water and bring them up to my eyes, rinsing them over and over until the burn starts to subside. Once my eyes begin to feel relief, my shoulder starts to ache from the repeated blows being delivered to it.

"Get out, you pervert!"

I'm awake enough now to know that I actually did hear a girl screaming, and now that girl is hitting me. In *my* bathroom.

I grab a hand towel and press it to my eyes while I shield her punches with my elbow.

"I was peeing, you sick bastard! Get out!"

Shit, she hits hard. I still can't really see her, but I can recognize fists when they're flying at me. I grab both of her wrists to keep her from assaulting me even more.

"Stop hitting me!" I yell.

The bathroom door that leads to the living room swings open and my left eye is working enough that I can tell Brennan is standing there. "What the hell is going on?" He walks toward us and removes my hands from her wrists and then stands between us. I bring the towel back to my eyes and squeeze them shut.

"He barged in on me while I was peeing!" the girl yells. "And he's naked!"

I open one eye and glance down. I am, in fact, completely naked.

"Jesus, Warren. Put on some clothes," Brennan says.

"How was I supposed to know I'd be attacked in my own bathroom?" I say, pointing at her. "Why the hell is she using my bathroom, anyway? Your guests can use *your* bathroom."

Brennan immediately holds up two defensive palms. "She didn't spend the night with me."

"Gross," the girl mutters.

I don't know why Ridge thought it would be a good idea to rent a four-bedroom apartment. Even though one of the bedrooms is empty, that's still two people too many. Especially when guests spend the night and don't know about the designated bathrooms.

"Look," I say, pushing both of them toward the door that leads to the living room. "This is my bathroom and I'd like to use it. I don't care where she slept or who she slept with; she can use your bathroom. This one's mine."

Brennan holds up a finger and turns to face me. "Actually," he says, "this is a *shared* bathroom. With *that* bedroom." He points to the door that leads to the other bedroom. "And that bedroom now belongs to . . ." He points to the girl. "Bridgette. Your new roommate."

I pause.

Why did he just call her my roommate?

"What do you mean, *roommate*? No one asked me if I wanted a new roommate."

Brennan shrugs. "You rarely pay rent, Warren. You don't really have a say in who lives here."

He knows I don't pay rent because I help manage their band, but Ridge does take on the brunt of the financial expenses. He makes a good point, unfortunately.

This isn't good. I can't share a bathroom with a girl.

Especially a girl with that good of an arm. And especially a girl with all that bronzed skin.

I look away from her. I hate that she's hot. I hate that she's a brunette, because I really like her long, light brown hair and the way it's pulled back, all messy and shit.

Dammit!

"Well, this has been a really fun bonding moment," Bridgette says, walking toward me. She shoves my shoulders, pushing me back toward my bedroom. "Now wait your turn, *Roomie*."

The bathroom door closes in my face and I'm standing in my room again. Still naked. And maybe a little emasculated.

"You can leave, too," I hear her say to Brennan, right before the door to the living room slams shut. Seconds later, the water begins running in the shower.

She's in the shower.

My shower.

She's probably taking off her shirt right now, tossing it on the floor, pulling her panties down over her hips.

I'm fucked.

My apartment is my sanctuary. My man cave. The only place I can go where my life isn't ruled by women. My boss is a woman, all my professors are women, my sister and my mother are both women. Once Bridgette steps into my shower and makes it her own with all her girly shampoos and razors and shit, I'm screwed. That's *my* shower.

I walk to Ridge's bedroom and flip the light switch a couple of times to give him warning that I'm coming in, since he's deaf and can't hear me knocking or stomping toward his room like a kid about to tattle on his little brother.

I flip the switch two more times and then swing his door open. He's lifting up onto his elbows, groggy-eyed. He sees the anger on my face and he begins to laugh, incorrectly assuming I'm here about the pepper-juice prank.

I hate that I fell for it. I'm such a deep sleeper though, and he gets me every damn time.

"That prank was stupid," I sign to him. "But I'm not here because of that. We need to talk."

He sits up in bed and reaches over to tilt his alarm clock so that he can check the time. He looks back at me, agitated. "It's six-thirty in the morning," he signs. "What the hell do you want to talk about at six-thirty in the morning?"

I point in the direction of the new roommate's bedroom.

Bridgette.

I hate her name.

"You let a *girl* move in?" I make the sign for roommate and continue. "Why in the world would you let a *girl* move in with us?"

Ridge makes the sign for Brennan's name. "That's all him. I don't think he would have accepted no for an answer."

I laugh. "Since when are girls important to Brennan?"

"I heard that," Brennan says from behind me. "*And* saw you sign it."

I face him. "Good. So answer the question."

He glares at me and then looks at Ridge. "Go back to sleep. I'll handle the five-year-old." He motions for me to follow him into the living room, turning out Ridge's bedroom light as he exits.

I like Brennan, but the fact that we've known each other for so long makes me feel like he's my little brother sometimes. My *annoying-as-fuck* little brother. My little brother who thinks moving his women into our apartment is a good idea.

"It's just for a few months," Brennan says, continuing toward the kitchen. "She's in a rough spot and needs a place to stay."

I follow Brennan into the kitchen. "Since when did you start providing rescue homes? You don't even let girls spend the night when you're done with them, much less move in with you. Are you in love with her or something? Because if that's the case, this is the stupidest decision you've ever made. You'll get tired of her in a week, and then what?"

Brennan faces me and calmly holds up a finger. "I told you earlier, it's not like that. We aren't together and we never will be together. But she's important to me and she's in a tough spot and we're going to help her, okay?" He takes a bottle of water out of the fridge and opens the cap. "It won't be that bad. She's in school and works full-time, so she'll hardly ever be here. You won't even notice."

I groan, frustrated, and run my hands down my face. "This is great," I mumble. "The last thing I need right now is some chick taking over my entire bathroom."

Brennan rolls his eyes and begins walking back toward his bedroom. "It's a *bathroom*, Warren. You're acting like a little shit."

"She *hit* me!" I say in defense.

Brennan turns and cocks an eyebrow. "See what I mean?" He walks into his bedroom and closes the door behind him.

The water turns off in the shower, and I hear the curtain slide open. As soon as the door to her bedroom shuts, I walk toward the bathroom. *My* bathroom. I try to open the door from the living room, but it's locked from the inside. I walk through my bedroom and check that door, but it's locked, too. I walk out of my room, straight into her bedroom. My eyes catch a glimpse of her before she screams and pulls a towel in front of her.

"What the hell are you *doing*?"

She picks up a shoe and tosses it at me. It hits me in the shoulder, but I don't even flinch. I ignore her and walk into the bathroom and slam the door shut. I lean against it, lock it behind me, and then close my eyes.

Dammit, she's hot.

Why does she have to be hot?

And I know it was just a glimpse but . . . she shaves. *Everywhere.*

It's bad enough I have to share a bathroom with a girl, but now I have to share it with a *hot* girl? A hot girl who has a severe mean streak? A hot girl with a sick tan and hair so long and thick, it covers up her breasts when it's wet, and *shit, shit, shit.*

I hate Brennan. I hate Ridge. I also love them for doing this to me.

Maybe having her for a roommate could be a good thing.

"Hey, asshole!" she yells through the door. "I used all the hot water. Have fun."

Maybe not.

I walk to Brennan's room and swing open the door. He's packing a suitcase and doesn't even look at me when I stalk over to him.

"What now?" he asks, annoyed.

"I need to ask you something and I need you to be completely honest with me."

He sighs and turns to face me. "What is it?"

"Have you slept with her?"

He looks at me like I'm an idiot. "I already told you no."

I hate that he's acting so mature and calm about this situation, because my reaction is making me feel really immature. Brennan has always been the immature one. Since the moment I met Ridge . . . *God, how long ago was that? Ten years? I'm twenty-four, Brennan's twenty-one . . . yeah. Ten years.* I've been best friends with them for a decade, and this is the first time I've actually felt inferior to Brennan.

I don't like it. *I'm* the responsible one. Well, not as responsible as Ridge, obviously, but no one is. I do manage Brennan's band, and I do a hell of a good job of it, so why can't I seem to control my reactions right now?

Because. I know myself, and if I can't get rid of the new roommate right away, then I'll more than likely become infatuated with her. And if I'll be infatuated with her, I need to make sure Brennan *isn't.*

"You have to be honest with me, because I think you might be in love with her and I need you to tell me you're not, because I think I might want to kiss her. And touch her. A lot. Like, everywhere."

Brennan's hands fly to his forehead and he looks at me like I've lost my mind. He takes several steps back.

"Are you listening to yourself, Warren? I mean, *fuck,* man! You yell at me three minutes ago because you hate her and don't want her here, and now you're saying you want her? Are you bipolar?"

He makes a good point.

Jesus, what's wrong with me?

I pace the room, trying to figure out a solution. She can't stay here. But I want her to stay. I can't share a bathroom with her, but I don't really want anyone else to share a bathroom with her, either. I'm a little bit selfish, apparently.

I pause my frantic pacing and look at Brennan. "Why is she so *mean*?"

Brennan walks over to me and calmly places two hands on my shoulders. "Warren Russell, you need to calm the hell down. You're starting to freak me out."

I shake my head. "I know. I'm sorry, I just. I don't want to be attracted to a girl that you're involved with, so I need to know now if that's the case because we go too far back to let something like this mess us up. But you also know you can't just drop a girl that looks like her in my lap, and expect me not to go there in my head. And I just saw her naked and now I'm useless. Ruined. She's so damn perfect beneath all those clothes and . . ." I look up at him. "I just want to make sure I'm not stepping on any toes when I fantasize about her tonight."

Brennan stares at me, mulling over my admission. He pats me twice on the shoulder and returns to his suitcase. "She's mean, Warren. Probably the meanest girl I've ever met in my life. So if she murders you in your sleep, don't say I didn't warn you." He closes his suitcase and begins to zip it. "She needed a place to stay and we have an extra room. Her life makes mine and Ridge's look like a cakewalk, so go easy on her."

I take a seat on the edge of his bed. I'm trying to be sympathetic to the situation, but the business manager in me is skeptical. "She just called you out of the blue and asked if she could move in with you? Don't you think that's a little suspicious, Brennan? You don't think it has to do with the band finally making a name for itself?"

Brennan glares at me. "She's not an opportunist, Warren. Trust me on that. And hit on her if you want, I couldn't care less."

He walks toward the door and grabs his keys off the dresser. "I'll be back next week after the last show. Do you have our hotel rooms squared up?"

I nod. "I emailed you all the confirmation numbers."

"Thanks," he says as he walks out of the room.

I fall back onto the bed and hate the fact that Brennan isn't into her. That means she's fair game.

I was kind of hoping she wasn't.

But then I smile, because she is.

Chapter Two

"What are you doing?" Ridge signs.

I walk back to Bridgette's bedroom with another glass of water. Once I carefully place it on the floor with all the others, I come back to the living room. "She's lived here two weeks," I tell Ridge. "If she wants to be a roommate, she has to live with the pranks. It's the rule."

Ridge shakes his head disapprovingly.

"What?" I say defensively.

He sighs heavily. "She hardly seems like the type to embrace pranks. This will backfire on you. She hasn't even spoken to us since she moved in."

I disagree with a shake of my head. "She hasn't spoken to *you* because you're deaf and she doesn't know sign language. She hasn't spoken to me because I'm pretty sure I intimidate her."

"You *annoy* her," Ridge signs. "I don't think that girl is capable of being intimidated."

I shake my head. "I don't annoy her. I think she might be attracted to me and that's why she's avoiding me. Because she knows it's not a good idea for roommates to hook up."

Ridge points to her bedroom. "Then why are you making an effort to prank her? Do you *want* her to speak to you? Because if you think roommates shouldn't hook up, then you probably shouldn't be . . ."

I interrupt him. "I didn't say *I* think roommates shouldn't hook up. I said I think that's why she's avoiding me."

"So you want to hook up with her?"

I roll my eyes. "You don't get it. No, I don't want to hook up with her. Yes, I like staring at her ass. And I'm only pranking her because if she's going to live here, she needs to get used to it. When in Rome . . ."

Ridge throws his hands up in defeat and heads toward his room, just as the front door begins to open. I rush to my bedroom and shut the door before she sees me.

I sit on the bed and wait.

And I wait.

And I wait some more.

I lie down on the bed. I wait some more.

She never makes a sound. I don't hear her getting angry that I just filled over fifty cups of water and placed them strategically around her entire bedroom. I don't hear her stomping into the kitchen to pour them out. I don't hear her beating on my door to throw the cups of water at my face in retaliation.

I'm so confused.

I stand up and walk out of my bedroom, but she's not in the kitchen or living room. Her work shoes are by the front door where she keeps them, so I know she came home. I know she went into her room.

What a disappointment. Her lack of response makes me feel like my prank was a failure, when I know it wasn't. It was epic. There's no way she could have made it one foot into her room without having to move all those cups of water.

I stalk back to my bedroom and lie down on the bed.

I want to be pissed at her. I want to hate her for sucking at prank retaliation.

But I don't. I can't stop smiling because I love that her response caught me off guard. She's unexpected, and I like that.

• • •

"Warren."

Her voice sounds so sweet. I must be dreaming.

"Warren, wake up."

So, so sweet. Angelic, even.

I give myself a few seconds to adjust to her voice, to the fact that she's waking me up, to the randomness of her being at my bedroom door, calling out my name. I slowly open my eyes and roll onto my back. I lift up onto my elbows and look at her. She's standing in the doorway between the bedroom and our bathroom. She's wearing an oversized Sounds of Cedar T-shirt, and it doesn't even look like she's wearing anything underneath it.

"What's up?" I ask her.

She wants me. She totally wants me.

She folds her arms tightly over her chest. She tilts her head to the side, and I watch as her eyes narrow into tiny, angry slits. "Don't ever step foot inside my bedroom again. *Ass*hole." She straightens up and backs into the bathroom, slamming the door.

I glance at the clock, and it's two in the morning. That was an extremely delayed reaction to my prank. Was she just waiting for me to fall asleep so she could wake me up and yell at me? Is that her idea of revenge?

She's such an amateur.

I smile to myself and roll over, shifting on the bed. I gasp when a rush of water pours down on top of me.

What the fuck?

I look up, just as an empty cup falls from the edge of the headboard and hits me square between the eyes.

I close my eyes, ashamed that I didn't see that coming. I'm so disappointed in myself. And now I'll have to sleep on towels, because my mattress is soaking wet.

I throw the covers off and swing my legs over the bed, only for my feet to be met with even more cups of water. I knock several of them over in my attempt to stand and it creates a sort of domino effect. I bend over and try to stop them from falling over, but I just make it worse. She's placed them so close together, all over my bedroom floor, and I can't find a safe spot to step.

I try to reach for the nightstand while at the same time lifting my right leg so that it doesn't hit any more cups, but I lose my balance in the process and . . . *yes.* I fall down. Onto the remaining pile of cups that are full of water. Water that is now all over my carpet.

Touché, Bridgette.

• • •

I'm carrying the cups of water from my bedroom to the kitchen, back and forth, back and forth. Ridge is sitting at the table, staring at me. I know he wants to ask why the cups are now in my room, but he better not. I'm sure he can see by the look on my face that I don't need his *"I told you so."*

The door to Bridgette's bedroom opens and she walks

out with her backpack slung over her shoulder. I pause and stare at her for a few seconds. Her hair is pulled back into a ponytail. She has on a pair of jeans and a blue tank top. She's usually wearing her Hooters uniform, which, don't get me wrong, is fantastic. But this? Seeing her dressed down with her flip-flops on and no makeup is just . . . *Stop looking at her.*

"Good morning, Warren," she says, shooting daggers in my direction. She glances at the cups in my hands. "Sleep well?"

I smile at her with vengeance. "Screw you, Bridgette."

She crinkles up her nose and gives her head a quick shake. "No thanks," she says, heading toward the front door. "Oh, by the way. We're out of toilet paper. Also, I couldn't find my razor, so I hope you don't mind that I used yours." She opens the front door and turns to face me. "And . . ." She scrunches up her nose again. "I accidentally knocked your toothbrush into the toilet. Sorry. I rinsed it off for you, though."

She closes the door right when one of the cups of water flies out of my hand and meets the back of the door.

She's such a bitch.

Ridge calmly walks past me, straight to his bedroom. He doesn't even look at me, because he knows me better than anyone, and therefore, he knows not to speak to me right now.

I wish Brennan knew me that well, because he's laughing, making his way into the kitchen. Every time he glances up at me, he laughs even harder. "I know she's mean, but Christ, Warren. She *hates* you." He's still laughing as he opens the dishwasher to unload it. "I mean, really hates you."

I finish the trek across the living room and set the empty cups next to the sink. "I can't do this anymore," I say to him. "I can't live with a girl."

Brennan glances at me, amused. He doesn't think I'm serious.

"Tonight. I want her out tonight. She can move in with a friend, or with that sister of hers she's always on the phone with. I want her gone, Brennan."

He can see that I'm not kidding. He straightens up and presses his hands onto the counter behind him, eyeing me. He shakes his head. "She's not leaving."

He reaches down and closes the dishwasher and presses the button to start it. He begins to walk away so I follow after him. "You can't have final say in who lives here. I've tried for two weeks to get along with her, and she's fucking impossible."

Brennan glances at all the cups lining the countertop. "You think pranking her is making an effort to get along with her?" He looks back at me. "You have a hell of a lot to learn about women, Warren." He turns away from me and walks back toward his room. "She's not leaving. She's our roommate now, so *deal* with it."

He slams his door, and it pisses me off even more because I'm really tired of everyone slamming doors lately. I stomp across the living room and swing his door open. "Either she goes or I go!"

As soon as I say it, I regret it. Actually, I don't. I'm not going anywhere, but maybe the threat will change his mind. He shrugs.

"See ya," he says casually.

I turn around and punch the door. "Seriously, Brennan? You would let me leave over her?"

He stands and walks toward me, not stopping until we're eye to eye. "Yes, Warren. I would. So go think it over and let me know when you're moving out." His hand grips the door and he tries to close it in my face, but I slap my palm against it and push it back open.

"You're fucking her," I say.

"Stop it, already! I'm not fucking her."

My jaw is clenched tightly and I'm nodding my head slowly. That's the only explanation for why he's endlessly defending her. "I don't know why you won't just admit it, Brennan. It's fine. You're in love with Bridgette and you don't want her to move out. If you would just admit it, I'd stop."

Brennan's jaw tenses and he expels a quick, frustrated breath. He runs his hands through his hair, and that's when I see it. I see it written all over his face.

Brennan is in love with Bridgette.

I don't know how I feel about that, which makes no sense, since I'm trying to kick her out.

"Warren," he says calmly. He backs into the room and motions for me to step inside. I don't know why he thinks he needs privacy when the only other person in this apartment is Ridge. He closes the door behind me once I'm inside his bedroom. He puts his hands on his hips and stares at the floor for several seconds. When his eyes finally meet mine again, they're full of defeat.

I knew it.

"I'm not in love with Bridgette," he says calmly. "She's my sister."

Chapter Three

I'm pacing the room, holding my forehead, pausing every few feet to look at Brennan and shake my head, only to continue pacing again.

I liked it better when I thought he was fucking her.

"How?" I ask. "How is that even possible?" I pause again and face him. "And why didn't you guys tell me before now?" I feel slightly excluded, like Ridge and Brennan were trying to keep some big family secret from me. That isn't right, because *I'm* their family. They lived with me after they left home. My parents took them in and gave them a roof over their heads and food on the table.

"Ridge doesn't know," Brennan says. "And I don't want him to know until we find out for sure. We'll have a paternity test done soon, but our schedules just haven't worked out yet and it's kind of expensive."

Great. I can't keep secrets from Ridge. We've been best friends since we were ten. I've never kept a secret from him, especially one this big.

"Warren, swear to me you won't tell him. The last thing he needs right now is more stress, and if he finds out I've been in touch with our father, he'll take it personally."

My hands fly up in the air. "Your father, Brennan? Why in the hell would you ever want to contact that bastard again?"

He shakes his head. "I didn't. After Bridgette found out that her biological mother had an affair with our father, she found me and asked me to help her find him." He folds his arms over his chest and looks down at the floor. "I warned her, but she had to see it for herself. I won't be seeing my father again, but if Ridge knows I even took her to see him, he would think I was going behind his back to reach out to our parents, and I wasn't."

"What did your father say when you showed up after all these years?"

Ridge and Brennan moved in with me and my parents when they were only seventeen and fourteen, so it's been about seven years since either of them has had contact with their father.

Brennan shakes his head. "He hasn't changed. He barely said two sentences to us before he sent us on our way. I think it disappointed her so much, she'd be fine not having a paternity test completed if it weren't for Ridge and me possibly being her brothers. I think she just wants someone she can call family, which is why I'm helping her out with all this. I feel bad for her."

I can't believe this. I never would have guessed it. "She doesn't even look like either of you." Brennan and Ridge look almost identical, and they both look just like their father. If their father is the common link between them and Bridgette, you would think she'd have some form of similarity to them. Other than her brown hair, there's nothing about her that looks like Ridge or Brennan. Her green eyes aren't even close to their dark brown eyes, so if she is their sister, she must have taken a hundred percent after her mother. I could just be justifying the fact that I don't want them to look alike. That would be a little strange for me.

Brennan shrugs. "We still don't know for sure, Warren. If it turns out she's not his daughter, then Ridge will never even have to know about this."

I nod, knowing full well that Brennan is right. Ridge has enough on his plate having to deal with Maggie's issues, and until they know for sure, this isn't something he should have to stress over.

"What happens to Bridgette?" I ask him. "If it turns out she's not your sister."

Brennan shrugs. "Then I guess she's just our new roommate."

I sit down on the bed and try to soak everything in. This changes everything. If she's Ridge and Brennan's sister, she won't just be my roommate. She and her attitude and her tiny little Hooters shorts will be part of our lives forever.

I don't really know how I feel about that.

"Are you sure she's not just trying to swindle you?"

Brennan rolls his eyes. "That girl is just trying to survive, Warren. She's had a really fucked-up life, and even if it turns out we're not related, she just needs someone to give her a chance. So please. You don't even have to be nice to her. Just be understanding enough to allow her to live here."

I nod and fall back onto the bed. *Sister?*

"So," I say to Brennan. "I guess that means you definitely aren't into her. Which means I *can* be."

Brennan's pillow meets my face. "You're disgusting."

Chapter Four

Brennan was right. I'm disgusting. I've never felt more disappointed in myself than I have these past two weeks. Since the moment I found out she might be Ridge and Brennan's sister, I haven't been able to stop staring at her. I keep trying to pinpoint mannerisms they have in common, or physical features, but the only thing I've noticed is how hot she looks in that Hooters outfit.

Which, in turn, makes me disgusted with myself, because thoughts of her in her uniform lead to some really strange dreams. Last night I dreamt I walked into the apartment and she was standing in the kitchen in those tiny orange shorts with her midriff showing. But when my eyes made it to her face, it wasn't her face I was looking at. It was Brennan's. He was smiling at me with a shit-eating grin, and right when I started gagging, Ridge walked out of his room wearing the same Hooters outfit.

I woke up after that and had to immediately go to the bathroom and brush my teeth. I don't know why I thought brushing my teeth would help me, but whatever. This sibling thing is fucking with my head in more ways than it should. On the one hand, I think it would be cool if Ridge and Brennan had a sister. On the other hand, I don't want that sister to be Bridgette. Mainly because I'm skeptical of the reasons she's showing up out of the blue right when Brennan begins to make a name for himself. Does she have ulterior motives? Does she think he's made of money?

Because as the band's manager, I can assure her, he's not. The money the band brings in goes right back into promotion and travel expenses. It's at the point where they're putting in so much time and effort, if it doesn't start paying off during this next scheduled tour, it may be the last one they go on. Which is why I'm a little bitter when it comes to Bridgette, because I need Brennan's focus to be on Sounds of Cedar and Ridge's focus to be on writing the songs. I don't want them caught up in family drama.

But dammit. Those shorts.

I'm standing in my bedroom doorway, watching her. She's in the kitchen, talking on the phone while she makes herself something to eat. The phone is sitting on the counter and she's on speaker with whoever is on the other line.

Bridgette hasn't noticed I'm standing here, so until she does, I'm staying right here. Because seeing her have a normal, human conversation is something I've never witnessed before, and I can't stop watching. Which is strange, because how many times a day do I see people having typical interactions with other humans? It says a lot about Bridgette's personality that seeing her do something like this could actually be fascinating. She'd make an interesting anthropological study, considering she doesn't seem to conform to how society expects a young woman to act.

"I can't take living in this dorm," the voice on speaker says. "My roommate's a fruit loop dingus."

Bridgette tilts her head toward the direction of the

phone, but still doesn't turn around to see me. "You can make it until you graduate."

"And then we can get our own place?"

My ears perk up, hearing her mention the possibility of moving out. "We can't afford our own place," Bridgette says.

"We could if you would go back into doing porn films."

"It was one porn," Bridgette says defensively. "We needed the money. Besides, I was in it for all of three minutes, so will you please stop bringing it up."

Holy shit. *Please say the name, please say the name.* I have to know the name of this porn.

"Okay, okay," the girl says, laughing. "I'll stop bringing it up if you can promise I'll be out of the dorms in three months."

Bridgette shakes her head. "You know I don't make promises. And are you forgetting about the time we tried living together for three months? Because I'm still shocked either of us came out alive. We get along better with distance, and you're better off in the dorms, believe me."

"Ugh. I know you're right," the girl says. "I just need to get off my ass and get a job. How's that Hooters gig working out for you?"

Bridgette scoffs. "It's the worst job I've ever had." She turns around to pick up her phone and her eyes meet mine. I don't even try to hide the fact that I was listening to her conversation. She glares at me as she picks up the phone and holds it to her mouth. "I'll call you later, Brandi." She ends her call and slaps her phone against the counter. "What's your problem?"

I shrug. "Nothing," I say, straightening up and walking toward the kitchen.

Don't look at her shorts, don't look at her shorts.

"I just didn't realize you were capable of normal human interaction."

Bridgette rolls her eyes and picks up the plate of food she just finished preparing. She begins walking toward her bedroom. "I can be pleasant to people who deserve it."

When she reaches her door, she turns around and faces me. "I need you to drop me off at work in an hour. My car's in the shop." She disappears into her bedroom.

I grimace, because for some reason the thought of taking her to work excites me, and my excitement disappoints me. I feel like I'm two different people right now. I'm a guy who finds his new roommate insanely attractive, but I'm also a guy who can't stand to be around his bitchy new roommate.

I'm also a guy who's about to do some heavy research into the porn industry, because I have to find that movie. *Have* to. It's all I'm gonna be able to think about until I see it with my own eyes.

• • •

"What's Bridgette's last name?" I ask Brennan. I've texted him five times in the last half hour, trying to figure it out, but he hasn't texted me back, so now I'm on the phone with him. I'm sure a little Google search of her name could help me find the title.

"Cox. Why?"

I laugh. "Bridgette Cox? Seriously?"

There's a pause on his end of the line. "What's so funny? And why do you need her last name?"

"No reason," I say. "Thanks."

I hang up the phone without giving him an explanation. The last thing Brennan needs to know is that his possible sister was in a porn film.

But *Cox*? That's way too easy.

I spend the next fifteen minutes googling her name, looking for anything porn-related. I come up empty-handed. She must have used a fake name.

I slam my laptop shut when my bedroom door swings open. "Let's go," she says.

I stand up and slip on my shoes. "Ever heard of knocking?" I ask as I follow her through the living room.

"Really, Warren? Coming from the guy who's walked in on me in the bathroom no less than three times in the past two weeks?"

"Ever heard of locking doors?" I say in response.

She doesn't reply as she makes her way outside. I grab my keys off the bar and follow her. I am curious as to why she never locks the doors when she's in the shower. My first thought leads me to believe that maybe she likes it when I walk in on her. Why else would she leave them unlocked?

Come to think of it, she also wears that damn uniform way longer than she needs to. She puts it on a good two hours before going to work and she leaves it on just as long when she gets home. Most people spend as little time as possible in their work clothes, but Bridgette seems to like flaunting her ass in my face.

I pause at the bottom of the stairs and watch as her ass makes its way toward my car.

Holy shit. I think Bridgette is into me.

She turns around after she tries to open the locked door. She looks at me expectantly and I'm still frozen at the bottom of the stairs, staring at her, my mouth agape.

Bridgette likes me.

"Unlock the car, Warren. Jesus."

I lift the key fob and point it at the car to unlock the doors. Bridgette slides into her seat and flips the visor down, fingering at her hair. A smile slowly spreads across my face as I make my way to the driver's side.

Bridgette wants me.

This is gonna be fun.

After I back the car out, I keep half of my focus on the road and half of it on her legs. She has one propped up on the dash and she keeps running her hand up and down her thigh. I can't tell if she's doing it in a seductive way or because she likes the sound of her fingernails scraping over her panty hose.

I have to adjust in my seat and swallow the lump in my throat, because we've never actually been this close before for this long. The tension is thick, and I can't tell if it's all mine or if it's a shared tension. I clear my throat and do what I can to not make this the most awkward ten miles I've ever had to drive.

"So," I say, attempting to think of something to break the ice. "Do you like your job?"

Bridgette laughs under her breath. "Yes, Warren. I *love* it. I love when disgusting old men grab my ass night after night, and I especially love it when drunk guys think my boobs are an accessory and not an extension of my body."

I shake my head. I don't know why I thought it would be a good idea to speak to her. I exhale and don't bother asking her any more questions. She's impossible to talk to.

Silence engulfs the car for another two miles. I hear her sigh heavily and I turn and glance at her, but she's staring out the window. "The tips are good," she says quietly.

I smile and look back at the road. I smile, because I know that's as close to an apology as Bridgette is capable of giving. "That's good," I say to her, my way of telling her I accept her apology.

We're quiet until we reach her work. I stop out front and she gets out of the car and then leans down and looks at me. "I need you to pick me up at eleven tonight."

She slams the door shut without saying please or thank you or goodbye. And even though she's the most inconsiderate person I've ever met in real life, I can't stop smiling.

I think we may have just bonded.

• • •

After I make it home, the first thing I do is set timers on every single porn on pay-per-view. I spend the next few hours fast-forwarding through most of them, pausing it any time it lands on a girl that even remotely resembles her. I take into account that she may have been wearing a wig, so I can't rule women out simply based on their hair color.

Ridge takes a seat next to me on the couch and I consider putting the TV on caption for him, but I don't. Let's be honest, pornos aren't known for their riveting story lines.

Ridge elbows me to get my attention. "What's with this new fascination?" he asks, referring to the fact that I've done nothing today other than watch porn after porn.

I don't want to be honest, so I just shrug. "I like porn."

He nods his head slowly and then stands up. "I'm not gonna lie," he signs. "It's really awkward. I'll be out on my balcony if you need me."

I pause the TV. "You worked out any new songs yet?"

Ridge looks frustrated when I ask him this. He shakes his head. "Not yet." He walks away and I feel bad for asking. I don't know what's changed over the last few months, but he's not the same. He seems more stressed out than usual, and it makes me wonder if he and Maggie have been fighting. He says they're fine, but he's never had a problem writing music for the band before, and everyone knows the number one source for musical inspiration comes from relationships.

Ridge and Brennan are both musically inclined and I've always been a little bit jealous in that regard. Granted, I'm jealous of Ridge in a lot of ways. He just seems to have been born with a certain level of maturity, and I've always envied that about him. He's not impulsive like I am and he also seems to take people's feelings into consideration more than I do. I know Brennan has always looked up to him and I definitely do, too, so seeing him struggling with whatever is going on in that head of his is tough. He knew what he was getting into when he began dating Maggie, so I'm not sure if he's growing unhappy in his relationship with her or if maybe he's concerned she's unhappy with him. Whatever it is, I'm not sure what I can do to help him.

I don't think I *can* help him.

I give my focus back to the TV and fast-forward through at least three more films before I realize it's already eleven and I'm late picking up Bridgette.

Shit. Time flies when you're watching porn.

I spend the next several minutes in fast-forward, making it the ten miles to Hooters in record time. When I pull up, she's standing outside with her arms folded across her chest, shooting daggers at my car. She swings the door open and climbs in. "You're late."

I wait until she slams the door before pressing on the gas. "You're welcome for the ride, Bridgette."

I can feel the anger radiating from her. I don't know if it's simply because I'm late picking her up or because she had a shitty night at work, but I'm not about to ask. When we pull into the complex, she jumps out of my car before I even have it in park. She stalks up the stairs and slams the front door shut.

When I reach the apartment, she's already in her bedroom. I try to be understanding, but this is just . . . *it's fucking rude.* I give her a ride to and from work and all she does is bitch at me? You don't have to be taught manners to know how inappropriate that kind of behavior is. Hell, I'm one of the most inconsiderate people I know, and I would never treat someone like she's treating me.

I walk to my bedroom and head straight for the bathroom. She's already in there, standing at the sink, washing her face. "Again with the failure to knock?" she says with a dramatic roll of her eyes.

I ignore her and walk to the toilet. I lift the lid and unzip my pants. I try to keep my smile in check when I hear her scoff at the fact that I just started taking a piss with her in the bathroom.

"Are you serious?"

I continue to ignore her comments and flush the toilet when I'm finished. I leave the lid up on purpose and step over to the sink, right next to her. *Two can play at this asshole game, Bridgette.*

I grab my toothbrush and squirt toothpaste on it and then start brushing my teeth. She elbows me when I get in the way of the sink, attempting to push me aside. I elbow her right back and continue brushing. I look up at our reflection in the mirror and like what I see. I'm several inches taller than her. My hair is darker than hers, and my eyes are brown compared to her greens. We complement each other, though. Standing next to each other like this, I can see how we could make a good-looking couple. We'd probably even make some good-looking children.

Shit.

Why am I allowing thoughts like this to fester in my brain?

She finishes wiping the makeup from her face before grabbing her own toothbrush. Now we're both fighting for sink space, brushing with more force than our teeth have probably ever been brushed. We take turns angrily spitting into the sink, throwing elbows at each other between every turn.

When I'm finished, I rinse off my toothbrush and put it back in the holder. She does the same. I cup my hands under the stream of water and bend forward to take a sip when she shoves me aside, causing me to splash water all over the counter. I wait until she has water in her own hands, then I shove her arms, watching the water splash everywhere.

She grips the counter and takes a deep, calming breath. It doesn't help, though, because she splashes her hand through the faucet stream, sending a handful of water straight at my face.

I close my eyes and try to put myself in her shoes. Maybe she's had a rough day. Maybe she hates her job. Maybe she hates her life.

Whatever her reason for acting the way she does doesn't excuse the fact that she still didn't say thank you for the ride. She's treating me like I ruined her life, and all I've done is try to accommodate her.

I open my eyes and don't even look at her. I reach over, turn the sink faucet off, and then grab the hand towel and begin drying my face. She's watching me closely, waiting for me to retaliate. I take a slow step toward her, towering over her. She presses her back against the sink and keeps her eyes focused on mine as I lean forward.

Our chests are almost touching now. I can feel the heat radiating from her as her lips slowly part. She's not pushing me away this time. In fact, it looks like she's daring me to keep going. To come closer.

I place my hands on either side of her, locking her in. She still doesn't resist and I know if I tried to kiss her right now, she wouldn't resist that, either. Under any other circumstance, I *would* be kissing her right now. My tongue would be as far into that mouth as I could get it, because *fuck it's a nice mouth.* I don't know how so much venom can spew from lips as soft as hers.

"Bridgette," I say, very calmly.

I can see the roll of her throat as she swallows, still looking up at me. "Warren," she says, her voice a mix between resolved and desperate.

I smile at her, just inches from her face. The fact that she's allowing me this close only proves that my theory earlier this afternoon is correct. She wants me. She wants me to touch her, to kiss her, to carry her to my bed. I wonder if she's as mean in the bedroom as she is out of the bedroom.

I lean in another inch and she gasps quietly, trading glances between my eyes and my lips. I pull my bottom lip into my mouth, slowly sliding my teeth across it. She watches my mouth with fascination. My heart is in my throat and my palms are sweating, because I'm not sure I can do this. I'm not so sure I can resist her.

I lean in even closer, reaching around her with my right hand until I find the mouthwash on the counter. Just when our lips would meet if I were to kiss her, I pull back and step away, removing the lid from the mouthwash. I keep my eyes focused on hers and take a sip before putting the lid back on it and setting it down on the counter.

I can see the desire in her eyes become swallowed up by fury. She's pissed at me, pissed at herself. Possibly even embarrassed. When she sees I was teasing her, the corners of her eyes crinkle with her intense glare. I step up to the sink and spit the mouthwash out, wiping my mouth with the hand towel again. I turn toward my bedroom. "Goodnight, Bridgette."

I close the door and lean against it and squeeze my eyes shut. Her bedroom door slams shut and I blow out a steady breath. I've never been more turned on than I am right now. I've also never been more proud of myself than I am right now. Walking away from that mouth and those hungry eyes was the hardest thing I've had to do, but also the most important. I have to keep the upper hand, because that girl has way too much power over me, and she doesn't even know it.

I turn out my bedroom light and walk to my bed, trying to get the image of what almost just happened out of my head. After several minutes, I give up trying to fight it. I decide to use the thoughts of her to my advantage as I slip my hand into my boxers, thinking about those orange shorts. That mouth. The small gasp of breath she took when I leaned in toward her.

I close my eyes and think about what could have happened if I wasn't so stubborn. If I would have just kissed her. I also think about the fact that she's just a few feet away, hopefully just as sexually frustrated as I am right now.

Why does she have to be so damn mean? Mean girls are my weakness, and I think I just now figured that out.

Chapter Five

It's been three days since our moment in the bathroom. I've noticed she keeps the doors locked now, which is fine. I'm sure she's pissed off that she allowed herself to have a moment of weakness. She doesn't seem like the type to give in as easily as she almost did.

Either way, I can't decide if I made the right move. Half of me rejoices in the fact that I was able to walk away, but the other half of me can't believe how stupid I was for passing up an opportunity like that. I could have had her, and now I more than likely won't ever. But it's for the best, because the last thing I need is to hook up with a roommate who could potentially be the sister of my best friend. But she makes it hard, pun intended, when she walks into the living room looking like she does right now. She's not in her work clothes, but what she does have on doesn't make it any better. She's wearing a thin tank top over a barely there pair of pajama shorts, and she's walked between me and the TV more times than I can count.

Shit.

Now she's heading toward me with books in her hands.

Shit.

She's sitting on the couch. Next to me. In that thin tank top. Without a bra.

I can handle this. I force my eyes on the TV, still in

search of whatever porn she was in. I could just ask her, but that's not a good idea. If she knows I know she was in a porn film, she'd probably do everything she could to make sure I never find out.

She leans forward and picks up the remote, and then points it at the TV to mute it. I don't know who she thinks she is, but if she doesn't want to hear the TV, she can go to her room. I grab the remote and turn the sound back on. She sighs and opens one of her textbooks and begins reading.

I pretend I'm paying attention to the TV, but I can't stop stealing glances at her, because *holy shit, I can't believe I walked away from her*. I'm an idiot.

She grabs the remote and mutes the TV again, possibly because one of the girls was screaming at the top of her lungs. I wonder if Bridgette is loud during sex? Probably not. She's more than likely stubborn, refusing to give up any of her sounds.

I unmute the TV again and she reaches her breaking point. "I'm trying to study, Warren. For fuck's sake, you still get the same effect when it's on mute."

I eye her curiously. "How would you know? Are you a porn expert?"

She glances at me, a flash of suspicion in her eyes. "Can you please, for one night, forgo your addiction so I can study in peace and quiet?"

Bridgette said "please."

"Go study in your bedroom," I say.

Her mouth presses into a tight, thin line. She pushes her book off her lap and stands. She walks toward the TV and reaches behind it, pulling the plug. After returning to the couch, she pulls her book back onto her lap and resumes studying.

I don't know how I ever got beyond her horrible attitude enough to even be attracted to her. She's vile. I don't care how good she looks, she'll never find anyone who can put up with her personality.

"You can be a real bitch sometimes, you know that?"

She releases an exasperated breath. "Yeah, well. You're addicted to porn."

I laugh under my breath. "At least I wasn't *in* a porn."

Her eyes swing in my direction. "I knew you were eavesdropping."

I shrug. "I couldn't help it. You were having a conversation like you were an actual human being. It was fascinating."

Her focus falls back onto the pages of the textbook. "You're an asshole."

"You're an opportunist."

She slams her book shut and turns to face me on the couch. "An opportunist? Are you kidding me?"

I pull my knee up and turn and face her. "You don't think it seems a little fishy that you show up out of the blue and claim to be the long-lost sister to the most popular local band in Austin?"

She looks capable of murder. "Warren, I suggest you stop making accusations against people you know absolutely nothing about."

I grin, because I know that got to her. I might come out victorious again.

"I've learned enough about you to know you don't deserve to be trusted." I pick up her book and put it back in her lap and point to her bedroom. "Now take your homework and go back to your borrowed room."

"*My* borrowed room? You don't even pay rent, Warren."

"Neither do you, Bridgette."

"All you do is watch porn and stare at my ass. You're a lazy pervert."

"All you do is *flaunt* your ass and fantasize about me kissing you."

"You're disgusting," she says. "As a matter of fact, *watch* the porn. I'm sure you need all the pointers you can get."

Okay, that's low. She can insult my laziness, my finances, my new porn addiction, but she cannot insult my bedroom skills. Especially when she doesn't have firsthand experience. "I don't need pointers to please a woman, Bridgette. I was born with natural talent."

She's eyeing me like she's about to punch me, but I can't stop staring at her mouth, hoping she insults me again. Somewhere between being called an asshole and this moment, I've become more turned on than I've ever been in my life. I'm hoping she's about to storm off to her bedroom because I've already met my quota for restraint when it comes to her.

She licks her bottom lip, and I have to grip the couch cushion to keep myself from attacking that mouth. Her eyes are focused intensely on mine, and we're both breathing so heavily from our verbal attacks, I can taste her breath on my lips.

"I hate you," she says through clenched teeth.

"I hated you first," I hiss back.

Her focus falls on my mouth and as soon as I see the tiniest flash of desire in her eyes, I lunge forward. I grab her face and press my lips to hers as I shove her back against the couch. She's pushing me away with her knees while pulling me to her with her hands. My tongue forces through the barrier of her lips and she devours me in response. I kiss her hard, and she kisses me even harder. I'm pulling at a fistful of her hair while she scratches down my neck with her fingernails. *Fuck,* it hurts. *She* hurts.

I want more.

I'm hovering over her and then pressing myself against her, pulling her knee up so she can wrap it around my waist. Her hands are in my hair, and I don't want her to move out. I want her to stay. I want her to be my roommate forever. She's the best fucking roommate I've ever had and, my God, she's so *nice.* How did I ever think she was mean? She's so, so sweet, and her lips are sweet and *Bridgette, I love your name.*

"Bridgette," I whisper, wanting to say her name out loud. I don't know how I hated her name before this moment, because it's the most beautiful name I've ever said out loud.

I pull away from her mouth and begin working my way down her sweet, sweet neck. As soon as I make it to her shoulder, she begins to push me away with her hands.

Just like that, I snap back to reality and separate from her willingly.

I move to the other end of the couch, needing the space to wrap my head around *what the hell just happened?*

She quickly sits up on the couch. She wipes her mouth and I run my hands through my hair, doing whatever I can to process this.

She's an evil vixen. I close my eyes and squeeze my forehead, trying to figure out how I just lost complete control of myself simply because I was kissing her. I think of all the lies that were just passing through my head as my dick tried to convince me she was actually a decent person.

I'm weak. I'm so weak, and she just gained the upper hand again.

"Don't do that again," she says, angry and breathless.

Her voice makes me wince. "You started it," I say defensively.

Did she? I can't remember. It might have been mutual.

"You kiss like you're trying to resuscitate a dead cat," she says, disgusted.

"You kiss like you *are* a dead cat."

She pulls her knees up to her chest and wraps her arms around them. She looks extremely uncomfortable in the silence, so it doesn't surprise me when she spits out another insult. "You probably fuck like a limp noodle."

"I fuck like I'm Thor."

I'm not looking at her, but I know that comment had to make her smile. If she's even capable of smiling. The silence grows heavier and neither of us moves, making it even more apparent that what just happened was a mistake.

"Why do you taste like onions?" she asks.

I shrug. "I just ate pizza."

She glances into the kitchen. "Is there any left?"

I nod. "It's in the fridge."

She immediately stands up to walk to the kitchen, and I hate that I'm staring at her shirt. I can see her nipples poking through the thin fabric, and I want to point at her and say, *"I did that! That's all me!"*

Instead, I close my eyes and try to think about whatever

will stop my wanting to follow her into that kitchen and bend her over the counter. Luckily, Ridge's bedroom door opens, so I give my full attention to him as he walks into the living room. He pauses when he sees me sitting on the couch. He glances at the TV that isn't even on. "Why do you look so guilty?"

I shake my head shamefully. "I think I just made out with Bridgette," I sign.

Ridge looks at Bridgette, who is standing in the kitchen with her back to us. He shakes his head in disappointment. Or confusion.

"Why?" he asks, perplexed. "Did she do it willingly?"

I grab one of the couch pillows and throw it at him. "Yes, she did it willingly, asshole. She wants me."

"Do you want her?" He seems genuinely shocked, like he didn't see this coming at all.

I shake my head. "No, I don't want her," I sign. "But I feel like I need her. So bad. She's so . . ." I pause my hands for a few seconds before continuing. "She's the best worst thing that's ever happened to me."

Ridge backs up until his hand is on the front door. "I'm going to Maggie's for the night," he signs. "We'll pray for you."

I flip him off as he makes his way out. When I turn back to face Bridgette, she's walking toward her bedroom. She passes the TV and doesn't even have the audacity to plug it back in.

I plug in the TV, because there isn't a doubt in my mind now. I *have* to find that porno, because after experiencing that kiss, I'm addicted. Addicted to all things Bridgette.

• • •

I barely slept last night. Being in the same apartment with her, knowing Ridge and Brennan were both gone, was too much. It took all I had not to make an excuse to knock on her bedroom door. But I'm learning how her mind works, and I know she'd turn me down in a heartbeat just to stay in control.

And now, Ridge and Brennan are both still gone and she's at work and I've exhausted all the porn on pay-per-view. I can't keep track of how much porn I've watched in the past two weeks. It's ridiculous. How many could there possibly be? And I've narrowed it down to the ones that have been recorded in the last few years, because she had to be over eighteen when she filmed it. She's twenty-two now, so that's four years of porn films to sift through.

Oh, my God. I'm obsessed.

I'm like a stalker.

I *am* a stalker.

The front door swings open and Bridgette walks in. She slams it shut so hard, I flinch. She walks to the kitchen and begins opening cabinets and banging them shut. She finally rests her palms on the bar and looks straight at me. "Where the hell do you keep the alcohol?"

Bad day, I guess.

I stand up and walk over to the sink. I open the cabinet beneath it and take out the bottle of Pine-Sol. I don't even bother grabbing her a glass. She looks like the type who can take a good swig.

"Are you trying to kill me?" she asks, staring at the bottle in my hands.

I push it into her hand. "Ridge thinks he's clever by hiding it in old cleaner bottles. He doesn't like it when I drink all his alcohol."

She brings the bottle to her nose and winces. "Is whiskey the only thing you have?"

I nod. She shrugs and brings the bottle to her lips, tilts her head back, and takes a long swig.

She hands the bottle back to me as she wipes her mouth with the back of her hand. I take a sip from the bottle myself and then hand it back to her. We do this several times until her anger seems to have subsided, as much as anger can subside in Bridgette's world. I put the top back on the bottle and return it to the cabinet.

"Bad day?" I ask.

She leans against the counter and pulls at the elastic of her orange shorts. "The worst."

"Want to talk about it?"

She looks up at me through her lashes and then rolls her eyes. "No," she says flatly.

I don't push it. I don't even know that I really want to know about her day. Anything and everything seems to set her off, so she's probably pissed over something stupid, like a red light on her way home. It has to be exhausting to respond to all aspects of life with so much anger.

"Why are you always so mad?"

She laughs under her breath. "That's easy," she says. "Assholes, stupid customers, a shitty job, worthless parents, crappy friends, bad weather, annoying roommates who don't know how to kiss."

I laugh at the last comment, which I'm sure was supposed to be a dig, but it felt more like an underhanded flirt.

"How are you so happy all the time?" she asks. "You think everything is funny."

"That's easy," I say. "Great parents, being lucky enough to have a job, loyal friends, sunny days, and roommates who starred in porn films."

She glances away quickly in an attempt to hide a smile that almost appeared on her face. God, I wish she would let that smile out, because I'm dying to see what it looks like. As long as she's lived here, I'm not sure that I've ever seen her smile.

"Is that why you watch so much porn? Because you're hoping to find out which one I was in?"

I don't nod, but I don't shake my head, either. I lean my hip into the counter and fold my arms over my chest. "Just tell me the name of it."

"No," she says quickly. "Besides, I was just an extra. I didn't even really do anything."

An extra. That helps narrow down my search a little.

"*Didn't really* do anything doesn't mean *didn't.*"

She rolls her eyes at me, but she's still standing here, so I keep going. "Were you naked?"

"It was a porn, Warren. I wasn't wearing a sweater."

That means yes.

"Did you have sex on camera?"

She shakes her head. "No."

"But you made out with a guy?"

She shakes her head again. "Wasn't a guy."

Holy fuck.

I turn around and grip the bar with one hand while

making the form of a cross over my body with the other. When I turn back around, she's still standing in the same spot, but she actually looks relaxed. She should drink whiskey every day.

"So you're telling me you made out with another girl? And it's documented somewhere? On film?"

The corner of her mouth curls up into a ghostly smile.

"You smiled."

She stops smiling immediately. "I did not."

I take a step toward her and nod my head. "Yes, you did. I made you smile."

She begins to shake her head in disagreement, so I slip my hand behind her neck. Her eyes widen, and I'm almost positive she's about to push me away, but I can't help it. *That smile.*

"You *did* smile, Bridgette," I whisper. "And you need to own it, because it was fucking beautiful."

She gasps in shock right before my lips crash against hers. I don't think she was expecting this kiss to happen, but she certainly isn't objecting. Her mouth is warm and responsive and when I part her lips with my tongue, she actually lets me.

I don't know if it's the whiskey or her, but my heart is thrashing around in my chest like a caged beast. I slide my hands down her back until they meet her ass and I squeeze as I pick her up and set her back down on the bar.

Our lips separate, and we stare at each other silently, each of us hesitant to believe that the other isn't about to walk away again. When I realize that neither of us seems to want to stop this, I bring my hands up to her cheeks and lean in again, taking her lips between mine.

This is different from our kiss the other night. Our first kiss was quick and frantic, because we knew that's where it would end.

This one is slow and deep, and feels like it's just the beginning of what we're about to experience tonight. This time when I leave her mouth to taste her neck, she doesn't push me away. She pulls me closer, wanting me to kiss her harder.

"Warren," she whispers, tilting her neck to the side, allowing me free rein of her skin. "If I have sex with you, you have to promise you won't get clingy afterward."

I laugh, but I don't move away from her neck. "If you have sex with me, Bridgette, *you're* the one in danger of becoming clingy. You'll want so much more of me, I won't be able to tell the difference between you and Saran Wrap."

She laughs, and I pull away from her. I look down at her mouth and then into her eyes. *"My God."*

She shakes her head, confused. "What?"

"Your laugh." I kiss her on the lips. "Fucking phenomenal," I whisper into her mouth. I lift her off the counter and keep her wrapped around me as I make my way across the living room. As soon as we're in my bedroom, I close the door and push her against it. I keep her pressed against the door with my body while I remove my shirt. I find the hem of her shirt and begin to pull it over her head. "I can't tell you how many times I've fantasized about this, Bridgette."

She helps me pull her shirt over her head. "I haven't fantasized about it at all," she says.

I smile. "Bullshit."

I lift her again and carry her to the bed. As soon as I lay her on it and begin to crawl on top of her, she pushes my shoulders and shoves me onto my back. Her hands meet the button on my jeans and she undoes them. I attempt to take control again by pushing her onto her back, but she's not having it. She straddles me and places her hands on my biceps, pushing my arms against the bed. "I make the calls," she says.

I don't argue. If she wants to be in charge, I'll absolutely let her.

She sits up straight and brings her hands around to her back to undo her bra. I lift up and begin to reach around to assist her, but her hands are back on my arms in a flash. She pushes me to the mattress again. "What did I just say, Warren?"

Holy shit. She's not kidding.

I nod and focus my attention back to her bra as she lifts up and unfastens it. She slides the straps slowly down her arms and I can't keep my eyes off her. I want to touch her, to help her, to be the one to remove her bra, but she's not allowing me to do anything.

My breath catches in my chest when she flings the bra away.

My God, she's perfect. Her breasts are the perfect size, appearing as if they would fit right in the palms of my hands. But I wouldn't know, because I'm not allowed to touch them.

Am I?

I hesitantly lift my hands to feel the softness of her skin, but she immediately shoves my arms away from her, back to the bed.

God, it's torture. Her breasts are *right here*, inches from me, and I can't even touch them.

"Where are your condoms?"

I point to the nightstand on the opposite side of the bed. She slides off me and I watch her closely as she walks to my nightstand. She opens the drawer and sifts around until she finds one. She puts it between her teeth as she walks back toward the foot of the bed. She doesn't climb back on top of me. Instead, she hooks her thumbs into the waistband of her shorts and begins to shimmy out of them.

I'm harder than I've ever been, and I can feel my pulse throbbing throughout my whole body. She needs to hurry the hell up and climb back on top of me.

She leaves her panties on as she bends over and begins to pull my jeans the rest of the way off. She hooks her hands in my underwear and pulls them down as well, the condom wrapper still dangling between her teeth. Her hair is the perfect length, trailing lightly over my skin like feathers every time she leans over me.

Once all my clothes are off, her eyes focus on the hardest part of me. A smile tugs at her lips and her eyes meet mine. She pulls the condom out of her mouth.

"Impressive," she says. "This definitely explains your inflated ego."

I take the insult with the compliment, because I already know Bridgette isn't the type to dish them out.

She straddles me again, still wearing her panties. She leans forward and presses her palms into my forearms. Her mouth meets mine, and her breasts press against my chest, causing me to groan. She feels incredible. So good. I'm worried now, because we haven't even had sex yet and I can already tell I'm ruined.

I can feel her wetness through her panties as she torturously slides up and down, up and down, as slow as she possibly can. Her tongue is in my mouth, and I keep trying to grab the back of her head, or grip her by the waist, but every time I move, she stops me.

I imagined she would be bossy in the bedroom, but nothing like this. She won't even let me touch her, and it's fucking killing me.

"Open your mouth," she whispers into my ear. I do, and she places the condom wrapper between my teeth. I bite down on it and she uses her own teeth to grip the other end of it as she pulls away from me, tearing the wrapper open between both our mouths.

Okay, that was hot.

So hot.

We should quit our jobs and do this full-time.

She pulls out the condom and sits straight up. She looks down and licks her lips as she slides the condom over me and I moan, because her hands are *fuck. They're too much. I want them everywhere.*

I understand how guys can say stupid shit in the throes of passion, because I want to say so much to her right now. I want to tell her I love her and that we're soul mates and that she should marry me, because her hands make me think stupid, stupid, untrue thoughts like this.

She lifts up higher on her knees and pulls her panties to the side, leaving them on as she begins to lower herself on top of me.

It's official. She's the best roommate I've ever had in my life.

She winces slightly when she begins to take me inside

her, and I feel kind of bad that it hurts her. But not bad enough to stop myself from lifting my hips and sliding into her the rest of the way.

As soon as we're flush together, we moan in unison.

I've never felt anything like it.

It's as if her body contours perfectly to mine, fitting every line and curve and dip. Neither of us moves an inch while we fill the room with heavy gasps, giving ourselves a moment to adjust to the sheer perfection we just created.

"Fuck," I whisper.

"Okay," she replies.

She begins to move, and I don't know what to do with myself. My hands want to hold her by the waist as she slides up and down, but I also know I'm not allowed to touch her. My eyes take her in as she continues her movements, her perfect, methodical, sweet movements.

After several minutes of watching her on top of me with her eyes closed and her lips parted, I give up. I can't not touch her. My hands grip her waist and she tries to pull them away but I just grip harder, lifting her when she rises and pulling her down when she falls. She gives up trying to fight me after seeing how much better my strength can make it feel.

I want to hear her moan and I want to hear her fall apart on top of me, but she's holding it all back, just like I knew she would.

I slide my hands up her back and pull her forward until our mouths meet. I keep one hand on the back of her head and one on her waist as she continues her rhythm on top of me.

I curve my hand around her hip and slowly slide it over her stomach, until I'm touching her. I slide a finger between us, separating her, feeling her warmth and wetness surround me. She moans into my mouth and I begin to rub her, but she immediately stops moving. She grabs my wrist and pulls it away from her, slapping my arm against the mattress again.

Her eyes open and focus firmly on mine as she slowly begins to move again. "Keep your hands on the mattress, Warren," she warns.

Dammit, she's making this difficult. I need to feel her again, and when I'm done touching her, I want to taste her. I want that wetness and warmth all over my tongue.

But first, I'll let her have her way. I close my eyes and stop trying to take control. I focus on her tightness, swallowing me up. I focus on the fact that each time her body meets mine, I'm as deep inside her as I can possibly go.

She leans forward and her breasts dance back and forth across my chest as she moves on top of me.

Heaven is *definitely* for real.

My legs begin to tense and my hands are searching for something to grip as I feel myself building. She can sense I'm near release, so she tightens around me and her thrusts become faster and harder. I keep my eyes closed as my body begins to shake beneath her.

I want to cuss and groan, and let her know how good this feels as I release inside of her, but I don't make a single noise. If I'm not allowed to touch her while I come, then she's not allowed to hear how much I fucking love every second of it.

She continues to move over me as I quietly succumb to the tremors. When it's over, she comes to a stop on top of me. I open my eyes and look up at her and catch her smiling down at me. As soon as she realizes I'm looking at her, the smile is gone.

I want her to collapse against my chest. I want to roll her onto her back and take her in my mouth until she's screaming my name out in ecstasy, rather than anger.

Instead, she slowly slides off of me. She stands and turns toward the bathroom. "Goodnight, Warren."

The door closes behind her and I'm lying here in complete confusion. I would be running after her right about now, but I'm still too weak to move.

I give myself time to regroup, and then I remove the condom and toss it into the bathroom trash can on my way to her bedroom. I swing open the door just as she's crawling into her bed. As soon as her head meets her pillow, I'm on top of her, kissing her. As expected, she pushes me away.

"What did I say about being clingy?" she says, pulling her face from mine.

"I'm not being clingy," I say, kissing my way down her neck. "We're not finished."

She pulls away even farther and pushes my face back. "I'm pretty sure we finished, Warren. About three minutes ago."

"*I* finished," I say, looking her in the eyes. "But *you* didn't finish." I can feel her resistance as she attempts to roll over.

"Warren, stop," she says, pushing me away.

I don't pull away from her. Instead, I wrap my arm around her and slowly move my hand across her stomach.

That's when she slaps me.

I immediately pull back and look down at her in shock.

She pushes me away and scoots up on her bed until her

back meets the headboard. "I said stop," she says, defending her slap.

I work my jaw back and forth, not sure what to do. In all my years of experience with girls and even in all the recent porn I've been watching, this isn't how sex usually goes. People are selfish by nature and the fact that she doesn't even want me to get her off is confusing the hell out of me.

"Am I . . ." I pause and look at her. "Am I misreading something here? Because I thought . . ."

"We fucked, Warren. It's over, now go to sleep."

I shake my head. "No, Bridgette. *You* fucked. *You* did all the work and you didn't even get to enjoy it. I don't understand why you won't let me touch you."

She groans, frustrated. "Warren, it's fine. It was fun." She looks away from me. "I just don't like the other part, so go to bed."

She doesn't like the other part? The part where she has an amazing, mind-blowing orgasm?

"Okay," I say. "I'll go to bed."

"Thank you," she mutters.

"But first," I say, holding up my finger. "I need to know something."

She rolls her eyes. "What?"

I lean toward her and look at her with fascination. "Is this how sex *always* is with you? You have to be in complete control, to the point where you don't even allow someone to get you off?"

She kicks at me with her foot, trying to get me to leave her bed. "I'm not discussing my sex life with you, Warren. Go back to your room."

She scoots down on her bed until her head meets her pillow. She rolls over until her back is to me and she pulls the covers up over her head.

Holy shit. This is . . . I don't even know what to think. I've never met anyone like her. She has some serious control issues.

"Bridgette," I whisper, needing her to roll over and talk to me again. She ignores me, but I can't leave because this conversation needs to happen. "Are you telling me you've never had an orgasm during sex?"

The covers fly off her head and she rolls onto her back. "It's never been an issue with anyone until you," she says angrily.

I laugh and shake my head and for some reason, feel extremely happy about this. Because she's apparently been with some really selfish assholes in the past, and I'm about to show her what she's been missing.

She pulls the covers back over her head and faces the opposite direction again. Rather than stand and walk back to my room like I know she wants me to do, I lift the covers and slide in behind her. I wrap my arm over her, pressing my palm against her stomach, pulling her against my chest.

She practically growls at me. "Believe it or not, I'm perfectly happy with my sex life, and I don't need you to *Oh, my God.*" She stops mid-rant as soon as I cup her between the legs.

I rest my cheek against hers. "I need you to shut up, Bridgette."

She doesn't move, so I roll her onto her stomach and slide on top of her. I pin her arms beneath my hands, just like she did me earlier. “Please don’t resist me,” I whisper into her ear. “I want to be in control, and I want you to do what I say.” I run my tongue across her ear and watch as the chills break out on her neck. “Understood?”

Her breaths are shallow, and she squeezes her eyes shut with her nod.

“Thank you,” I tell her. I kiss my way down her neck and shoulder, and then work my kisses slowly across her back. Her entire body is tense and knowing that she’s never experienced an orgasm at the hands of another guy already has me hard again.

I reach down to her thighs and spread her legs with my hand. She buries her face into her pillow and it makes me smile. She’s never been this vulnerable with someone else, and she doesn’t want to give me the pleasure of seeing how much she enjoys it.

I keep my eyes focused on her anyway as I slowly push two fingers inside of her, waiting for her to moan into her pillow.

She doesn’t make a sound, so I pull them out and reenter her with three fingers this time.

I press my forehead into her pillow, right next to her face, and I wait for the sounds to escape.

Nothing. I laugh quietly, because I really have my work cut out for me.

I pull my hand away from her and flip her onto her back. Her eyes are still closed tightly so I grab her jaw and press my lips to hers. I kiss her hard and deep, until she begins to kiss me back with just as much anger. She pulls at my hair and spreads her legs for me, wanting me to bury myself inside of her.

I do. I push her panties aside and shove into her so hard and fast, she lets out a moan and *my God, I need more of that. So much more.* But I don't have on a condom, and this time isn't about me, so I pull out of her. I take one of her breasts in my hands and bring it to my mouth.

I slowly kiss my way down her stomach, and the lower I get, the tenser her body grows. I can feel her hesitation, and part of me wants to devour her immediately, but part of me needs to know that I'm not going too far, too fast. I can tell by the stiffness in her posture that she's nervous now. I position both my hands on her waist and look up at her. She's chewing nervously on her bottom lip and her eyes are terrified.

"Have you never let anyone do this to you?" I whisper.

She releases her bottom lip with the shake of her head.

I pull her hips down several inches on the bed. "You're too stubborn for your own good." I lift her and begin to lower my mouth to her, but she pulls back and sits up.

I grip her hips and pull her back down. "Lie back and close your eyes, Bridgette."

She continues to look at me with fear in her eyes, refusing to lie back down, so I lift up onto the palms of my hands. "Will you please stop being so stubborn and just relax? *Fuck*, woman. I want to give you the best ten minutes you've ever had in your life, but you're making it really difficult."

She bites her lip hesitantly, but she does as I say and slowly lowers herself to the bed, relaxing into her pillow.

I smile triumphantly and press my lips to her stomach again. I start just below her belly button and trail slow kisses all the way down until I meet her panties. I hook my fingers into the waistband and pull them down, over her hips, over her thighs, and I continue to slowly remove them until I'm at her ankles. Once I toss them on the floor, I lift her leg and press a soft kiss against her ankle, then her calf, then the inside of her knee, repeating the kisses all the way up her thigh, until I'm inches from sliding my tongue against her. As soon as I position my mouth over her, I can feel her warmth beckoning me.

"Warren, please . . ." she begins to protest. As soon as the word *please* leaves her mouth, my tongue slides against her, separating her. She lifts her hips several inches off the bed and cries out, so I grip her waist and pull her back down to the bed.

She's sweet and salty, and as soon as my mouth is against her, I'm convinced she could satiate every ounce of hunger I'll feel for the rest of my life.

She cries out again, still trying to pull away from me. "What . . . God . . . Warren . . ."

I continue to lick her, devour her, run my tongue over every bare part of her so that I leave no inch of her untasted. Her hands find their way back to my hair just as my fingers find their way back inside of her. I'm filling her, consuming her with my tongue, and she's taking every ounce of me she can get. She's no longer trying to scoot away from me. Now she's pressing my face into her, begging me to go faster.

Her hands leave my hair and meet her headboard as she grips it tightly and locks her legs around my shoulders. I keep my fingers buried inside of her as she cries out my name with each tremor that racks her body. I continue to please her until her shudders subside and her moans fade into silence.

I kiss the inside of her thigh as I pull my fingers out of her. I kiss all the way up her stomach until I'm pressed against her again, wanting to slide inside of her and stay the night.

I want to kiss her, but I don't know if she'd want that. Some girls prefer not to be kissed afterward, but my mouth is aching with a need to feel her lips against mine.

Apparently she wants the same thing, because she doesn't even hesitate when she pulls my face to hers and kisses me with a moan. There's so much pressure in every inch of my body, because I want to take her again. The only thing that can relieve that pressure is to push into her, which is exactly what I do.

She lifts her hips and meets my thrusts and I know I should stop. I have to stop.

I don't know why I can't stop.

I've never been inside a girl without a condom before, but she makes me stupid. She renders my conscience useless, and all I can think about is how incredible she feels.

And also how much I need to stop.

Stop, Warren. Stop.

I somehow pull out of her and press my face against her chest, gasping for air.

It hurts. God, it hurts. I live in the next room, where there's a drawer full of condoms, but I'm not sure I'd make it that far if I tried to stand.

She pulls my face back to hers and presses her lips to mine. She slides her hands down to my lower back and she pulls me against her, pressing her warmth against me as she urges me to move with her.

She feels incredible. It's not the same as being inside her, but the way she's moving against me feels pretty damn close. I close my eyes and bury my face against her neck as I work to increase the pace between us.

I grab a fistful of her hair and tilt her face to mine as I look down on her, watching as we both grow nearer to yet another release. She winces and I feel the first of her shudders pass through her. "Warren," she whispers. "Kiss me."

I do.

I cover her mouth with mine and drown out her moans with my own as I feel the warmth of my release spread between us. I'm holding her as tight as I can, kissing her as hard as I can.

All my weight is against her now that I'm physically incapable of holding myself up for another second. Her hands slide from my neck and fall to the bed. I'm too weak to speak, or I would be telling her how amazing she is. How good she feels. How perfect her body is and how she just single-handedly got the upper hand for all of eternity.

I can't speak, though. My eyes fall shut from pure exhaustion.

Pure, blissful exhaustion.

• • •

"Warren."

I try to open my eyes, but I can't. Or I just don't want to. I don't think I've ever experienced as deep of a sleep as the one I'm being torn from right now.

Her hand is on my shoulder and she's shaking me. I lift my head and turn to face her, curious if she's ready for another round. I smile at her through sleepy eyes.

"Go to your room," she says, kicking me with her feet. "You're snoring."

My eyes fall shut again but they fly open when her cold feet meet my stomach. She uses the strength of her legs to try and push me out of her bed. *"Go,"* she groans. "I can't sleep."

I somehow push myself into a standing position. I look down at her and she rolls onto her stomach, flips her pillow over, and sprawls out across her mattress.

I shuffle my way across her bedroom, through our bathroom and to my own bed. I fall onto it and close my eyes, taking all of three seconds to fall right back to sleep.

Chapter Six

I'm convinced that I've never slept as well as I did last night. And even though she kicked me out of her bed, I still feel victorious. Like royalty.

After I'm showered and dressed, I join Ridge in the kitchen. He's cleaning up what looks like breakfast, which is odd, because neither of us ever cooks breakfast. But then I understand when Maggie emerges from his room.

"Morning, Maggie," I say to her with a smile.

She eyes me cautiously. "What's with you?"

Right at that moment, Bridgette's bedroom door opens. We all watch her walk into the living room. She pauses when she looks up and sees us all staring at her.

"Morning, Bridgette," I say with a triumphant smile. "Sleep well?"

She sees the look on my face and immediately rolls her eyes. "Screw you, Warren." She walks into the kitchen and begins rummaging through the refrigerator, searching for something to eat. I watch her the entire time, until Ridge taps me on the shoulder.

"You had sex with her?" he signs.

I immediately shake my head in defense. "No," I sign back. "Maybe. I don't know. It was an accident."

Maggie and Ridge both laugh. He grabs Maggie's hand and pulls her toward his bedroom. "Come on," he signs. "I don't want to be in here when Bridgette realizes her mistake."

I watch them retreat back to Ridge's room, and then I turn and face Bridgette. She's glaring at me.

"Did you just tell him we had sex?"

I find myself once again shaking my head. "He already knew. I told him the other day."

Bridgette tilts her head to the side. "We had sex last *night*. How did you tell him before it happened?"

I grin. "I had a good feeling."

She lets her head drop back in defeat, until she's staring up at the ceiling. "I knew it was a bad idea."

"It was a *great* idea," I interject.

She looks at me with as much seriousness as she can muster. "It was a onetime thing, Warren."

I hold up two fingers. "It was twice, actually."

She makes a face that lets me know just how much I'm irritating her. "I'm serious, Warren. We're not doing it again."

"Thank God," I say, slowly stepping toward her. "Because it was awful, wasn't it? I could tell you weren't enjoying it." I continue across the kitchen until I'm less than a foot from touching her. "You especially weren't enjoying the part when you were on your back, and my tongue was . . ."

She slaps her hand over my mouth to shut me up. She's looking at me, narrow-eyed. "I'm serious, Warren. This changes nothing. We aren't a couple. In fact, I'll probably bring other guys home and you need to be prepared for that."

She removes her hand from my mouth and I disagree. "You will not."

She looks at me with a competitive gleam in her eyes. "I will. This is why I warned you not to get clingy."

Ha. She thinks this is clingy? If she smiles and laughs like she did last night, she'll find out just how clingy I can be.

"If you don't want me to want you anymore, it's not that hard," I tell her. "Just don't smile at me." I lean forward until my lips are at her ear. "If you don't smile at me, I won't have the urge to do all those bad things to you. Because your smile is incredible, Bridgette."

I pull away slowly and look down at her. She's attempting to control the rise and fall of her chest, but she's not fooling me. I grin, and the faintest of smiles appears on her lips. I reach my hand up and touch the corner of her mouth with my finger. "You're such a tease."

She pulls away from me and calmly pushes against my chest. She grabs her drink and returns to her bedroom without another word.

I press my head against the cabinet door and sigh heavily. What have I done? What in God's name have I done to myself?

• • •

Bridgette and I both had the day off today, and I was positive that after our interaction this morning, and especially after last night, that she'd be all over me by nightfall. However, she completely ignored me. She stayed in her room most of the day, and she wouldn't even acknowledge me. Now it's after eleven at night. I have to be at work tomorrow morning, and I know she has an early class, so my hope for a round three is swiftly dwindling.

She even locked the door when she took a shower earlier.

I sit on the edge of my bed and contemplate the night before, going over every single move in my head, wondering where I went wrong. The only thing I can conclude is that I did nothing wrong. I did everything right, and this scared her, because she's not used to guys taking control over her. I made her feel weak.

She doesn't like to feel weak. She obviously has serious power issues and I messed with her head. This should probably make me feel guilty, but actually I'm proud. I love that I got to her. I love that I'm slowly figuring her out. And the best part is, I have a feeling that she'll be coming back for a repeat. Maybe not tonight, but she'll be back, because she's human. Every human has a weakness and I think I just discovered what hers is.

Me.

I crawl under the covers and close my eyes, but I can already tell I won't be able to sleep. It's as if last night awakened this hunger inside of me and if I don't feed it every night before I go to bed, I'll never fall asleep. I count sheep, I count stars, I repeat Bible verses in my head that I learned when I was five. None of it works, because I'm still here an hour later and I'm still wide awake.

I wonder if *she's* awake.

I wonder if she would open her door if I knocked.

I toss the covers off and begin to walk to my door, but immediately U-turn to the nightstand for a condom. All I have on are boxers, so I slip it beneath the elastic band and open my bedroom door.

Boobs.

Her boobs.

They're right here.

Her hand is in the air, poised to knock on my door. She looks just as shocked that I opened it as I am that she's standing here. She's wearing a black lace bra and the tiniest pair of panties I've ever seen in my life. She lowers her arm and we stare at each other for a solid five seconds before I'm pulling her inside, slamming my door and pushing her up against it. Her tongue is in my mouth faster than I can slip my hand beneath her bra.

"Is this what you sleep in?" I say against her mouth, pulling the straps of her bra down.

"Yes," she says breathlessly. She tilts her head and pushes my face against her neck. "But sometimes I sleep naked."

I groan and press myself against her, ready to sink myself inside her. "I like it." I spin her around until her chest is pressed against the door and her back is to me. I wrap my arm around her and grab one of her breasts while I slide my other hand down to her ass. She's in a thong. A teeny, tiny, black, lacy, beautiful thong. I rub my hand over her and then slip my fingers beneath the thin veil of fabric, pulling it down to her knees. I watch as the thong falls to her ankles and she kicks it aside.

I position myself directly behind her and run my hands down her back and to her waist. "Put your palms against the door."

She doesn't move them right away. I can feel her hesitation. I'm sure she doesn't want to hand over control again, but she needs to realize she lost control the second she showed up at my bedroom door.

I watch as she slowly presses her palms against my bedroom door. I lean forward and brush her hair away from her neck, dropping it over her shoulder. "Thank you," I whisper against her neck. I pull her hips until she's flush against me, and then I remove my boxers and open the condom.

"Bend over a little more," I tell her.

She does. She's such a fast learner.

I wrap my fingers in her hair and twist my hand around until I have a fistful of it, and then I tug just enough to get her to lift her face. She whimpers when I do this, and that little whimper is all it takes for me to push into her, as far as I can go until she's completely full.

"Make that sound again," I whisper.

She doesn't, so I tug at her hair. The noise escapes her throat and it's so beautiful and full of desire. I pull out and push back into her, and the same sound passes her lips. *I can't take it.* I don't know if I can do this standing up, because that sound is making me dizzy.

I cover one of her hands with mine and squeeze, giving myself the wall support I need to continue moving in and out of her. Every time she whimpers, I push into her a little bit harder. She begins to whimper, over and over, occasionally replacing that sound with my name, and *I already know I'm gonna sleep like a rock tonight.*

Right when I feel myself growing close to release, I pull out of her and reposition her so that her back is against the door. I lift her legs and wrap them around my waist, sliding back inside her with ease. I keep one arm wrapped around her waist to hold her up and my other hand pressed against the door for support. My tongue is fighting hers, and I'm swallowing every sound she's willing to give me.

Her hands are gripping my neck, so I reach behind me and pull one of her hands away. I press her palm against her chest and slide it slowly down her stomach. My forehead meets hers, and I look her hard in the eyes. "Touch yourself."

Her eyes grow wide, and she begins to shake her head. I place my hand on top of hers and I look down at where are bodies join together. I move her hand a few more inches until her fingers are right where I want them. "Please," I breathe out, desperately.

I need my hand for support, so I pull it away and press it against the door beside her head. I'm still holding her around the waist with my other arm and slowly pushing in and out of her. Our foreheads are still pressed together, but now my eyes are planted on her hand as she timidly begins to move her fingers in a slow, circular motion.

"Holy shit," I exhale. I watch her for a minute longer, until she starts to relax against her hand, and then I move my eyes back to her face. I pull away and stare down at her, watching as her head falls back against the door. Her eyes are closed and her lips are slightly parted and all I can feel in my heart is *kiss her, kiss her.*

My lips come down gently against hers and she moans softly into my mouth. I tease her lips with the tip of my tongue, sliding it across her top lip and then her bottom. Her moans are becoming more frequent, and the more I press her against the door, the better I can feel her hand moving between us.

I can't believe this is real life. I can't believe she lives five feet away from me and she's willing to give me this part of her. I'm the luckiest man in the world.

She starts to whimper again, but this time my mouth is resting against hers and I take in every single one of the sounds she makes. She tilts her face more and more to mine, wanting me to kiss her hard, but I'm enjoying this too much. I love the way she looks right now, eyes closed, mouth open, heart exposed. I don't want to kiss her. I want to keep my eyes open and watch every second of this.

I stop moving inside her and wait for her to finish, because if I keep moving, I won't last another second. She begins to open her eyes, wondering why I stopped, so I lean in to her ear. "You're almost there," I whisper. "I just want to watch you."

She relaxes again and I continue to watch her, soaking up every whimper and every moan and every movement she makes like I'm a sponge and she's my water.

As soon as her legs begin to tighten around my waist, I grip her hips with both hands and resume moving inside her. Her whimpers turn into moans, and her moans turn into my name and it takes us all of ten seconds before we're both shaking and gasping for breath and kissing and groping and then finally, sighing.

Her body weakens in my arms and she lays her head against my chest. I bring my hand up to her neck and kiss her softly on top of the head.

After a solid minute of working to catch our breath and regain the ability to move, I slowly begin to pull out of her. She lowers her feet to the floor and looks up at me. She's not smiling, but I can see the calmness behind her eyes. This was exactly what she needed. Exactly what *I* needed.

"Thank you," she says, matter-of-factly.

I grin. "You're welcome."

She ducks her head as soon as she begins to smile, and slips under my arm. She enters the bathroom and closes the door behind her. I lean against the wall and slide down to the floor, completely unable to will my legs to make it back to the bed. If I didn't have to wait on her to finish in the bathroom, I'd fall asleep right here on the floor.

Chapter Seven

Three solid weeks.

Twenty-one nights.

Over thirty times we've had sex.

Absolutely zero interaction during the day.

I don't really understand her. I don't know her well enough to know what sets her off or, in turn, what makes her so quiet. I don't know why she refuses to treat what's going on between us like it's anything remotely significant, but I'm not complaining. I mean, come on. We have sex every night and I don't have to dote on her during the day. I would have the perfect setup if I didn't want just a little bit more from her. But until I can get to another level with Bridgette, I know nothing better come in between us. Especially a new roommate, which is what I'm afraid might happen. Brennan has officially gone on tour and moved out, which means his room is now up for grabs. I can't take the idea of Bridgette's sister moving in, which is something I've heard them discussing on the phone. I don't know what or whom Ridge has in mind, but I for sure don't think I can take the possibility of another guy moving in. As much as I want to pretend I'm as casual with this arrangement as Bridgette is, if another guy even looks at her ass in those shorts, I won't be able to refrain from beating his ass. And I'm not even the type of guy who fights other guys, but Bridgette makes me want to fight everyone. Even the nerdy guys. I'll hit all the humans if it means keeping up the arrangement I've got going with her.

Which is why I can't stop staring at the couch right now. There's a person on it. I think it's a girl, because I see blond hair peeking out from under the pillow pulled over her face, but it could be a long-haired guy. A guy I don't want to be our next roommate. I continue to watch the couch, waiting for the person to wake up. I'm loud enough in the kitchen to wake up the whole apartment, but whoever is on this couch is sleeping like a rock.

I finish pouring my bowl of cereal and bring it into the living room. Since whoever this is has decided to take up residence where I eat breakfast, I take a seat on the floor, right in front of the couch. I begin eating, crunching as loud as I can.

I wonder if she or he is a friend of Bridgette's.

No, Bridgette didn't bring anyone home last night. I know this because I picked her up after I got off work and we came straight home and went straight to my bed. Come to think of it, we didn't even turn on the living room lights, so I'm pretty sure whoever this is was probably on the couch last night, we just didn't notice.

Oh, man. I wonder if we were loud? We never have to worry about how loud we are when Ridge is home.

A groan comes from beneath the pillow and the body rolls over, facing me so I can see it is, in fact, a girl. I continue to sit on the floor, eating my cereal. I watch her attempt to open her eyes.

"Who are you and why are you asleep on my couch?" I finally ask her.

Her whole body jerks at the sound of my voice. She lifts the pillow and backs away, making eye contact with me. I have to stifle a laugh, because someone has written *Someone wrote on your forehead* on her face with a Sharpie.

It was more than likely Ridge, so I do what I can to avoid looking at it and stare at her eyes instead.

"Are you the new roommate?" I say with a mouthful of cereal.

She shakes her head. "No," she says. "I'm a friend of Ridge's."

Hmmm. Didn't see that one coming.

"Ridge only has one friend. Me."

She rolls her eyes and sits up on the couch. She's cute. *Very impressive, Ridge.*

"Jealous?" she asks, stretching into a yawn.

"What's his last name?"

"Whose last name?"

"Your very good friend, Ridge."

She sighs and her head falls against the back of the couch. "I don't know Ridge's last name," she says. "I don't even know his middle name. The only thing I know about him is he's got a mean right hook. And I'm only asleep on your couch because my boyfriend of two years decided it would be fun to screw my roommate and I really didn't want to stick around to watch."

I like this girl. She could give Bridgette a run for her money. And I don't mean with *me,* I just mean because Bridgette is mean and probably doesn't meet a lot of girls who would stand up to her. This could be fun. "It's Lawson," I say. "And he doesn't have a middle name."

I hear Bridgette's bedroom door open and I immediately turn around to face her. She's still wearing my boxer shorts from last night, but she's put her own T-shirt over them. *God, she looks good.* "Good morning, Bridgette. Sleep well?"

She looks at me briefly and rolls her eyes. "Screw you, Warren."

Which, in Bridgette speak means, *Yes, Warren. I slept like a baby, thanks to you.*

"That's Bridgette," I whisper, turning back to the girl on the couch. "She pretends to hate me during the day, but at night she *loves* me."

The girl laughs and makes a face like she doesn't believe me.

"Shit!" Bridgette yells. I turn around in time to watch her catch herself by grabbing the bar. "Jesus Christ!" She kicks one of the suitcases that are still on the floor next to the bar. "Tell your little friend if she's staying here she needs to take her shit to her room!"

My little friend? I turn to face the girl on the couch again, wide-eyed. I think Bridgette already has an issue with this girl. All the more reason to make sure she becomes the new roommate, because I like an angry Bridgette. I'm also willing to bet a jealous Bridgette will be a lot more clingy, which could work in my favor. I turn and glare at Bridgette from where I'm seated. "What am I, your bitch? Tell her yourself."

Bridgette glances at the girl on the couch, then points to the suitcase she almost tripped over. "GET . . . YOUR . . . SHIT . . . OUT . . . OF . . . THE . . . KITCHEN!" she says before marching back to her bedroom.

I slowly turn my head to face the girl again. "Why does she think you're deaf?"

She shrugs. "I have no idea. She came to that conclusion last night and I failed to correct her."

I laugh. What a perfect prank, and I didn't even have to think of it. "Oh, this is classic," I say to her. "Do you have any pets?"

She shakes her head.

"Are you opposed to porn?"

"Not opposed to the principle of porn, but slightly opposed to being *featured* in one." I nod, because that's probably a good thing. At least I won't have double the reason to watch every porn I can get my hands on.

"Do you have annoying friends?"

"My best friend is a backstabbing whore and I'm no longer speaking to her."

"What are your showering habits?"

She laughs. "Once a day, with a skipped day every now and then. No more than fifteen minutes."

"Do you cook?"

"Only when I'm hungry."

"Do you clean up after yourself?"

"Probably better than you," she says, glancing at my shirt, which I've used for a napkin several times during this conversation.

"Do you listen to disco?"

"I'd rather eat barbed wire."

She's perfect for us.

"All right, then," I tell her. "I guess you can stay."

She sits up straighter and pulls her legs onto the couch. "I didn't realize I was being interviewed."

I look at her suitcase and then back at her. Most people don't travel with all their belongings, and if she's in search of somewhere to live, I want it to be here so I can ensure the new roommate doesn't have a dick. "It's obvious you need a place to stay, and we've got an empty room. If you don't take it, Bridgette wants to move her sister in next month and that's the *last* thing Ridge and I need."

"I can't stay here," she says, shaking her head.

"Why not? From the sound of it, you're about to spend the day searching for an apartment anyway. What's wrong with this one? You won't even have to walk very far to get here."

The door to Ridge's bedroom opens and I can see the girl's eyes widen slightly, as if she's nervous. That's probably not a good sign for Ridge, but he's so hung up on Maggie, adding this chick as a roommate shouldn't be an issue for any of us. I wink at her and stand up to walk my bowl back to the kitchen. I speak and sign at the same time. "Have you met our new roommate?"

Ridge glances at her and then looks back at me. "Yeah," he signs. "She needs a place to stay, so I'll probably just let her use Brennan's room. Or if you want, she can take your room and you can take Brennan's, so we both aren't having to share a bathroom with girls."

I shake my head. "No way are you putting me further away from Bridgette. Our bathroom sex is my favorite."

Ridge shakes his head. "You're pathetic." He walks back to his room and I look at our new roommate.

"What did he say?" she asks, nervously.

"Exactly what I thought he'd say," I tell her. I walk to my room and grab my keys off the dresser. I glance into the bathroom and see Bridgette at the sink. I swing the door open and give her a quick kiss on the cheek. She tries to pull away from me, but I also see the smile tugging at her lips.

My eyes fall to the black Sharpie sitting next to the sink. I pick it up and eye Bridgette suspiciously. She shrugs her shoulders and I laugh.

I didn't think she had it in her, but after the water cup prank and now this, I fear I might have met my match. At least the new roommate is being hazed early.

I close the bathroom door and head back out into the living room. "He says you two already worked out a deal." I point to Brennan's old room. "Heading to work now. That's your room if you want to put your stuff in it. You might have to throw all Brennan's shit in the corner, though." I open the door and step outside, but turn around before I close it. "Oh. What's your name?"

"Sydney."

"Well, Sydney. Welcome to the weirdest place you'll ever live."

I close the door behind me, feeling slightly guilty that I may have swayed this roommate thing a little in my favor. But seriously. Not only does this ensure our new roommate won't be putting the moves on Bridgette, it also makes for an interesting dynamic. Two girls in a prank war may be the best thing that ever happened to Ridge and me.

Chapter Eight

"So, what's with the new roommate?" I sign to Ridge when I walk in the door.

"She lives in the complex. Her boyfriend cheated on her and she needed a place to stay."

I walk over to the table he's seated at and pull the chair out. "She still here?"

He looks up from the laptop and nods. "Yeah, she'll probably be here for a few weeks, at least. That okay?"

Something is off with him. When you've known someone most of your life, you can almost feel their unease. This Sydney girl makes him nervous, and I don't know why.

"Is Maggie okay with it?"

His attention quickly moves back to his laptop. He nods his head and stops signing. I push my chair out and glance at the door to see if Bridgette's shoes are where she always keeps them. They aren't. I tap Ridge on the shoulder. "Where's Bridgette?" I sign.

He shifts in his seat. "Out."

"Out where?"

He shrugs. "Warren, do you really want to know? Because you aren't going to like it."

I sit in the chair again. "Hell yes, I want to know. Where is she?"

He leans back in his chair and sighs. "A guy picked her up about three hours ago. It looked like they were going out."

"Out," I sign. "Out like on a date?"

He nods.

I suddenly want to punch Ridge, but I know he has nothing to do with it. I stand up and push the chair back under the table.

She's on a date. Bridgette is on a fucking date.

This is such bullshit. Why didn't I set boundaries? Why didn't I tell her she couldn't see other guys?

What if she brings him back here? She will. She's so mean, she probably will.

I grab my keys and sign to Ridge that I'll be back in a little while.

I'll fix this.

Somehow.

• • •

I'm seated on the couch two hours later when the door opens. As expected, she doesn't walk in alone. A guy is following behind her, way too close. His hand is on her lower back as she slips her shoes off at the door and looks straight at me. "Oh. Hey, Warren."

She points to me. "Guy, this is Warren. Warren, this is Guy."

I look at him. At all six-metrosexual-douchebag-feet of him. "Your name is *Guy*?"

He doesn't respond. He just looks at Bridgette like he's a little uncomfortable that he just walked into her apartment and a guy is sitting on her couch. I bet he'd be really uncomfortable to know what I was doing on this same couch with Bridgette just twenty-four hours ago.

"Warren," Bridgette says in a sickeningly fake, sweet voice. "Do you mind giving us some privacy?" She glances toward my bedroom, silently asking if I'll go wait it out in there while she flirts in my living room with *Guy*. I narrow my eyes at her. She's doing this on purpose. She's testing me, and I'm about to ace this test.

"Sure will, Bridgette," I say with a smile. I stand up and walk over to Guy, reaching out for his hand. "Good to meet you," I say to him. He smiles and his apprehension eases when he sees I've loosened up. "You kiddos have fun. I'll leave the bathroom door unlocked in case either of you needs to use it." I point toward the bathroom, planting the seed.

Please, let him have to use the restroom. Please.

Bridgette can see that my last comment was out of character. She squints her eyes at me as I retreat to my room. I close the door and stay right next to it. I'm not about to miss a second of this. If she's going to try and test me or torture me by bringing another guy home, she has to expect I'll eavesdrop on their entire conversation.

I stand with my ear pressed to the door for at least fifteen minutes. In those fifteen minutes, I hear him go on and on about everything he's good at.

Baseball.

Football.

Tennis.

Trivia. (He actually forced her to quiz him.)

Work. (He's a salesman. He's the best, apparently. Highest sales for the last four quarters.)

He's a world traveler, *of course.*

He speaks French, *of course.*

Bridgette yawns four times during their conversation. I feel like this act she's putting on is exhausting her more than it is me.

"Mind if I use your restroom?" Guy says.

Finally.

A few seconds later, I hear the door close to the restroom and I immediately open my bedroom door and walk to the kitchen. Bridgette is seated on the couch with her feet propped up on the coffee table. "You look bored to death," I tell her.

"He's riveting," she says with a fake smile. "I'm having so much fun, I'll probably ask him to stay the night."

I smile, knowing that won't happen. "He'll never agree to that, Bridgette," I tell her. "In fact"—I look down at my wrist and tap it—"I'm pretty sure he'll be leaving as soon as he exits the restroom."

She sits up straight on the couch and then comes to a quick stand. She stalks over to me, pointing her finger, pushing it against my chest. "What did you do, Warren?"

The bathroom door opens and Guy walks out. Bridgette faces him with her obnoxious, fake smile. "Want to hang out in my room?" she says, walking toward him.

He glances at me and I shake my head, quickly. For all he knows, I'm just warning him, man-to-man, that he better run while he still can.

I can tell he's terrified after seeing what all I've planted in the restroom. He glances at the door and back at Bridgette. "Actually, I was just about to leave," he says. "I'll call you."

The next few seconds are the most awkward seconds I've ever seen play out between two people. He reaches in for a handshake, she goes in for a hug, he backs away, afraid she's about to try to kiss him, and his eyes grow wide with fear. He rushes around her and heads straight for the door. "Nice to meet you, Warren. I'll call you later, Bridgette."

And he's gone.

She slowly turns to face me. Her eyes are as sharp as diamonds. I'm scared they're sharp enough to slit my throat. I wipe the smile from my face and walk toward my bedroom. "Good night, Bridgette."

Nice try, Bridgette.

Nice try.

• • •

"Son of a bitch!"

My bathroom door swings open and she marches straight toward my bed. I was studying, but I quickly throw my books aside when I see her coming at me. She jumps onto the bed, standing, and walks across it. She holds her hands up in the air and that's when I notice she's holding something. I notice it too late, though, because the cream squirts out of the tube and onto the top of my head.

"*Hemorrhoid* cream?" she yells, tossing it aside. She grabs another tube of cream that was tucked under her arm.

"*Wart* remover?" She squeezes it onto my pillow. I'm trying to cover my head with the blanket, but she's getting the stuff everywhere. I pull her legs out from under her and she falls on the bed, then she starts kicking me, and throwing the tubes at me.

"Cold sore relief?" She squirts that one right in my face. "I can't believe you put all these in our bathroom! I swear to God, you're a little boy, Warren. A jealous little boy!"

I pull the rest of the tubes from her hands and I wrestle her onto her back, locking her arms to the mattress.

"You're such an *ass*hole," she yells.

I struggle to hold her still. "If I'm an asshole, then you're a coldhearted, calculating, ruthless *bitch!*"

She grunts, trying to free herself from my grip. I refuse to budge, but I also do my best to remove the anger from my voice and speak to her calmly.

"What was that about, Bridgette? Huh? Why the hell did you bring him here?"

She stops struggling long enough to smile in my face. Knowing that my jealousy makes her smile pisses me off even more. I hold both of her wrists with one hand and reach beside her head, grabbing a tube of the cream. I flip the lid open and squirt it in her hair. She starts thrashing beneath me and *God, I'm so mad at her.*

Why would she do that?

I grab her jaw and hold her face so she'll look at me. She realizes she's not overpowering me physically, so she relents. Her chest is heaving and she's gasping for breath. I can see anger in her eyes. I have no idea what gives her the right to be mad, when she's the one fucking with my head.

I lower my forehead to hers and close my eyes. "Why?" I say, breathless. The room grows quiet. "Why did you bring him here?"

She sighs and turns her head. I pull back and look down on her, convinced I see more pain in her features than anger. Her voice is quiet when she speaks. "Why'd you let another girl move in today?"

I know that was hard for her, because her question proves that she cares. That question proves that I wasn't the only one fearing a new roommate would come between us. She's scared I'll move on. She's scared that Sydney is going to come between us, so she tried to hurt me first.

"You think things might change between us just because another girl moved in?" I ask her. She looks over my shoulder so she doesn't have to look me in the eyes. I tilt her jaw and make her look at me. "Is that why you brought him here?"

Her eyes narrow and she tightens her lips, refusing to admit she was hurt.

"Just say it," I beg. I need her to say it out loud. All I need is for her to admit she brought him here because she was hurt and scared. I need her to admit that there's an actual heart inside her chest. And that sometimes it beats for me.

Since she won't admit it, I'll admit it *for* her. "You've never let anyone close enough to where their absence could hurt you. But it would hurt you if I left you, so you wanted to hurt me first." I press my lips closer to her ear. "You did," I whisper. "Seeing you walk through that door with him hurt like hell. But I'm not going anywhere, Bridgette, and I'm not interested in anyone else. So that little game you tried to play backfired, because from now on, the only man you're allowed to bring home is the one who already lives here." I slowly pull back and look her in the eyes. "Understood?"

In true Bridgette form, she refuses to answer. But I also

know that her refusal to answer is her way of saying I'm right and that she agrees.

She's breathing so much heavier than she was a few minutes ago. I'm almost certain I am, too, because it doesn't feel like my lungs are working anymore. I can't inhale, no matter how hard I try, because the need to kiss her has taken over my passageways. *I need her air.*

I force my mouth against hers and I kiss her with a possessiveness I didn't even know was in me. I kiss her so desperately, I forget that I'm still mad at her. My tongue dives into her mouth and she takes it, giving me her own desperate kiss in return, grabbing at my face, pulling me closer. I can feel her in this kiss like I've never felt her before. It's probably the best kiss I've ever experienced with her, because it's the first kiss with actual emotions behind it.

Even though it's the best kiss, it's also one of the shortest. She shoves me away from her. She's out of my bed, out of my bedroom, and out of my line of sight as the bathroom door slams behind her. I roll onto my back and stare up at the ceiling.

She's so confusing. She's so frustrating. She's so damn unpredictable.

She's nothing I've ever wanted in a girl. And absolutely everything I need.

I hear the water in the shower start running, so I immediately roll off the bed and walk into the bathroom. My heart tightens a little when the doorknob turns and I realize she didn't lock it behind her. I know this sign means she wants me to follow her. What she wants me to do once I'm inside this bathroom is a mystery, though. Does she want me to take her against the shower wall? Does she want me to apologize to her? Does she want me to talk to her?

I don't know with her. I never know. So, I do what I always do and wait for her to show me what she needs. I walk into the bathroom and grab a towel to wipe all the damn cream out of my hair. I get as much out as I can and then close the lid to the toilet and take a seat on it, listening quietly as she continues her shower. I know she knows I'm in here, but she doesn't speak. I'd even take her insults right now if it meant she would say something to alleviate the silence.

I lean forward and clasp my hands between my knees. "Does this scare you, Bridgette?"

I know she hears me, but she doesn't answer. *That means yes.*

I let my head fall into my hands and I vow to remain calm. This is how she relates. She doesn't know any different. Somehow, over the course of her twenty-two years, she's never learned how to love, or even communicate, really. That's not her fault.

"Have you ever been in love before?"

It's a slightly generic question. I don't ask if she could fall in love with me *specifically*, so maybe the question won't piss her off.

I hear a relenting sigh come from behind the shower curtain. "I think it takes *being* loved in order to know *how* to love," she says quietly. "So I guess that's a no."

I wince at her answer. What a sad, sad answer. One I wasn't expecting.

"You can't really believe that, Bridgette."

Silence follows. She doesn't reply.

"Your mother loved you," I say to her.

"My mother gave me to my grandmother when I was six months old."

"I'm sure your grandmother loved you."

A quiet, pained laugh comes from the shower. "I'm sure she did, but not enough to stay alive for more than a year. After she died I lived with my aunt, who made it very obvious that she didn't love me. My *uncle* did, though. Just in all the wrong ways."

I squeeze my eyes shut and allow her words to sink in. Brennan wasn't kidding when he said she's had a rough life. And she's so casual about it, like she's just accepted that this is the kind of life she was given and there's nothing she can do about it. A mixture of anger and sadness consumes me.

"Bridgette . . ."

"Don't bother, Warren. I've dealt with my life the only way I know how. It works for me, and I don't need you or anyone else to try and figure me out, or fix me. I am who I am and I've accepted that."

I clamp my mouth shut and don't offer her words of advice. I wouldn't know what to say anyway. I feel awful for wanting to prod her with more questions after that revelation, but I'm not sure when I'll get this side of her again. Bridgette doesn't open up easily, and now I can see why. She doesn't seem to have had anyone to open up to, so this might be a first for her.

"What about your sister?"

Bridgette releases a sigh. "She's not even my real sister. We're stepsisters, and we didn't even grow up in the same house."

I should stop with the questions. I know I should, but I can't. To know that she's probably never spoken or heard the words "I love you" from anyone in her life is affecting me way more than I imagined it could.

"I'm sure you've had boyfriends who have loved you in the past."

She laughs a really sad laugh, and then she just sighs an even sadder sigh. "If you're planning on asking me questions like this all night, I'd much rather you just fuck me."

I cover my mouth with my hand, absorbing her words like a knife to the chest. She seriously can't be this broken. No one can be this alone, can they?

"Have you ever loved *anyone*, Bridgette?"

Silence. Complete silence until her voice shatters it like glass. "It's hard to fall in love with assholes, Warren."

That's a comment from a girl who's been jaded way too many times. I stand up and slide the shower curtain open. She's standing beneath the stream of water. Mascara has streaked its way down her cheeks.

"Maybe you just haven't met the right asshole yet."

She immediately lets out a quick burst of laughter, along with a few tears. Her eyes are sad, and her smile is appreciative, and for the first time she's completely bare. It's as though she's holding her heart out to me, begging me not to break it. The vulnerability she's showing me right now is something I'm almost positive she's never shown anyone else. No other man, at least.

I step into the shower. She looks at me in shock as my clothes quickly become drenched. I take her face in my hands, and I kiss her.

I don't kiss her fast.

I don't kiss her rough.

I don't kiss her hard.

I press my lips to hers with such delicacy; I want her to feel everything she's ever deserved to feel at the hands of someone else. She deserves to feel beautiful. She deserves to feel important. She deserves to feel cared for. She deserves to feel respected. She deserves to feel like there's at least one other person in this world who accepts her for exactly who she is.

She deserves to know how *I* feel, because I feel all of those things. And maybe a little more.

Chapter Nine

Since that day in the shower, things have changed between us.

Not that she had this miraculous personality shift or that she's actually nice to me during the day. In fact, she's still pretty damn mean to me most of the time. She also still thinks Sydney is deaf, which is almost unbelievable that the prank has gone on for this long. So I can't even say that my excitement over pranking her has changed.

What *has* changed are our nights together.

The sex.

It's different now. Slower. Way more eye contact. Way more kissing. Way more buildup. Way more kissing. So much kissing, and not just on the mouth. She kisses me everywhere, and she takes her time when she does it. And she enjoys it.

She still isn't the type to want to cuddle afterward, and she always kicks me out of her bed before the sun comes up.

But still, it's different. That night in the shower tore a wall down between us. Because I know that every night when I have her in bed, she gives me a part of herself that no one else has ever seen. And that's enough to keep me happy for a long damn time.

I just hope today doesn't ruin that.

We both have the day off and that doesn't happen very often between both of our jobs and school. I have a few errands to run and I asked her to go with me, which might be a little strange. We've been sleeping together for a few months now, but this is the first time we've ever actually done anything that didn't involve sex.

Which also makes me wonder if I should ask her out on a date eventually. I know she's not a typical girl, but surely she likes some of the same things other girls do, like being taken out on dates. But she's never hinted that she wants me to take her on one, and frankly, I'm scared to ask her. I feel like our setup is perfect for both of us and if we start throwing dates into the mix, it'll screw it all up.

That includes daytime dates. Like today. Like what we're about to do.

Shit.

"So," Sydney says. She's seated on the couch next to me. I'm watching porn, naturally, because Bridgette still refuses to give me the name of the one she was in. Sydney doesn't mind it, though. She's focusing on her homework, oblivious to the fact that I'm kind of having a minor internal freak-out over the fact that I may or may not have just invited Bridgette on a daytime date to run errands.

"What's up with Bridgette?"

I glance at Sydney and she's still focusing on her textbook, making notes.

"What do you mean?"

Sydney shrugs. "She's just so . . . mean."

I laugh, because it's true. Bridgette can be awful. "She can't help it," I say. "She's had a rough life."

"So has Ridge," Sydney says, "but he doesn't bite people's heads off when they try to speak to him."

"That's because Ridge is deaf. He can't yell at people, it's physically impossible for him."

Sydney looks up at me and rolls her eyes, laughing. She elbows me in the ribs, just as Bridgette walks out of her bedroom. Bridgette glares at Sydney and I hate that she still assumes there could ever be something between Sydney and me. I like her, and I think she's cool, but I have a feeling Ridge would put a stop to that in a heartbeat.

Which isn't a good thing, considering Ridge has Maggie. But those are issues I don't feel like getting involved in at the moment, because *my* issue is glaring right at me. "Please don't tell me you invited your little girlfriend," Bridgette says, shifting her eyes toward Sydney.

Sydney is really good at this prank thing. She doesn't even bat an eye as Bridgette talks about her. She just goes on pretending she can't hear a word Bridgette says. I'm pretty sure Sydney has gone on this long with the prank because it's a whole lot easier than having to actually *speak* to Bridgette.

"She's not coming," I say, standing up. "She has plans."

Bridgette turns away, giving her attention to the purse she has just slung over her shoulder. I walk up to her and wrap my arms around her from behind. "I'm kidding," I whisper in her ear. "I didn't invite anyone else to run errands with me today but you."

Bridgette's hand meets my forehead, and she pushes me away from her. "I'll stay here if you expect today to be like this."

I take a step back. "Like what?"

She points at me. "You. Touching me. Kissing me. PDA.

Gross." She walks to the front door and I clutch my hand to my heart and wince at Sydney.

"Good luck," she mouths as I make my way to the door.

Once we're in my car and it's moving away from the apartment, Bridgette finally speaks. "So where are we going first? I need to go to Walgreens before we come back."

"First, we go to my sister's house, then we go to the bank, then we go to Walgreens, then we go eat lunch, then we go home."

Her hand flies up and she holds up a finger. "What did you just say?"

I repeat myself. "First we go to my sister's house, then we go to . . ."

"Why in the *hell* are you taking me to your sister's house? I don't want to meet your sister, Warren. We aren't that kind of couple."

I roll my eyes and grab the hand she's holding up in protest. "I'm not bringing you as my girlfriend. You can stay in the damn car for all I care. I just need to drop off a package at her house."

This actually eases her apprehension. She relaxes into the seat and flips her hand over so that I can slide my fingers through hers. I look down at our hands and seeing them linked together on the seat between us feels like I just went further with her than the night we first had sex.

She would have never let me hold her hand back then. Hell, she would have never let me hold her hand last month. But we're holding hands now.

Maybe I should ask her out on a date.

She pulls her hand from mine and I immediately glance

up at her. She's staring straight at me. "You were smiling too much," she says.

What?

I reach over and grab her hand again and pull it back to me. "I was smiling because I like holding your hand."

She yanks her hand back. "I know. That's why I don't want you to hold it."

Goddammit. She's not winning this one.

I reach across the seat again, swerving the car in the process. She tries to shove her hand beneath her legs so that I can't grasp it, so I pull at her wrist instead. I release the steering wheel and reach across with both hands now, steering with my knee. "Give me your hand," I say through clenched teeth. "I want to hold your damn hand." I have to grab the wheel to steer us back into our lane. Once we're no longer in danger of crashing, I slam on the brakes as I pull over to the side of the road. I throw the car in park and lock the doors so she can't run. I know how she works.

I lean across the seat and pry her hand away from being tucked against her chest. I grab her wrist with both hands and I pull her toward me. She's still trying to fight me by pulling her hand away, so I release her and look her directly in the eye. "Give. Me. Your. Hand."

I'm not sure if I just scared her a little, but she relaxes and allows me to grab her wrist. I put her wrist in my left hand and I hold up my right hand in front of hers. "Spread your fingers."

She makes a fist instead.

I pry open her fist, then force our fingers to intertwine. I hate that she's being so resistant. She's pissing me the hell off. All I want to do is hold her damn hand and she's making such a big deal out of it. We're doing everything backward in this relationship. Couples are supposed to start out holding hands and going on dates. Not us. We start out fighting, end up screwing, yet we apparently haven't even made it to the point where we can hold hands. If things continue at this rate, we'll probably move in together before we even go on our first date.

I squeeze her hand until I know she can't pull away from me. I scoot back to my seat and I put the car in drive with my left hand and then ease back onto the road.

We drive the next several miles in silence, and she occasionally tries to ease her hand from mine, but each time she does it I squeeze a little tighter and get even more agitated with her. She's gonna hold my damn hand whether she likes it or not.

We hit a red light and the lack of movement outside the car and the lack of conversation inside the car shifts the mood tremendously, thickening the air with tension and . . . *laughter?*

She's laughing at me.

Figures.

I slowly tilt my head in her direction, giving her a sidelong glance. She's covering her mouth with her free hand, trying not to laugh, but she is. She's laughing so hard that her body is shaking.

I have no idea what she finds so funny, but I'm not laughing with her. And as much as I want to turn away and punch the steering wheel, I can't stop watching her. I watch the tears form at the corners of her eyes, and I watch her chest heave when she attempts to catch her breath. I watch her lick her lips as she tries to stop herself from smiling so much. I watch her run her free hand through her hair as she sighs, coming down from her fit of laughter.

She finally looks at me. She's no longer laughing, but the residue is still there. The smile is still on her mouth and her cheeks are still a shade pinker than normal, and her mascara is smudged at the corners of her eyes. She shakes her head, keeping her focus on me. "You're insane, Warren." She laughs again, but only for a second. The fact that I'm not smiling is making her uncomfortable.

"Why am I insane?"

"Because," she says. "Who throws that big a fit over holding someone's hand?"

I don't move a muscle. "*You* do, Bridgette."

The smile slowly leaves her face, because she knows I'm right. She knows that she's the one who made a big deal out of holding hands. It was me who wanted to show her how easy it was.

We both look down at our hands as I slowly pry my fingers away from hers and release my grip. The light turns green as I grab the steering wheel and press on the gas. "You sure do know how to make a guy feel like shit, Bridgette."

I give my full attention back to the road and rest my left elbow on the window. I cover my mouth with my hand, squeezing the stress out of my jaw.

We make it three blocks.

Three blocks is all it takes for her to do the most considerate thing she's ever done for me since the moment I met her.

She reaches to the steering wheel and takes my hand.

She pulls it to her lap and slides her fingers between mine. She doesn't stop there, though. Her right hand slides over the top of my hand and she strokes it. She strokes my fingers and the top of my hand and my wrist and back down to my fingers. She stares out her window the whole time, but I can feel her. I can feel her speaking to me and holding me and making love to me, all in the motion of her hands.

And I smile the entire way to my sister's house.

• • •

"Is she older or younger than you?" Bridgette asks when I turn off the ignition.

"Ten years older."

We both exit the car and begin walking toward the house. I didn't ask her to come with me, but the fact that she didn't wait in the car is proof that another wall has been torn down between us.

I walk up the steps, but before I knock on the door, I turn and face her. "What do you want me to introduce you as?" I ask her. "Roommate? Friend? Girlfriend?"

She glances away and shrugs. "I don't care, really. Just don't make it weird."

I smile and knock on the door. I immediately hear tiny footsteps and squealing and things falling and *shit, I forget how crazy it is over here.* I probably should have warned her.

The door swings open and my nephew, Brody, jumps up and down. "Uncle Warren!" he yells, clapping his hands. I open the screen door, set the package my mother sent for my sister on the floor and immediately swoop Brody up. "Where's your mom?"

He points across the living room. "In the kitchen," he says. His hand meets my cheek and he makes me face him. "Wanna play dead?"

I nod and set him down on the carpet. I motion for Bridgette to follow me inside, and then I fake stab Brody in the chest. He falls to the floor in a dramatic display of defeat.

Bridgette and I both stand over him as he writhes in pain. His body convulses a few times and then his head falls limp to the carpet.

"He dies better than any four-year-old I've ever seen," I say to Bridgette.

She nods, still staring down at him. "I'm in awe," she says.

"Brody!" my sister yells from the kitchen. "Is that Warren?"

I begin walking in the direction of the kitchen and Bridgette follows me. When I round the corner, Whitney has Conner on her hip and she's stirring something on the stove with her other arm.

"Brody's dead, but yeah, it's me," I say to her.

As soon as Whitney glances at me, cries come from the baby monitor next to the stove. She sighs, exasperated, and motions for me to come to the stove. I walk over to her and take the spoon from her hands. "It has to be stirred for at least another minute, then remove the burner from the pan."

"You mean remove the pan from the burner?"

"Whatever," she says. She pulls Conner off her hip and walks toward Bridgette. "Here, hold Conner. I'll be right back."

Bridgette instinctively holds out her hands and my sister

shoves Conner at her. Bridgette's arms are outstretched, as far from her body as she can get them. She's holding Conner under his armpits, staring at me wide-eyed.

"What do I do with it?" she whispers. Her eyes are filled with terror.

"Have you never held a kid before?" I ask in disbelief. Bridgette immediately shakes her head.

"I don't know any kids."

"Me a kid," Conner says.

Bridgette gasps and looks at Conner, who is staring right back at her with just as much terror and fascination. "It talked!" she exclaims. "Oh, my God, you talked!"

Conner grins.

"Say *cat*," Bridgette says.

"Cat," Conner repeats.

She laughs nervously, but is still holding him like he's a dirty towel. I remove the pot from the burner and turn it off, then walk over to her. "Conner's the easy one," I tell her. "Here, hold him like this." I pull him around to her hip and wrap her arm behind him, securing him against her waist. She's trading nervous glances between Conner and me.

"He won't shit on me, will he?"

I laugh and Conner giggles. He slaps her chest twice and kicks his legs. "Shit on me," he says, still laughing.

Bridgette's hand clamps over her mouth. "Oh, my God, he's just like a parrot," she says.

"Warren!" Whitney yells from the top of the stairs.

"I'll be right back."

Bridgette shakes her head and points to Conner. "But . . . but . . . *this* . . ." she stutters.

I pat her on top of her head. "You'll be fine. Just keep him alive for two minutes." I scale the steps and Whitney is standing in the doorway to the nursery. She's wiping her neck with a rag.

"He pissed in my face," she says. She looks so frazzled. I want to hug her, and I would if she weren't covered in infant piss. She hands me the baby. "Take him downstairs while I jump in the shower, please."

I lift him out of her hands. "No problem."

She begins to head to her room, but pauses right before I make it back to the stairs. "Hey," she says. I turn and face her. "Who's the girl?" she signs.

I love that she signs this, so Bridgette has no chance of hearing her ask. Having a family that is all fluent in sign language definitely comes in handy.

"Just my roommate," I sign back to her, shrugging it off. She smiles and walks into her room. I walk down the stairs holding the baby against my chest. I step over Brody, who is still playing dead on the floor. When I make it to the doorway in the kitchen, I pause. Bridgette has sat Conner on the kitchen island. She's standing right in front of him so that he doesn't fall and she's holding up her fingers, counting with him.

"Three. Can you count to three?"

Conner touches his finger to the tips of hers. "One. Two. Twee," he says. They both start clapping and he says, "Me now."

Bridgette begins to count his fingers this time. I lean my head against the doorframe and watch her interact with him.

I don't know why I've never spent time with her outside

of the bedroom before this. I could add up all the things she's done to me at night, and I'm positive I wouldn't trade today for all of that combined.

This is the Bridgette that *I* see. The part of her she gives to me. And now that I'm watching her, I see that she's very capable of giving it to others who deserve it.

"Do you stare at all your roommates like this?" Whitney whispers in my ear. I spin around, and she's standing behind me, watching me watch Bridgette. I shake my head and look back at Bridgette. "No. I don't."

As soon as I say it, I regret saying it. Whitney will be texting me within the hour, wanting to know all the details. How long I've known her, where she's from, if I'm in love with her.

Time to leave.

"Ready, Bridgette?" I ask, handing the baby back to Whitney.

Bridgette glances up at me and then back to Conner. She actually looks a little sad that she has to say goodbye.

"Bye, Bwidjet," Conner says to her with a wave. Bridgette gasps and turns to face me.

"Oh, my God! Warren, he said my name!"

She turns back to Conner, and he's still waving. "Shit on me," he says.

Bridgette immediately picks him up and sets him down on the floor. "Ready," she says quickly, walking away from him and toward the front door.

Whitney is pointing at Conner and looking at me, "Did he just say . . ."

I nod. "I think he did, Whit. You need to watch your

language around your kids." I give her a quick kiss on the cheek and head for the front door.

Bridgette is standing over Brody, looking down at him. "Seriously impressive."

He's in the exact same position we left him in. "I told you he dies better than anyone I know." I step over him and hold the front door open for her. We walk outside and she doesn't even flinch or pull away when I slide my hand through hers. I walk her to the passenger side door, but before I open it, I turn her to face me and I press her against the car. My hand touches her forehead and I wipe away a wisp of hair.

"I never thought I wanted kids," she says, glancing back at the house.

"But you do now?"

She shakes her head. "No, not really. But maybe if I could have Conner. At that age, for like a year, maybe two. Then I'd probably get tired of him and not want him anymore, but a year or two out of my life might be fun."

I laugh. "So why don't you kidnap him and bring him back when he's five?"

She faces me again. "But you would know it was me who took him."

I smile down at her. "I would never tell. I like you better than I like him."

She shakes her head. "You love your sister too much to do that to her. It would never work. We'd have to kidnap someone else's kid."

I sigh. "Yeah, you're probably right. Besides, we should probably kidnap a celebrity's kid. That way we could get ransom out of it and never have to work again. We could give the kid back, take the money, and spend the rest of our lives having sex all day."

Bridgette smiles. "You're so romantic, Warren. No other guy has ever promised me a kidnapping and ransom."

I tilt her chin up so that her mouth is positioned closer to mine. "Like I said, you just haven't met the right asshole." I press my lips to hers and kiss her, briefly. I keep it PG in case Brody has come back to life and is watching us.

I reach behind her and open the door. She walks around me to climb inside, but before she does, she stands on her tiptoes and kisses me on the cheek.

To Brody or anyone else watching, that was just a kiss on the cheek. But knowing Bridgette like I know her, that was a whole lot more than just a kiss. That was her saying she doesn't need anyone else.

That kiss on the cheek means we're official.

That kiss on the cheek means I have a girlfriend.

Chapter Ten

"So you think it's official because she kissed you on the cheek?" Sydney says, confused. She doesn't get it. She's like everyone else and sees Bridgette at face value, which is fine. Bridgette gives people a pretty rough face value, and that's Bridgette's right.

I stop trying to explain to Sydney my relationship with Bridgette. Besides, I kind of like that no one gets it. And even though we had this really crazy, nonsexual experience with the hand-holding and the cheek kissing the other day, it hasn't affected us in the bedroom. In fact, last night we moved past the slow and steady streak we've been on and played out a fantasy of mine that involved her Hooters uniform.

"You should try to get a job at Hooters," I tell Sydney. I know she's been looking for work, and even though it doesn't seem up her alley, the tips really are good.

"No, thanks," she says. "I wouldn't be caught dead in those shorts."

"They're actually very nice shorts. Soft. Stretchy. You'd be surprised. And last night when Bridgette was pretending she was serving me a platter of hot wings, I reached down and . . ."

"Warren," Sydney says. "Stop. I don't care. How many times do I have to tell you I don't care about your sex life?"

I frown. Ridge doesn't really like to hear about it, either, and I can't tell Bridgette because she's a part of the story and it would just be redundant. I miss Brennan. He always listened.

Bridgette's bedroom door opens, and I watch as her eyes search the living room for me. I can see a hint of a smile, but she's good at making sure I'm the only one who sees it.

"Good morning, Bridgette," I say to her. "Sleep well?"

Her eyes fall on Sydney, who's seated next to me on the couch again. She looks away, but not before I see a flash of hurt on her face.

"Screw you, Warren," Bridgette says, turning her attention toward the refrigerator.

Still, after holding hands and kissing my cheek, she thinks I'd ever mess with another girl?

I watch her as she slams stuff around in the kitchen, angrily. "I don't like how she's up your ass all the time," Bridgette says. I immediately turn to Sydney and laugh, because for one, she still thinks Sydney can't hear her, and two, I can't believe she just said that to me. If that isn't her laying claim to me, I don't know what is.

I love it.

"You think that's funny?" Bridgette says after spinning around. I quickly shake my head and lose my smile, but she throws her hand in Sydney's direction. "The girl obviously has it bad for you, and you can't even respect me enough to distance yourself from her until I'm out of the house?" She turns her back to us again. "First she gives Ridge some sob story so he'll let her move in, and now she's taking advantage of the fact that you know sign language so she can flirt with you."

I don't know who to feel worse for, Bridgette or Sydney. Or *myself.* "Bridgette, stop."

"*You* stop, Warren," she says, turning back around to face me. "Either stop crawling in bed with me at night or stop shacking up on the couch with *her* during the day."

I knew it was coming, but I hoped I wouldn't be here when it finally did.

Sydney reaches her breaking point and slaps her book against her thighs. "Bridgette, please!" she yells. "Shut up! Shut up, shut up, shut up! Christ! I don't know why you think I'm deaf, and I'm definitely not a whore and I'm not using sign language to flirt with Warren. I don't even know sign language. And from now on, please stop yelling when you speak to me!"

I'm scared to look at Bridgette. I feel torn, because I want to high-five Sydney for finally standing up for herself, but I want to hug Bridgette because I know this has to be hard for her. I suddenly feel like the prank was the worst prank in the history of pranks.

I glance up just in time to see a flood of hurt wash over Bridgette's face. She marches to her room and slams her door.

This is going to be impossible to fix. Sydney just single-handedly ruined my entire relationship with that outburst.

Okay, it wasn't all her. I played a huge part in it, too.

My chest hurts. I don't like this. I don't like the silence, and I don't like the fact that I'm about to have to go make this right. I put my hands on my knees and begin to stand. "Well, there goes my chance to act out all the role-playing scenes I've been imagining. Thanks a lot, Sydney."

She pushes her book off her lap and stands up. "Screw you, Warren."

Ouch. Double hurt.

Sydney walks over to Bridgette's bedroom door and knocks. After a few seconds, she cautiously slips inside and closes the door behind her.

If she somehow fixes this, I'll be indebted to her forever.

I sigh and run my hand through my hair, knowing this is my fault. I glance over at Ridge and he's staring at me. "What'd I miss?" he signs.

I slowly shake my head in shame. "Bridgette found out Sydney's not deaf and now Bridgette hates me. Sydney went to Bridgette's room to try and fix things because she feels guilty."

Confusion clouds Ridge's face. "Sydney?" he signs. "What does *she* have to feel guilty for?"

I shrug. "Going along with the prank, I guess. She feels bad that it embarrassed Bridgette."

Ridge shakes his head. "Bridgette deserved it. If anyone should be apologizing, it should be her. Not Sydney."

Why is he defending Sydney like he's her overprotective boyfriend? I glance at Bridgette's bedroom door, shocked that I actually hear a conversation going on in her room, rather than a catfight. Ridge waves his hand in the air to get my attention again.

"Bridgette isn't yelling at her, is she?" he signs. He looks worried, and frankly, that concerns me.

"You sure do seem to care a lot about Sydney's well-being," I sign.

His jaw tightens, and I know I probably shouldn't have

said anything. I can't help it, though. I've been through a lot with Ridge and Maggie, and I don't want him screwing things up just because he might find another girl attractive.

I can tell he doesn't want to take the conversation in that direction, so I redirect it back to me.

"No, neither of them are yelling," I sign. "But Bridgette *will* be as soon as she walks back out of her bedroom. She'll more than likely move out now, and I'll never be able to crawl out of bed again because . . ." I clasp my hand to my chest, "She's gonna take my heart with her."

He knows I'm being dramatic, so he rolls his eyes and laughs, turning to face his laptop again. The door to Bridgette's bedroom swings open, and she marches out.

I didn't prepare for this. I knew she'd be mad, but I'm not sure I can defend myself against her physically if we were in a real fight.

I sit up straight and watch in fear as she walks swiftly toward me. She kneels down onto the couch and slides her leg across my lap, straddling me.

I'm so confused.

Her hands meet my cheeks and she sighs. "I can't believe I'm falling in love with such a stupid, stupid asshole."

My heart wants to rejoice, but my mind is pulling on the reins.

Falling in love.

With an asshole.

A stupid, stupid asshole.

Holy shit! That's *me!*

I wrap my hands around her head and pull her mouth to mine at the same time that I stand up and begin making my way into my bedroom. I shut the door behind us and walk over to the bed and drop her on it. I take off my shirt and throw it on the floor.

"Say it again." I slide on top of her and she smiles, touching my face with the palms of her hands.

"I said I'm falling in love with you, Warren. I think. I'm pretty sure that's what this is."

I kiss her again, frantically. Those are the most beautiful words I've ever heard come out of another human. I pull back and look at her again. "But you wanted to kill me five minutes ago. What changed?" I lift up onto my hands. "Did Sydney pay you to say that? Is this a prank?" My heart stops. Bridgette shakes her head.

I would die. I would literally die if she took them back. I would die so much better than Brody dies, because my death would be *actual* death.

"I just . . ." Bridgette pauses, searching for the right words. "I've been thinking this whole time that maybe you were messing around with Sydney. But after talking to her, I know that's not true. And she also mentioned that one night when you were drunk, you said you might love me. And that just . . . I don't know, Warren."

God, I love this. I love her nervousness. I love her hesitation. I love that she's talking to me so openly. "Tell me, Bridgette," I say quietly, urging her to finish what she was saying. I roll onto my side and lift up onto my elbow. I brush the hair away from her forehead and lean forward to kiss it.

"When she said that, it made me feel . . . *happy.* And I realized that I'm never happy. I was an unhappy child and I'm an unhappy adult and nothing in my life makes me feel the way you do. So I just . . . I think that's what this feeling is. I think I'm falling in love with you."

A small droplet of a tear escapes from the corner of her eye, and as much as I want to bottle it up and save it for all of eternity, I pretend not to notice it, because I know that's what she would prefer. I kiss her lips again before pulling back and looking her directly in the eyes. "I'm falling in love with you, too."

She smiles and reaches her hand up to the back of my head, slowly pulling my mouth to hers. She kisses me softly and then gently pushes me onto my back. She eases herself on top of me and presses her hands against my chest.

"I think I should clarify that I never said I was *in* love with you. I just said I was *falling* in love with you. There's a difference."

I grab her by the hips and pull her closer. "The only difference between *falling* in love and *being* in love is that your heart already knows how you feel, but your mind is too stubborn to admit it." Then I whisper in her ear. "But take all the time you need. I have nothing but patience for you."

"Good, because I'm not telling you I love you yet. Because I don't. I might be on my way to that point, but anything could derail that."

I can't help but smile and kiss her after that little disclaimer.

After a few more minutes of kissing, she turns her head to the side and holds up a finger, silently asking me to stop. She pulls away and sits up on the bed, hugging her knees. She lays her head on her arms and squeezes her eyes shut.

She's quiet for several moments, and her reaction is unusual for her. She looks guilty. She doesn't ever look guilty because she's always too angry to feel any sense of guilt.

"What's the matter?" I ask her.

She quickly shakes her head. "I'm the worst person in the world," she whispers. She turns her head toward mine, slowly. I don't like the look on her face.

She begins to scoot off the bed and I feel my heart dragging behind her. "It was a prank, Warren," she says softly as she stands.

I rise up onto my elbows. "What do you mean?"

She turns to face me and her eyes are so full of shame, she can't even look at me without wincing. "I was trying to get back at you for letting me think Sydney was deaf." She opens the bathroom door and looks down at her feet. "I said all that because I was mad at you, not because it's really how I feel. I'm not falling in love with you, Warren."

I think you're standing on my heart, Bridgette.

She glances over her shoulder into the bathroom, and then back at me. "I didn't mean to take it that far. This is really awkward. I'm gonna go back to my room now." She closes the door behind her.

I'm too numb to feel. Too numb to move. Too numb to process the words that just came out of her mouth. My throat hurts, my stomach hurts, my chest hurts, even my fucking lungs hurt and *oh, my God*, it hurts so much.

I fall back to the bed and bring two fists to my forehead.

"Hey, Warren," she says from the doorway.

I look up at her and she still looks just as guilty. She waves her hand back and forth between us. "That whole thing that just happened? That was . . ." Her frown transforms into a shit-eating grin. "*That* was actually the prank!"

She runs and jumps on the bed, and begins dancing around me. "You should have seen your face!" She's laughing and jumping, bouncing every aching part of me up and down on the bed.

I want to kill her.

She falls to her knees and leans over me, pressing her lips to mine. When she pulls back, I don't want to kill her anymore. My whole body is miraculously healed by her smile. I feel better than I've ever felt. I feel stronger, more alive, happier, and somehow more in love with her than I was five minutes ago. I pull her against me. "That was a really good prank, Bridgette."

She laughs. "I know. It was the best."

I nod. "It really was."

I hold her for several quiet minutes, replaying the entire scene in my head. "God, you're such a bitch."

She laughs again. "I know. A bitch who finally met the right asshole."

Chapter Eleven

Guess who woke up in Bridgette's bed again this morning?

Me.

And guess who'll be falling asleep in Bridgette's bed tonight?

That's right. *Me.*

Both of those things are great, but not as great as this moment. Right now.

We're both seated on the couch, and she's lying between my legs with her head on my chest. We're watching a movie where the actors actually stay dressed for the entire film. But it's not really important what film it is, because Bridgette's cuddling with me.

This is a first, and it's incredible, and I love how she makes me appreciate such simple, mundane things.

Both of us glance at the door when we hear a key being inserted into the lock. The door opens and Brennan walks in. I immediately sit up on the couch, because he's supposed to be in Dallas tonight. He has a show tomorrow, and I'm positive I booked him a hotel for the right night.

Bridgette sits up on the couch and looks at him. He smiles at her, but it's a forced smile. He reaches for his back pocket and pulls out a sheet of paper. He holds it up. "This came today," he says.

Bridgette squeezes my hand and that's when I realize he's holding the test results. I've known Brennan long enough to know by his reaction that he's not happy about the results. I just don't know if that's a good thing or a bad thing for Bridgette.

"Just tell me," she whispers.

Brennan looks down at his feet and then up to me. The look in his eyes is enough for Bridgette to know that she's not any closer to figuring out who her real father is than she was a few months ago.

She inhales a deep breath, and then stands up. She mutters a "thank you" to Brennan and begins heading toward her bedroom, but he grabs her by the arm and pulls her to him. He wraps his arms around her and gives her a hug, but in true Bridgette fashion, she doesn't allow it to last more than two seconds. She begins to cry, and I know that Bridgette doesn't want anyone to see her cry. She ducks her head and rushes to her room.

Brennan tosses the paper on the counter and runs his hands through his hair. "This sucks, man," he says. "I felt like she really needed it to be true, and instead, it just adds to all the shit she's had to deal with her whole life."

I sigh and drop my head against the couch. "You sure about the results? There's no way they could have messed up?"

Brennan shakes his head. "She's not his daughter. And in a way, I'm happy for her because who would want him for a dad? But I know she liked the idea of finally having a little bit of closure."

I stand up and squeeze the back of my neck. "I don't think closure is the only thing she was hoping for." I point to her bedroom. "I'm gonna go check on her," I tell him. "Thanks for coming all this way to tell her."

Brennan nods, and I make my way into her bedroom. She's curled up on the far side of her bed, facing opposite from the door.

I'm not good at consoling, so I'm not sure what I can say to make her feel any better. Instead, I just climb onto the bed and scoot in behind her. I wrap my arm over her and grab her hand.

We lie like this for several minutes, and I let her get all her tears out. When it doesn't sound like she's crying anymore, I press a kiss into her hair.

"He would have been a horrible father, Bridgette."

She nods. "I know. I just . . ." She sucks in a rush of air. "I like it here. I feel like all of you accept me for who I am, and that's never happened before. And now that Brennan knows I'm not his sister, what happens now? Do I just leave?"

I squeeze her tighter, hating that she even thinks that's an option. "Over my and Brody's dead bodies. No way am I letting you go anywhere."

She laughs and wipes at her eyes. "You guys don't have to be nice to me out of pity."

I roll her onto her back and shake my head in confusion. "Pity? This isn't pity, Bridgette. I mean, yeah, I feel bad for you. Yeah, it might have been cool if you were their sister. But it doesn't change anything. The only thing those test results would have changed is that you'd go from not knowing who your real father is to having one of the worst fathers in the world." I kiss her on the forehead. "I don't care whose sister you are, I love you the same."

Her eyes widen, and I can feel her body stiffen in my arms. I didn't say I was falling in love this time.

I just told her I loved her. Like, actively. And yes, those three words could probably make her flip out more than any other three words in the English language, but I can't take it back. I *won't* take it back. I love her, and I've loved her for months now and I'm tired of being too scared of her reaction to say it.

She begins to shake her head. "Warren . . ."

"I know," I interject. "I said it. Get over it. I love you, Bridgette."

Her expression is void of any emotion right now. She's absorbing it. She's waiting to see how those words make her feel, because I'm not sure if she's ever heard them before.

Her jaw grows tense, and she places her hands against my chest. "You're a liar," she snaps, attempting to roll out from under me.

Here we go again.

I pull her back to the mattress while she attempts to squirm away. "You're exhausting, you know that?" I roll her onto her back and she begins to nod, frantically.

"That's right, Warren. I'm exhausting. I'm mean. I always see the glass half empty, and if you think telling me you love me will make me nicer and less exhausting, you're wrong. You can't change me. Everyone wants to change me, but I am who I am, and if you think me telling you that I love you, too, will make me shit out unicorns and rainbows, you're wrong. I *hate* unicorns and rainbows."

I drop my face to her neck and I start to laugh. "*Oh, my God,* I can't believe you're mine." I kiss her on the cheek, and then I kiss her on the forehead, and then her nose and her chin and her other cheek. I look back at her eyes full of confusion.

"I don't *want* you to change, Bridgette. I'm not in love with who you *could* be, or who you *used* to be, or who the world *says* you should be. I'm in love with *you*. Right now. Just like this."

She's still guarded and defensive, so I pull her closer to me and wrap my arms around her, hugging her tightly. "Stop," I whisper in her ear. "Stop telling yourself that you aren't lovable, because it's pissing me off. I don't care if you aren't ready to admit how you really feel about me yet, but don't you dare dismiss how I feel about you. Because I love you." I kiss her on the side of the head, and I say it again. It feels so good to finally say it. "I love you, Bridgette."

She pulls away just enough for me to see her face. Her eyes are rimmed with tears.

"Bridgette, I love you," I say again, this time looking her straight in the eyes. I can feel her struggling internally. Part of her wants to enjoy this moment, and part of her is trying to hold up that last wall that still stands between us.

"I love you," I whisper again.

One of the tears escapes from her eyes, and I'm afraid she's about to break and push me away like she always does. I press my lips against hers, and I inhale deeply. I touch her cheek and wipe away her tear with my thumb.

"You're the most genuine person I know, Bridgette. So whether you think you deserve love or not, it doesn't matter, because I can't help it. I fell in love with you, and I'm not sorry for it."

Another tear falls from her eyes.

A smile forms on her lips.

A laugh escapes her mouth, and her chest begins to shake because she's laughing and crying and kissing me. And I kiss her right back, crashing right through the last wall that stood between us.

She wraps her hands in my hair and rolls me onto my back, still with her lips pressed to mine. I open my eyes and she backs away from my mouth, still smiling. She begins to shake her head in slow disbelief. "I can't believe I'm in love with such a stupid, stupid asshole."

I'm not sure this sentence could mean more to any other man in the world.

"I love you, Warren."

I can't even tell her I love her back, because hearing those words come out of her mouth has left me completely speechless. But I don't think she cares, because her lips are on mine so hard and fast, I wouldn't be able to speak anyway.

I'm in love with Bridgette.

Bridgette is in love with me.

All is finally right in the world.

We continue to kiss while we remove each other's clothes. Neither one of us is in control this time. She makes love to me at the same time I make love to her, and no one is in charge. No one is calling the shots. It's completely equal now. She feels about me how I feel about her and when we're finished, she whispers, "I love you, Warren."

And I say, "I love you, Bridgette."

And no one argues.

She lies peacefully in my arms and doesn't try to kick me

out of her bed. Just the thought of having to go back to my room and sleep alone seems ridiculous, and I'm not sure I ever want to sleep alone again.

I stroke her arm with my fingers. "I have an idea," I whisper against her hair.

She shakes her head. "I'm not doing anal."

I laugh and pull back. "*What?* No. Not that. Not yet, anyway." I push her off me and sit up, pulling her to a seated position. I take both of her hands in mine, and I look her very seriously in the eyes. "I think we should move in together."

Her eyes widen in shock and she's looking at me like I've lost my mind. Maybe I have. "We already live together, dumbass. And we hardly have to pay rent. We'd be broke if we got our own place."

I dismiss her concerns with a shake of my head. "I don't mean into a new apartment. Move into my bedroom with me. We're together every night anyway."

She's still shaking her head. "Why would I want to do that?"

"Because," I say to her, brushing her hair behind her ear. "It's romantic."

"No, Warren, it's dumb."

I fall back onto the bed, frustrated. She drops to my side and glares down at me. "Why would I want to move all my clothes into your tiny closet? That's so stupid. I have way too much closet stuff."

"Fine," I tell her. "You can keep all your clothes in your own closet, but move everything else into my room."

She drops her forehead to my chest. "I don't *have* any other stuff. I have a bed. That's it."

I tuck my finger under her chin and lift her eyes to mine. "Exactly. Move your bed to my room. We both have full-size beds. Putting them together would be like having a king, and we'd have more room to have sex, and when we're finished you can roll over to your side of the bed and I can watch you sleep."

She considers my proposal for several quiet moments, and then smiles. "This is so dumb."

I sit up and pull her off the bed. "And romantic. Come on, get dressed. I'll help you."

We put our clothes back on and begin tossing the blankets and pillows off her bed. We lift the mattress and begin scooting it out the door, into the living room, and toward my room. Ridge and Brennan are both sitting on the couch, staring at us.

"What the hell are you doing?" Brennan asks.

I press my hip against the mattress so I can sign back to them. "Bridgette and I are moving in together."

Ridge and Brennan look at each other, then back at me. "But . . . you already *live* together," Brennan says.

I dismiss them with a wave of my hand, and we finish moving Bridgette's mattress next to mine. Once her bed is remade, she falls onto hers and I onto mine. We roll until we're facing each other. She rests her head on her arm and sighs.

"We've lived together for two minutes, and I'm already sick of your face."

I laugh. "I think you should move out. We got along so much better before this."

She flips me off, so I grab her hand and link my fingers through hers. "I need to ask you something else."

She falls onto her back. "So help me God, Warren, if you ask me to marry you I'll cut your nuts off."

"I don't want to marry you," I say. "Yet. But . . ."

I crawl over to her part of our home and lie next to her. "Will you go on a date with me?"

She looks away from me and stares up at the ceiling. "Oh, my God," she whispers. "We've never been on a date before?"

"Not a real one."

She slaps a hand to her forehead. "I'm such a whore. I already moved in with you and we haven't even been on a date?"

"You're not a whore," I say to her with mock reassurance. "We haven't even had sex . . . *oh, wait.*" I grimace. "You *are* such a whore. A huge, slutty whore who wants me to try anal with her tonight."

She laughs and shoves me in the chest.

I shove her back.

She shoves me harder.

I push her until she's at the edge of her bed.

She lifts her legs to kick me.

I kick her back, pushing her off the bed until she's lying on the floor. After several quiet seconds, I scoot to the edge of the mattress and look down at her. She's still lying flat on her back in the same position she landed.

"You could give Brody a run for his money," I tell her. She reaches up a hand to hit me, but I grab it and pull it to my mouth. I kiss the top of it and hold her hand while I lock eyes with her.

She's in an unusually agreeable mood right now, which leads me to believe that maybe . . . *just maybe* . . .

"I have one more question, Bridgette."

She cocks an eyebrow and slowly shakes her head. "I'm not telling you the name of that porn."

I drop her hand and roll onto my back. "Fuck."

Maybe not.

Acknowledgements

A huge thank-you to so many people. First, my family. Without you I could never finish anything. To my publisher, Atria Books, and Judith Curr, for not saying no when I said, "I want to write a novella about Warren. And I want it to be a surprise!" A special thanks to my editor, Johanna Castillo, for being the absolute best! I say it with every book, but we really are a great team. To my brand-new publicist, Ariele, for being top-notch at her job. Yer er der berst, Erererl! And to my agent, Jane Dystel, and her team of amazing people. To Murphy and Stephanie for always keeping my head above water. And last but not least, my readers. Without you, none of the people just mentioned would have a job, including me. Your passion for reading gives us the ability to live our passion. For that, we ALL thank you!

This book is for every single member of
Colleen Hoover's CoHorts.

Except the murderers.
This book isn't for those two.

Maybe Now

Prologue

Maggie

I set the pen down on the paper. My hand is shaking too much to finish filling it out, so I inhale a few quick breaths in an attempt to calm my nerves.

You can do this, Maggie.

I pick up the pen again, but I think my hand is shaking worse than before I put it down.

"Let me help you with that."

I look up to see the tandem instructor smiling at me. He grabs the pen and picks up the clipboard, then takes a seat in the chair to my right. "We get a lot of nervous first-timers. It's easier if you just let me fill out the paperwork because your handwriting probably won't be legible," he says. "You act like you're about to jump out of an airplane or something."

I'm immediately put at ease by his lazy smile, but become nervous all over again when I realize I'm a horrible liar. Lying on the medical section would have been a lot easier if I were filling it out myself. I'm not sure I can lie out loud to this guy.

"Thanks, but I can do it." I try to take back the clipboard, but he pulls it out of my reach.

"Not so fast"—he quickly glances down at my form—"Maggie Carson." He holds out his hand, still holding the clipboard out of my reach with his other hand. "I'm Jake, and if you're planning on jumping out of a plane at ten thousand feet while at my mercy, the least I can do is finish your paperwork."

I shake his hand, impressed with the strength behind his grip. Knowing these are the hands I'm about to entrust my life to eases my mind a tiny fraction.

"How many tandem jumps have you completed?" I ask him.

He grins, then returns his attention to my paperwork. He begins flipping through the pages. "You'll be my five hundredth."

"Really? Five hundred sounds like a big deal. Shouldn't you be celebrating?"

He brings his eyes back to mine and loses his smile. "You asked how many tandem jumps I've completed. I don't want to celebrate prematurely."

I gulp.

He laughs and nudges my shoulder. "I'm kidding, Maggie. Relax. You're in good hands."

I smile at the same time I inhale a deep breath.

He begins to scroll through the form.

"Any medical conditions?" he asks, already pressing his pen to the box marked *no*. I don't answer him. My silence prompts him to look up at me and repeat his question. "Medical conditions? Recent illnesses? Any crazy ex-boyfriends I should be aware of?"

I smile at his last comment and shake my head. "No crazy exes. Just one really great one."

He nods slowly. "What about the other part of the question? Medical conditions?" He waits for my answer, but I fail to give him anything other than a nervous pause. His eyes narrow and he leans forward a little bit more, eyeing me carefully. He's looking at me like he's trying to figure out answers to more than just what's on the questionnaire he's holding. "Is it terminal?"

I try to hold my resolve. "Not really. Not yet."

He leans in even closer, looking at me with an expression full of sincerity. "What is it, then, Maggie Carson?"

I don't even know him, but there's something calming about him that makes me want to tell him. But I don't. I look at my hands, folded together in my lap. "You might not let me jump if I tell you."

He leans into me until his ear is close to my mouth. "If you say it quietly enough, there's a good chance I might not even hear it," he says in a hushed voice. A wave of his breath caresses my collarbone, and I'm immediately covered in chills. He pulls back slightly and eyes me as he waits for my response.

"CF," I say. I'm not sure he'll even know what CF means, but if I keep it simple he might not ask me to elaborate.

"How are your O_2 levels?"

Maybe he does know what it means. "So far so good."

"Do you have a doctor's release?"

I shake my head. "Last-minute decision. I tend to be a little impulsive at times."

He grins, then looks back to the form and checks no on medical conditions. He glances at me. "Well, you're lucky, because I happen to be a doctor. But if you die today, I'm telling everyone you lied on this questionnaire."

I laugh and nod in agreement, appreciative he's willing to shrug it off. I know what a big deal that is. "Thank you."

He looks at the questionnaire and says, "Why are you thanking me? I didn't do anything." His denial makes me smile. He continues to scroll down the list of questions, and I answer them honestly until we finally make it to the last page. "Okay, last question," he says. "Why do you want to skydive?"

I lean over him to glance at the form. "Is that really a question?"

He points to the question. "Yep. Right here."

I read the question, then give him a blunt answer. "I guess because I'm dying. I have a long bucket list of things I've always wanted to do."

His eyes harden a little, almost as if my answer upset him. He returns his attention to the form, so I tilt my head and lean over his shoulder again and watch as he writes down an answer that isn't at all the one I gave him.

"I want to skydive because I want to experience life to the fullest."

He hands me the form and the pen. "Sign here," he says, pointing to the bottom of the page. After I sign the form and give it back to him, he stands up and reaches out for my hand. "Let's go pack our chutes, Five Hundred."

• • •

"Are you really a doctor?" I yell over the roar of the engines. We're seated directly across from each other in the small airplane. His smile is huge and full of teeth so straight and white, I would bet money he's actually a dentist.

"Cardiologist!" he yells. He waves a hand around the interior of the airplane. "I do this for fun!"

A cardiologist who skydives in his spare time? Impressive.

"Your wife doesn't get upset that you're so busy all the time?" I yell. *Oh, God. That was such an obvious, cheesy question.* I cringe that I even asked that out loud. I've never been good at flirting.

He leans forward and yells, "What?"

He's really going to make me repeat myself? "I asked if your wife gets upset that you're so busy all the time!"

He shakes his head and unbuckles his safety harness,

then moves to the seat next to me. “It’s too loud in here!” he yells, waving his hand around the interior of the airplane. “Say it one more time!”

I roll my eyes and begin to ask him again. “Does . . . your . . . wife . . .”

He laughs and presses a finger to my lips, but only briefly. He pulls his hand away and leans toward me. My heart reacts more to this quick movement of his than it does to the fact that I’m about to jump out of this airplane.

“I’m kidding,” he says. “You looked so embarrassed after the first time you said it, I wanted to make you say it again.”

I slap him on the arm. “Asshole!”

He laughs and stands up, then reaches for my safety harness and presses the release latch. He pulls me up. “You ready for this?”

I nod, but it’s a lie. I am absolutely terrified, and if it weren’t for the fact that this guy is a doctor and he does things like this for fun—and he’s really hot—I’d probably be backing out right about now.

He turns me until my back is to his chest and connects our safety harnesses together until I’m securely fastened to him. My eyes are closed when I feel him pull my goggles on. After several minutes of waiting for him to finish prepping us, he walks me forward toward the opening of the airplane and presses his hands against either side of the opening. I am literally staring down at clouds.

I squeeze my eyes shut again, just as he brings his mouth close to my ear. "I don't have a wife, Maggie. The only thing I'm in love with is my life."

I'm somehow smiling during one of the scariest moments of my life. His comment makes the question worth the three times he had me repeat it. I tighten my grip around my safety harness. He reaches around me and takes both of my hands, then lowers them to my side. "Sixty more seconds," he says. "Can you do me a favor?"

I nod, too scared to disagree with him right now since I've practically placed my fate in his hands.

"If we make it to the ground alive, will you let me take you to dinner? To celebrate being my five hundredth time?"

I laugh at the sexual undertone in his question and look over my shoulder. "Are tandem instructors allowed to date their students?"

"I don't know," he says with a laugh. "Most of my students are men, and I've never had the desire to ask one of them out."

I stare straight ahead again. "I'll let you know my answer when we land safely."

"Fair enough." He pushes me a step forward, then intertwines his fingers with mine, spreading our arms out. "This is it, Five Hundred. You ready?"

I nod as my pulse somehow begins to beat even more rapidly than before, and my chest tightens with the fear consuming me, knowing what I'm about to willingly do. I feel his breath and the wind against my neck as he inches us to the very edge of the plane's opening.

"I know you said you want to skydive because you're dying," he says, squeezing my hands. "But this isn't dying, Maggie! This is living!"

With that, he shoves us both forward . . . and we jump.

Chapter One

Sydney

As soon as I open my eyes, I immediately roll over to find the other side of my bed empty. I grab the pillow Ridge slept on and pull it to me. It still smells like him.

It wasn't a dream. Thank God.

I still can't wrap my head around last night. The concert he orchestrated with Brennan and Warren. The songs he wrote for me. That we were finally able to tell each other how we really felt without guilt being attached to those feelings.

Maybe that's where this new sense of peace comes from—the absence of all the guilt I've always felt in his presence. It was hard falling in love with someone who was committed to someone else. It was even harder trying to prevent it from happening.

I roll out of bed and scan the room. Ridge's shirt is next to mine on the floor, so that means he's still here. I'm a little nervous to walk out of my bedroom and see him. I don't know why. Maybe because he's my boyfriend now, and I've barely had twelve hours to adjust to it all. It's so . . . official. I have no idea what it will be like. What our lives together will be like. But it's an excited nervous.

I reach down and grab his T-shirt, then pull it over my head. I make a detour to the bathroom to brush my teeth and wash my face. I debate fixing my hair before I walk into the living room, but Ridge has seen me in worse conditions than the present one. We used to be roommates. He's seen me in *way* worse conditions.

When I open the door to the living room, he's there, seated at the table with a notebook and my laptop. I lean against the doorframe and watch him for a while. I'm not sure how he feels about it, but I love that I can watch him unabashedly without him hearing me enter the room.

He pulls a frustrated hand through his hair at one point, and I can tell by the stiffness of his shoulders that he's stressed. Work stuff, I assume.

He eventually catches sight of me, and that seeing me in the doorway seems to ease his stress completely erases all my nervous energy. He stares for a moment and then drops his pen on the notebook. He smiles and scoots his chair back to stand, then makes his way across the living room. When he reaches me, he grabs me and pulls me against him, pressing his lips against the side of my head.

"Good morning," he says, pulling back.

I will never grow tired of hearing him speak. I smile at him and sign, "Good morning."

He looks at my hands and then back at me. "That is so damn sexy."

I grin. "You speaking is so damn sexy."

He kisses me, then pulls away and heads to the table. He grabs his phone and texts me.

Ridge: I have a ton of work to catch up on today and I really need my own laptop. I'm going to head back to my apartment so you can get ready for work. Want me to come over tonight?

Sydney: I drive by your place on my way home from work. I'll just stop by on my way home.

Ridge nods and picks up the notebook he was writing in. He closes my laptop and walks back to me. He wraps his arm around my waist and pulls me against him, pressing his mouth to mine. I kiss him back, and we don't stop, even when I hear him toss the notebook on the bar. He lifts me up with both arms, and a few seconds later, we're across the living room and he's lowering me onto the couch, and then he's on top of me and I'm pretty sure I'm going to get fired this week. There's no way I can tell him I'm already late for work when I'd rather be fired than have to stop kissing him.

I'm being dramatic. I don't want to get fired. But I've waited so long for this and don't want him to leave. I start counting to ten, promising myself that I'll stop kissing him and get ready for work when I reach ten. But I make it all the way to twenty-five before I finally press against his chest.

He pulls back, smiling down at me. "I know," he says. "Work."

I nod and do my best to sign what I'm saying. I know I'm not getting it all right, but I spell out the words I don't know yet. "You should have chosen this coming weekend to sweep me off my feet rather than a work night."

Ridge smiles. "I couldn't wait that long." He kisses my neck and then starts to roll off me so I can get up, but he pauses and stares at me appreciatively for a moment.

"Syd," he says. "Do you . . . feel . . ." He pauses, then pulls out his cell phone. We still have a huge communication barrier in that he doesn't feel completely comfortable speaking full conversations out loud yet, and I don't know enough sign language to hold a full conversation at a decent pace. I'm sure until we both get better, texting will remain our primary form of communication. I watch him text for a moment, and then my phone pings.

Ridge: How do you feel now that we're finally together?

Sydney: Incredible. How do you feel?

Ridge: Incredible. And . . . free? Is that the word I'm looking for?

I'm still reading and rereading his text when he immediately begins typing out another one. He's shaking his head, like he doesn't want me to take his previous text the wrong way.

Ridge: I don't mean free in the sense that we weren't free before we reunited last night. Or that I felt tied down when I was with Maggie. It's just . . .

He pauses for a moment, but I respond to him before

he replies because I'm pretty sure I know what he's trying to say.

Sydney: You've been living a life for others since you were a kid. And choosing to be with me was kind of a selfish choice. You never do things for yourself. Sometimes putting yourself first can feel freeing.

He reads my text, and as soon as his eyes flick to mine, I can see we're on the same page.

Ridge: Exactly. Being with you is the first decision I've made simply because I wanted it for myself. I don't know, I guess I feel like I shouldn't feel this good about it. But I do. This feels good.

Even though he's saying all of this like he's relieved he finally made a selfish choice, there's still a wrinkle between his furrowed brows, like his feelings are also accompanied by guilt. I reach my hand up and smooth it out, then cup his face. "Don't feel guilty. Everyone wants you to be happy, Ridge. Especially Maggie."

He nods a little, then kisses the inside of my palm. "I love you."

He said those words numerous times last night, but hearing them again this morning still feels like he's saying them for the first time. I smile and pull my hand from his so I can sign, "I love you, too."

This all feels so surreal—him actually being here with me after so many months of wishing it could be this way. And he's right. It felt so stifling being apart from him, yet feels liberating now that he's here. And I know he isn't saying all of what he just said because he felt like his life with

Maggie was in any way something he didn't want. He loved her. Loves her. What he's feeling is the result of spending an entire life making decisions that were in the best interest of others and not himself. And I don't think he regrets any of it. It's just who he is. And even though I was a selfish decision he finally made for himself, I know he's still the same selfless person he's always been, so there's going to be some residual guilt there. But people need to put themselves first sometimes. If you aren't living your best life for yourself, you can't be your best self for those in your life.

"What are you thinking?" he asks, brushing my hair back.

I shake my head. "Nothing. Just . . ." I don't know how to sign what I want to say, so I grab my phone again.

Sydney: This all feels surreal. I'm still trying to soak it all in. Last night was completely unexpected. I was starting to convince myself that you were getting to a point where you didn't think we could be together.

Ridge's eyes shoot to mine, and he laughs a little, like my text was completely absurd. Then he leans forward and gives me the softest, sweetest kiss before replying.

Ridge: I haven't been able to sleep for three months. Warren forced me to eat because I was anxious all the time. I've thought about you every minute of every day, but I kept my distance because you said we needed time apart. And even though it killed me, I knew you were right. Since I couldn't be with you, I forced myself to write music about you.

Sydney: Are there any songs I haven't heard yet?

Ridge: I played all my new songs for you last night. But I've been working on one. I've been stuck because the lyrics didn't feel quite right. But last night after you fell asleep, the lyrics started flowing like water. I wrote them down and sent them to Brennan as soon as I got them down on paper.

He wrote an entire song after I fell asleep last night? I narrow my eyes at him and then reply.

Sydney: Have you even slept yet?

He shrugs. "I'll nap later," he says, brushing his thumb over my bottom lip. "Keep an eye on your email today," he says as he leans in for another kiss.

I love it when Brennan makes rough cuts of the songs Ridge writes. I don't think I'll ever get tired of dating a musician.

Ridge rolls off the couch and then pulls me up with him. "I'll leave so you can get ready for work."

I nod and kiss him goodbye, but when I try to walk to my bedroom, he doesn't release his grip on my hand. I turn around, and he's looking at me expectantly.

"What?"

He points to the shirt I have on. *His* shirt. "I need that."

I look at his T-shirt and laugh. Then I pull the shirt off—slowly—and hand it to him. He's eyeing me up and down as he takes his shirt and pulls it over his head. "What time did you say you're coming over tonight?" He's still staring at my chest when he asks this question, completely unable to look me in the eyes.

I laugh and push him toward the door. He opens it and slips out of my apartment, but not before stealing another quick kiss. I close the door behind him and realize for the first time since the day I moved out of my old apartment, I finally feel like I'm no longer resentful for the turmoil Hunter and Tori caused.

I am absolutely, without a doubt, so grateful for Hunter and Tori. I would live through the Tori/Hunter heartache a million times over if Ridge was always my final result.

• • •

A few hours later, I get an email from Brennan. I duck into a bathroom stall at work with my headphones and click on the email with the subject line, "Set Me Free." I lean against the wall, press play on my phone, and close my eyes.

"Set Me Free"

I've been running 'round
I've been laying down
I've been underground with the devil
You've been saving me like a ship at sea
Saying follow me to the light now

So here we go
A little more
Something I've been waiting for

Here we go

A little more

You set me free

Shook the dust right off me

Locked up tight you found the key

And now I see

Ain't no place I'd rather be

I got you and you got me

You set me free

Hard to know the cost of it

But when you've lost something

Then you know there's a price tag

Think you might have been born to

Be my come through when

I can't keep it all together

So here we go

A little more

Something I've been waiting for

Here we go

A little more

You set me free

Shook the dust right off me

Locked up tight you found the key

And now I see

Ain't no place I'd rather be
I got you and you got me
You set me free

I was sitting low
I didn't know where I could go
Thought the bottom was the ceiling
No remedy to heal it
A Hail Mary to a sin
A new start to an end

You set me free
Shook the dust right off me
Locked up tight you found the key
And now I see
Ain't no place I'd rather be
I got you and you got me
You set me free

I stand completely silent after the song ends. There are tears running down my cheeks, and it isn't even a sad song. But the meaning behind the lyrics Ridge wrote after falling asleep next to me last night mean more to me than any other lyrics he's ever written. And even though I understood what he was saying this morning when he said he feels free for the first time, I didn't realize just how much I identified with what he was feeling.

You set me free, too, Ridge.

I pull the headphones out of my ears, even though I want to put the song on repeat and listen to it for the rest of the day. On my way out of the bathroom, I catch myself singing the song out loud in the empty hallway with a ridiculous smile on my face.

"Ain't no place I'd rather be. I got you and you got me . . ."

Chapter Two

Maggie

I think about death every minute of every hour of every day of my life. I'm almost positive I think about death more than the average person. It's hard not to when you know you've been given a fraction of the time almost everyone else on earth has been given.

I was twelve when I started to research my diagnosis. No one had ever really sat me down and explained to me that cystic fibrosis came with an expiration date. Not an expiration date on the illness, but an expiration date on my life.

Since that day, at only twelve years old, I look at life completely differently than I looked at it before. For example, when I'm in the cosmetics section of a store, I look at the age cream and know that I'll never need it. I'll be lucky if my skin even starts to wrinkle before I die.

I can be in the grocery section, and I'll look at the expiration dates on food and wonder which one of us will last longer, me or the mustard?

Sometimes I receive invitations in the mail for a wedding that's still a year out, and I'll circle the date on the calendar and wonder if my life will last longer than the couple's engagement.

I even look at newborn babies and think of death. Knowing that I'll never live to see a child of my own grow into adulthood has erased any desire to ever have a child.

I'm not a depressed person. I'm not even sad about my fate. I accepted it a long time ago.

Most people live their lives as if they'll live until they're one hundred years old. They plan their careers and their families and their vacations and their futures as if they'll be around for all of it. But my thoughts work differently from most people's, knowing that I don't have the option to pretend I'll live until I'm one hundred years old. Because I won't. Based on the current state of my health, I'll be lucky to live another ten years. And that's precisely why I think about death every minute of every hour of every day of my life.

Until today.

Until the moment I jumped out of the plane and I looked down on an earth that seemed so insignificant that I couldn't help but laugh. And I couldn't stop laughing. The entire time we were falling, I laughed hysterically until I started crying because the experience was beautiful and exhilarating and far exceeded my expectations. The entire time I was plummeting toward the earth at over one hundred miles per hour, I didn't once think about death. I could only think of how lucky I was to be able to feel that alive.

Jake's words kept repeating in my head as I was pushing against the wind. *This is living!*

He's right. This is the most I've ever lived, and I want to do it again. We've only been on the ground for all of a minute. Jake's landing was impeccable, but I'm still harnessed to him and we're sitting on the ground, my feet out in front of me as I try to catch my breath. I appreciate that he's given me a quiet moment to soak it all in.

He begins to unlatch us and stands up. I'm still sitting when he walks around in front of me and blocks the sun with his height. I look at him and am slightly embarrassed that I'm still crying, but not enough to try to hide it.

"Well?" he says, holding out his hand. "How was it?" I take his hand, and he pulls me up as I use my other hand to wipe the tears away from my cheeks. I sniff and then laugh. "I want to do it again."

He laughs. "Right now?"

I nod vigorously. "Yeah. That was incredible. Can we do it again?"

He shakes his head. "The plane is booked for the rest of the afternoon. But I can put you on the schedule for my next day here."

I smile. "I would love that."

Jake helps me remove my harness, and I hand him my

helmet and goggles. We go inside, and I change out of my gear. When I make it back to the front counter, Jake has printed out pictures and downloaded a video of the skydive for me.

"I sent it to the email address you have on file," he says, handing me a folder with the pictures inside it. "Is the address on your form your correct home address?"

I nod. "Yeah. Should I be expecting something in the mail?"

He glances up from the computer and smiles at me. "No, but you can expect me at your front door tonight at seven."

Oh. He was serious about celebrating tonight. Okay, then. I just got super nervous all of a sudden. I don't react, though. I smile at him and say, "Will this be a casual or formal celebration?"

He laughs. "I could make a reservation somewhere, but honestly, I'm more of a pizza-and-beer kind of guy. Or burgers or tacos or anything that doesn't require me to wear a tie."

I smile, relieved. "Perfect," I say, backing away from the counter. "See you at seven. Try not to be late."

I turn and walk toward the door, but before I exit, he says, "I won't be late. In fact, I want to show up early."

• • •

Ridge and I dated for so long, that I don't even remember the last time I've stressed over what to wear on a date. Aside from his infatuation with front-clasping bras, I don't even think Ridge paid attention to what underwear I wore. But here I am, digging through my dresser, trying to search for anything that matches or doesn't have holes or isn't tailored to fit a grandmother.

I can't believe I don't have any cute panties.

I open my bottom drawer full of stuff that, for whatever reason, I'd convinced myself I'd never wear. I sift through unmatched socks and gag-gift crotchless panties until I come across something that makes me forget about my search altogether.

It's a folded sheet of paper. I don't have to open it to know what it is, but I walk to my bed and open it anyway. I sit and stare at the list I started writing over ten years ago, back when I was only fourteen.

It's a bucket list of sorts, although back then I didn't know what the term "bucket list" meant. Which is why I titled it *Things I Want to Do Before I Turn Eighteen.* The *Before I Turn Eighteen* part of the title is marked out because I spent my eighteenth birthday in the hospital. When I got home, I was bitter at the whole world, and that I hadn't marked anything off my list. So I scribbled out the end of the title and changed it to *Things I Want to Do. Maybe One of These Days . . .*

There are only nine things on the list.

1) Drive a race car.
2) Skydive.

3) See the Northern Lights.
4) Eat spaghetti in Italy.
5) Lose $5,000 in Vegas.
6) Visit the caves in Carlsbad Caverns.
7) Bungee jump.
8) Have a one-night stand.
9) Visit the Eiffel Tower in Paris.

I look over the list and realize that out of the nine things I hoped for as a teenager, I have only done one. I went skydiving. And I didn't even do that until today, yet it ended up being the best moment of my life.

I reach to my nightstand and grab a pen. I cross out the second item on my list.

Eight more things remain on my bucket list. And honestly, they're all doable. Maybe. If I can somehow prevent myself from catching an illness while I travel, every single thing on this list is doable. Number eight might even be doable tonight.

I don't know how Jake would feel about being checked off as an item on my bucket list, but I don't think he'd complain too much about being the other half of my one-night stand. It's not like I'm going to let anything come of this date tonight, anyway. The last thing I want is another situation where I'll feel like I'm a burden to someone. The thought of being someone's irresistible one-night stand has me way more excited than the prospect of being someone's terminally ill girlfriend.

I fold the list and put it in the drawer of my nightstand. I walk over to my dresser and grab a random pair of panties. I don't even care what they look like. If all goes as planned, I won't even be wearing them long enough for Jake to care what they look like. I'm pulling on my jeans when I receive a text.

Ridge: Mission successful.

I smile when I read the text. It's been several months since we ended things, but Ridge and I still text occasionally. As hard as it was to see our relationship come to such an unexpected end, it would be even harder to lose his friendship. He and Warren are the only two friends I've had for the past six years of my life. I'm grateful that even though our relationship didn't work out that it doesn't mean our friendship can't. And yes, it's weird discussing Sydney with him, but Warren has been keeping me up to date on all things Ridge, even in the areas I don't care to be up to date on. In all honesty, I want Ridge to be happy. And as angry as I was when I found out he'd kissed Sydney, I still like the girl. It's not like she showed up with evil intentions and tried to steal him from me. She and I actually got along, and I know they both tried to do the right thing. I'm not sure we'll ever get to a point where we'll all hang out as friends. That would be too weird. But I can be happy that Ridge is happy. And since Warren filled me in on their plan to trick Sydney into going to a bar last night so Ridge could convince her to be with him, I've been curious how it would all turn out. I told Ridge to text me if their plan was successful last night, but I don't think I want the details. I can accept that she's a part of his life now, and I really am happy for him. I just don't think I'll ever be in the position to want the details.

Maggie: That's great, Ridge!

Ridge: Yeah, that's all we'll say about that because it's still too weird discussing it with you. Any word on the thesis yet?

I'm glad we're on the same page. And I can't believe I forgot to tell him the good news.

Maggie: Yes! Found out yesterday. Got a 5!

Before he responds, there's a knock at my front door. I look at the time on my phone and it's only 6:30. I toss the phone on my bed, walk to the living room, and look through the peephole. Jake wasn't kidding when he said he might show up early. I haven't even finished getting ready.

I back up to the mirror in my hallway and yell, "Just a sec," while I check my reflection. Then I rush back and look through the peephole again. Jake is standing with his hands in the pockets of his jeans, looking out over my front yard as he waits for me to open the door. It's honestly a bit surreal, knowing I'm about to go on a date with this guy. He's a freaking doctor! Why is he even single? He's really cute. And so tall. And successful. And . . . is that a . . .

I swing open the door and step outside. "Holy shit, Jake. Is that a Tesla?" I don't mean to be rude, but I brush right past him and walk straight to his car. I hear him laugh behind me as he follows me to the driveway.

I'm not a car fanatic by any means, but one of my neighbors dates a guy who drives a Tesla, and I'd be lying if I said I wasn't a tad bit obsessed with these cars. But I don't know my neighbor well enough to go ask her if I can go for a ride in her boyfriend's car.

I run my hand over the sleek black hood. "Is it true they don't have engines?" I spin around, and Jake is watching me with amusement as I ogle his car instead of him.

He nods. "Want to see under the hood?"

"Yes."

He pops the hood with his key fob and then steps next to me to open it. There's nothing but an empty trunk inside, lined with carpet. No engine. No transmission. There's just . . . nothing.

"So there's no engine at all in these cars? You never have to fill up with gas?"

He shakes his head. "Nope. There's not even oil that needs changing. Only upkeep is the brakes and tires, really."

"How do you keep it charged?"

"I have a charger in my garage."

"You just plug it in at night like you're charging a phone?"

"Basically."

I turn back toward the car, admiring it. I can't believe I get to ride in a Tesla tonight. I've been wanting to ride in one for two years. If I had updated my bucket list at all in the past few years, this would definitely be something I'd be crossing off it tonight.

"They're really good for the environment," he says, leaning against the hood. "No emissions."

I roll my eyes. "Yeah, yeah, that's nice. But how fast does it go?"

He laughs and crosses his feet at the ankles. His voice is intentionally low and sexy when he raises a brow and says, "Zero to sixty . . . in 2.5 seconds."

"Oh my God."

He nods at the car. "You want to drive it?"

I glance at the car and then back at him. "Really?"

His smile is sweet. "Actually . . . let me make a phone call," he says, pulling out his phone. "I might can get us in over at Harris Hill."

"What's Harris Hill?"

He raises the phone to his ear. "A public racetrack in San Marcos."

I cover my mouth with my hand, trying to hide my excitement. What are the chances that I'll mark a third of my bucket list off in one day? Skydiving, race-car driving, *and* a possible one-night stand?

Chapter Three

Ridge

I open my eyes and stare at the ceiling. My first thought is of Sydney. My second thought is that I can't believe I fell asleep on the couch in the middle of the afternoon.

I barely slept last night, though. Actually, I've barely slept for the entire past week. I was so anxious leading up to the show I had planned for Sydney last night, not knowing how she would react to it. And then, after she reacted better than I ever imagined and we ended up at her place, I still couldn't sleep because I couldn't stop texting Brennan lyrics. He's probably got enough material from last night alone to make three songs out of.

When I left Sydney's apartment this morning, my plan was to come home and catch up on work, but I couldn't concentrate on anything because I was so exhausted. I finally lay down on the couch and turned on *Game of*

Thrones. I'm probably the last person to start the series, but Warren has been trying to get me to catch up to him for months. He's on season three, and I made it through the first three episodes of season one today before I passed out.

I wonder if Sydney has watched it. If not, I'd much rather start it over and watch it with her.

I pick up my phone and have two unread texts from Warren, one from Maggie, one from Brennan, and one from Sydney. I go straight to Sydney's text first.

Sydney: I listened to the song. It made me cry. It's really good, Ridge.

Ridge: I think you're just partial because you're in love with me.

She texts back immediately.

Sydney: Nope. I'd love the song even if I didn't know you.

Ridge: You're not good for my ego. What time will you be here?

Sydney: On my way now. Will Warren and Bridgette be there?

Ridge: Pretty sure they both work tonight.

Sydney: Perfect. See you soon.

I close out my texts to Sydney and open Warren's text.

Warren: Brennan sent me the new song. I like it.

Ridge: Thanks. Started Game of Thrones today. I like it.

Warren: IT'S ABOUT DAMN TIME! Have you made it to the episode where they decapitate Stark in front of his daughters yet?

I press my phone to my chest and close my eyes. I hate him sometimes. Like really hate him.

Ridge: You are a fucking asshole.

Warren: Dude, it's the best episode!

I toss my phone on the coffee table and stand up. I walk to the kitchen and open the refrigerator to search for a way to get revenge on him. I hope Warren is kidding. Ned Stark? Really, George?

There's a block of one of Bridgette's fancy cheeses in the drawer. I pull it out and open the packaging. It's some sort of white cheese with fancy pieces of spinach or something in it. Smells like shit, but it looks just like a bar of soap once the wrapping is removed. I take it to Warren's bathroom, remove his bar of soap from the shower, and replace it with the cheese.

Ned gets decapitated? I swear to God, if that actually happens, I'm throwing away my television.

When I walk back to the living room, my phone is lighting up on the coffee table. It's a text from Sydney, telling me she just parked. I walk to the door and open it, then make my way down the stairs. She's making her way up, and as soon as I see the smile on her face, I forget all about the decapitation I'm praying is a just a terrible prank Warren is pulling on me.

We meet in the middle of the staircase. She laughs at my eagerness when I push her against the railing and kiss her.

God, I love her. I swear, I don't know what I'd have done if she hadn't signed "when" last night. I'm sure I'd still be sitting on that stage, playing every sad song I could think of while I drank every last drop of alcohol in the bar. But not only did the worst-case scenario not happen—the best-case scenario happened. She loved it and she loves me and here we are, together, about to spend a perfect, boring night at my apartment doing nothing but eating takeout and watching television.

I pull away from her, and she reaches up to wipe lip gloss off my mouth.

"Have you ever watched *Game of Thrones*?" I ask her.

She shakes her head.

"Do you want to?"

She nods. I grab her hand and walk up the stairs with her. When we get inside, she goes to use the bathroom and I pick up my phone. I open the unread text from Maggie.

Maggie: Yes! Found out yesterday. Got a 5.

Ridge: Why am I not surprised? Congratulations! Hope you're doing something to celebrate.

Maggie: I did. Went skydiving.

Skydiving? I hope she's kidding. Skydiving is the last thing she should be doing. That can't be good for her lungs. I start to respond to her, but I pause in the middle of my text. This is the one thing she disliked the most about me. My constant worrying. I have to stop stressing about her doing things that might make her situation worse. It's her life, and she deserves to live it however she wants.

I delete my response to her. When I look up from my phone, Sydney is standing at the refrigerator, watching me. "You okay?" she asks.

I stand up straight and slide my phone into my pocket.

I don't want to talk about Maggie right now, so I smile and save it for another day. "Come here," I say to her.

She smiles and walks over to me, sliding her arms around my waist. I pull her to me. "How was your day?"

She grins. "Excellent. My boyfriend wrote me a song."

I press my lips to her forehead, then hook my thumb beneath her chin, tilting her face up to mine. As soon as I start to kiss her, she grabs my shirt and starts walking backward toward my bedroom. We don't break the kiss until she's falling onto my bed and I'm climbing on top of her.

We kiss for several minutes with our clothes on, which I would rectify, but it's nice. We didn't really fall in love in a typical way, so we went from a kiss that filled us with weeks of guilt, to a three-month stretch of not communicating at all, to a night of making up and making love. We were nothing at all and then suddenly all in. It's nice taking it slow right now. I want to spend the rest of the night kissing her because I've thought about kissing her like this for three months straight.

She rolls me onto my back and then slides on top of me, breaking our kiss. Her hair is falling around her face, so she moves it out of the way by sliding it over her shoulder. She kisses me softly on the mouth and then sits up, straddling me so she can sign.

"Last night feels like . . ." She pauses, struggling to sign the rest, so she speaks it. "It feels like forever ago."

I nod in agreement and then lift my hands to teach her

how to sign the word *forever*. I say it out loud as she signs it. When she gets it right, I nod and sign, "Good job."

She falls to my side and lifts up onto her elbow. "What's the sign for the word *deaf*?"

I make the motion for the word, sliding my hand across my jaw and toward my mouth.

She drags her thumb from her ear to her chin. "Like that?"

I shake my head to let her know she got it wrong. I lift up onto my elbow, then take her hand to tuck in her thumb and straighten out her index finger. I press it to her ear and slide it over her jaw, toward her mouth. "Like that," I tell her. She repeats the sign for *deaf* with perfection. It makes me smile. "Perfect."

She falls back onto her pillow and smiles up at me. I love that she studied sign language for the three months we were apart. As mad as I am at Warren for ruining *Game of Thrones* for me, I'll never be able to repay him for everything he's done to help Sydney and me learn to communicate without so many barriers. He really is a good friend . . . when he isn't being a complete asshole.

She's picked up ASL so fast. Every time she signs something, I'm impressed all over again. It makes me want her to sign everything from now on, and it makes me want to voice all the words I ever say to her.

"My turn," I say. "How do you make the sound a cat makes?"

There are so many words I still don't understand, and

animal sounds are a huge portion of that. Maybe I struggle with knowing how they should sound because it's impossible to read lips when the sound is coming from a cat or a dog.

"You mean meow?" she asks.

I nod and press my fingers against her throat so I can feel her voice when she says it. She repeats the word, and then I give it my best attempt. "Me . . . oh?"

She shakes her head. "First part sounds like . . ." She signs the word *me*.

"Me?"

She nods. "Second part . . ." She lifts her hand to sign the letters *Y*, *O*, and *W* while saying them out loud again. I keep my palm pressed against her throat.

"Again," I say.

She enunciates slowly. "Me . . . yow."

I love the way her lips form a circle at the end of the sound. I bend down and kiss her before trying to speak the sound again. "Me . . . yow."

She grins. "Better."

I say it faster. "Meow."

"Perfect."

I start to ask her why *meow* is used in certain instances, but I forget how new she is at signing, and her eyes grow big with her confusion as she tries to follow along with my hands. I lean over her and grab my phone and type out my question.

Ridge: Why is the word MEOW sometimes used to depict

when something is sexy? Does the word make a sexy sound when it's spoken?

She laughs and her cheeks blush a little when she says, "Very."

I find that interesting.

Ridge: Is it also sexy when a person barks like a dog?

She shakes her head. "No. Not at all."

The verbal form of the English language is so confusing. But I love learning more about it from her. It's the first thing that drew me to her beyond the physical attraction. Her patience with my inability to hear and her eagerness in wanting to know all about it. There aren't a lot of people like her in this world, and every single time she signs for me, it reminds me how lucky I am.

I pull her closer and lean toward her ear. "Meow." When I pull back, she's no longer smiling. She's looking at me like that was the sexiest thing she's ever heard. She confirms my thoughts by sliding her fingers through my hair and pulling my mouth to hers. I roll on top of her and part her lips with my tongue. Just as I start to give her a deeper kiss, I feel the vibration of her moan, and then I'm a goner.

And so are our clothes. So much for taking it slow tonight.

Chapter Four

Sydney

I follow the path of Ridge's finger with my eyes as he runs it back and forth over my stomach. We've been lying like this for five minutes now, him running his fingers in soft circles over my skin while he watches me. Every now and then, he kisses me, but we're both too exhausted for round two.

I don't even know how he's still awake. He barely slept last night at my house because he stayed up writing that song for me, and then as soon as I got here an hour and a half ago, we came straight to the bedroom and have stayed fairly busy. It's almost eight, and if I don't eat dinner soon, I'm going to fall asleep right here in his bed.

My stomach growls, and Ridge laughs, pressing his palm flat against my stomach. "You hungry?"

"You felt that?"

He nods. "Let me shower, and then I'll figure out dinner." He kisses me and rolls off the bed, heading for his bathroom. I find his T-shirt and pull it on before heading to the kitchen for something to drink. When I open the refrigerator, someone behind me says, "Hi."

I yelp, and then I swing the refrigerator door wide open and try to hide my undressed bottom half behind it. Brennan is sitting on the couch, grinning.

So are the other two guys from his band, whom I've still yet to be formally introduced to.

Brennan tilts his head. "The first night I met you, you weren't wearing a shirt. And now a shirt is all you're wearing."

I can't recall ever being this mortified in my life. I didn't even put my panties on, and even though Ridge's shirt covers my ass, I don't know how to make it from here all the way back to his bedroom without losing my last shred of dignity.

"Hi," I say, sticking my arm up over the door with a pathetic wave. "Do you guys mind looking away so I can find some jeans?"

All three of them laugh, but they look at the wall to spare me a few seconds to run back to Ridge's room. As soon as I start to swing the refrigerator door shut, the front door flies open, and Warren stomps into the apartment. I pull the refrigerator door open again to continue shielding myself.

Bridgette storms into the apartment behind Warren,

and then Warren slams the door. "Go!" he says, waving her away as she storms across the living room toward their bedroom. "Go hide in your room and give me the silent treatment like you always do!"

Bridgette slams their bedroom door. I look back at Warren, who is staring at Brennan and the other two guys on the couch. "Hey," he says, still not noticing me. "What's up?"

None of them are looking at Warren because I asked them to turn toward the wall, so Brennan is still staring at the wall when he says, "Hey, Warren."

"Why are you staring at the wall?"

Brennan points toward the refrigerator, but continues to stare at the wall. "Waiting for her to run back to Ridge's room so she can put some clothes on."

Warren swings his attention to me, and his eyes immediately light up. "Well, what a sight for sore eyes," he says, tossing his keys on the bar. "I know I see you all the time, but it's good to finally see you back in this apartment."

I swallow, doing my best to remain stoic. "It's . . . good to be back, Warren."

He points at the refrigerator door. "You really shouldn't stand there with the door open like that. Ridge makes me split the bills with him now, and you're wasting a lot of electricity."

I nod. "Yeah. Sorry. But I sort of don't have any pants on, and if you'd walk over there and stare at the wall with those guys, I'll shut the door and go back to Ridge's room."

Warren tilts his head and then takes two steps toward me and leans to the right like he's trying to look around the refrigerator door.

"See?" Bridgette yells from across the room, standing in Warren's now-open doorway. "This is exactly what I'm talking about, Warren! You flirt with everyone!" Their door slams again.

Warren rolls his head and sighs, then walks toward their bedroom. I use the opportunity to make a mad dash back to Ridge's bedroom. I shut the door and lean against it, covering my face with my hands.

I'm never going back out there.

I make my way toward Ridge's bathroom just as he opens the door. There's a towel wrapped around his waist, and he's drying his hair with another towel. I rush toward him and wrap my arms around him, burying my face against his chest as I squeeze my eyes shut. I just start shaking my head until he pulls me away from his chest so he can look at me. I can't even imagine what he's seeing because I'm groaning and frowning and laughing at my embarrassment.

"What happened?"

I point to the living room and then sign, "Your brother. Warren. The band. Here." Then I motion toward my half-naked body and the fact that my butt cheeks are practically hanging out of his T-shirt. He eyes me up and down and then glances toward the living room, then looks at me again, squinting like he's remembering something. "The first time you met Brennan . . . you were wearing just a bra. Now you're wearing—"

"I *know*," I groan, falling onto his bed. Ridge starts laughing while he pulls on his jeans. Then he leans forward, and I think he's going to kiss me, but instead he just slips his shirt over my head and pulls it off me. He's fully dressed, and I'm even more naked than I was when I walked into the living room. He hands me my clothes, and I know he wants to officially introduce me to the band, but I want to curl up into a ball and hide until everyone leaves.

I force myself to suck it up and get dressed because Ridge is smiling at me like this entire thing amuses him, and his smile makes me forget how embarrassed I am. The kiss he gives me when he pulls me toward the door makes me forget it even more.

When we walk back into the living room, Brennan is now sitting on the bar with his legs dangling, swinging back and forth. He grins at me, and it's unnerving how much he and Ridge look alike yet carry themselves so differently. Ridge walks me to the couch where the other two members of Sounds of Cedar are standing up to shake my hand.

"Spencer," the tall brunette one says. He's the drummer. I know this because I've seen them play. I've just never actually been introduced to them.

"Price," the other one says, shaking my hand. He plays lead guitar and sings backup vocals, and while the star of the band is definitely Brennan, I think Price gives him a run for his money. He's got the rock-star swagger down, even though their music isn't typically rock. It's got a more pop/alternative vibe. But he could probably pull off any sound because he's so charismatic onstage. Brennan sometimes takes a step back and lets him shine.

"I'm Sydney," I say, with a lot of forced confidence. "It's so good to finally meet you guys. I'm a huge fan of the band." I wave my arm across them and over to Brennan. "It's so impressive how fast you guys get stuff recorded."

Price laughs and says, "Sydney, we're all huge fans of yours. Ridge went through a pretty long dry spell until you came along."

My eyes widen, and I look over at Ridge, who is looking at Brennan, who is signing everything everyone is saying. Ridge immediately looks back at me, and then at Price.

"Dry spell?" Ridge says out loud.

"*Lyrical* dry spell," Price says, clarifying what he meant. "I meant lyrical." Now Price looks embarrassed.

God, this is so awkward.

"I'm hungry," Brennan says, slapping his hands on the bar on either side of him. "Has anyone eaten?"

"Chinese sounds good," I suggest.

Brennan picks up his phone and looks at it. "A girl who knows what she wants. I like it." He pulls the phone to his ear. "Chinese it is. I'll just order a shit-ton of everything."

I try not to stare at him too hard. I just can't get over how much he looks like Ridge physically, but with a completely different personality. Ridge is responsible and mature, and Brennan seems like he doesn't give a shit. About anything. It's like he doesn't have a single care, yet his older brother takes on the burden of caring about every single thing.

"So, Bridgette and I are fighting, if you didn't notice," Warren says, taking a seat on the couch and scrolling through his texts. He looks up at me. "She says I flirt with other people too much."

I laugh. "You do."

Warren rolls his eyes and mutters, "Traitor. You're supposed to be on my side."

"There are no sides when it's a discussion of facts," I say. "You flirt with me. You flirt with Bridgette. You flirt with the old lady who lives in my apartment building. Hell, you even flirt with her dog. You're a flirt, Warren."

"He flirts with me," Spencer says.

Warren is still scrolling through his texts when he reads something that makes him pause. He laughs a little and then looks over at Ridge and Brennan. "Maggie went skydiving today."

My breath catches at the mention of her name. Naturally, I look over at Ridge, who is leaning against the bar next to Brennan. Brennan covers his phone with his hand and says, "Good for her."

Ridge just nods, expressionless, and says, "I know. She told me earlier." He glances at me for a brief second and then looks down at his phone.

My mouth feels dry. I press my lips together. There was a moment earlier, when I came out of the bathroom and saw Ridge holding his phone with a torn expression. I had no idea what had caused him to react like he was. I assumed it was work.

But . . . it wasn't work. It was Maggie. He was worried about Maggie.

I don't like how I'm feeling right now. I pull my phone out of my pocket and try to busy myself, but I'm standing awkwardly in the middle of the living room. Brennan ends his call to the Chinese place, and Warren and Ridge are both looking at their phones. I suddenly feel out of place. Like I don't belong in this living room with these people in this apartment. Brennan signs something to Ridge without speaking, and then they start a silent conversation with Warren that's too fast for me to keep up with, which makes me think they don't want me to know what they're saying. I try to ignore them, but I can't help but look when Warren says, "You worry too much, man."

"Typical Ridge," Brennan says. As soon as he says that, Brennan looks at me and then at Ridge and then stiffens a little. "Sorry. Is that weird? We shouldn't talk about Maggie. That's weird." He looks over at Warren, who brought up the entire conversation. "Shut the fuck up, Warren."

Warren brushes off Brennan's comment with a flippant wave in my direction. "Sydney's cool. She's not a PSYCHOTIC JEALOUS GIRLFRIEND LIKE SOME PEOPLE!" he yells toward his bedroom.

Two seconds later, Bridgette swings open the door and says, "I'm not your girlfriend. I broke up with you."

Warren looks offended. And confused. He holds up his hands. "When?"

"Right now," Bridgette says. "I'm breaking up with you right now, asshole." She slams the door, and sadly, no one really pays it much attention. Some things haven't changed a bit around here. Warren doesn't even get up from the couch to chase after her.

I feel my phone vibrate, so I look at the text.

Ridge: Hi.

I glance over at him, and he's sitting on the bar now, next to Brennan. They're both swinging their legs, seated the same way, and Ridge looks completely adorable as he smiles at me. The looks he gives me are intoxicating. He motions for me to come stand with him, so I walk over to him. He spreads his legs wider, turning me until my back is against his chest. He kisses me on the side of my head and wraps his arms around my shoulders.

"Hey, Sydney," Brennan says. "Did Ridge play you the song Price wrote?"

I glance at Price and then back at Brennan. "No, which one is it?"

Brennan signs for Ridge to play me the song, so Ridge holds his phone in front of me and searches his files.

"'Even If Your Back Was Turned,'" Price says from the couch.

"We just recorded it last week," Brennan says. "I like it. I think it'll do well. Price wrote it for his mommy."

Price throws a pillow in Brennan's direction. "Fuck

you," he says. He looks at me and shrugs. "I am a momma's boy."

I laugh, because he doesn't look like your typical momma's boy.

Ridge finds the song and presses play. He sets the phone on his thigh and then wraps his arms around me again as I listen. Almost as soon as it starts to play, a text notification goes off on Ridge's phone. I look down at it.

Maggie: Guess what? I'm finally riding in a TESLA!!!

Ridge must see the text as soon as I hear it and read it, because his legs stop swinging and he stiffens. We're both looking at the phone, and I know he's waiting on my reaction, but I don't know how I should react. I don't even know what I'm supposed to be feeling right now. It's just all too weird. I reach over and swipe up on her text so it'll disappear. Then I pause the song and say to Price, "I'll listen to it later. It's too loud in here."

Ridge wraps his arm tighter around my waist as he picks up his phone and begins texting with one hand. I don't know if he's responding to her or not, but I guess it's not my business. Is it? I don't even know if I should be mad. I don't think I'm mad. *Confused* is a better word for it. Or maybe *uncomfortable* is the best way to describe what I'm feeling.

Ridge pulls on my hand so I'll turn and look at him. I'm still standing between his legs, but this time I'm facing him, looking at him, trying not to let him read my thoughts. He puts his phone in my hand, and when I look at it to read whatever he's written in his note app, he lowers his forehead to mine.

She's my friend, Sydney. We text sometimes.

As I'm reading the note on his phone, his hands are sliding softly down my arms in a comforting gesture. It's amazing how much more he can communicate nonverbally as a result of being so stifled by his verbal communication. By pressing his forehead to mine as I read what he typed, it's as if he's silently saying, *We're a team, Sydney. You and me.*

And the way he's sliding his hands down my arms is equivalent to a thousand verbal reassurances.

I expected that he still talks to Maggie. What I didn't expect was for it to bother me like it is. But it's not because I think Ridge and Maggie are in the wrong. It's because I feel like I'll always be the girl who came between them, no matter how friendly they remain. I can be friendly with every single friend Ridge ever has, but I'm not sure I could ever be friends with Maggie, so the fact that he *is* friends with her makes me feel like a third wheel to that friendship.

It's a strange feeling. And one I don't like, so I can't help but have a noticeable reaction. Especially to Ridge. He notices every nonverbal reaction I have because that's the focus of his communication.

I hand Ridge's phone back to him and force a smile, but I know my feelings are probably written all over my face. He pulls me in for a reassuring hug and then kisses the side of my head. I press my face against his neck and sigh.

"God, you two are so cute together," Brennan says.

"It makes me want a girlfriend. For like a whole week, maybe."

His comment makes me laugh. I pull away from Ridge and turn around, leaning my back into him again.

"You're about to have one for more than a week," Spencer says. "Sadie's opening for us for the next two months."

Brennan groans. "Don't remind me."

I welcome the distraction. "Who is Sadie?"

Brennan looks at me pointedly and says, "Sadie is Satan."

"Her name is Sadie Brennan," Warren says, standing up. "Not to be confused with Brennan Lawson. Coincidence that they share part of a name, and also a coincidence that Brennan thought she was a groupie the first time he met her."

Brennan grabs a roll of paper towels off the bar and throws them at Warren. "It was an honest mistake."

"I think this is a story I need to hear," I say.

"No," Brennan says firmly.

At the same time Brennan says *no*, Warren pipes up and says, "I'll tell it." He flips one of the table chairs around backward and sits down, facing us. "Brennan has a routine," Warren says and signs. "Sounds of Cedar isn't a widely known band, but locally, you know, they have a decent following. Quite a few fangirls who come to the meet and greets after the shows."

Warren is signing everything for Ridge, so it makes me laugh when Brennan's head falls back and he groans, then signs, "Shut up," at the same time he says it. It'll never get old that they sign everything for Ridge. It's like it's second nature, and they don't even realize they're doing it. That's my goal. I want to learn to communicate that way to the point where Ridge and I have absolutely no barriers.

"Sometimes after the shows, if Brennan thinks a girl is cute, he'll slip her a note with his hotel information, asking if she wants to chat in private. Five times out of ten, they show up an hour later at his hotel room door."

"Ten times out of ten," Brennan corrects.

God, he and Ridge are so different.

Warren rolls his eyes and continues, "Sadie happened to be one of the girls he slipped a note to. But what he didn't know was that she wasn't at his meet and greet as a fan. She was there looking to talk with him about a gig. And what she didn't know is that Brennan slips someone his number after every show with the intention of hooking up. She thought he slipped her a note because he wanted to chat with her about opening for the band on our upcoming tour. So when she showed up at his hotel room that night, let's just say there was a lot of confusion."

I look at Brennan, and he's running his hand down his face like he's embarrassed. "Dude, I hate this story."

He might hate it, but I'm enjoying the hell out of it. "What happened?"

Brennan groans. "Can't we just end the story here?"

"No," Warren says. "This is where it gets good."

Brennan looks so embarrassed, but he continues the story himself. "Let's just say it took her a few seconds to realize what I assumed she was there for, and it took me more than a few seconds to realize she wasn't there because she wanted me to take off her shirt."

"Oh no. That poor girl."

Brennan makes a face. "Poor girl, my ass. I told you she's Satan. She makes Bridgette look like an angel."

"I heard that," Bridgette yells from her room. Brennan shrugs. "It's true."

"She's not that bad," Price says to Brennan. "She just hates *you*."

"But . . . she's opening for you guys on the next tour? She must not hate you too much," I say.

Brennan shakes his head. "No, she definitely hates me. But she also has mad talent. That's the only reason why she got the gig."

"Do you have any of her songs?" I ask. "I want to hear one."

Brennan scoots closer to us and hands me his phone after pulling up a YouTube video. Ridge scoots me over and hops off the bar to set out plates for the Chinese food. I can't help but stare at the video on Brennan's phone in complete awe. The girl is really pretty. And she's super talented. I watch the first video, and then another, and then a third before I realize Brennan hasn't moved a muscle. He can pretend he isn't into her all he wants, but he holds his breath through every video, never taking his eyes off the screen.

We're watching the fourth video when the food arrives. We all make our plates and sit around the table. It's the first meal Ridge and I have eaten together as a couple.

He's sitting right next to me with his left hand on my thigh. We've eaten a lot of meals at this table together while forcing ourselves to sit as far apart from each other as we possibly could. It feels good to finally be able to touch him—sit close to him—and not fight everything inside me that was growing.

I like this.

The door to the bathroom between Warren and Bridgette's old bedroom swings open. Bridgette is standing in a towel, sopping wet from the shower. Her eyes scan the table until she finds Warren, and then she tosses something at him, hitting him in the chest. Whatever it is falls onto his plate. Then the door slams.

Everyone looks at Warren. He picks up the block of whatever she just threw at him and stares at it for a second. Then he sniffs it. His head slowly turns toward Ridge.

"Cheese? You put *cheese* in my shower?"

I look at Ridge, and he's attempting to force back a smile.

Warren sniffs the cheese again and then takes a small bite of it. I cover my mouth with my hand, trying not to gag. *Does he not realize that Bridgette had to rub that block of cheese on some part of her body before realizing it wasn't soap?*

Warren sets the cheese on his plate like he just received a free course with his meal.

As disgusting as some of them are, I've missed their pranks so much. I squeeze Ridge's leg to let him know that was a clever one.

When we finish eating, I text Ridge and tell him I should go. I have an early day tomorrow, and it'll be after ten by the time I get home. I tell all the guys goodbye, and Ridge walks me down. When we reach my car, he opens my door but doesn't kiss me goodbye. He waits for me to sit, and then he walks around to the passenger side and takes a seat.

He grabs my phone, which I just placed in the console, and hands it to me.

Ridge: You okay?

I nod, but he doesn't look convinced. I don't know how to say, *Stop having friends!* without feeling a little like Bridgette.

Ridge: Does it bother you?

He doesn't even have to specify what he's talking about. We both know. And I don't know how to answer him. I don't want to be that jealous girlfriend who takes issue with every single thing, but how can I not be jealous when there's still a part of me that's envious of Maggie?

Ridge: Please be honest, Syd. I want to know what you're thinking.

I sigh, thankful he cares enough to talk about it but also wishing we could brush it under the rug at the same time.

Sydney: It's uncomfortable. It bothered me that you seemed so worried about her. But it would also bother me if you didn't care. So it's just . . . weird. It's going to take time to get used to, I guess.

Ridge: I do worry about her. And I care about her. But I am not in love with her, Sydney. I'm in love with you.

When I finish reading his text, he leans across the seat and takes my face in his hands. "I love you."

The sincerity in his expression makes me smile. "I know you do. I love you, too."

He stares at me for a moment, searching for any remaining doubt in my expression. Then he kisses me goodnight. When he gets out of the car, he takes the stairs two at a time. He reaches the top and texts me again.

Ridge: Let me know when you make it home safe. And thank you.

Ridge: For being you.

When I look up, he smiles and then disappears inside his apartment. I watch his door for a moment and then drop my phone in my purse, just as someone knocks on my window. I jump and press my hand to my chest. When I look out my window, I roll my eyes.

You've got to be kidding me.

Hunter is standing at my driver's-side window, looking at me expectantly. I forgot he even frequented this apartment complex. I guess that means he's still with Tori. I stare at him for a moment and feel absolutely nothing. Not even anger.

I put my car in reverse and back up, pulling away from the complex without looking back. The only way to look now is forward.

• • •

Ridge: You asleep?

I look at the time stamp on his text. He just sent the message two minutes ago. I pull the towel off my head and run my fingers through my hair before I text him back.

Sydney: Nope. Just got out of the shower.

Ridge: Oh yeah? So you're naked?

Sydney: I have a towel on. And no, you aren't getting a pic.

Ridge: I don't want a pic. I want you to open your front door and let me in.

I glance toward the living room, then look back down at my phone. *He's here?* I only left his apartment an hour ago. I rush to the living room with worry in the pit of my stomach. I hope nothing is wrong. Surely Hunter didn't do anything stupid after I pulled away.

I look through the peephole, and there he is, staring at the door. I leave the living room light off since I'm opening the door with only a towel on. Ridge slips inside my apartment. I close the door. It's dark, and I'm suddenly no longer wearing a towel. Ridge's mouth is on mine, and my back is against the living room wall.

Ridge isn't really the type to just show up without telling me first, but I don't mind it.

I don't mind it *at all.*

What I do mind is that he's dressed and I'm not.

I pull off his shirt and unbutton his jeans. His mouth is everywhere, but his hands have me caged against the wall. He kicks off his pants and then picks me up, wrapping my legs around his waist. He starts toward the bedroom, but realizes we're way closer to the couch, so he turns and lowers me to the sofa.

We're still kissing when he lowers himself on top of me, and then he's inside me and it's incredible. I am so in love with this man.

He stops kissing me for a moment, so I let my head fall back onto the cushion, and I relax as he kisses my neck. When he reaches my mouth again, he pulls back and stares down at me. He brushes my hair back, and there's just enough light from the window shining down on us so that I can see every emotion in his eyes. He's looking at me with so much feeling when he says, "I love you, Sydney." He pauses above me so that I'm focused on his words and nothing else. "I love you more than I have ever loved anyone."

I close my eyes because the impact of his words hits me everywhere. I had no idea how much I wanted those words. *Needed* those words. And he knows I would never ask him to admit that or compare us to his last relationship, but here he is, wanting to diminish any shred of doubt I might have had while at his apartment tonight. I repeat his words silently, never wanting to forget this moment. This feeling. *I love you more than I have ever loved anyone.*

His warm mouth presses gently against mine, and his tongue slides past my lips, delicately searching for mine. When I kiss him back, I wrap my hand in his hair and pull him as close as I can. For the next several minutes, Ridge proves to me just how much I mean to him without speaking or signing another word.

Even when it's over, several minutes go by with our lips still connected. Every time he tries to stop kissing me, he can't. It's just one kiss after another after another. He eventually buries his face against my neck and sighs against my skin. "Can I spend the night with you?"

His question makes me laugh. I don't know why. It just feels like it's a given at this point. As soon as I nod, he grabs my arms and pulls me up with him, then lifts me and carries me to the bedroom. He lays me on the bed and then crawls under the covers with me, wrapping his bare legs around me. I love that neither of us are dressed. This is a first.

I kiss him on the nose and want to sign to him, but it's dark. He also can't read lips in the dark, so I grab my phone.

Sydney: That was completely unexpected.

Ridge: Do you prefer your boyfriend to be more predictable?

Sydney: I prefer my boyfriend to be you. That's really my only requirement. Just be Ridge Lawson and you can date me.

Ridge: I'm pretty good at being Ridge Lawson. You're in luck.

We are so cheesy. I hate us and love us.

Sydney: Unexpected or predictable, I like all the versions of you.

Ridge: I like all the versions of you, too. Even if the rest of our lives were predictable, I'd never get tired of you. We could live the same day over and over and I'd just ask for more.

Sydney: Like Groundhog Day. I feel the same way.

Ridge: You make routine something I actually look forward to. If you told me you wanted us to go wash dishes together right now, I'd get excited.

Sydney: What if I asked you to do laundry with me? Would that excite you?

The light from our phones makes it possible for me to see him when he looks at me. He nods slowly, like the thought of doing laundry with me turns him on. I grin and look back at my phone.

Sydney: Would you look forward to eating the same meal every single day?

Ridge: I would if I were eating it with you.

Sydney: Would you be able to drink the same drink every single day?

Ridge: If I were drinking it with you, I would still be thirsty for it on my deathbed.

Sydney: Oh, that's a good line. Keep going.

Ridge: If I could hear music, I would listen to the same song over and over and never tire of it as long as I was listening to it with you.

I laugh.

Sydney: I see you still have the same self-deprecating deaf jokes you've always had.

Ridge reaches out and touches my mouth. "And you have the same beautiful smile you've always had." His thumb runs over my bottom lip, but his eyes grow intense as he stares at my mouth. "Same smile . . . same laugh." He pulls his hand from my mouth and lifts up. "This feels like a song," he says. As soon as he says it, he rolls over and turns on the lamp. "Paper?" He opens my top drawer. He doesn't find paper, but he finds a pen. He faces me with a look of urgency. "I need paper."

I roll off the bed and walk to my desk. I grab a legal pad and a book for him to place it on. He grabs them out of my hands before I'm even seated back on the bed; then he starts writing lyrics. I've missed this so much. He writes a few sentences, and I lean over his shoulder and watch him.

Same seats on the couch
Same drinks when we go out
Same smile, same laugh
You know I'll never get enough of that

He pauses for a moment, then he looks at me. He smiles and hands me the pen. "Your turn." It feels like old times. I take the pen and the legal pad and think for a moment before adding my own lines.

Same clothes on the floor
Same dog at our door
Same room, same bed
I wouldn't wish for anything instead

He's staring at the lyrics when he hops off the bed and starts looking around the floor. "Jeans?" he says. I point to the living room. He nods, like he forgot we came to my bedroom naked. He points over his shoulder. "Guitar. My car." He rushes out of my room, and a minute later, I hear him walk out my front door. I look at the page and read through the lyrics again. I have two more sentences written when he makes it back to my bedroom with his guitar.

When everything is changing
Baby you're written in stone

He sets his guitar on the bed and looks over the lyrics, then motions for the pen. He tears out the lyrics and starts writing out chords and notes on another page. This is my favorite part. This is the magic—watching him hear a song that doesn't even have sound and doesn't even exist yet. The pen is flying over the paper frantically. He pulls the lyrics back in front of him and starts adding to them.

Feels like we made it
Got something of our own
Maybe it's predictable
But I can't complain
With you and me
All I need
Is more of the same
More of the same

He hands me the notepad and pen and picks up his guitar. He starts playing, and I'm reading the lyrics, wondering how he does this with such little effort. Just like that, he's created a new song. An entire song from nothing more than a few sentences and a little inspiration.

I begin to write another verse while he plays the chords.

Same songs in the car
We never need to go too far and I won't leave you alone
Just stay the same baby I've always known that
When everything is changing
Baby you're written in stone
Feels like we made it
Got something of our own
Maybe it's predictable
But I can't complain
With you and me
All I need is more of the same
More of the same

When I finish writing the chorus again, he reads it all. Then he hands me the lyrics and leans back against my headboard. He motions for me to sit between his legs, so I crawl over and turn my back toward him as he pulls me against him and wraps his guitar around us. He doesn't even have to ask me to sing the song. He starts playing, leaning his head against mine, and I start singing the song for him so that he can perfect it.

The first time he played for me, we were sitting like this. And just like that first day, I am completely in awe of him. His concentration is inspiring, and the way he creates such a pleasing sound that he can't even hear makes it hard for me to focus on the lyrics. I want to turn around and watch him play. But I also like that we're wrapped together on my bed and I'm caged against him by his guitar, and every now and then, he kisses the side of my head.

I could do this every night with him and still want more of the same.

We sing and play the song about three times, and he pauses to make notes between each run-through. After the fourth and final time, he tosses the pen on the floor and then pushes his guitar to the other side of the bed. Then he turns me around so I'm straddling his lap. We're both smiling.

It's one thing for a person to find their passion, but it's another thing entirely to be able to share that passion with the person you're passionate about.

It's fun and intense, and I think we're both realizing for the first time that we get to do this together all the time. Write songs, kiss, make love, be inspired to write more songs.

Ridge kisses me. "This is my new favorite song."

"Mine, too."

He slides both hands to my cheeks and bites his lip for a second. Then he clears his throat. "With you and me . . . all I need . . . is more of the same."

Oh my God. *He's singing.* Ridge Lawson is serenading me. And it's terrible because he's so out of tune, but a tear falls from my eye because it's the most beautiful thing I've ever witnessed or heard or felt.

He wipes my tear away with his thumb and smiles. "That bad, huh?"

I laugh and shake my head, and then I kiss him harder than I've ever kissed him because there is no way I can verbally express my love for him right now. Instead, I love him silently. He doesn't even break the kiss when he reaches behind him and turns off the lamp. He pulls the covers over us and then tucks my head under his chin as he wraps himself around me.

Neither of us says *I love you* before we fall asleep.

Sometimes two people share a silent moment that feels so deep and so powerful, a simple phrase such as *I love you* risks losing all prior meaning if spoken aloud.

Chapter Five

Maggie

I've only taken three bites of my burger, but I push the plate away from me and lean back. "I can't finish this," I mutter, letting my head fall back against the booth. "I'm sorry."

Jake laughs. "You jumped out of an airplane for the first time ever and then drove a car in circles for an hour straight. I'm surprised you're able to eat anything at all."

He says this with an empty plate sitting in front of him while scarfing down a milkshake. I guess when you're used to jumping out of planes and driving fast cars, the adrenaline doesn't jack with your equilibrium to the point that you feel like the world is spinning inside your stomach.

"It was fun, though," I say with a smile. "It's not every day I cross two things off my bucket list."

He scoots both of our plates to the edge of the table and leans forward. "What else is on your bucket list?"

"Vegas. The Northern Lights. Paris. The usual." I fail to tell him that he's who I hope will be number eight on my list. We've had so much fun tonight, I want to do it again. But I also don't, simply because we had so much fun tonight. I've spent the entirety of my adulthood in a relationship. I don't want that again. Even if he is too good to be true. "Why are you single?" I ask him.

He rolls his eyes like the question embarrasses him. He pulls his glass of water in front of him, sipping from it in order to avoid it for a few seconds longer. When he lets the straw fall away from his lips, he shrugs. "I'm usually not."

I laugh. That's expected, I suppose. A skydiving, Tesla-driving, good-looking cardiologist doesn't sit home every Friday night. "Are you a serial dater?"

He shakes his head. "The opposite, actually. I just got out of a relationship. A really long relationship."

I didn't expect that answer. "How long did you date her?"

"Twelve years."

I sputter a cough. "Twelve years? How old are you?"

"Twenty-nine. Started dating her in high school."

"Can I ask what ended it? Or do you want to change the subject?"

Jake shakes his head. "I don't mind talking about it. I moved out about six months ago. We were engaged, actually. I proposed four years ago. We never got around to planning the wedding because we were waiting until we finished our residencies."

"She's a doctor, too?"

"Oncologist."

Jeez. I suddenly feel so . . . young. I just barely finished my thesis, and here he is with an ex-fiancée who went through medical school with him and saves lives. I pull my drink to my lips and take a sip, attempting to wash down all my insecurities.

"Was it a mutual breakup?" I ask him.

He looks down at his hands briefly. A flash of guilt takes over his expression before he responds. "Not really. I realized about twelve years too late that I didn't want to spend the rest of my life with her. I know that sounds bad after being with her for so long. But for some reason, choosing to spend the rest of my life with her was a lot easier than breaking up with her."

Why am I feeling everything he's saying? I find myself wanting to raise my arm and say, *Amen*, like I'm in church. "I can absolutely relate to what a hard decision that must have been."

Jake leans forward, folding his arms on the table. He tilts his head in thought for a moment, then says, "I had a moment before I ended it. I remember asking myself what I would regret more. Ending something that was good so I didn't end up with regrets? Or spending the rest of my life regretting that I didn't have the courage to end something simply because I was afraid of regret? Either choice would have left me with some form of regret, so I chose to end it. And it was hard. But I'd rather regret ending something good than be what prevents her from finding something great."

I stare at him a moment, but I have to break my stare because I'm starting to have that feeling again. That I want him to be more than a one-night stand.

"How long were you and your boyfriend together?" he asks.

"Almost six years."

"Were you the one who ended it?"

I think about his question for a moment. From the outside looking in, I'd say I was. But being in it . . . I'm not so sure. "I don't know," I admit. "He fell in love with another girl. And it wasn't like it was some torrid, scandalous affair. He's a good person, and he would have chosen me in the end. But he would have chosen me for the wrong reasons."

Jake looks surprised. "He cheated on you?"

I hate that word. I find myself shaking my head, even though he did. Ridge cheated on me. It makes him sound malicious, which he is not. "*Cheating* is such an ugly term to describe what happened." I think about it for a moment as I stir my straw around in my glass. Then I look up at Jake and say, "He . . . connected with someone else on a deeper level, I think. To call him a cheater feels like an insult he doesn't deserve. He crossed a line with someone he connected with. We'll just leave it at that."

Jake watches me for a moment, reading my expression. "You don't have to talk about it if you don't want to. I just find it fascinating that you don't sound like you hate him."

I smile. "He's one of my best friends. And he tried to do the right thing. But sometimes the wrong thing is the right thing."

Jake fights a smile, like he's impressed with this conversation, but he doesn't want to show it. I like that. I like how interesting he is. And I like that he seems to find me interesting.

He's still staring, like he wants to hear more, so I continue. "Ridge writes lyrics for a band. About two years ago, the band released a new song, and I'll never forget the first time I heard it. Ridge always sent me the songs ahead of their release, but for some reason, he never sent me this particular song. After I downloaded it and listened to it, I immediately knew why he never sent it. It's because he wrote it about us."

"A love song?"

I shake my head. "No. It was kind of the opposite. Sort of a falling-out-of-love song, about a couple who needed to move on from each other but didn't know how. It wasn't until I heard that song that I realized he felt the same way I did. But neither of us was in a place to admit that to the other at the time."

"Did you ever ask him about it?"

"No. I didn't have to. I knew it was about me as soon as I heard the first line."

"What was the line?"

"'I keep on wondering why I can't say bye to you.'"

"Wow," Jake says, leaning back. "That's definitely telling."

I nod. "I don't know why we waited so long after that to end it. I guess it's like you said. Things between us were good, but I knew he'd found something great in another girl. And he deserved better than just good."

Jake's expression is stoic as he watches me silently for a few seconds. But then he smiles with a shake of his head. "How old are you?"

"Twenty-four."

He makes a face like he's impressed. "You're a little young to have life figured out so well."

His compliment makes me smile. "Yeah, well, I have a shorter life span than everyone else. I have to cram a lot into a smaller time frame."

I almost regret making a joke about having a terminal illness, but it doesn't dismay him at all. In fact, it makes him smile. *God, I hate how much I like him already.*

"Is this your first date since Ridge?" he asks. I nod, and he says, "Mine, too."

I think about that for a moment. If he hasn't dated since his breakup, that means he hasn't dated another girl since high school. And I probably shouldn't open my mouth, but the sentence is already coming out. "If you dated your ex for twelve years, that means you've only been with—"

"Her," he says, matter-of-fact. "That is correct."

And here we are, somehow discussing sexual partners over dinner on a first date. And somehow, the conversation isn't at all uncomfortable. Conversation with him has been great, actually. There hasn't been a lull all night. Not even while I was driving his car one hundred miles per hour in circles around a racetrack.

There also hasn't been a lull in our chemistry. There were a couple of times tonight when I thought he might kiss me—and I absolutely would have let him—but he'd grin and step away from me like he enjoys the feeling of torture. I guess that would make sense. He's an adrenaline junkie. Adrenaline and attraction feel very closely related.

He's staring at me right now, and I'm staring at him, and I don't know exactly what it is that's taken over me at the moment. A little bit of adrenaline. Attraction. Maybe even infatuation. Whatever it is, I have a bad feeling about it. I don't know Jake well enough, but I think the intense look on his face suggests he feels it, too.

I break eye contact with him and clear my throat. "Jake . . ." I lift my eyes, meeting his stare again. "I don't want a relationship. At all. Not even remotely."

My words have no visible impact on him. He simply presses his lips together and then, a moment later, asks, "What do you want?"

I lift my shoulders in a slow, unsure shrug. "I don't know," I say, dropping my shoulders again. "I wanted to have fun with you on our date. And I did. I am. But I'm not sure it's a good idea if we go out again."

I wish I could explain to him all the reasons why I don't want to go on another date with him. But there are way too many reasons not to go on another date, as opposed to only one reason why I should.

Jake squeezes the back of his neck and then leans forward, folding his arms over the table again. "Maggie," he says. "I've been out of practice when it comes to this whole dating thing. But . . . I feel like you like me. Do you like me? Or am I just blinded to your disinterest because I'm insanely attracted to you?"

Ugh. I can't help the smile that forces its way out. I can also feel myself blushing over the fact that he's insanely attracted to me. "I do like you. And . . ." This is so hard for me to say. Flirting is so foreign to me. "I'm insanely attracted to you, too. But I don't want to date you after tonight. It's nothing personal. I want to live in the moment, and right now, another serious relationship is not a part of my moment. I've been there, done that. I have other plans for my life."

Jake looks both intrigued and disappointed by my answer, if that's even possible to feel both things at once. He nods and says, "So this is it? I leave a tip on the table and then I drive you home and drop you off and we never see each other again?"

I bite my bottom lip, because knowing it's now or never makes me nervous. I either use this moment to mark off another item on my bucket list, or I wake up tomorrow regretting that I was too scared to ask him to come over.

I'm not scared. I can do this. I am Maggie fucking Carson. I am the girl who jumped out of an airplane and raced a sports car in the same day.

I swallow the last shred of shyness and look him in the eyes. "This date doesn't have to end when we pull into my driveway."

I can see the immediate change in his demeanor. I can see his intrigue and his attraction and his hope, all settled behind his eyes that are staring at my mouth. He lowers his voice a little and says, "When, exactly, does it have to end?"

Holy shit. This is actually happening. Bucket list item number eight, practically in the bag.

"How about we just live in the moment?" I suggest. "And then when that moment is over, you go home, and I fall asleep."

The corners of his mouth curl into a grin. Then he pulls out his wallet and lays a tip on the table. He stands up and offers me his hand. I slip my fingers through his, and we leave the restaurant, living in the moment and not a second beyond it.

Chapter Six

Maggie

I roll over to see if he's gone as soon as I open my eyes.

He is.

I run my hand over his pillow, wondering how someone can feel so full of emptiness.

Last night was . . . well . . . It was bucket-list-worthy, that's for sure. As soon as we left the restaurant, we headed to my house. He let me drive. We talked about cars, my thesis, that I want to try bungee jumping. He offered to take me, but realized he was essentially asking me out on another date, so he corrected himself and told me a place he thinks I should try. When we got to my house, we were both laughing as we walked inside because the sprinklers came on as soon as we got out of the car, the spray of water hitting us both right in the face. I walked to my kitchen and grabbed a hand towel to dry my face. Jake followed me, and when I handed him the towel to use, he tossed it over his shoulder and reached for me, kissing me like he'd been waiting to do it since the moment he'd laid eyes on me.

It was unexpected, but wanted, and even though I felt every single thing while his mouth was on mine, I was also full of uncertainty. I've only been with two people sexually in my life, and I was in love during both of those relationships. This was the first time I was about to have sex with someone I wasn't in love with. I wasn't sure what to expect, but knowing he didn't either made me feel more at ease. I kept reminding myself of that with every new part of my neck he kissed.

After about fifteen minutes of full-on making out with him, something switched in me. I don't know how he did it, but he was so attentive and into it that all my concerns and insecurities eventually fell away with my clothing. By the time we made it to the bedroom, I was all in. And then he was all in, in more ways than one.

It was everything. Afterward, we rolled onto our backs, and just when I thought he was getting ready to leave, he turned his head and looked at me. "Are there rules to one-night stands I'm not aware of? Are we only allowed to have sex once?"

I laughed, and then he was on top of me again, and as much fun as it was the first time, the second time was even better. It was intense. And slow. And perfection.

He didn't roll onto his back after the second time. He rolled onto his side and wrapped his arms around me and whispered, "Goodnight," before kissing me. I liked that he said *goodnight* instead of *goodbye*, because it took the focus off the fact that we both knew he'd be leaving before I woke up.

I just assumed I'd wake up in a state of euphoric bliss today. Not a state of melancholy.

Feeling a little down about it being over isn't necessarily a bad thing, though. It means I couldn't have chosen a better person to have my one-night stand with. Had it been anyone else, I don't think I would have enjoyed it as much as I did. And if I hadn't enjoyed it, I wouldn't feel like I'd have the right to cross it off my bucket list.

So yes, it sucks that I can't find anything wrong with him. But it would suck even more to fall back into something I'll just want out of eventually. I can't put myself in another position where someone will become obligated to take care of me.

It's not a good feeling, knowing someone has convinced themselves they're more in love with you than they are simply because you're dependent on them. I'd rather feel melancholic than pathetic.

I grab the pillow Jake slept on—the same pillow I was just rubbing in longing—and I throw it off my bed. I'll throw it in the trash later. I don't even want to smell him again.

I walk over to my dresser and grab my bucket list. I mark out number eight and then look over the list again. I suddenly feel accomplished, knowing number eight was probably the one thing on my bucket list I was certain I would never have the guts to do.

Maggie fucking Carson. You are a badass.

I fold the list and set it on top of my dresser. I open the second drawer, then grab a pair of panties and a tank top and pull them on. I need to go visit my grandfather today while I have the opportunity, but first I need waffles and a shower.

Waffles before shower. I'm way too excited for waffles after not having been able to eat much last night.

I might even go get a manicure today. I'm staring down at my nails when I walk into my living room. But then I freeze when I smell bacon. I slowly raise my head to find Jake standing at my kitchen stove.

Cooking.

He spins around to reach for a plate and sees me. He grins. "Morning."

I don't smile. I don't speak. I don't even nod a greeting in return. I stand there and stare at him and wonder how a twenty-nine-year-old man could honestly not understand the meaning behind one-night stand. *Night* being the key word. There's not supposed to be a morning included in that definition.

I look at my tank top and underwear and suddenly feel modest, even though he spent enough time on top of me last night that he probably has every inch of my body memorized. But still, I wrap my arms around myself.

"What are you doing?" I ask.

Jake is watching me, a little unsure of himself after seeing my reaction to him still being here. He looks at the stove and then at me, and I swear he deflates right in front of me.

"Oh," he says, suddenly seeming out of place. "You thought . . . Okay." He starts nodding and immediately reaches to the stove and turns off the burner. "My bad," he says, not looking at me. He grabs a glass that's next to the stove and takes a quick drink. When he faces me again, he can't even look at me. "This is awkward. I'll go. I just . . ." He finally makes eye contact with me. I wrap my arms around myself even tighter because I hate that I've created such an awkward moment when he was obviously trying to do something nice.

"I'm sorry I made this awkward," I say. "I just wasn't expecting you to still be here."

Jake nods, walking toward me to grab the shoes he kicked off next to the couch last night. "It's fine. I misread things, obviously. I know you made yourself clear last night. But that was before we . . . twice . . . and it was . . ."

I press my lips together.

His shoes are now on his feet, and he stands, eyeing me. "Wishful thinking, I guess." He points at my front door. "I'm gonna leave now."

I nod. It's probably for the best. I just ruined every good thing about last night.

Actually, *he* ruined every good thing about last night. I walked into my living room accepting that I'd never see him again, and he ruined it by assuming I wanted him to stay and cook me breakfast.

He reaches for the front door, but before he opens it, he pauses. When he turns around, he stares at me for a moment, then walks back over to me. He stops about two feet away and tilts his head. "Are you positive you don't want to see me again? There's no wiggle room for me to convince you to give this one more shot?"

I sigh. "I'll be dead in a few years, Jake."

He takes half a step back, but doesn't take his eyes off me. "Wow." He brings a hand to his mouth and runs it over his jaw. "You're really using that one?"

"It's not an excuse. It's a fact."

"A fact I'm very aware of," he says. His jaw is hard, and now he's mad. *See?* If he would have just left before I woke up, this would have ended perfectly! Now, when he leaves, we're both going to be frustrated and full of regret.

I take a step forward. "I'm dying, Jake. *Dying.* What's going to come of this? I don't ever want to get married. I don't want children. I have no desire for another relationship where I'll eventually become someone's burden. Yes, I like you. Yes, last night was incredible. And that's exactly why you should have left already. Because I have things I want to do, and falling in love and fighting with someone about how I live the last few years of my life is not something that's ever been on my bucket list. So thank you for last night. And thank you for attempting to cook me breakfast. But I need you to leave."

I blow out a frustrated breath and then immediately look at the floor because I hate the look in his eyes right now. Several seconds pass, and he doesn't respond. He stands there and soaks in everything I said. He eventually takes a step back, and then another. I look up, and he looks away, turning toward the front door. He opens it and steps outside, but before he closes it, he looks straight at me.

"For the record, Maggie. I was just making you breakfast. I wasn't proposing."

He shuts the door, and my house has never felt emptier than it does in this moment.

I hate this. I hate everything I just said to him. I hate how much I wish it weren't the truth.

I hate this stupid fucking illness.

And I hate that I said all that and made him leave before he could even finish cooking the damn bacon. I stare at the pan and then walk over to it and throw the entire pan in the trash.

I lean against the bar and can't help but pout. Is Jake ending a relationship twelve years too late better or worse than me ending a relationship completely and entirely too early? He's someone I could love. *If* I had the life to love him in.

I bring my hands up to the back of my head and press my elbows together, bending over. I try to stop myself from being so disappointed. But the fact that I'm disappointed over a guy I met twenty-four hours ago disappoints me even more. I take a few minutes to recover, then force myself upright.

I grab the box of waffles I had intended to have for breakfast from the freezer. Only now, I'm not nearly as excited to eat them.

Chapter Seven

Ridge

Sydney swings open my bedroom door. I'm sitting at my desk, finishing up a website for a client, when she goes straight to my bed and falls face-first onto the mattress.

Rough day, I guess.

It's probably my fault because I stayed another night at her house last night. Maybe I should give her a night to catch up on her sleep. Outside of her job, we've been together almost nonstop since Monday. I know it's only Friday, but we get exhausted being together. In the best way.

I'll make sure tonight is a little more relaxing than the last few nights. We can take the *chill* out of *Netflix and chill* and literally just watch TV shows all night. Then I'll let her sleep in as long as she wants tomorrow. Hell, I'll probably sleep in *with* her.

I walk over to the bed and lie down beside her. I brush

her hair out of her face, and she opens her eyes and grins at me, despite looking exhausted.

"Bad day?" I ask her.

She shakes her head and rolls over onto her back. She lifts her hands to sign, but whatever she wants to say, she doesn't know how to sign. "Midterms," she finally says.

I tilt my head. "Midterms?" She nods.

"You had midterms this week?"

She nods again.

Now I feel like an asshole. I grab my phone and text her.

Ridge: Why didn't you tell me? I wouldn't have stayed at your apartment.

Sydney: Mine were Monday, so no worries. Your timing Monday night was impeccable. It's just that I work at the library and it's insane during midterms. The students are insane. The professors are insane. I'm so happy it's Friday.

Ridge: Me too. Let's do nothing tonight but watch TV. I need to find out if Ned really gets decapitated.

Sydney: Who?

Shit. Warren is rubbing off on me. I don't want her to know I just spoiled season one of *Game of Thrones.*

Ridge: Oh, nothing. Talking about The Walking Dead.

Sydney stares at her phone for a second, confused.

Sydney: I don't remember that from The Walking Dead.

She watches *The Walking Dead.* Great. Now I want to have sex, and I already told her we'd be lazy tonight.

Sydney's attention moves away from me and toward my bedroom door. "Someone is knocking," she signs.

I climb off the bed and head to the living room. Through the peephole, I notice it's a girl with a FedEx uniform on. I open the door, and she hands me a package. Once I've signed for it, I walk the package to the bar and wait for Sydney as she walks into the kitchen. I read the label, and it's addressed to me, but there's no return address.

Sydney leans over me and then signs, "You got a present?"

I shrug. I'm not expecting anything that I can remember, but I open the package and there's another package inside of it. Knowing Warren, he probably sent me a roll of toilet paper with his face all over it. I start to pull the tape off, but I notice Sydney walk around me, toward the living room. When I glance up at her, she's holding her phone up, aiming her camera in my direction.

"Are you recording me?"

She nods and gives me a sweet smile. "The present is from me."

"You bought me something?"

Her shy smile is so fucking adorable. Every time I think I'm too exhausted to even think about picking her up and throwing her on my bed, she does something that completely reinvigorates me and makes me feel like I could run a marathon.

I look back down at the package and feel bad that she got me a gift. I suck at gifts. Shit, what if she's the type who gives the best gifts? I'm the guy who once bought his nine-year-old brother a hamster for Christmas, but didn't realize it had died in the box. Brennan opened it and cried the entire day.

And this beautiful girl has *me* as her boyfriend.

Although this gift is hard as shit to open. I set it on the bar and yank at the lid.

A sudden cloud of dust bursts out of the container and hits me in the face. It happens so fast, I can't even close my mouth in time. I step back from whatever the hell was in that container, and I start spitting. *What the hell just happened?*

I walk to the sink and run my hands under the water, then wet my face. When I pull my hands back, they're sparkling like a fucking unicorn.

Glitter. Everywhere.

On my arms, my shirt, my hands, the counter. In my mouth. I look over at Sydney and she's rolling on the floor with laughter. Tears are in her eyes, she's laughing so hard.

She glitter bombed me.

Wow.

I guess that means the prank war has recommenced.

I wash my mouth out and then calmly walk to the bar, where the explosion just happened. I scoop a handful of glitter into my palm. *Two can play this game.* Her laughter hasn't let up at all. I think she's laughing even harder now that she sees me up close. I'm sure I look fantastic in sparkles.

I've read the word *squeal* before and know that it's a form of laughter, but I have no idea what it sounds like at all. As soon as I tip my hand over and watch the glitter fall all over her, I'm almost positive that's what she's doing. *Squealing.*

She clutches her stomach and falls onto her back. A tear falls down her cheek.

My God. I'd give anything to be able to hear her right now. I spend so much time trying to imagine what her voice and her laughter and her sighs sound like, but there isn't enough imagination in one person to come close to what I know it probably sounds like.

She sees the look on my face and suddenly stops laughing. Her eyebrows pull together when she signs, "Are you angry?"

I smile and give my head a slight shake. "No. I just really wish I could hear you right now."

Her expression relaxes a little. Saddens, even. She pulls in her bottom lip for a second as she stares up at me. Then she reaches her hand up and grabs mine, pulling on it. I lower myself to the floor, sliding my knee between her legs.

I might not be able to hear her like I wish I could, but I can smell her and taste her and love her. I run my nose over her jaw until my lips reach hers. When I brush my lips against hers, her tongue slips into my mouth, soft and inviting. I return the action, searching her mouth for remnants of laughter.

She's an incredible communicator when it comes to her kiss. Her kiss sometimes says more to me than anything she could ever sign or text or speak. Which is why I immediately know when she's distracted. I don't even have to hear it. She hears it for me, and then I feel her reaction and I just know. I pull back and look down at her, just as her attention moves to Warren and Bridgette's bathroom door. I look up, and Bridgette is walking out of the bathroom. She pauses and looks at us, lying on the living room floor together, covered in glitter.

And then she does the unthinkable.

Bridgette smiles.

Then she steps over us and walks away. When she leaves the apartment, I look down at Sydney, wondering if she's just as shocked as I am by that exchange. Her eyes are wide as she looks back at me. She starts laughing again. I quickly press my ear to her chest, wanting to feel it, but her laughter fades too quickly. I bring my hand to her waist and start tickling her. I feel her start laughing again, so I keep tickling her because it's the closest I can get to hearing that laugh.

Her phone is next to me on the floor, so when it lights up, I naturally glance at it. I stop tickling her when I see the name and the message that appear on the screen.

Hunter: Thank you, Syd. You're the best.

She hasn't noticed her phone. She's still laughing and trying to squirm away from me, so I sit back on my knees and pick up her phone. I hand it to her as I'm standing up to walk away. I try to bite down my anger as I grab a rag and begin wiping the glitter off the bar. I glance at her to see her reaction, but she's sitting cross-legged now, responding to that fucker's text.

Why is she talking to him?

Why does it seem like they're somehow miraculously on good terms?

"Thank you, Syd"? Why is he calling her *Syd*, like he has any right to be that casual with her after what he did to her? And why is she sitting so casually like this is okay? I grab my phone.

Ridge: Let me know when you're finished chatting with your ex. I'll be in the shower.

I don't look at her as I head to my bedroom and then my bathroom. I pull open the shower curtain and turn on the water, and then take my shirt off. I swear, I just want to make loud noises. It's not very often I feel the need to be loud, but in situations like this, I know it probably feels good to be able to groan so that I can hear my frustrations leaving my body. Instead, I toss my shirt at the wall and unbutton my jeans with nowhere for my noise to go.

When the bathroom door opens, I regret not locking it because I really need a minute. Or two or three. I glance at Sydney, and she leans against the door frame and raises an eyebrow.

"Seriously?"

I stare at her expectantly. What does she want me to say? Does she expect me to be okay with this? Does she expect me to smile and ask her how Hunter is doing?

Sydney hands me her phone and scrolls up on her texts to Hunter so I can read them. I have no desire to read them, but she uses both of her hands to force mine around her phone, and then she motions for me to read them. I look down at the string of messages.

Hunter: I know you don't want to speak to me. I don't blame you for driving away the other night. And believe me, I would leave you alone, but I gave you all my financial forms to give to your dad to look over during our company's merger last year. It's almost April and I need them for taxes. I called his office and they said they sent them back with you a few months ago.

Sydney: They're in Tori's apartment in my old bedroom. Look in the red folder at the top of the closet.

Hunter: Found them!

Hunter: Thank you, Syd. You're the best.

Sydney: Can you delete my number now?

Hunter: Done.

I lean against the sink and rub a hand down my face. She immediately starts texting me when I hand her back her phone, so I check my phone.

Sydney: I realize my situation with Hunter is different from your situation with Maggie, but I have been extremely accommodating to the friendship you chose to keep, Ridge. EXTREMELY ACCOMODATING! But you are being a hypocritical tool right now. It's very unattractive.

I blow out a breath of mixed relief and regret. She is absolutely right. I'm a hypocritical tool.

Ridge: You're right. I'm sorry.

Sydney: I know I'm right. And that little apology doesn't really make me any less angry with you.

I glance at her and swallow because I haven't seen her this angry in a very long time. I've seen her upset and frustrated, but I don't think I've seen her this angry since the morning she woke up in my bed and found out I had a girlfriend.

Why did I have to react that way? She's right. She's been nothing but patient with me, and the first chance I have to show her the same trust and patience in return, I stomp out of the room in a tantrum.

Ridge: I was jealous and in the wrong. 100% wrong. Actually, I was so wrong, I think I stretched the limit of 100%. I was 101% wrong.

I look at her, and I'm thankful I can read her nonverbal cues so well. Even though she tries to hide it, I can see her relax a little with that text. So I send her another one. I'll text her apologies all night if I have to in order to get rid of this tension I caused.

Ridge: Remember when we used to tell each other our flaws so it would help fight our attraction for each other?

She nods.

Ridge: One of my flaws is that I never knew I had a jealous streak until I had you to be jealous over.

She doesn't smile, but she does lean against the counter next to me. Our shoulders touch, and it's such a subtle thing, but it means so much right now.

Sydney: My flaw is that I forgive too easily and I can't stay mad.

She may find that to be a flaw, but I couldn't be more grateful for that side of her. Especially right now. She lifts her eyes and shrugs a little, like she's already over it. I give her a quick kiss on her forehead.

Ridge: My flaw is that I'm covered in glitter. I somehow even got it . . .

I pull at the flap of my jeans. "Down there," I say. She starts laughing. And I smile because *fuck Hunter*.

I have the absolute best girlfriend there ever was to walk this earth.

Sydney: My flaw is that I kind of already forgot why we were fighting because you're so cute when you sparkle.

Ridge: We're fighting because you are perfect and I don't deserve you.

Sydney rolls her eyes and then sets down her phone. I stand up straight and place my phone on top of hers, pushing them to the back of the counter. I move in front of her, and she grips the counter at her sides, looking at me with glitter in her lashes and her hair. Such a beautiful girl. Inside and out. I lower my mouth to hers while bringing my hands to the front of her jeans. I unzip and unbutton them and then continue to kiss her as I undress her.

I pull her into the shower with me, and for the next half hour, I apologize profusely with my mouth.

Chapter Eight

Maggie

I've spent seventeen nights in the hospital this past year alone.

I've been to visit my doctor more times than that. Since the day I was born, I've been at appointments to check my health more times than I've gone grocery shopping.

And I'm sick of it.

Sometimes when I arrive at my doctor's office, I sit there and stare at the building, wondering what would happen if I drove away and never went back. What would happen if I stopped having tests administered? What would happen if I stopped receiving treatment for every single cold I'm afflicted with?

I'd get pneumonia. That's what would happen. Then I would die. At least I'd never have to go back to a doctor's office. The nurse takes the blood pressure cuff off my arm. "It's a tad high."

"I had a lot of sodium for breakfast." I pull my sleeve back down. My blood pressure is high because I'm here. At the doctor. They call it white-coat syndrome. Anytime I have my blood pressure checked inside a doctor's office, it's high because of nerves. But outside of a doctor's office, it's fine.

I lick my lips, trying to moisten them. My mouth is dry from the nervous energy of being here. I don't want to be here. But here I am. No turning back now.

The nurse hands me a gown and tells me I can change when she leaves the room. I look down at the gown and cringe.

"Is this necessary?" I ask, holding up the gown.

She nods. "It's a requirement. We'll probably run a few tests today, and your chest needs to be easily accessible."

I nod and watch as she slips my chart in the door slot and starts to pull it shut. She smiles reassuringly. "Doctor will be in shortly," she says. She has a look of pity about her, like she wants to hug me. I get that a lot. Especially from the really sweet nurses. I remind them of when they were in their formative years, young and vibrant and full of life. And they try to imagine themselves in my shoes at this age, and their eyes fill with pity for me. I'm used to it. Sometimes I even pity myself, but I don't think that's related to the illness. I think, as humans, we all have a degree of self-pity.

I blow out a breath, more nervous than I've ever been

to be in a doctor's office. My hands are shaking when I pull off my shirt. I hurry up and put on the gown and then sit on the exam table. It's cold in here, so I rub my hands over my arms, fighting the chills. I press my knees together and then squeeze them with my hands, trying my best not to think about the reason I'm here. I sweat when I'm nervous. I don't want to be sweaty.

I feel my chest tighten, and then my throat becomes itchy and I start to cough. I cough so hard, I have to stand up and walk over to the sink to balance myself. There's a knock on the door in the middle of one of my coughing fits, and I turn around to find the nurse peeking her head in.

"You okay?"

I nod, still coughing. She walks over to the sink and takes a cup and then fills it with water. But I don't need more liquid in my throat right now. I take the cup and thank her, but I wait until my coughing subsides before I take a sip. She leaves the room again. I walk back over to the exam table, and as soon as I sit, there's another knock at the door.

This is it.

The door begins to open and my heart starts to pound so hard; I'm relieved no one is checking my blood pressure at the moment. He flips my chart open before he looks up. He pauses as soon as he opens it, probably because he's shocked to see my name on the chart.

I knew he'd be surprised. Hell, *I'm* surprised I worked up the courage to come here.

Jake immediately lifts his head and looks at me. I realize there are probably much better ways to reach out to him, but I feel like my undeniable attraction should be just as dramatic as my denial of him was. I still feel a little guilty for how we left things a few days ago. But since he walked out my front door, I've done nothing but mope, because the time we spent together was so good. Fun. Easy. I haven't stopped thinking about him. Especially his parting words.

I was just making you breakfast. I wasn't proposing.

I've flip-flopped all week about this. Sure, he was just making me breakfast. But when a good-looking doctor cooks you breakfast, that breakfast turns into lunch and then dinner and then breakfast again, and then trips together on the weekends and then grocery shopping together, and then all that eventually turns into being the emergency contact at the hospital.

So yeah, he was just cooking me breakfast. But because of how much I like him, that's not where it would have ended. And the idea of him feeling forced to care for me makes me sad to think about.

But on the other hand, I can't stop thinking about him. And when I think about him, I get this empty pit in my stomach that distracts me and makes everything I want out of life seem to pale in comparison to the thought of spending time with him. But the idea of setting ourselves up for emotional investment just makes me sad since I know it won't end well. So what do I do? What choice do I make? Avoid him and be sad? Or embrace him and be sad?

Either way, I'll be sad.

So . . . here I am. Faking a need to see a cardiologist just so I can let him know I overreacted. And also to let him know that bungee jumping alone just sounds boring.

I can see the surprise on Jake's face, but he holds it in well. He glances at my chart again. "According to this, you're here because you're experiencing excessive heart palpitations."

I can see the grin he stifles before looking back at me.

I nod. "Something like that."

Jake's eyes scan me from head to toe for a moment, and then he sets the chart on the counter and pulls his stethoscope to his ears. He straddles a chair and sits, rolling toward me.

"Let's take a listen."

Oh, God. I'm not *really* having heart palpitations. He knows it was just an excuse to show up here. Now he's about to listen to my heart just to be an ass because he knows I'm nervous right now. And it's going to be beating stupid fast because he's even better-looking today with his white coat and stethoscope, straddling a rolling chair. If he actually listens to my heartbeat right now, he might call for a defibrillator.

He rolls his chair right up to the exam table. Right up to me. We're eye to eye now as he lifts the stethoscope and places it over my heart. He closes his eyes and lowers his head as if he's actually concentrating on my heartbeat.

I close my eyes because I have to calm down. Him listening to my heartbeat is making me completely transparent. I keep my eyes closed, even when he pulls the stethoscope away from me. There's a quiet pause, and then in a low voice, he says, "What are you doing here, Maggie?"

I glance at him, and his eyes are searching mine. I suck in a deep breath and then slowly release it before saying, "I'm trying to live in the moment."

He sighs, and he's so stoic right now, I can't tell if it's a good sigh. But then I feel his hand on my knee, his thumb brushing over the top of it. He searches my face and then reaches up and tucks a lock of hair behind my ear. "That's all I want," he says. "A few moments here and there. I'm not asking for your entire timeline."

I stare at him, completely infatuated with his mouth and his blue eyes and the words that he just said. I nod a little, but I don't really have anything to say. I just want him to kiss me. And so he does.

He takes my face in both of his huge, warm hands and presses his lips to mine as he stands, kicking the chair away from him. I sigh against his lips. I grip the collar of his white coat and take his tongue as he pushes my knees apart and slides in front of me. I'm so thankful I was forced to put this gown on. I wrap my legs tightly around his waist as he lowers me to the exam table and leans over me, kissing me with extreme urgency. But he breaks that kiss with the same urgency seconds later, breathing heavily, looking down on me with heated eyes. He shakes his head. "Not here."

I nod. I wasn't expecting this to happen here. I can tell

he's about to pull back, but then he pauses, looking at me with so much hunger, I can practically see his ethics melt right to the floor. He kisses me again, and the way his hand is sliding up my thigh has me forgetting that he's a doctor and we're in a clinic and I'm technically on record as his patient now. But none of that matters because his hands feel so good, and his mouth even better, and I've never had so much fun visiting a doctor before.

He's making his way to my neck when he pauses and glances at the door. He immediately pulls me up, giving my gown a quick tug over my thighs. He spins toward the sink and turns on the water.

The door opens, and I swing my head toward the nurse who is now standing in the doorway. Jake is casually washing his hands, trying to pretend he didn't just have his hand halfway up my thigh and his tongue all the way down my throat. I'm trying to catch my breath, but his hands and his kiss have left my already weak lungs aching for air. I'm practically gasping.

The nurse gives me another concerned, pitiful look. "You sure you're okay?"

After my coughing fit earlier and now this, she probably thinks I'm near my deathbed. I nod quickly. "I'm fine. Just . . . shitty lungs. Side effect of CF."

I hear Jake clear his throat, attempting to cover a laugh. He gives his full attention to the nurse.

"They need you in three," she says. "Kind of urgent."

Jake gives her a nod. "Thanks, Vicky. Be right there."

When she closes the door, Jake covers his face with his hand. When he looks up at me, he's grinning. He pushes off the counter and walks past but turns toward me. "Put your clothes back on, Maggie," he says, backing toward the door. "I'll come over tonight and take them right back off."

I'm smiling so stupidly when he leaves the room. I hop off the table and walk over to the chair to retrieve my clothes. Feeling another coughing fit coming on, I cover my mouth, still unable to stop smiling. I'm so glad I showed up here.

I clear my throat, but it doesn't help. Pressing my hand on the counter for more balance doesn't do anything, either, because here it is. *Hello, old friend.* I can feel it about to happen before it actually happens. I always do.

As soon as the room begins to spin, I allow my knees to buckle so the impact isn't as hard when I hit the floor.

Chapter Nine

Jake

My father took me to Puerto Vallarta when I was ten, just so I could jump out of an airplane.

I'd begged him to take me skydiving with him since I learned how to talk, but it's not so easy in Texas to give your child legal permission to jump out of an airplane.

He was an adrenaline junkie, just like the child he had created. Because of that, I basically lived at the jump zone where he spent all of his free time. Most dads golf on Sundays. My dad jumped out of airplanes.

By the time I graduated high school, I had already completed four hundred fifty of the five hundred jumps it took to qualify as a tandem instructor. But because of the turn my life took during my senior year, it was several years to finish those last fifty jumps. I finally became certified as a tandem instructor right out of med school. And even though Maggie was my five hundredth tandem jump, I've probably taken that leap at least three times that amount doing it solo since the age of ten.

Even with that much experience, that five hundredth tandem jump felt like the most terrifying jump I'd ever taken. I'd never been nervous to jump out of a plane before then. I've never worried that my chute wouldn't open. I've never once been concerned for my life until that moment. Because if that particular jump didn't end well, that meant dinner with Maggie was off the table. And I *really* wanted to take her to dinner. I'd planned to ask her out since the moment I laid eyes on her as I walked into the facility that day.

My immediate reaction to her surprised me. I can't even remember the last time I was attracted to someone like that. But the second I saw her, something in me woke up. Something I knew was there, but had never been rattled until then. I hadn't looked at a girl and felt that way in so long, I forgot how stupefying attraction could be.

She was standing at the counter, taking paperwork from Corey, who was on schedule to jump tandem with her. As soon as I realized she was there alone, I waited until she took a seat to fill out her paperwork, and then I begged Corey to let me take over and be the one to jump with her.

"Jake, you're barely here once a month. This isn't even your job," he said. "I'm here every day because I actually need the money."

"You can have the fee," I said. "I'll give you the credit. Just let me have this one."

When I told him he could keep the money for none of the work, he made a face like I was an idiot and then waved his hand toward Maggie. "All yours," he said, walking away.

I felt triumphant for a split second, until I looked back at her, sitting in the chair, all alone. Skydiving is such a monumental moment in the lives of most people who do it. Most first-timers never come alone. They almost always have people with them who are experiencing their own monumental moment by also jumping, or they have people with them waiting on the ground for when they survive the jump.

In all honesty, she was the first first-timer I'd ever seen show up completely alone, and her independence both intrigued and intimidated me. Since the moment I walked up to her and asked if she needed help filling out the forms, nothing has changed when it comes to the situation inside my chest. It's been days, and I'm still filled with that same nervous energy. I'm still intrigued. Still intimidated.

And I have no idea how to move forward.

That's why I'm stuck in this hallway, right outside the hospital room where they brought her two hours ago.

I was dealing with another patient when Vicky found Maggie and dealt with the entire situation without my even being aware. She didn't tell me until I finished up with two more patients and Maggie had already been gone for an hour.

Vicky said she noticed it was taking Maggie a while to get dressed and exit the room, so she went to check on her.

Maggie was on the floor, just recovering from a blackout. Vicky tested her sugar levels immediately and then sent staff with her over to the hospital. The clinic I work at is adjacent to our hospital, so we're used to having to transport patients. I'm just not used to the medical emergencies also feeling like a *personal* emergency.

Since the moment Vicky informed me of what happened, I haven't been able to concentrate. I finally had a colleague take over so I could come check on Maggie. Now that I'm in the hallway, standing in front of her room, I'm not sure how to feel or what to do or how to approach this entire situation. We've been on one date with the potential of another. But now she's in the hospital and in the exact vulnerable situation she was scared she'd be in when it came to us.

Her being constrained by her illness. Me being here to witness it.

I step aside when the door to her hospital room opens. A nurse walks out, heading for the nurse's station. I follow her. "Excuse me," I say, touching her shoulder. She pauses, and I point at Maggie's room. "Have you notified this patient's family yet?"

The nurse glances at the name on my coat and says, "Yes. Left a voice mail as soon as she was brought in." She looks down at the file. "I thought she was Dr. Kastner's patient."

"She is. I'm her cardiologist. She was at my clinic when her condition worsened, so I'm just checking in."

"You're from cardiology?" she asks without looking up from the file. "We're aware of the CFRD, but have nothing on file about heart issues."

"It was just a preventative checkup," I say, backing away before she gets too nosy about my nosiness. "I just wanted to make sure her family was notified. Is the patient alert?"

The nurse nods, but also makes a face like she's annoyed that I'm questioning her ability to do her job. I turn and walk back toward Maggie's room, pausing just outside the door. Once again, I fail to walk in because I don't know her well enough to know what kind of reaction she would prefer from me right now. If I walk in and try to pretend her passing out in my office wasn't a big deal, she might be put off by my casualness. If I walk in and act like I'm concerned, she might use that concern as a weapon against us.

I think if we were more than just one overnight date in, the next few minutes might not matter as much. But since we've only been on one date, I'm almost positive she's in there right now regretting showing up at my office and regretting that I'll see her in such a vulnerable state, and possibly even regretting that she even walked into my life on Tuesday. I feel like my next moves are extremely crucial to how all of this will turn out.

I don't think I've ever worried this much about how to act in front of someone. I normally have the attitude that if someone doesn't like me, that's not going to matter to me or my life, so I've always just done and said what I feel like doing and saying. But right now, with Maggie, I'd give anything to have a handbook.

I need to know what she needs from me in order for her not to push me away again.

I put my hand on the door, but my phone begins to ring as soon as I start to push it open. I quickly back up so she isn't aware I'm right outside her door. I walk a few feet down the hallway and pull my phone out of my pocket.

I smile when I see that it's Justice, trying to FaceTime me. I'm relieved to have a few minutes more to prepare before walking in to see Maggie.

I accept the call and wait the several seconds it usually takes for the FaceTime to connect us. When it finally does, it's not Justice's face I see on his phone. His screen is covered by a piece of paper. I squint to see it, but the grade is too blurry.

"It's too close to your phone," I tell him.

He pulls the paper back a few inches, and I can see the number eighty-five circled in the top right-hand corner.

"That's not too bad for a night of horror movies," I say.

Justice's face is on the screen now. He looks at me like I'm the child and he's the parent. "Dad, it's a B. My first B all year. You're supposed to yell at me so I'll never make another B again."

I laugh. He's looking at me so seriously, like he's more disappointed that I'm not furious with him than he is disappointed in getting his first B. "Listen," I tell him as I lean against the wall. "We both know you know the material. I'd be mad if you didn't study, but you did. The reason you got a B is because you went to bed too late. And I already yelled at you for that."

I woke up at three o'clock this morning and heard the television on in my living room. When I went to turn it off, Justice was on the couch with a bowl of popcorn, watching *The Visit*. He's obsessed with M. Night Shyamalan. His obsession is mostly my fault. It started when I let him watch *The Sixth Sense* when he was five. He's eleven now, and the obsession has only gotten worse.

What can I say? He takes after his father. But as much of me as he has in him, he's also very much his mother's child. She stressed over every paper and every homework assignment throughout high school and college. I once had to console her because she was crying over receiving a ninety-nine on a paper when she was aiming for a perfect score.

Justice has that overachieving side to him, but it's constantly warring with that side of him that wants to stay up late and watch scary movies when he isn't supposed to. When I dropped him off at school today, I had to wake him up when I pulled into the drop-off lane.

I knew his math test wasn't going to end well when he wiped the drool off his mouth, opened the door to get out of my car, and said, "Goodnight, Dad."

He thought I was dropping him off at his mother's house. I laughed when he got out of the car and realized it was a school day. He turned back to the car and tried to open the door. I locked it before he could climb back inside the car and beg me for a skip day.

I cracked the window, and he stuck his fingers inside and said, "Dad, please. I won't tell Mom. Just let me sleep today."

"Actions have consequences, Justice. Love you, good luck, and stay awake."

His fingers slipped out of the window, and he backed up, defeated as I drove away.

I watch my phone as he wads up the paper and tosses it over his shoulder. He rubs his eyes and says, "I'm going to ask Mr. Banks if I can get a redo."

I laugh. "Or just accept the eighty-five. It's not a terrible grade."

Justice shrugs and then scratches his cheek. "Mom went out with that guy again last night." He says it so casually, like the possibility of a stepdad doesn't deter him. That's a good thing, I guess.

"Oh yeah? Did he call you *squirt* and tousle your hair again?"

Justice rolls his eyes. "No, he wasn't so bad this time. I don't think he has kids, and Mom told him people don't call eleven-year-olds *squirts*. But anyway, she wanted me to ask you if you were busy tonight because they're going out again."

It's still a little weird, hearing about Chrissy's dates from the child we created together. This is new territory I don't know how to deal with, so I do my best to make it seem like it's not weird. It was my decision to end things with her, and it wasn't easy. Especially since we share a child. But knowing that Justice was the only reason we were still together just didn't seem fair to any of us. Chrissy took it hard in the beginning, but only because we were all comfortable with the life we shared. But there was a void, and she knew it.

When it comes to loving someone else, I've always believed there should be a level of madness buried in that love. An I-want-to-spend-every-minute-of-every-day-with-you madness. But Chrissy and I have never had that kind of love. Our love is built on responsibility and mutual respect. It's not a maddening, heart-stopping love.

When Justice was born, we felt that maddening love for him, and that was enough to hold us over through high school graduation, college, medical school, and most of our residencies. But when it came to what we felt for each other, it was the type of love that was too thin to attempt to stretch it out over an entire lifetime.

We separated over a year ago, but I didn't get my own place until about six months ago. I bought a house two streets away from the house we'd raised Justice in. The judge gave us joint custody with an outline of who gets him and when, but we haven't once stuck to that. Justice stays with both of us a fairly equal amount, but it's more on his terms than either of ours. With our houses being so close, he just goes back and forth whenever he feels like it. I actually prefer that. He's adjusted really well, and I think this way of letting him control most of the visitation has made our separation a smooth transition for him.

Sometimes *too* smooth.

Because, for some strange reason, he thinks I want to know about his mother's dating life, when I'd rather be kept in the dark. But he's only eleven. He's still innocent in almost every sense, so I like that he keeps me up to date on the half of his life I'm no longer a part of.

"Dad," Justice says. "Did you hear me? Can I stay at your house tonight?"

I nod. "Yeah. Of course."

I told Maggie I'd go to her place tonight, but that was before . . . *this*. I'm almost positive they'll keep her overnight for monitoring, so my Friday night is wide open. Even if it weren't, it would have become wide open for Justice. I work a lot, and I have a lot of hobbies, but that all comes second to him. Everything comes second to him.

"Where are you?" Justice leans in, squinting at the phone. "That doesn't look like your office."

I turn the phone and face it toward the empty hallway, angling it at Maggie's door. "I'm at the hospital visiting a sick friend." I face the phone back at myself. "If she wants to see me."

"Why wouldn't she?" Justice asks.

I stare at him a moment, then shake my head. I didn't mean to say that last part out loud. "It's not important."

"Is she mad at you?"

This is too weird, talking to him about a girl I went

on a date with who isn't his mother. As casual as he may be about it, I'm not sure I'll ever feel comfortable talking to him about my dating life. I pull the phone closer to my face and raise an eyebrow. "I'm not talking to you about my dating life."

Justice leans forward and mimics my expression. "I'll remember this conversation when I start dating."

I laugh. Hard. He's only eleven, and he's already got more wit than most adults. "Fine. If I tell you about her, will you promise you'll tell me the first time you kiss a girl?"

Justice nods. "Only if you don't tell Mom."

"Deal."

"Deal."

"Her name is Maggie," I say. "We went on a date Tuesday, and I'm pretty sure she likes me, but she didn't want to go out with me again because her life is hectic. But now she's in the hospital, and I'm about to go see her, but I have no idea how to act when I walk through that door."

"What do you mean you don't know how to act?" Justice asks. "You're not supposed to act or pretend around other people. You always tell me to be myself."

I love it when my parenting advice actually sinks in with him. Even if my own advice isn't sinking in with me. "You're right. I should just walk in there and be myself."

"Your *real* self. Not your doctor self."

I laugh. "What does that even mean?"

Justice cocks his head and makes a face at the phone that looks just like a face I probably make a lot of the time.

"You're a cool dad, but when you go into doctor mode, it's so boring. Don't talk about work or medical stuff if you like her."

Doctor mode? I laugh. "Any other advice before I go in there?"

"Take her a Twix bar."

"A Twix?"

Justice nods. "Yeah, if someone brought me a Twix, I'd want to be friends with them."

I nod. "Okay. Good advice. I'll see you tonight and let you know how it goes."

Justice waves and then ends the FaceTime.

I slide my phone into my pocket and walk toward Maggie's door. *Just be yourself.* I stand in front of the door and inhale a calming breath before knocking. I wait for her to say, "Come in," before I open the door. When I walk farther into the room, she's curled up on her side. She smiles when she sees me and lifts up onto her elbow.

That smile is everything I needed.

I walk over to her bed as she adjusts it, raising the head of it a little bit. I sit in the empty chair next to the bed. She tucks her arm under her head and rests on her pillow. I reach over and rest my hand on the side of her head, then lean in and give her a soft peck on the mouth. When I pull back, I have no idea what to say. I lay my chin on the bed rail and run my fingers through her hair while I stare at her.

I love how I feel when I'm near her. Full of adrenaline,

like I'm in the middle of a nighttime skydive. But even though I'm full of adrenaline and I'm touching her hair and she smiled at me when I walked in the door, I can see in her eyes that my chute is about to fail and I'm about to free-fall alone, with nothing ahead of me but an ugly impact.

Her gaze flits away for a moment. She pulls her oxygen mask to her mouth and inhales a cycle of air. When she pulls it away, she forces another smile. "How old is your child?"

I narrow my eyes, wondering how she knows that about me. But the quietness in the room reveals the answer. Everything happening outside this door can be heard very clearly.

I pull my hand from her hair and lower it to her hand that's resting on her pillow. I trace a soft circle around where the IV is taped to her skin. "He's eleven."

She smiles again. "I wasn't trying to eavesdrop."

I shake my head. "It's fine. I wasn't trying to hide that I have a kid. I just didn't know how to bring it up on a first date. I'm a little protective of him, so I feel like I should guard that part of my life until I'm positive it's something I want to share."

Maggie nods in understanding, flipping her hand over. She lets me trace the skin on her wrist for a moment. She watches my fingers as they trickle over her palm, down her wrist, until they reach the IV again. Then she looks back up at me again. "What's his name?"

"Justice."

"That's a great name."

I smile. "He's a great kid."

I continue touching her hand, but it's quiet for a while. I don't want to delve even deeper into this conversation because I know it's going to go where I don't want it to go. But at the same time, if I don't keep talking, she might take the floor and begin to tell me, once again, why she doesn't want any part of this.

"His mother's name is Chrissy," I say, filling the void. "We started dating because we had a lot in common. We both wanted to go to med school. We had both been accepted to UT. But then I got her pregnant senior year. She gave birth to Justice a week before our high school graduation."

I stop tracing her skin and slide my fingers through hers. I love that she lets me. I love the feel of her hand wrapped around mine.

"It's impressive that the two of you had a newborn in high school and still somehow managed to become doctors."

I appreciate that she recognizes how hard that was for us. "There was a stretch during her pregnancy where I looked into other careers. Easier ones. But the first time I laid eyes on him, I knew that I never wanted him to think he was a hindrance to our lives in any way, simply because we had him so young. We did everything we could to make sure we stuck to our goals. It was a challenge, two teenagers trying to make it through premed with an infant. But

Chrissy's mom was—*is*—a lifesaver. We couldn't have done it without her."

Maggie squeezes my hand a little when I finish talking. It's gentle and sweet, like she's silently saying, *Good job.* "What kind of father are you?"

No one's ever asked me to evaluate my own ability as a parent. I think about it for a moment and then answer the question with complete honesty. "An insecure one," I admit. "With most jobs, you know right away if you're going to be good at them or not. But with parenting, you don't really know if you're good at it until the child is grown. I'm constantly worried I'm doing everything wrong, and there's no way to know until it's too late."

"I think your worry about whether you're a good father is testament that you shouldn't worry."

I shrug. "Maybe so. But even still, I worry. Always will."

There's a moment of hesitation on her face when I mention how much I worry about him. I want to take it back. I don't want her to think I have too much on my plate. I want her to think about right now and right now only. Not tomorrow or next week or next year. But she is. I can see it in the way she's staring at me—wondering how she could possibly feel okay with fitting herself somewhere in my life. And I can see in the way she looks away from me and focuses on everything *but* me that she doesn't see herself fitting in at all.

She was already hesitant when she thought my biggest concern outside of work was if the weather was right for skydiving. And even though she showed up at my office today, ready to give it a chance, I can see that finding out about Justice has not only changed her mind, but filled her with even more resolve than she held as she was kicking me out of her house.

I release her hand and bring mine back up to the side of her head, running my thumb over her cheek in order to bring her attention back to me. When she finally looks up at me, her mind is made up. I can see it in all the pieces of broken hope that are floating around in her eyes. It's amazing how someone can convey so much in one look.

I sigh, sliding my thumb over her lips. "Don't ask me to leave."

Her eyebrows draw apart, and she looks absolutely torn between what she wants and what she knows she needs. "Jake," she says. She doesn't follow my name up with anything else. My name lingers in the air, heavy with weariness.

Not only do I know I can't change her mind, but I'm not sure I should even try to. As much as I want to see her again and as much as I want to get to know her better, it's not fair of me to beg. She knows her situation better than anyone. She knows what she's capable of, and she knows what she wants her life to look like. I can't argue all the reasons why she shouldn't push me away, because I'm almost positive I'd have the same outlook if our roles were reversed.

Maybe that's why we're both being so quiet. Because I understand her.

The mood is thick in the room. It's full of tension and attraction and disappointment. I try to imagine what it would be like to love her. Because if spending one night with her can fill a room with this much angst, I can only imagine that this is what the beginning of a maddening love would feel like.

I've finally found someone I think could one day fill the void in my life, but to her, she feels that by being in my life, her absence would one day *create* a void. It's ironic. *Maddening.*

"Have you seen Dr. Kastner yet?"

She nods but doesn't elaborate.

"Has anything changed with your condition?"

She shakes her head, and I can't tell if she's lying. She answers too quickly.

"I'm fine. I probably need to rest, though."

She's asking me to leave, but I want to tell her that even though I barely know her, I want to be here for her. I want to help her cross those last several items off her bucket list. I want to make sure she keeps living and doesn't continue to focus on the fact that she may not have as much time as everyone else.

But I say nothing, because who am I to assume she won't have a completely fulfilled life if she doesn't allow me to be a part of it? That's something only a narcissist would think. The girl in front of me right now is the same girl who showed up alone to skydive for the first time this week. So I will respect her choice and I will walk away for the exact same reason I was drawn to her in the first place. Because she's an independent badass who doesn't need me to fill a void. There are no voids in her life.

And here I am wanting to selfishly beg her to fill mine.

"You were on a roll with your bucket list," I say. "Promise me you'll knock off some more items."

She immediately begins to nod, and then a tear slips from her eye. She rolls her eyes like she's embarrassed. "I can't believe I'm crying. I barely know you." She laughs, squeezing her eyes shut, and opens them again. "I'm being so ridiculous."

I smile at her. "Nah. You're crying because you know if your situation were different, you'd be falling for me right about now."

She lets out a sad laugh. "If my situation were different, I would have started that free fall back on Tuesday."

I can't even follow that up with anything. I lift out of my chair and lean forward to kiss her. She kisses me back, holding on to my face with both hands. When I pull back, I press my forehead to hers and close my eyes.

"I almost wish I'd never met you."

She shakes her head. "Not me. I'm grateful I met you. You ended up fulfilling a third of my bucket list."

I lean away and smile at her, wishing more than anything that I was selfish enough to try to change her mind. But simply knowing the one day I spent with her meant something to her is enough for now. It has to be.

I kiss her one last time. "I can stay until your family gets here."

Something changes in her expression. She hardens a little. She shakes her head and pulls her hands from my head. "I'll be fine. You should go."

I nod, standing up. I don't even know anything about her family. I know nothing about her parents, or whether she has brothers and sisters. I sort of don't want to be here when they get here. I don't want to meet the most important people in her life if I don't have the chance to someday *be* one of them.

I squeeze her hand one more time, looking down on her while trying to hide my regret. "I should have brought you a Twix."

She makes a confused face, but I don't clarify. I step back, and she gives me a small wave. I wave back, but then I turn without saying goodbye. I walk out of the room as fast as I can.

As someone who has craved the feeling of adrenaline my entire life, I haven't always made the smartest decisions. Adrenaline makes you do stupid shit without putting too much thought into your actions.

It was stupid of me at thirteen to crash my first dirt bike because I wanted to know what it felt like to break a bone.

It was stupid of me at eighteen to have sex with Chrissy when we didn't have a condom, simply because it felt thrilling and we ignorantly assumed we were immune to the consequences.

It was stupid of me at twenty-three to jump backward off a cliff I wasn't familiar with in Cancún, relishing in the buzz of not knowing if there were rocks beneath the surface of the water.

And it would be stupid of me at twenty-nine to beg a girl to jump headfirst into a situation that might end up being that maddening love I've been craving my whole life. When a person sinks into a love that deep, they don't come back out of it, even when it ends. It's like quicksand. You're in it forever, no matter what.

I think Maggie knows that. And I'm positive that's why she's pushing me away again.

She wouldn't push someone away so adamantly if she weren't scared her death would also kill *them*. I can take that assumption with me as I go, at least. The assumption that she saw something in us that had enough potential that she felt the need to end it before we both sank.

Chapter Ten

Ridge

I'm at the sink straining pasta, watching Sydney walk around the kitchen and living room as she points at things and signs them. I correct her when she's wrong, but she's mostly been right. She points at the lamp and signs, "Lamp." Then the couch. The pillow, the table, the window. She points at the towel on her head and signs, "Towel."

When I nod, she grins and then pulls the towel off her head. Her damp hair falls around her shoulders, and I've imagined more times than I'd like to admit what her hair smells like fresh out of the shower. I walk over to her and wrap my arms around her, pressing my face against her head so I can inhale the scent of her.

Then I go back to the stove, leaving her standing in the living room, looking at me like I'm weird. I shrug as I pour the Alfredo sauce into the pan of noodles. Someone grips my shoulder from behind me, and I know immediately that it's Warren. I glance at him.

"Is there enough for me and Bridgette?"

I don't know why we didn't do this at Sydney's apartment. It's a lot more peaceful over there for me, and I can't even hear. I can only imagine how much more peaceful it is for Sydney.

"There's plenty," I sign, realizing just how much I need to take Sydney out on a real date. I need to get her out of this apartment. I will tomorrow. I'll take her on a twelve-hour date tomorrow. We'll eat lunch and then go to the movies and then dinner, and we won't have to see Warren and Bridgette at all.

I'm taking the garlic bread out of the oven when Sydney rushes to the bathroom. At first, it concerns me that she just ran to the bathroom, but then I remember our phones are still on the counter. She must have a phone call.

She returns a moment later to the kitchen with her phone to her ear. She's laughing as she talks to someone. Probably her mother.

I want to meet her parents. Sydney hasn't told me a whole lot about them, other than her father is a lawyer and her mother has always been a stay-at-home mom. But she doesn't seem put out when she speaks to them. The only people I've met in her life are Hunter and Tori—and I'd like to forget I ever met them—but her family is different. They're her people, so I want to know them, even if it's to tell them they've raised an exceptional woman who I love with all my heart.

Sydney smiles at me and signs, "Mom," as she points to her phone. Then she slides my phone across the bar to me. I press the home button and see that I have a missed call and a voice mail. It's rare that I get phone calls, because everyone who knows me knows I can't answer the phone. I usually only receive text messages.

I open my voice mail app to read the transcription, but it says, "Transcription not available." I put my phone in my pocket and wait for Sydney to finish her phone call. I'll just have her listen to the voice mail and let me know what it says.

I turn off the stove and the oven and set plates out at the table, along with the pans of food. Warren and Bridgette both magically appear as soon as dinner is ready. They're like clockwork. They disappear when it's time to clean or pay bills, but show up every time there's food to be eaten. If they ever move out, they're both going to starve.

Maybe *I* should move out. Let them have this apartment and see how fun it is having to pay bills on time. One of these days I will. I'll move in with Sydney, but not yet. Not until I've met everyone in her family and not until she's had the chance to live on her own for a while like she's always wanted.

Sydney ends her phone call and sits down at the table next to me. I slide my phone to her and point to the voice mail. "Can you listen to that?"

She asked me earlier this afternoon to start signing everything I say to her, so I do. It'll help her learn faster. I grab her plate as she listens to the voice mail, and I fill it with pasta. I throw a piece of garlic bread on it and set it in front of her, just as she pulls the phone away from her ear.

She stares at the screen for a second and then looks at Warren before looking at me. I've never seen this look on her face before. I'm not sure how to read it. She looks hesitant, worried, and somehow sick, and I don't like it.

"What is it?"

She slides my phone back to me and grabs the glass of water I poured for her. "Maggie," she says, forcing my heart to a stop. She says something else, but she doesn't sign it, and I'm not able to read her lips. I swing my eyes to Warren, and he signs what Sydney just said.

"It was the hospital. Maggie was admitted today."

Everything sort of just stops. I say *sort of* because Bridgette is still making her plate of food, ignoring everything happening. I glance at Sydney again, and she's taking a drink of her water, avoiding my gaze. I look at Warren, and he's staring at me like I should know what to do.

I don't know why he's acting like it's my choice to direct this scene. Maggie is his friend, too. I look at him expectantly and then say, "Call her."

Sydney looks at me, and I'm looking at her, and I have no fucking idea how to handle this situation. I don't want to seem too worried, but there's no way I can find out Maggie is in the hospital and not be worried. But I'm equally concerned about how this is making Sydney feel. I sigh and reach for Sydney's hand under the table while I wait for Warren to get in touch with Maggie. Sydney slides her fingers through mine, but then props her other arm on the table, covering her mouth with her hand. She turns her attention to Warren, just as he stands up and starts talking into the phone. I watch him and wait. Sydney watches him and waits. Bridgette scoops up a huge portion of pasta with her bread and takes a bite.

Sydney's leg is bouncing up and down. My pulse is pounding even faster than her leg. Warren's conversation is dragging, taking what feels like forever to finish. I don't know what is being said, but in the middle of the conversation, Sydney winces and then pulls her hand from mine and excuses herself from the table. I get up to follow her, just as Warren ends the call.

Now I'm standing in the middle of the living room about to rush after Sydney, but Warren starts to sign. "She passed out at a doctor's office today. They're keeping her overnight."

I blow out a breath of relief. The hospitalizations for her diabetes are the best-case scenarios. It's when she contracts a virus or a cold that it usually ends up taking weeks for her to recover.

I can tell by the look on Warren's face that he's not finished speaking yet. There's something he hasn't said. Something he said to Maggie that upset Sydney enough for her to walk away. "What else?" I ask him.

"She was crying," he says. "She sounded . . . scared. She needs our help, but she wouldn't tell me more than that. I told her we're on our way."

Maggie wants us there.

Maggie *never* wants us there. She always feels like she's inconveniencing us.

Something else must have happened.

I cover my mouth with my hand, my thoughts frozen.

I turn to walk toward my bedroom, but Sydney is standing in the doorway with her shoes on and her purse over her shoulder. She's leaving.

"I'm sorry," she says. "I'm not leaving because I'm mad. I just need to process all this." She waves her hand flippantly around the room, then drops it to her side. She doesn't leave, though. She simply stands there, confused.

I walk over to her and take her face in my hands because I'm confused, too. She just squeezes her eyes shut when I press my forehead to hers. I don't know how to handle this situation. I have so much to say to her, but texting isn't fast enough, and I'm not sure I can speak everything I want to say or that everything I say would even be understandable to her. I pull away from her and grab her hand, then walk her back to the table.

I motion for Warren to help us communicate if we need him. Sydney sits in her chair, and I scoot mine to where I'm right in front of her. "Are you okay?"

She seems at a loss for how to answer that question.

When she finally does, I can't understand her, so Warren signs for me. "I'm trying, Ridge. I really am."

Just seeing the pain when she speaks makes her my only focus. I can't leave her like this. I look at Warren. "Can you go by yourself?"

He looks disappointed by my question. "You expect me to know what to do?" He tosses his hands up in frustration. "You can't stop being there for her just because you have a new girlfriend. We're all Maggie has, and you know it."

I'm just as frustrated by Warren's answer as I am my own question. Of course I'm not going to stop being there for Maggie. But I don't know how to be there for both her and Sydney right now. I didn't really think ahead when Maggie and I split up. I doubt she thought ahead, either. But Warren is right. What kind of person would that make me if I just walked out on the girl who has depended solely on me for the past six years when it comes to her medical needs? Hell, I'm still her emergency contact. That shows how much of a support system she has in her life. And I can't send Warren alone. He can't even take care of himself, much less Maggie. I'm the only one who knows her medical needs. Her entire medical history. The medications she takes, the names of all her doctors, what to do in an emergency, how to operate her respiratory equipment at her house. Warren would be lost without me.

As if Sydney's thoughts are on the same track as mine, she speaks to Warren, and he signs for me. "What do you normally do when this happens?"

"Normally, when this happens, Ridge goes. Sometimes we both go. But Ridge always goes. We help her get home, pick up her prescriptions, make sure she's settled, she gets mad because she doesn't think she needs any help, and after a day or two, she usually forces us to go back home. The same routine we've had since her grandfather could no longer care for her."

"Does she not have anyone else?" Sydney asks. "Parents? Siblings? Cousins? Aunts, uncles, friends? A really reliable mailman?"

"She has relatives she doesn't know very well who live out of state. None that would drive to pick her up at the hospital. And none that know anything at all about how to handle her medical condition. Not like Ridge does."

Sydney looks exasperated. "She really has no one else?"

I shake my head. "She's spent all her time focusing on college, her grandparents, and her boyfriend for six years. We are literally all she has."

Sydney absorbs my answer and then nods slowly, like she's trying to be understanding. But I know it's a lot to take in. She's probably spent the last several months trying to convince herself that Maggie and I wouldn't get back together. I doubt she's even thought far enough ahead to realize that even though Maggie and I are no longer in a relationship, I'm still her primary caregiver when she's not in the position to care for herself.

I know she tolerates the occasional text messages, but

because Maggie hasn't had any episodes for the past several months, this part of Maggie's and my new friendship has yet to be navigated. I've been so focused on just getting Sydney to give me a chance, it hasn't occurred to me until this second that Sydney might not be okay with that.

The realization hits me with the weight of a thousand bricks. If Sydney isn't okay with this, where does that leave us? Will I be able to walk away from Maggie completely, knowing she has no one else? Would Sydney actually put me in a position to choose between her happiness and Maggie's health?

My hands start to shake. I feel the pressure coming at me from all sides. I grab Sydney's hand and lead her to my bedroom. When I close the door, I lean against it and pull her to my chest, squeezing her, scared to death that she's about to put me in an unthinkable situation. And I wouldn't blame her. Asking her to be supportive of such an unusual relationship with the girl I was in love with for years is basically asking her to be heroic.

"I love you," I say. It's the only thing I have the strength to say right now. I feel her sign the words back to me against my chest. She clings to me and I cling to her, and then I feel her start to cry in my arms. I press my cheek to the top of her head and hold her, wanting to take away every ounce of ache she's feeling in her heart right now. And I could. I could text Maggie right now and tell her it's too much for Sydney and that I can't be a part of her life anymore.

But what kind of person would that make me? Could

Sydney even love a guy who would completely cut someone out of his life like that?

And if Sydney asked me to do it—if she asked me never to speak to Maggie again—what kind of person would that make *her* if her jealousy won out over human decency?

She's not that type of person. And neither am I. That's why we're both standing in the dark, wrapped around each other while she cries. Because we know what will eventually happen tonight. I'll leave to take care of Maggie. And it won't be the last time, because Maggie will likely need me until Maggie doesn't need me anymore. And that's a thought I don't feel like processing right now.

I know I've tried to do right by them, but I haven't always *been* right. Part of me feels like this is Karma. I'm being forced to hurt Sydney because I hurt Maggie. And hurting either of them hurts me.

I lift her head from my chest and kiss her, holding her face in my hands. Her eyes are sad, and tears are staining her cheeks. I kiss her again and then say, "Come with me."

She sighs and shakes her head. "It's too soon for that. She wouldn't want me there."

I brush her hair back and kiss her twice on the forehead. She backs up a step and reaches into her pocket for her phone. She types out a text, but my phone is still on the table, so she hands me hers so I can read her text.

Sydney: If you go, I'm probably going to cry myself to sleep. But she's in the hospital, Ridge. And she's all alone. So if you don't go, she'll probably cry herself to sleep, too.

I type out a text to her in return.

Ridge: Your tears mean more to me, Sydney.

Sydney: I know. And as much as this situation sucks and as much as it hurts, the fact that you're torn right now because you don't want to abandon her makes me think more of you than I already do. So go, Ridge. Please. I'll be okay as long as you come back to me.

I hand her back her phone and then run my hands through my hair. I turn away from her and face the door, squeezing the back of my neck. I try to hold it in, but in all my twenty-four years, I have never felt this depth of love from anyone. Not Maggie. Certainly not my parents. And as much as I love Brennan, I'm not sure I've ever felt this depth of love from my own brother.

Sydney Blake, without a doubt, loves me harder than I've ever been loved. She loves me more than I deserve, and in this moment, more than I can even handle.

I wish there were a sign in ASL that could convey my need to hold her even more than a hug can, but there isn't. So I turn and hug her and press my face into her hair. "I don't deserve your compassion. Or your heart."

• • •

She helps me pack.

I let the moment sink in and respect it for what it is. My new girlfriend is helping me pack so that I can go make sure my ex-girlfriend isn't alone in the hospital tonight.

The entire time Sydney is replenishing items in my

duffel bag, I keep distracting her, pulling her to me, kissing her. I don't think I've ever loved her more than I do in this moment. And even though I won't be here tonight, I want her in my bed. I grab her phone and type out a message in the notes app.

Ridge: You should stay here tonight. I want to smell you on my pillow tomorrow.

Sydney: I planned on it. I still need to eat and then I'll clean up the kitchen.

Ridge: I can clean tomorrow. Eat, but leave the mess for me. Or maybe Bridgette will finally contribute.

She rolls her eyes with a laugh after that message. We both know what a stretch it is. We walk into the living room, and Warren and Bridgette are still at the table. Warren is scarfing down his food with a backpack hanging on his chair. Bridgette is sitting across from him, staring at her phone. When she looks up, she seems a little shocked that Sydney and I are walking out of the bedroom together. I guess she wasn't expecting this to end so amicably.

"Ready?" Warren signs.

I nod and walk to the table to grab my phone. Warren walks around the table to give Bridgette a kiss, but she turns her face so that he can only kiss her on the cheek. He rolls his eyes and stands up straight, grabbing his backpack as he walks away from the table.

"Is she mad at you?" I sign.

Warren looks confused. He looks back at Bridgette and then looks at me. "No. Why?"

"She refused to kiss you goodbye."

He laughs. "That's because she just *fucked* me goodbye."

I glance at Bridgette, who is still looking down at her phone. Then I look back at Warren. He smiles with a shrug. "We're quick."

Bridgette looks up from her phone and glares at Warren. He rolls his eyes and starts backing away from me, toward the door. "I have to learn how to stop speaking out loud when I sign to you." He glances at Sydney and gives her a once-over. "You okay with all this?" he asks.

Sydney nods, but then both of them look at Bridgette. Bridgette begins speaking—which is unusual—so I look back at Warren, and he signs everything Bridgette is saying.

"Take it from me, Sydney," she says. "Some men come with heavy baggage, like five kids and three different baby mommas. But Ridge and Warren's baggage is just an ex-girlfriend they sometimes have slumber parties with. Let them go play with their Barbie. We'll stay here and get drunk and order pizza with Warren's debit card. Ridge's pasta sucked, anyway."

Wow.

That's the most Bridgette has ever spoken at one time. Sydney looks at me, wide-eyed. I'm not sure if she's wide-eyed because Bridgette spoke so much or because she just invited Sydney to hang out with her. Either is unprecedented for Bridgette.

"Must be a full moon," Warren says. He walks to the

front door and opens it. I look down at Sydney and wrap my arm around her waist, pulling her against me. I dip my head and press my mouth to hers.

She kisses me back, pushing me toward the door. I tell her I love her three times before I'm finally able to close the door. And as soon as we get to Warren's car, I pull out my phone and text her as we're driving away.

Ridge: I love you, I. FUCKING. LOVE. YOU. SYDNEY.

Chapter Eleven

Maggie

I am craving a Twix so bad right now. *Dammit*, Jake.

I couldn't hear the majority of his conversation with his son when he was out in the hallway earlier. I heard words here and there and could tell he was talking to a child, so when I heard the word *dad*, it all made sense.

I suddenly understood why he seemed so alpha male on the surface, but also somehow had an extremely adorable, romantic side to him. I knew he loved fast cars and extreme sports, but on our date, I couldn't help but wonder what must have forced him to settle down and take his career seriously like he had.

That something turned out to be Justice.

I still don't know why Jake made that Twix comment, but now the only things on my mind are the speed at which Jake rushed out of this hospital room . . . and Twix.

I reach over to my nightstand and grab my phone. I don't know which one of them is driving, so I open up a group text between the three of us.

Maggie: I really need a Twix.

Warren: A Twix? Like the candy bar?

Maggie: Yes. And a Dr Pepper, please.

Ridge: Warren, stop texting and driving.

Warren: It's cool, I'm invincible.

Ridge: But I'm not.

Maggie: Are you guys almost here?

Ridge: Five minutes away. We'll stop at the store before we get there, but we're only getting you a Diet Dr Pepper. You need to watch your blood sugar. Need anything else?

Maggie: I think we're way overdue for an AMA.

Ridge: Nope. I don't think so.

Warren: Did someone say AMA? (And I'll get you a Twix, Maggie.)

Ridge: No.

Warren: LET'S DO IT!!! Be out front in five minutes, Maggie!

Ridge: Don't, Maggie. We'll be up there in five minutes.

Warren: No, we'll be out front in five minutes.

I ignore Ridge's concern and choose to side with Warren. I throw the covers off me, feeling the first flicker of happiness since Jake walked into this room. God, I've missed them so much. I look around the room to make sure I won't be leaving anything behind. My doctor left about half an hour before Jake showed up, so I'm not due for another visit from her until morning. This is the perfect time to make my escape. I reach down to remove my IV, knowing exactly what Ridge is thinking right now.

AMA is the acronym for when a patient leaves a hospital Against Medical Advice. I've only been able to successfully sneak out of a hospital twice in all my years, but Warren and Ridge were there for both escapes. And it's not as irresponsible as Ridge is making it seem. I'm an expert when it comes to IVs and needles. And I know they're only keeping me overnight to be monitored. Not because I'm in any immediate danger. I have been more congested today than normal, but my blood sugars are stable now, and that's the only reason I'm here right now. Stable enough to eat at least a *bite* of a Twix bar. And the last thing I want to do is lie in a hospital bed all night while getting absolutely no sleep.

I'll contact the hospital in the morning and apologize, letting them know it was a family emergency. My doctor will be pissed, but I piss her off a lot. She's used to being irritated with me.

When she was here earlier, she started to get invasive about my "support system" since my health has been on somewhat of a decline this year. She's been my primary doctor for ten years now, so she knows everything about my situation. I was raised by my grandparents, who are no longer taking care of me. My grandmother passed away, and my grandfather was recently put in hospice. My doctor knows about Ridge and our recent breakup because he's almost always with me at my appointments and anytime

I'm in the hospital. But she's noticed his sudden absence in my life, because she asked about it during my last visit with her. And then today, she asked again because no one was with me in the hospital this time.

After hearing her concern today, for a split second it made me regret pushing Ridge away in the end. I'm not still in love with him, but I do love him. And part of me, when I start to worry about being alone, thinks maybe I made a mistake. Maybe I should have held on to his love and loyalty. But *most of me* knows that ending our relationship was the right thing to do. He would have conveniently remained in a mediocre relationship with me for the rest of my life if I hadn't forced him to look at our relationship through a magnifying glass instead of his rose-colored glasses.

Our relationship wasn't a healthy one. He was stifling me, wanting me to be someone I didn't want to be. I was growing resentful under the weight of his protection. And I always felt guilty. Every time he dropped everything he was doing for me, I felt guilty for pulling him away from his life.

Yet . . . here we are, in the same predicament.

I don't think I realized how alone I was outside of him while I was dating him. It was when we finally separated that I truly realized he and Warren were all I had. It's part of the reason I agreed they could come tonight. I think the three of us need to really sit down and have a heart-to-heart about this entire situation. I don't want Ridge to feel like he's all I have when I do have an emergency. But in reality . . . he *is* all I have. And I don't want that to hinder his relationship with

Sydney in any way. I mean, I know I have Warren, too. But I think Warren needs more care than even I do.

My life is starting to feel like a merry-go-round, and I'm the only one on the ride. Sometimes it's fun and exciting, but sometimes I feel like puking and I want it all to just stop. I realize I focus on all the negative way more than I should, but part of me wonders if it's because my situation is so unusual. Most people have huge support systems, so they can live normal lives with this illness. My support system was my family, and that's now nonexistent. Then my support system became Ridge. Now? It's still Ridge, but with different rules. The last few months of dissecting my situation have been eye-opening. And it puts me in weird funks. I used to feel stifled, but never alone.

I wish I could find a good mental balance. I want to do things, see things, live a normal life. And sometimes there are stretches where I do that and it's all fine. But then I have days or weeks where the illness reminds me that I'm not in full control.

Sometimes I feel like I'm two different people. I'm Maggie, the girl who chases down items on her bucket list at one hundred miles per hour, the girl who turns down hot doctors because she wants to be single, the girl who sneaks out of hospitals because she enjoys the thrill, the girl who broke up with her boyfriend of six years because she wants to live her life and not be held down.

The girl who feels full of life, despite her illness.

And then there's this quieter version of Maggie, who's

been looking back at me in the mirror these last few days. The Maggie who lets her worries consume her. The Maggie who thinks she's too much of a burden to date a man she's completely into. The Maggie who has moments of regret for ending a six-year relationship, even though it absolutely needed to end. The Maggie who allows her illness to make her feel like she's dying, despite her being very much alive. The Maggie whose doctor was so concerned about her today, she called in a prescription for antidepressants.

I don't like this version of myself. It's a much sadder, lonelier me, and luckily only appears once in a blue moon. The original version of myself is what I strive to be at all times. Most of the time that's who I am. But this week . . . not so much. Especially after the visit with my doctor today. She's never seemed as concerned for me as she was today. Which makes me more concerned than I've ever been. Which is why I just pulled out my IV, am changing out of this gown, and am about to sneak out of this hospital.

I need to feel like the original Maggie for a few hours. The other version is exhausting.

The walk out of my room and down the hallway is surprisingly uneventful. I even pass one of the shift nurses in the hospital, and she just smiles at me like she has no idea she refilled my IV solution an hour ago.

When I step off the elevator and into the lobby, I can see Warren's car idling outside. I'm instantly filled with adrenaline as I rush across the lobby and out the doors. Ridge steps out of the passenger seat and opens the door for me. He forces a smile, but I can see it all over his face. He's angry that I'm leaving before being discharged. He's angry that Warren is encouraging it. But unlike pre-breakup Ridge, he says nothing. He holds his tongue and holds the door as I climb quickly inside. He closes my door, and I'm putting on my seat belt when Warren leans across the seat and kisses me on the cheek.

"Missed you."

I smile, relieved to be in this car. Relieved to see both him and Ridge. Relieved to be getting the hell out of this hospital. Warren reaches between us and holds up a Twix and a Diet Dr Pepper. "We brought you dinner. King-size."

I immediately open the package and pull out one of the bars. I say, "Thank you," with a mouthful of chocolate. I hand Warren one of the four bars just as he hits the gas and drives away from the hospital. I turn around, and Ridge is sitting in the middle of the backseat, looking out the window.

His gaze meets mine, and I hand him one of the Twix bars. He takes it and smiles at me. "Thank you," he says.

My mouth falls open so far, chocolate almost falls out of it. I laugh and cover my mouth with my hand. "You"—I look at Warren—"He spoke." I look back at Ridge. "You're speaking?"

"Pretty cool, huh?" Warren says.

I'm dumbfounded. I have never heard him speak a single word. "How long have you been verbalizing?" I sign.

Ridge shrugs like it isn't a big deal. "A few months."

I shake my head, completely in shock. His words are exactly how I imagined they would sound. Our relationship with the deaf culture is what ultimately brought all of us together. Warren's parents. Mine and Ridge's hearing loss. But Ridge's hearing loss is much more profound. Mine is so mild, it doesn't even hinder my life in any way. Which is why, for years, when we were together, I did all of his speaking for him. Even though we could both communicate using ASL, I still wanted so badly for him to learn to speak out loud. I just never really pushed him because I don't know what it's like to have profound hearing loss, so I didn't know what it was that was holding him back.

I guess he figured it out, though. And I want to know every detail. I'm excited for him. This is huge! "How? Why? When? What was the first thing you said out loud?"

Something immediately changes in his expression. He becomes guarded, like it's not something he wants to talk to me about. I glance at Warren, who is staring straight at the road like he just purposefully checked out of this conversation. I look back at Ridge, but he's looking out the window again.

And then I get it.

Sydney.

She's why he's talking now.

I suddenly feel envious of them. Of her. It makes me wonder what it was about her that made him overcome whatever obstacle it was that had held him back. Why wasn't I enough of a motivator to ever make him want to say things to me out loud?

And here she is again: the insecure, depressing version of myself.

I grab the Diet Dr Pepper and take a drink, trying to drown this sudden onslaught of jealousy. I'm happy for him. And I'm proud of him. It shouldn't matter what spurred him to want to learn how to communicate in more ways. All that matters is that he is. And even though my chest still burns a little, I'm smiling. I turn back around and make sure he can see the pride in my expression.

"Have you cussed out loud yet?" I sign.

He laughs, wiping the corner of his mouth with his finger. "*Shit* was my first cuss word."

I laugh. Of course it was. He liked watching me say that word when I was angry. I realize speaking words out loud without being able to hear them probably isn't as satisfying as being able to hear your own voice, but it has to feel a little good, finally being able to cuss out loud.

"Call Warren an asshole," I say.

Ridge looks at the back of Warren's head. "You're an asshole."

I cover my mouth with my hand, completely in shock that Ridge Lawson is verbalizing. It's like he's this whole new person.

Warren looks over at me, taking the steering wheel with his knee so that he can sign what he's saying for Ridge. "He isn't a toddler. Or a parrot."

I punch Warren in the shoulder. "Shut up. Let me enjoy this." I look back at Ridge and rest my chin on the headrest. "Say fuck."

"Fuck," he says, laughing at my immaturity. "Anything else? Damn. Goddamn. Motherfucker. Hell. Son of a bitch. Bridgette."

I die with laughter as soon as he includes her name in his string of profanity. Warren flips him off. I turn around and face the road again, still laughing. I take another sip of my drink and then relax against the seat with a sigh.

"I've missed you guys," I say. Only Warren knows I've said it.

"We've missed you, too, Maggot."

I roll my eyes, hearing that nickname again. I look over at him but make sure my headrest is a barrier between me and Ridge so that he can't read my lips. "Is Sydney mad that he came?"

Warren glances over at me briefly and then stares back at the road. "*Mad* isn't the right word. She did react, but not like most people would have reacted." He pauses for a moment and then says, "She's good for him, Maggie. She's just . . . *good*. Period. And if this whole situation weren't so damn weird, I feel like you would really like her."

"I don't *dis*like her."

Warren looks at me out of the corner of his eye. He smirks. "Yeah, but you won't be getting manicures together and going on road trips with her anytime soon."

I laugh in agreement. "That's for damn sure."

Ridge leans forward between the seats and grips both the front headrests. He looks at me, and then he looks at Warren. "Rearview mirrors," he says. "It's like a sound system for deaf people." He leans back in his seat. "Stop talking about us like I'm not right here."

Warren laughs a little. I just sink into my seat, ruminating over that last sentence.

Stop talking about us like I'm not right here.

Stop talking about us . . .

Us.

He refers to himself and Sydney as an *us* now. And he speaks out loud. And . . . I take another sip of my drink because this isn't quite as easy to swallow as I assumed it would be.

Chapter Twelve

Sydney

I don't know what's more awkward: watching Ridge leave to go stay the night with his ex-girlfriend, or sitting in his apartment alone with Bridgette.

As soon as Warren and Ridge left, Bridgette's phone rang. She answered it and walked to her bedroom without acknowledging me. It sounded like she may have been talking to her sister, but that was an hour ago. Then I heard her shower start running.

Now, here I am, cleaning their kitchen and doing their dishes. I know Ridge told me not to worry about it, but I won't be able to sleep if I know there's food out all over the counter.

I'm loading the last of the silverware when Bridgette walks out of her room with pajamas on. Her phone is to her ear again, but this time she's looking at me. "You aren't, like, gluten-free or vegetarian, are you?"

Wow. We're really doing this. And wow. I'm actually a little bit excited. I shake my head. "I've never met a slice of pizza I didn't like."

Bridgette places the phone on the bar and puts it on speaker as she opens the refrigerator and pulls out a bottle of wine. She hands it to me, expecting me to open it, so I take it and look for the bottle opener.

"Pizza Shack," a guy says, answering her call. "Will this be carry-out or delivery?"

"Delivery."

"What can I get you?"

"Two large pizzas with everything. One thick crust, one thin."

I open the wine bottle while she continues to order. "Do you want all the meats?"

"Yeah," Bridgette says. "Everything."

"You also want feta cheese added?"

"I said I want everything."

There's a tapping sound, like fingers against keys, while the guy takes a moment to enter the order. "Do you want pineapple?"

Bridgette rolls her eyes. "I've said *everything* like three times. All the meats, all the vegetables, all the fruits. Whatever you have, just put it on there and bring us the damn pizza!"

I pause and glance over at her. She makes a face at me like she's on the phone with the biggest idiot in the world. Poor guy. He doesn't ask her any more questions. He takes her address, and she gives him Warren's debit card number before she ends the call.

I'm curious to see what kind of pizzas we're about to get. I pray that restaurant doesn't have sardines or anchovies. I pour two glasses of wine and hand Bridgette one. She takes a sip and then folds her arms over her chest, holding the wineglass to her lips as she looks me up and down.

She's very pretty, in a sexy way. I can see why Warren is so drawn to her. They really are the most interesting couple I've ever met. And when I say *interesting*, I don't necessarily mean that as a compliment.

"I used to hate you," Bridgette says, matter-of-fact. She leans against the bar and takes another drink of her wine.

So casual, like this is how people are supposed to interact with other people. She reminds me of one of my friends from childhood. Her name was Tasara, and she said anything and everything that was on her mind. I swear, she spent more days in detention than she did in class. I think that's why I was drawn to her, though. She was mean, but she was honest.

It's one thing when you're mean and you lie. But it's a lot more endearing when you're just brutally honest.

Bridgette doesn't seem like the type to waste time on lying, and for that reason, her comment doesn't offend me. And if I'm going to dissect her words, I have to acknowledge that her sentence was past tense. She *used* to hate me. That's probably the best compliment I'll ever get from her.

"You're starting to grow on me, too, Bridgette."

She rolls her eyes, then walks past me to the cabinet below the sink. She reaches for the Pine-Sol bottle that holds the liquor, and then grabs two shot glasses. *The wine isn't enough?*

She pours the shots and, as she hands me one, she says, "That wine isn't strong enough. I get really awkward when people are nice to me. I'm gonna need liquor for this."

I laugh and take the shot glass from her. We raise them at the same time, and I make a toast. "Cheers to women who don't need their boyfriends in order to have a good time." We clink our shot glasses together before downing the liquor. I don't even know what it is. Whiskey, maybe? Whatever. As long as it does the job.

She pours us another shot. "That toast was way too cheerful, Sydney." We hold up our glasses again, and she clears her throat before speaking. "Cheers to Maggie and her mad skills at remaining friends with both of her ex-boyfriends, to the point that they are somehow still at her beck and call, even when sex isn't involved."

I'm dumbfounded as she clinks her glass against mine and then downs her shot. I don't move my shot glass. When she sees her words have made me speechless, she pushes my shot glass toward my mouth and uses her fingers to tilt it up. I finally down it.

"Good girl," she says. She takes the shot glass from me and hands me my wineglass. She pulls herself up onto the bar and sits cross-legged. "So," she says. "What do girls do when they hang out like this?"

She is so unlike anyone I've ever spent time with as an adult. She's like an entirely different class of animal. There are amphibians, reptiles, mammals, birds, fish—and then there's Bridgette. I shrug and laugh a little, then pull myself up onto the kitchen bar across from her. "It's been a long time since I've had a girls' night, but I think we're supposed to bitch about our boyfriends while we talk about Jason Momoa."

She cocks her head. "Who is Jason Momoa?"

I laugh, but she looks at me like she's clueless. Oh my God. She's serious? She doesn't know who Jason Momoa is? "Oh, Bridgette," I say with pity. "Really?"

She still has no clue who I'm talking about. I grab my phone but don't feel like jumping off the bar to enlighten her. "I'll text you his picture."

I find a picture of him and text it to her. I've only ever sent her one text in the history of knowing her. Sending her a second one practically makes us best friends now.

When I've hit send, I go back to my messages and open up a missed text from Ridge. He sent it five minutes ago.

Ridge: Just letting you know that Maggie didn't want to stay at the hospital tonight so she talked Warren into helping her sneak out. We're taking her home and we'll probably stay there just to make sure she's fine. Are you okay with that? Also, are you having fun with Bridgette?

I read his text twice. I want to be casual about it all, despite my warring emotions, but I'm scared if I'm *too* casual, he'll run to her anytime she misses him. But if I'm not casual enough, I'll be disappointed in my inability to empathize with Maggie's situation. I don't know how to respond, so I do the unthinkable and look up at Bridgette.

"Ridge says they're taking Maggie home. She left before she was discharged. Now he and Warren are probably staying the night at her house."

Bridgette is staring at her phone. "That's shitty."

I agree. But I don't know which part she thinks is shitty. Maggie asking them to come when it doesn't seem like a medical emergency? Ridge saying they might stay the night? Or the entire situation as a whole?

"Does it ever bother you that she and Warren are so close?"

Bridgette immediately lifts her head. "Fuck yeah, it bothers me. Warren flirted with her every time she was here. But he also flirts with you and every other woman he comes across. So I don't know. For the most part, I trust him. Besides, my Hooters uniform would slide right off that shapeless figure of hers, and that uniform is Warren's favorite thing about me."

That explanation was going in such a good direction before it took a nosedive. I don't even know why I asked how she reacts to their situation, because theirs is so different from ours. Warren dating Maggie for a few weeks when she was seventeen hardly compares to Ridge spending six years of his life with her up until a few months ago.

Bridgette must see the worry in my expression while I stare back down at the text. "I really don't think you should stress about it," she says. "I've seen how Ridge is with Maggie, and I've seen how Ridge is with you. It's like comparing chopsticks and computers."

I look at her, confused. "Chopsticks and computers? How is that—"

"Exactly," she says. "You can't compare them because they're incomparable."

That . . . somehow . . . makes complete sense. And makes me feel so much better. I think about the glitter bomb and how Bridgette smiled at me and Ridge when we were laughing together on the floor. I can't believe I've never hung out with this girl before. She's actually not so mean when you peel back all the layers of . . . *mean*.

"Holy. Shit." Bridgette is staring at her phone, and based on how she says those two words, it can only mean one thing. She opened the pic I just sent. "Who is this exemplary specimen of man that has somehow never been introduced into my life?"

I laugh. "*That* is Jason Momoa."

Bridgette brings her phone up to her face and licks her phone screen.

I cringe and laugh at the same time. "You're as gross as Warren."

She holds up her hand. "Please don't mention his name while I stare at this man. It's ruining my moment."

I give her a moment to search him on Google Images while I finish off my glass of wine and reopen my text from Ridge. I type out a response to him and try to avoid the elephant in the room. Or would it be elephant in the *phone*, since Ridge and I aren't in the same room?

Yeah, okay, I think I might be a little buzzed.

Sydney: Glad Maggie is feeling okay. And Bridgette is not so bad, actually. It's weird. Like we're in another dimension.

Ridge: Wow. Is she having a legitimate conversation with you like a normal human?

Sydney: Normal is a stretch. But yeah. She's mostly giving me advice about you. ;)

Ridge: That's unsettling.

Sydney: Good. I want you to feel unsettled until I see you tomorrow.

Ridge: Don't worry, I do feel unsettled. I feel a lot of things. I feel guilty because I left you alone. Worried that you're sad. Lonely because I'm here and not with you. But mostly I feel grateful because you make difficult situations so much easier for everyone involved.

I bring my hand to my mouth and trace my smile. I love that he says exactly what I need to hear.

Sydney: I love you.

Bridgette: Tell Ridge goodbye. This is my time.

I glance up at Bridgette, who is looking at me with severe boredom. I laugh.

Sydney: Bridgette says I can't talk to you anymore.

Ridge: Better do what she says. No telling what the consequences are. I love you. Goodnight. I love you. Goodnight.

Sydney: You said that twice.

Ridge: I mean it even more than that.

I close out the texts, still smiling, and then place my phone facedown on the bar. Bridgette is pouring herself another glass of wine.

"Can I ask you a personal question?" she says.

"Sure." I hop off the bar and grab the wine from her, then turn and refill my glass.

"Does he . . . moan?"

I spin around at that question. "Excuse me?"

Bridgette waves her hand, dismissing my shock. "Just tell me. I've always wondered if he makes noises during sex since he can't hear anything."

I choke out a laugh. "You wonder what my boyfriend sounds like during sex?"

She tilts her head and glares at me, rolling her head. "Oh, come on. Lots of people wonder that about deaf people."

I shake my head. "No, I'm confident most people *don't* wonder that, Bridgette."

"Whatever. Just answer the question."

She's not going to stop. My face and neck feel flushed, but I don't know if it's because of all the alcohol or if it's because she just asked such a personal question. I take a long drink and then nod. "He does. He moans and grunts and sighs, and I don't know why, but the fact that he's deaf makes all his noises that much more of a turn-on."

Bridgette grins. "That is so hot."

"Don't call my boyfriend's sex noises *hot*."

She shrugs. "You shouldn't have made them sound so hot, then." She spends the next several minutes looking up images of Jason Mamoa. And even though I've seen them all, she holds up her phone and shows me each one like she's doing me a favor.

The doorbell eventually rings, and Bridgette suddenly looks happier than I've ever seen her look. She rushes toward the door with starved excitement, like she didn't just eat an entire plate of Alfredo pasta two hours ago. "Grab money for a tip, Syd. I don't have any."

She is perfect for Warren. Absolutely perfect.

Chapter Thirteen

Ridge

It's the first time I've been to Maggie's house since the night we broke up. It's a little weird, but it could be worse. Warren has always had this magical ability to make sure he's weirder than any situation ever could be. And that's exactly what's happening right now. He just raided Maggie's freezer and refrigerator and is standing in her kitchen, dipping soggy microwaved fish sticks into chocolate pudding.

"You eat some of the grossest stuff," Maggie says, opening her dishwasher.

I'm sitting on Maggie's couch, watching them. They're laughing, making jokes. Maggie is cleaning her kitchen as Warren messes it up. I stare at Maggie's wrist—at the hospital bracelet still attached to it—and try not to be upset that I'm here. But I *am* upset. I'm annoyed. If she's well enough to sneak out of a hospital and clean her kitchen, what am I even doing here?

Maggie grabs a paper towel and covers her mouth with it while Warren beats her on the back a few times. I noticed in the car that she was coughing a lot. Back when we were dating and I'd notice she was coughing, I would put my hand on her back or her chest to feel how bad of a cough it was. But I can't do that anymore. All I can do is ask her if she's okay and trust that she isn't downplaying her health.

This coughing fit lasts for an entire minute. She probably hasn't used her vest at all today, so I stand up and walk to her bedroom. It's on the chair by her bed. I grab the vest and the generator it's attached to, and walk it to the couch to hook it up in the living room.

She's supposed to use it two to three times a day to help break up the mucus in her lungs. When a person has cystic fibrosis, it causes their mucus to thicken, which then causes blockage to major organs. Before these vests were invented, patients relied on other people to do manual chest percussions, which meant beating on the back and chest several times a day to break up all the mucus.

The vests are a lifesaver. Especially for Maggie, because she lives alone and has no one to administer chest percussions. But she's never used it as much as she should, and that used to be a huge point of contention between us. I guess it still is, because here I am, hooking it up, about to force her to use it.

After I get it hooked up, Maggie taps me on the shoulder. "It's broken."

I look back down at the generator and power it on. Nothing happens. "What's wrong with it?"

She shrugs. "It stopped working a couple of days ago. I'll take it in Monday and trade it in."

Monday? She can't go an entire weekend without it. Especially if she's already coughing like she is. I sit on the couch to try to figure out what's wrong with it. Maggie walks back into the kitchen and says something to Warren. I can tell by his body language and the way he looks over at me that she said something about me.

"What did she say?"

Warren looks at Maggie. "Ridge wants to know what you just said."

Maggie glances over her shoulder at me and laughs, then faces me. "I said you haven't changed."

"Yeah, well, neither have you."

She looks offended, but honestly, I don't care. She's always tried to make me feel guilty for worrying about her. Clearly, nothing has changed, and my concern still annoys her.

Maggie seems irritated by my response to her. "Yeah, it's kind of impossible to stop having cystic fibrosis."

I stare at her, wondering why she's in such a shit mood. Probably for the same reason I am. We're having the same arguments we've always had, only this time there isn't a relationship between us to fall back on and cushion our feelings.

I'm annoyed that she left the hospital, but now that she's so unappreciative of us being here trying to help her, my anger is starting to build. My girlfriend was crying because I was leaving her, concerned about us, and now Maggie's scolding—*mocking*—me even though I came. *For her.*

I can't sit here and have this conversation. I stand up and unplug the generator, then carry everything back to her bedroom. Maggie and Warren can eat their sacrilegious combination of fish sticks and chocolate pudding, and I'll be in the other room, continuing to try to repair a vest that literally aids in keeping her alive.

I'm not even all the way into her room when I turn around and see that she's following me. I set the generator on the table next to the chair and sit down, pulling the table closer. I turn on the lamp next to the chair. Maggie is still standing in the doorway.

"What is your problem, Ridge?"

I laugh, but not because anything about tonight is funny. "What did you eat this morning before you passed out from low blood sugar?" Maggie's eyes narrow. I'm asking her this because she probably can't even remember. Hell, she probably didn't even eat. "Have you even checked your glucose levels since you ate half of a king-size Twix bar?"

I can tell she's about to yell. When she's really angry at me, she signs and yells. It used to turn me on. Now I would just give anything to be able to yell back at her.

"You have no right to comment on the food I consume,

Ridge. In case you don't remember, I'm not your girlfriend anymore."

"If I don't get a say in how you take care of yourself, then why am I here?" I stand up and walk closer to her. "You don't take care of yourself and you end up in the hospital, and then you call Warren, crying and scared. We drop everything to be there for you, but as soon as we get there, you leave the hospital without being discharged! Forgive me if I have better things to do than come running every time you're irresponsible!"

"You didn't have to come, Ridge! I didn't even know the hospital called you guys. And I didn't cry to Warren on the phone or tell him I was scared! He asked if I wanted company, and I told him yes because I thought we could all figure this stupid situation out like grown adults! BUT I GUESS NOT!" She slams the door on her way out of her bedroom.

I pull it right back open. I don't do it to follow Maggie, though. I go straight to the kitchen and look at Warren. "Why did you tell me she cried and that she was scared?" Maggie is standing on the other side of me, her arms crossed, while she glares at Warren. He's holding a soda, looking back and forth at both of us. His eyes finally land on me.

"I exaggerated. It's not a big deal. You wouldn't have come otherwise."

I force myself to inhale a calming breath. It's either that or I'm going to punch him.

"It's a long drive from Austin to San Antonio," Warren says. Besides, we needed to be together. The three of us. We have to figure out how to deal with all of this going forward."

"All of this?" Maggie says. She motions to herself. "You mean me? We have to figure out how to deal with *me*? I guess this proves I really am nothing but a burden to you guys."

She isn't yelling anymore. She's only signing. But even though I can tell she's hurting and upset, I'm still not convinced things would be different if she would take all this a little more seriously like I've been trying to get her to do for the last six years.

"You're not a burden, Maggie," I sign. "You're selfish. If you took care of yourself and monitored your blood sugar and used your vest like you're supposed to and—I don't know—maybe didn't jump out of fucking *airplanes*, none of us would even be arguing. I've put Sydney in an awkward situation that she wouldn't be in right now if you'd just take better care of yourself."

Warren covers his face with his hand like I just screwed up.

Maggie rolls her eyes with exaggeration. "Poor Sydney. She really is the victim in all of this, isn't she? Gets the man of her dreams *and* she's healthy. Poor *fucking* Sydney!" She turns her attention on Warren. "Don't ever force him to come take care of me again! I don't need him to take care of me. I don't need either of you to take care of me!"

Warren raises an eyebrow, but remains stoic. "With all due respect, you kind of *do* need us, Maggie."

I squeeze my eyes shut and look down. I know that had to hurt her, and I don't want to watch the sting. When I open my eyes again, she's marching to her bedroom. She slams the door. Warren turns and punches the refrigerator. I walk to the table by the couch and grab Warren's car keys.

"I want to leave." I toss Warren his keys, but his eyes dart up to Maggie's bedroom door. He rushes across the living room and swings the door open. Naturally, I rush with him because I can't hear whatever it is he just heard.

Maggie is in her bathroom, hugging the toilet, vomiting. Warren grabs a washcloth and bends down next to her. I walk over and sit on the edge of the tub.

This happens when she has too much buildup in her lungs. I'm sure right now, it's a combination of that and not using her vest for several days, and all the yelling she just did. I reach over and pull her hair back until it stops. It's hard for me to be upset with her right now. She's crying, leaning against Warren.

I don't know what it's like to be the one with this illness, so I probably shouldn't be judging her actions so harshly. I only know what it's like to be the one to care for someone with this illness. I used to have to remind myself of that all the time: No matter how frustrated I get, it's nothing compared to what she must go through.

It looks like I still need that reminder.

Maggie won't even look at me the whole time we wait with her to see if her episode is over. She doesn't even look at me when we're convinced it is over and Warren helps her to her bedroom. It's her way of giving me the silent treatment. She used to refuse to look at me when she was mad because she didn't want to give me the chance to sign to her.

Warren gets her in the bed, and I take her generator back to the living room. Once Maggie is settled, Warren leaves her door halfway open while he comes back to the living room and takes a seat on the couch.

I'm still pissed that he lied about their phone call in order to guilt me into coming. But I also understand why he did it. The three of us do need to sit down and figure this out. Maggie doesn't want to be a burden, but until she buckles down and makes her health her primary focus, she'll never be as independent as she wishes she could be. And as long as she's dependent, it's the two of us who will be taking care of her.

I know we're all she has. And I know that Sydney understands that. I would never walk away from Maggie completely, knowing how much she needs someone in her corner. But when you do things that continue to belittle and even disrespect the efforts of those in your corner, eventually you're going to lose your team. And without your team, eventually you lose the fight.

I don't want her to lose the fight. None of us do. Which is why Warren and I stay, because she needs a treatment. And that can't happen until I repair her vest.

Warren watches TV for the next hour, getting up once to take Maggie a glass of water. When he comes back into the room, he waves his hand to get my attention.

"Her cough sounds bad," he says.

I just nod. I already know. It's why I'm still trying to work on this vest.

It's after two a.m. when I finally figure out the issue. I found an old generator she used to use in her hallway closet. I switch out the power cords and can get it to kick on, but it won't stay on unless I'm holding the cord with my fingers.

Warren is asleep on the couch when I take the vest to Maggie's bedroom. Her lamp is still on, so I can see that she's still wide awake. I walk over to her bed and plug in the generator and hand her the vest. She sits up and slips it on.

"There's a short. I have to hold the cord while it's powered on or it'll cut off."

She nods, but she doesn't say anything. We both know this routine. The machine runs for five minutes, and then she has to cough to clear out her lungs. I run it for another five minutes and then let her take another coughing break. The routine continues for half an hour.

When the treatment is over, she slips off the vest and continues to avoid eye contact with me as she rolls over. I lay it on the floor, but when I look back at her, I can tell by the movement in her shoulders that she's crying.

And now I feel like an asshole.

I know I get frustrated with her, but she isn't perfect. Neither am I. And as long as we're doing nothing but arguing and pointing out each other's shortcomings, we're never going to get her health on the right track.

I sit next to her on the bed and squeeze her shoulder.

It's what I used to do when I felt helpless to her situation. She reaches up and squeezes my hand, and just like that, the argument is over. She rolls over onto her back and looks up at me.

"I didn't tell Warren on the phone that I was scared."

I nod. "I know that now."

A tear falls from her eye and slides down into her hair. "But he's right, Ridge. I am scared."

I've never seen this look on her face before, and it completely guts me. I hate this for her. I really do. She starts crying harder and rolls away from me. And as much as I want to tell her it wouldn't be so scary if she'd stop acting like she was immune to the effects of her illness, I don't respond. I wrap my arm around her because she doesn't need a lecture right now.

She just needs a friend.

• • •

I made Maggie do a second treatment in the middle of the night last night. I'm pretty sure I fell asleep somewhere in the middle of her second treatment, because I woke up at eight o'clock this morning and realized I was on her bed. I know Sydney wouldn't be comfortable with that, so I moved to the couch. I'm still on the couch. Facedown. Trying to sleep, but Warren is shaking me.

I reach for my phone and look at the time, not expecting it to be noon. I sit up immediately, wondering why he let me sleep so long.

"Get up," he signs. "We need to get Maggie's car and drop it back off here before we head back to Austin."

I nod, rubbing the sleep from my eyes. "We need to go to the medical supply store first," I tell him. "I want to see if they can give her a generator until hers gets repaired."

Warren signs, "Okay," and walks to the bathroom.

I fall back against the couch and sigh. I hate how this whole trip has gone. It's left me with an unsettled feeling, which, funny enough, is exactly what Sydney was hoping for. I smile, knowing she got her way and she doesn't even realize it. I haven't spoken to her since all the fighting between me, Maggie, and Warren last night. I open my texts to her and notice she hasn't texted since we talked last night. I wonder how her night with Bridgette went.

Ridge: Heading back soon. How was your sleepover?

She begins texting back immediately. I watch the text bubbles appear and disappear several times until her text comes through.

Sydney: Apparently not as eventful as yours.

Her text confuses me. I look at Warren, who is walking out of the bathroom. "Did you tell Sydney about the argument last night?"

"Nope," Warren says. "I haven't talked to either one of them today. My guess is that they're hungover and still in bed."

My chest tightens because her text is unlike her.

Ridge: What do you mean?

Sydney: Check Instagram.

I immediately close out my texts to her and open Instagram. I scroll down until I see it.

Son of a bitch.

Maggie posted a picture of us. She's making a silly face up at the camera and I'm next to her. In her bed. Asleep. The caption reads, "Haven't missed his snoring."

I fist my phone in both hands and pull it to my forehead, squeezing my eyes shut. *This. This* is why I should have stayed home.

I stand up. "Where's Maggie?"

Warren nods toward the hallway and signs, "The laundry room."

I walk to her laundry room and find her casually hanging up a shirt like she didn't just try to sabotage my relationship with Sydney with her petty Instagram post. I hold up my phone. "What's this?"

"A picture of you," she says, matter-of-fact.

"I see that. But why?"

She finishes hanging up the shirt and then leans against her washing machine. "I also posted a picture of Warren. Why are you so mad?"

I roll my head and throw my hands up in frustration. I'm confused why she did it in the first place, and now I'm confused as to why she's acting like it isn't a big deal.

She pushes off her washing machine. "I didn't realize we had rules to this friendship. I've posted pictures of all of us for six years. Are we catering our lives to Sydney now?" She tries to walk toward the door, but I step in front of it.

"You could show a little respect for our situation."

Maggie's eyes narrow. "Are you serious right now? Did you really just ask me to show respect to the relationship you're in with the girl you *cheated* on me with?"

That is not fair. We're past that now. At least I *thought* we were. "You could have posted any picture of me, but you chose to post one of me in your bed. A bed I was in because I stayed up for hours to make sure you were okay. Using that as an opportunity to throw my mistake back in my face is not fair, Maggie."

Her jaw hardens. "You want to talk fair? How fair is it that you're the one who had an emotional affair, but I'm the one who has to be sensitive about what I post on Instagram? How fair is it that I'm the bad guy for eating a Twix? I wanted a fucking *Twix*, Ridge!" She pushes past me, so I follow her. She spins around when she reaches her living room. "I forgot how I'm never allowed to have any fun when you're around. Maybe you shouldn't come back, because this is the worst day I've had in months!"

In all my years of knowing her, I've never been this mad at her. I don't know why I thought this could work. "If you have an actual emergency, let me know, Maggie. I'll be here for you. But until then, I can't be friends with you." I walk to the front door and swing it open, then face Warren. "Let's go."

Warren is standing in the living room, frozen, at a complete loss as to what to say or do. "What about Maggie's car?"

"She can take an Uber." I walk out of Maggie's house and head for Warren's car.

It takes him a few minutes to finally walk outside. I'm sure he was reassuring Maggie. Let him. Maybe he can reassure the unreasonable, but I sure can't.

When Warren finally makes it to his car, I open up my texts to Sydney. I don't even try to justify the picture with an excuse. I'll explain it all when we're face-to-face with her.

Ridge: I'm sorry she posted that, Sydney. I'm on my way back to my apartment now.

Sydney: No hurry. I won't even be at your apartment when you get here.

I get a separate text from Bridgette.

Bridgette: Dick. You're a dick. Dick, dick, dick.

Sydney: And don't bother coming to my apartment. Me and Bridgette are having another sleepover.

Bridgette: NO DICKS ALLOWED!

I close out the texts to both of them and lean my head against the seat. "Drive to Sydney's apartment first."

Chapter Fourteen

Maggie

I sit down on the couch after Warren closes the door. I stare at the floor.

I bury my face in my hands.

What is wrong with me?

I pushed Jake away. I pushed Ridge away. I even told Warren to get the hell out of my house when he stayed back and tried to get me to tell him why I was acting the way I was.

I don't know what's gotten into me this week. This isn't me. I, honest to God, don't want to be in a relationship with Ridge, but when I woke up this morning and saw him asleep next to me, it felt good to have him back. I've missed him. But not in a romantic way. I've just missed his company. And I started wondering if he missed my company, or if Sydney is all he needs now. Then I started feeling insecure again because he was here, even though he expressed just how much he didn't want to be here. And as I lay there and stared at him, I started thinking about the day I found all the messages between him and Sydney, and I got angry all over again.

I shouldn't have posted the picture. I know that. But I think I did it because I thought it would make me feel better in some twisted way. I missed him, I was angry at him, I was angry at myself. I feel like years of just trying to live despite this illness is catching up to me. Because Ridge is right. I don't take care of myself like I should, but it's because I'm sick of this illness, and sometimes I don't care if it wins. I really don't.

I pull out my phone and delete the picture; then I open a text to Ridge.

Maggie: It's been the shittiest week of my life. Tell Sydney I am so sorry. I deleted the picture.

I hit send and then power off my phone and lie down. I press my face into the couch and I cry.

The problem with hating yourself when you're all alone is that you have no one to remind you of any of your good qualities. Then you just hate yourself even more, until you sabotage anything good in your life and in yourself.

I'm at that point.

Maggie Carson. Not so much of a badass today.

Chapter Fifteen

Sydney

I had so much fun last night.

I ate Bridgette's disgusting pizza, and then she told me all about how she and Warren started dating. That only solidified my opinion of their weirdness. Then we watched *Justice League* and fast-forwarded through all the parts Jason Momoa wasn't in.

I don't remember much after that because we were several bottles of wine in. My sleep and my fun were both cut abruptly short today when Bridgette shook me awake and shoved Maggie's Instagram post in my face.

I'm more hurt than angry. I'm sure Ridge will have an excuse. He always does. But what's Maggie's excuse? I know, in a sense, I'm the other woman who came between them. I was the Tori in that situation. But I honestly thought we were all beyond that. From the way Warren and Ridge made it sound, she took it well and was even mature about it. But this feels so . . . *petty. Gross*, even.

I couldn't stand being in Ridge's apartment after seeing her post. The way I felt reminded me of the stark and pitiful misery I went through while I lived there. And the entire place smelled like pepperoni and anchovies. I told Bridgette I was going back to my place, and she went to her room to grab her stuff and told me she was going with me.

I think she might be just as upset as I am, because she brought another bottle of wine with her, and now we're drinking again, and it's barely two o'clock in the afternoon. But I don't mind that she's here. I actually prefer it, because I really don't want to be alone right now or I'll overanalyze this entire situation and come up with far-fetched reasons for him being on that bed before he can even explain himself.

Bridgette is sitting cross-legged on my bed. She reaches to the floor and grabs her purse, pulling her phone out of it. "That's it. I can't take it. I'm commenting on her Instagram post."

I try to pull her phone away. "Don't. I don't even want her to know I saw it. It'll serve her purpose."

Bridgette rolls onto her stomach to protect her phone from me. "That's why I said *I'll* comment. I'll say something to make her feel as insecure as she's trying to make you feel. I'll tell her she looks healthy. Everyone knows when you tell someone they look healthy, it really means fat."

"You can't say that to someone who is actually sick. And really skinny."

Bridgette groans and then rolls onto her back, tossing her phone aside. "She deleted it! Dammit!"

Thank God. I appreciate Bridgette's support, but I really don't need her wedging herself into Ridge's and my—and Maggie's—issues.

"You want me to call Warren and ask him what happened?" Bridgette sounds almost giddy. She would be one to thrive on drama.

And I'm not gonna lie. I've thought about calling Warren myself because I have so many questions. I know they're driving back right now and Ridge will probably come over and try to explain himself, but it would be nice to be a little enlightened beforehand so I know exactly how much and how loud I should yell at him when he arrives. Not that the decibel of my voice will matter in our argument, but it might make me feel better to scream at him.

Bridgette calls Warren and puts the phone on speaker.

"Hey, babe," he says as he answers.

"So, what the fuck happened last night?" Bridgette says.

Yeah, she doesn't know how to do anything with tact. Warren clears his throat, but before he starts speaking, I interrupt him.

"Are you signing this conversation for Ridge? I really don't want to talk to him right now."

"I'm driving," Warren says. "Kind of hard for me to drive, hold my phone, eat this cheeseburger, and sign everything I'm saying. Besides, he's staring out the passenger window, brooding."

Bridgette leans toward the phone. "Sydney and Ridge's relationship is in jeopardy, yet you guys had time to stop for burgers?"

"*I* stopped for a burger. Ridge won't eat until all is right in the world of Ridney."

I roll my eyes. "Well, then he's gonna be really hungry by tonight."

"He didn't do anything wrong, Sydney," Warren says. "I swear. That was all Maggie."

"He was asleep on her bed!" Bridgette says.

"Yeah, because he spent two hours repairing the generator to her vest and then had to hold the cord so she could use it. He didn't sleep all night, and when he finally did get a few hours of sleep, Maggie took a picture of him and went and pulled some really shady shit. I'm telling you, it was all Maggie. I've never seen her like this."

I glance up at Bridgette. I don't know if I can trust Warren. As if she can sense what I'm thinking, she says, "We're not stupid, Warren. Bros before hos. You would defend Ridge even if he murdered you."

"Hold on," Warren says. "I need to take a drink."

Bridgette and I wait and listen as he slurps down a drink. I fall back onto my bed, frustrated with Warren. With Ridge. With Maggie. But for once, I'm not at all frustrated with Bridgette.

"Okay," Warren says. "Here's what happened. After we left the hospital and got back to Maggie's house last night, it was an entire hour of them screaming at each other. It's like they both released years of aggression all at once, and there were so many insults coming from both sides. All of the—"

"Wait," Bridgette says. "Now I know for a fact you're lying."

"I'm not lying!" Warren says defensively.

"You said they were screaming at each other. Ridge can't scream, you idiot."

I press my hand to my forehead. "It's sort of a figure of speech in this situation, Bridgette. He was angry and he was signing. Warren refers to it as screaming." Bridgette shoots me a look of suspicion, like she still doesn't trust what Warren is saying. I give my attention back to the phone. "Why were they fighting?"

"Why *weren't* they fighting? Ridge was mad because he was there and she wasn't even that sick. He was mad she isn't taking her health seriously, and it's starting to inconvenience those around her. She was mad because he brought up the fact that she was inconveniencing you and putting a strain on your relationship with Ridge. I'm telling you, I've never seen them like this. And it wasn't the kind of fighting that me and Bridgette do, where we're just trying to get under each other's skin. This was legit *I'm fucking angry at you* fighting."

I close my eyes, hating the entire situation. I'm not pleased that they're fighting. That's helping no one. But it does explain why she posted that picture. It wasn't to get back at me. She was pissed at Ridge, and her best form of revenge on him is to involve me.

"And then they both got mad at me," he says. "All the yelling caused her to start vomiting, and then Ridge made her wear her vest, and he fell asleep on her bed during one of her treatments. As soon as he woke up, he went to the couch and slept for four hours until I woke him up and InstaGate happened. And that's the whole story."

I kick my legs on the mattress. "Ugh! I don't know who to be mad at! I just need to be mad at someone!"

Bridgette points to the phone and whispers, "Be mad at Warren. It's a great stress reliever." She raises her voice so he can hear her. "Why did they get mad at you?"

"Not important," Warren says. "We're pulling up to your apartment right now, Sydney. Let us in."

He ends the call, and I don't even know if I feel any better. I never thought Ridge was in Maggie's bed because he was cheating on me. I knew he probably had a valid excuse related to her health. But why couldn't they have been on the couch together, instead? Or the floor? Why did he have to fall asleep in a place where they've probably been intimate with each other for years?

I stand up. "I need more wine."

"Yep, yep. Wine," Bridgette says, following me to my kitchen.

When Ridge and Warren finally make it inside, I've just downed my second glass for the day. Warren walks in first, and then Ridge walks in. I hate how Ridge frantically searches for me and then looks relieved when he sees me. I just want to stay mad at him, but he makes it so hard with those kissable lips and apologetic eyes.

I know what I'll do. I just won't look at him. That way I won't succumb so easily to my forgiveness. I spin around so that I can't see Ridge or the door. I can only see Warren as he tries to hug Bridgette, but she pushes against his forehead.

Turning my back on Ridge doesn't do me any good, because he walks up behind me and wraps his arms around me, tucking his face into the space between my neck and shoulder. He kisses me softly on the neck and keeps his arms wrapped around me, apologizing without words.

I don't accept this apology. I'm still mad, so I remain stiff and don't react to his touch. Externally, anyway. Internally, I just combusted.

Bridgette downs the rest of her wine, then gives her attention to Warren. "Why were Ridge and Maggie mad at you?"

I want to hear Warren's answer, but Ridge releases me, turning me so that I'm face-to-face with him. He slides his hands to my cheeks and looks at me very seriously. "I'm sorry."

I shrug. "Still hurts."

Warren ignores Bridgette's question and walks toward me and Ridge. I glance over Ridge's shoulder as Warren touches his chest, looking somewhat guilty. "It was mostly my fault, Sydney. I'm really sorry."

"Figures," Bridgette says, walking to the kitchen for more

wine. She walks right between Ridge and me, separating us completely. "Just spill it, Warren."

Warren squeezes the back of his neck with his hand as he winces. "Well. Funny story . . ."

"I bet it's a riot," Bridgette deadpans.

Warren ignores her and continues, "I might have exaggerated about the phone call with Maggie. She wasn't crying, and she technically didn't beg us to come. I just knew if I didn't stretch the truth a little, Ridge wouldn't have gone."

Bridgette's mouth drops open. She makes a shocked sound and then looks at me, then back at Warren. "You wanted a sleepover with your ex-girlfriend, so you lied to everyone?"

"You're such an asshole, Warren," I say. Why would he lie and put Ridge in that situation yesterday? God, I am so angry at him. It feels good to finally have a solid target for my anger.

"Look," Warren says, throwing his hands up in the air. "Ridge and Maggie were way overdue for a conversation about this. I wasn't doing it to be malicious. I was trying to be helpful!"

"Yeah, sounds like the entire trip was a success," I say.

Warren shrugs, placing his hands on his hips. "There may not be a resolution yet, but Maggie needed to hear everything Ridge had to say. In fact, I think you'd be proud of him. After last night and everything he said to defend you, there isn't a doubt in my mind that he's one hundred percent aboard the Sydney train."

I fold my arms over my chest. "You mean you had doubts before last night?"

Warren looks up at the ceiling. "Not what I meant." He looks at Bridgette, and I can tell he's done with this day already. "Let's go. They need privacy. So do we."

Bridgette pulls out a chair at the bar and takes a seat. "No. I'm not finished with my wine."

Warren walks to the counter and grabs the bottle of wine. Then he takes her glass out of her hand and walks out the front door with it. Bridgette looks at the door and then at me. Then at the door and then at me again. Her eyes are full of panic. She points helplessly at the door. "Wine."

"Go," I say, walking around Ridge, toward the door. She rushes to the door, and I shut it behind her. When I turn back around, Ridge is leaning his head against the refrigerator, staring at me. I sigh and stare back at him, hating how tired he looks. As irritated as I am at Warren, I'm relieved he explained everything. I'm not as angry at Ridge.

Ridge pulls his phone out and starts to text me. I go to my room and get my phone and then head back to the kitchen as I read his text.

Ridge: I have no idea what's been happening for the last ten minutes. No one signed a single word of any of that and it's really hard to read lips when people are angry and moving around.

My shoulders drop when I read his text. I feel bad that we all just excluded him while we argued around him.

Sydney: To sum it up, Warren said you were innocent and he was guilty and Maggie was bitter and it was just a huge cluster-fuck of a slumber party.

Ridge reads the texts and then shrugs a shoulder.

Ridge: No matter the reason, I shouldn't have been on Maggie's bed without thinking about how that would make you feel. But for the record, I fell asleep during her treatment and then moved to the couch as soon as I woke up.

Sydney: Well, it wasn't soon enough. Because it bit you right in the ass.

Ridge: Whoever said Karma is a bitch must have never met her. Because Karma is very friendly and she follows me around everywhere I go. Everywhere. All the time.

I smile, but Ridge just looks so sad. I hate that we're in the position to have to make up after another argument, and we haven't even been together a week. I hope this isn't any indication of how the rest of our relationship is going to go. Of course, the first argument was all his fault, and he was being a tool. But this one . . .

I don't know. From what I gathered through Warren's explanation, Ridge really is making a huge attempt at putting me first. It's just hard when there are so many obstacles. *Oh man.* Did I just refer to Maggie as an obstacle? She's not an obstacle. Her recent *behavior* is the obstacle.

Ridge: Can I please kiss you? I need to. So bad.

I smile a little as I read his text. He must see it, because he doesn't even wait for me to look up and answer him. He just rushes toward me and lifts my face and then presses his mouth firmly to mine. He kisses me like he's starved for me. It's my favorite kind of kiss from him. It's so desperate and mostly one-sided from him that the strength behind his kiss ends up forcing me backward. He continues kissing me until my back is against the living room wall. But as desperate as it is, it's not a sensual kiss. It's just full of need. A need to feel me and know I'm not upset. A need for reassurance. A need for forgiveness.

After a good minute of him kissing me, he presses his forehead to mine. Still, even after I've let him kiss me, he seems distraught. I slide my hand up to his cheek and brush my thumb across it, bringing his eyes to mine.

"Are you okay?"

He inhales and then slowly exhales. He nods unconvincingly and then pulls me against him. I barely have time to wrap my arms around him when he bends down and slides an arm behind my knees and lifts me up. He carries me to the bedroom and lowers me to the bed.

Whatever is still bothering him can wait, because his mouth is on mine again. But this time his kiss isn't a need for my reassurance. It's just a need for me. He pulls his shirt over his head and then stands up and slides off my pajama bottoms. Then he's over me again, his tongue in my mouth, his hand sliding up my thigh, lifting my leg.

I want to hear him. Since the moment I described how hot his noises were last night, I've been craving them all. I unzip his jeans and slip my hand inside, pulling him out and guiding him inside of me.

His mouth is against my neck when I get his groan. It rumbles up his chest as he pushes into me, and then he sighs, softly, as he pulls out. He repeats the rhythm, and I close my eyes. The entire time he makes love to me, I remain quiet and listen to the sensual sounds of Ridge.

Chapter Sixteen

Ridge

There are three things that produce such beautiful sounds that countless poems have been written about them.

Oceans, waterfalls, and rain.

I've only been to the ocean once. Sounds of Cedar played a gig in Galveston two years ago, and I joined them for the trip. The morning after the concert, I walked to the beach. I took my shoes off and sat down in the sand and watched the sun rise.

I remember this feeling building inside me as I watched it. Almost like every negative emotion I've ever felt was evaporating with each new ray of sun that trickled out over the horizon.

It was a feeling of complete and utter awe, like nothing I had ever experienced. And as I sat there, I realized I was in awe of something that occurs every single day, and has occurred every single day since the very first sunrise. And I thought to myself, *How can something be so magnificent when it isn't even a thing of rarity?*

The sun and its rise and fall is the most expected, dependable, and repetitive natural occurrence known to mankind. Yet it is one of the few things that maintains a universal ability to render a man speechless.

In that moment, as I sat alone on the beach, my toes buried in the sand, my hands wrapped around my knees . . . I wondered, for the first time, if the sunrise made a sound. I was almost positive it didn't. If it did, I was sure I would have read about it. And I was sure there would be more poetry about the sound of the sunrise than there is about oceans or waterfalls or rain.

And then I wondered what that same sunrise must feel like to those who could hear the ocean as the sun broke itself free from the constraints of the horizon. If a soundless sunrise could mean so much to me, what must it mean to those who watch it as it's accompanied by the roll of the water?

I cried.

I cried . . . because I was deaf.

It's one of the few times I've ever felt resentful about this part of me that has limited my life so significantly. And it's the first and only time I've ever cried because of it. I still remember how I felt in that moment. I was angry. I was bitter. Upset that I had been cursed with this disability that hindered me in so many ways, even though most of my days were spent not even thinking about it.

But that day—that moment—gutted me. I wanted to feel the complete effect of that sunrise. I wanted to absorb every call of the seagulls flying overhead. I wanted the sound of the waves to enter my ears and trickle down my chest until I could feel them thrashing around in my stomach.

I cried because I felt sorry for myself. As soon as the sun had risen fully, I stood up and walked away from the beach, but I couldn't walk away from that feeling. The bitterness followed me throughout the entire day.

I haven't been back to the ocean since.

As I sit here with my hands pressed against the tile of the shower, the spray of the water beating down on my face, I can't help but think about that feeling. And how, until that moment, I never truly understood what Maggie probably feels on a daily basis. Bitter and hurt that she was dealt a hand in life that she's expected to accept with grace and ease.

It's easy for someone on the outside to look in and think that Maggie is being selfish. That she's not thinking about anyone's feelings but her own. Even I think that a lot of the time. But it wasn't until that day on the beach two years ago that I truly understood her with every part of my being.

My being deaf limits me very little. I'm still able to do every single other thing in the world besides hear.

But Maggie is limited in countless ways. Ways that I can't even fathom. My one bitter day on the beach alone when I truly felt the weight of my disability is probably how Maggie feels on a daily basis. Yet those on the outside of her illness would probably look at her pattern of behavior and say that she's ungrateful. Selfish. Despicable, even.

And they would be right. She is all those things. But the difference between Maggie and judgmental people who aren't Maggie is that she has every right in the world to be all those things.

Since the day I met her, she has been fiercely independent. She hates feeling as if she's hindering the lives of those around her. She dreams of traveling the world, of taking risks, of doing all the things her illness tells her she can't do. She wants to feel the stress of college and a career. She wants to revel in the independence the world doesn't think she deserves. She wants to break free of the chains that remind her of her illness.

And every time I want to scold her or point out everything she's doing wrong and all the ways she's hindering her own longevity, I only need to think back on that moment at the beach. That moment that I would have done whatever it took to be able to hear everything I was feeling.

I would have traded years of my life for just one minute of normalcy.

That's exactly what Maggie's doing. She just wants a minute of normalcy. And the only way she gets a moment of normalcy is when she ignores the weight of her reality.

If I could rewind the clock and start yesterday over again, I would do so many things differently. I would have included Sydney in that trip. I wouldn't have allowed Maggie to leave the hospital. And I would have sat down with her and explained to her that I want to help her. I want to be there for her. But I can't be there for her when she refuses to be there for herself.

Instead, I allowed every pent-up negative thought I've never said spill out all at once. It was truthful, yes, but the delivery was hurtful. There are much better ways to share your truth than to force it on someone so hard it injures them.

Maggie's feelings were hurt. Her pride was bruised. And while it's easy for me to say her actions warranted my reaction, it doesn't mean I don't regret that reaction.

I'm trying not to think about it, but it's consuming me. And I know the only thing that can alleviate everything I'm feeling is to talk to the one person in my life who understands my feelings more than anyone. But she's also the last person I want to subject to a discussion about Maggie.

I turn off the water in Sydney's shower. I've been in here for over half an hour, but I'm trying hard to figure out how to suppress everything I'm feeling right now. Sydney deserves a night untainted by my past relationship. This week has been tough, and she deserves one night of near perfection, where she is my sole focus and I am hers.

And I'm going to give her that.

I walk out of her bathroom in just a towel. Not because I'm trying to distract her from the homework she's currently doing on her bed, but because my pants are on her bedroom floor and I need them. When I drop the towel and pull on my jeans, she looks up from her homework with the tip of her pencil in her mouth, chewing on it with a grin.

I smile back at her because I can't help it. She pushes her books aside and pats the bed beside her. I sit down and lean back against the headboard. She slides her leg over me and straddles me, running her hands through my wet hair. She leans forward, kissing me on the forehead, and I'm not sure if she's ever done that before. I close my eyes as she plants soft kisses all over my face. She ends with a soft peck against my lips.

I just want to revel in this moment, so I pull her to me, not really interested in conversation or making out. I just want to hold her and keep my eyes closed and appreciate that she's mine. And she allows it for all of two minutes, but one of the advantages she holds over me is being able to hear the sighs I forget I'm even releasing.

This includes the heavy sigh that instantly causes her concern to resurface. She pulls back, holding my face with her hands. She narrows her eyes as if it's a warning that I better not lie to her.

"What is wrong with you? Be honest this time."

I'm not getting out of this without complete transparency. I slide my hands from her waist up to her shoulders. I squeeze them and then gently move her off me. "Laptops," I tell her.

We use our laptops for the serious conversations. The ones we know will require too much patience for signing or lipreading or text. I walk to her living room and grab my laptop out of my bag. When I make it back to her room, she's sitting against the headboard with her laptop, her eyes following me to my spot on the bed. I open up our messenger and begin the conversation.

Ridge: For the record, I wanted to avoid this conversation tonight. But I'm not sure there's a single emotion I can feel without you reading it.

Sydney: You're not as transparent as you seem to think you are.

Ridge: I only feel transparent to you.

Sydney: Well, let's see if you're right. I'm going to try and pinpoint what's bothering you.

Ridge: Okay. Are we taking bets? Because if you guess right, I'm taking you out on a date tonight. But if you guess wrong, you're going on a date with me tonight.

Sydney: ;) We've never been on a real date before.

Ridge: You better guess either right or wrong then, or we won't be going.

Sydney: Okay. I'm gonna take a stab at it, then. I can tell by your body language that your mind is somewhere else tonight. And based on the past twenty-four hours you've had, I'm going to assume your mind is on Maggie.

Ridge: I wish I could tell you you're wrong. But you're right. I just hope you know it's completely innocent. I just can't help but feel bad for everything I said to her.

Sydney: Have you spoken to her since you left her house today?

Ridge: She texted after I left and gave a two-sentence apology to both of us. But I didn't respond. I was too angry to respond. Now I don't know how to respond because I feel guilty, but also don't feel like she deserves any kind of apology from me. That's what confuses me. Why do I feel guilty if I don't feel like apologizing for what I did?

Sydney: Because. It bothers you that deep down inside, you know if you and Maggie were in any other situation, neither of you would speak again. You're both so different. If it weren't for her illness, the two of you probably would have ended your relationship long before y'all did. But that's not the situation, so she's probably having a hard time processing the fact that you're only in her life because you have to be.

I read her message, and I feel the truth dig straight into my bones. Sydney is right. Maggie's illness is the only reason we're still connected. As much as I know that, I haven't wanted to admit it. But there's me and there's Maggie and we're on opposite sides of the earth right now with this string called cystic fibrosis tying us together.

Ridge: You're right. But I wish you weren't.

Sydney: I'm sure she wishes it were different, too. How do you think that made her feel that you were at her house simply because you needed to be and not because you wanted to be?

Ridge: I'm sure that made her feel resentful.

Sydney: Exactly. And when people feel resentful, they act out. They say things they don't mean.

Ridge: Maybe so, but what was my excuse? I lashed out at her like I've never lashed out at anyone. And that's why I can't stop thinking about this situation, because I feel like I lost my patience with her.

Sydney: It sounds like you did. But I don't think you should regret it. Sometimes caring about someone means saying things you don't want to say, but that need to be said.

Ridge: Yeah. Maybe so.

Sydney: Your heart is my favorite thing about you, Ridge.

She really does love the side of me that Maggie never could. I think that's why it just works with Sydney and me. I finally have someone who is in love with the entirety of me.

Sydney: I won't lie, though. Sometimes your heart scares me.

Ridge: Why does it scare you?

Sydney: Because. I worry that Maggie is spiraling downward. And I know you worry about that, too. I'm scared your guilt and your worry are going to force you to get back together with her, just so you can fix her.

Ridge: Sydney . . .

Sydney: Hey, we're being uncomfortably honest right now.

I look at her, completely dumbfounded by that response. She looks up at me with a hint of fear in her expression, like she thinks I might actually agree with that asinine concern.

Ridge: Sydney, I would never leave you in order to fix her issues. I would be broken without you. Then who would fix me?

She reads my message, and I watch as she reaches a hand up to her laptop screen and runs her thumb over my words. Then she highlights the sentence and copies it. She opens a Word document and pastes it below a bunch of other messages.

I lean over to get a better view of her computer screen, but she hurries and closes out the Word program. I only got a half-second glance, but I could swear the title of the document said Things Ridge Says.

Ridge: Did that document have my name in the title?

Sydney: Maybe. Don't worry about it.

I glance down at her, and she's trying to stifle a smile. I shake my head, almost certain I know what she just did.

Ridge: Do you save things? Things I say to you? Like . . . you have an actual file of things I've said to you?

Sydney: Shut up. You act like that's weird. Lots of people have collections.

Ridge: Yeah, of tangible things, like coins or taxidermies. I don't think most people collect pieces of conversations.

Sydney: Fuck off.

I laugh and then highlight her sentence and copy it. I open a new Word file and paste it into the document, then save the file as Things Sydney Says.

She shoves me in the shoulder. I close my laptop and then shut hers, and slide them both to the other side of her. I wrap my arm around her and rest my chin on her chest, looking up at her. "I love you."

She raises an eyebrow. "Quick bean church."

I tilt my head. "Say that again. I'm pretty sure I misread your lips."

"Quit. Being. A. Jerk."

I grin at my bad lipreading and then kiss her chest. Then her neck. Then I peck her on the lips and pull her off the bed. "Time for our date. Let's get dressed."

She signs, "Where are we going?"

I shrug. "Where do you want to go?"

She grabs her phone while I'm putting on my shirt and she texts me.

Sydney: Would it be weird if we went back to that diner?

I try to recall a diner that we've been to, but the only one I can think of that she might be referring to is the one I took her to the first night we met in person. It was her birthday, and I felt bad that her day was so shitty, so I took her for cake.

Ridge: The one close to my apartment?

She nods.

Ridge: Why would that be weird?

Sydney: Because. It was the first night we met. And maybe going there on our first date would be sort of celebrating that moment.

Ridge: Sydney Blake. You have got to forgive yourself for falling in love with me. We've shared a lot of chapters that don't need to be torn out of our book simply because there are things in them you don't like. It's part of our story. Every single sentence counts toward our happy ending, good or bad.

Sydney reads my text and then slides her phone in her pocket like dinner is solidified thanks to that last text. She signs the next thing she says. "Thank you. That was beautiful. Bridge. Cloud. Pimple."

I laugh. "Was that supposed to be a real sentence?"

Sydney shakes her head. "I don't know how to sign a lot of words yet. I decided I'm just going to make random words up when I don't know how to sign what I really want to say."

I motion for her to get her phone out of her pocket.

Ridge: You said bridge, cloud, and pimple. LOL. What were you trying to sign?

Sydney: I didn't know how to sign that you are getting so lucky after this date tonight.

I laugh and wrap my arms around her, pulling her until her forehead meets my lips. Damn, I cannot get enough of my girl. I also can't get enough of the bridge, cloud, pimple.

• • •

We drove Sydney's car to my apartment because I didn't have my car, and we can't walk to the diner from her apartment like we could from mine. She insisted we walk like we did the last time we came here. Sydney ordered breakfast for dinner, but she also ate half my onion rings and three bites of my burger.

We decided to play twenty questions during dinner, so we used our phones instead of signing because it was hard to do that and eat at the same time. In the forty-five minutes we've been here, I haven't thought about my fight with Maggie. I haven't thought about how behind on work I am. I haven't even thought about that damn *Game of Thrones* spoiler. When I'm with Sydney like this, her presence absorbs all the bad parts of my day, and I find it so easy to concentrate on her and only her.

Until Brennan appears.

Now I'm concentrating on Brennan as he slides into the booth next to Sydney and reaches across the table for my last onion ring.

"Hi." He pops the onion ring into his mouth, and I lean

back in my seat, wondering what the hell he's doing here. Not that I mind. But it is our first official date, and I'm confused why he's crashing it.

"What are you doing here?" I sign.

Brennan shrugs. "I don't have anything scheduled tonight. I was bored and went to your apartment, but you weren't home."

"But how did you know we were here?"

"The app," he says, pulling my soda to him and taking a drink. I give him a look that lets him know I have no idea what he's talking about.

"You know," he says. "Those apps you can use to track people's phones. I track yours all the time."

What the hell? "But you have to set that app up with my phone."

Brennan nods. "I did like a year ago. I know where you are all the time."

That actually explains a lot. "That's weird, Brennan."

He leans back in his seat. "No, it isn't. You're my brother." He looks at Sydney. "Hi. Nice to see you fully clothed."

I kick him under the table, and he just laughs, then folds his arms over the table and speaks his next sentence. "You feel like writing something tonight?"

I shake my head. "I'm on a date with my girlfriend."

Brennan's shoulder's slump, and he falls back against the booth. Sydney looks back and forth between me and Brennan.

"A song?" she says. "You want to write a song tonight?"

Brennan shrugs. "Why not? I need more material, and I'm in the mood. My guitar is in my car."

Sydney perks up and starts nodding. "Please, Ridge? I want to watch you two write a song."

Brennan nods. "Please, Ridge?"

Brennan's begging does nothing to change my mind, but that's only because Sydney's begging already changed it. Besides, the whole time I've been on this date with Sydney, song lyrics have been swirling around in my head. Better to get them out now while I'm feeling it.

I pay the check, and we go outside to head back to the apartment, but Brennan points across the street at a park. He runs to his car and retrieves his guitar and stuff to write with. The three of us walk over to the park and find two benches across from each other. Brennan sits on one, and Sydney and I sit on the other.

Brennan turns his guitar over and presses the notepad to it. He writes on it for a few minutes and then hands it over to me. He's written out the music to a chorus he's working on, but there are no lyrics. I spend several minutes studying it. I can see Brennan and Sydney having a conversation while I look over the music and try to figure out how to add the first line of the chorus. He signs the first part of the conversation, but when he sees I'm not paying attention to either of them, he stops signing and they continue the conversation. I like that they're holding a conversation without me. It's not like the conversations people have where they forget to sign for me. It's just a conversation they're having because they know I need a while to focus on this song.

I think back to Sydney's and my conversation from earlier, and how she expressed a fear that I would someday take Maggie back because I want to fix everything going wrong in Maggie's life. I try to work that into a couple of sentences, but nothing sticks. I close my eyes and try to recall the exact words I said to her.

I would be broken without you. Then who would fix me?

I read that sentence over and over again. *Who would fix me?*

This is how I sometimes build a foundation for my lyrics. I think of a person. I think of a conversation with that person, or a thought I have about that person. And then I ask myself a question about that thought, then build a line of lyrics around the answer.

So . . . who *would* fix me? The only person who could mend my shattered heart would be Sydney.

I find my sweet spot in that answer and write down the lyric, "You're the only one who fixes me."

I tap my pencil on the page in the tempo of the music that Brennan wrote out for me. Brennan picks up his guitar and watches my pencil, then starts to play. I can see Sydney out of the corner of my eye as she pulls her knees up on the bench and wraps her arms around them, watching us. I look at her for a moment, waiting for thoughts of her to inspire another line. What do I want her to know when she hears this song?

I write down several sentences in no particular order,

and none of them rhyme, but they all remind me of Sydney. I'll build around them in a moment and make each of them into verses. I just need to get out the basic things I'm thinking.

There was a truth in you from the start.
I think you're pretty when you speak.
I bring the mess and you bring the clean.
Time will come and you will see.
You're the only one who fixes me.

I look up from the page, and Brennan is still playing, working through the tempo of the song that I just laid his chorus out to. Sydney is watching me, smiling. It's all I need to finish the lyrics. I move to the bench with Brennan and show him the lyrics, matched up with his chorus. He starts tweaking it while I finish the lyrics.

Almost an hour later, we have a complete song. It's the fastest the two of us have ever written together. Brennan hasn't sung any of the lyrics out loud yet for her, so I move to the bench with her and pull her against me before he plays her the full song. He begins strumming his guitar, and she wraps an arm around me, leaning her head against my shoulder.

Wake up early, go to bed late
That's what I do, that's my mistake
Tell me something and I forget
I'm not perfect, I'm far from it

I'm out the door fifteen too late
Thinking I'm early, but I make you wait
Don't wash my dishes for a week
But I think you're pretty when you speak

Ask around, you'll figure out
You're the one I'm thinking 'bout
Time will come and you will see
You're the only one who fixes me
You're the only one who fixes me

I bring the mess and you bring the clean
I think you're funny when you're mean
There was a truth in you from the start
And nothing can break this hold on my heart

Ask around, you'll figure out
You're the one I'm thinking 'bout
Time will come and you will see
You're the only one who fixes me
You're the only one who fixes me, yeah

Out of order, out of my mind
Had you waiting on a white lie
Took a minute but I finally found my way

Ask around, you'll figure out
You're the one I'm thinking 'bout

Time will come and you will see
You're the only one who fixes me

Ask around, you'll figure out
You're the one I'm thinking 'bout
Time will come and you will see
You're the only one who fixes me
You're the only one who fixes me, yeah

When Brennan finishes playing the song, Sydney doesn't move right away. She's curled up to me, her hand fisted in my shirt. I think she must need a moment to absorb that.

When she finally pulls away from my chest, there are tears in her eyes, and she wipes them away with her fingers. Brennan and I wait for her to say something, but she just shakes her head. "Don't make me talk right now. I can't."

Brennan smiles at me. "Speechless. Your girl approves." He stands up and says, "I'm gonna head to your apartment and get this one recorded on my phone while it's fresh in my head. Want a ride?"

Sydney nods and grabs my hand. "Yes. But we aren't staying at Ridge's. We have to go back to my apartment. It's important."

I give her a confused look.

She shoots me an adamant look in return. "Bridge, cloud, pimple. Now."

I smile as she pulls me toward Brennan's car.

I think she loved that song.

Chapter Seventeen

Sydney

Ridge and Brennan have both exited Brennan's car, but I'm still sitting in the front passenger seat, looking at the car parked next to ours. It's Hunter's car. But it's not Hunter shutting the back door. It's Tori. Which is why I'm frozen to my seat, because I wasn't expecting to see her, and I really don't want her to see me. I'm certain it won't end up with me punching her again, but I still have no desire to talk to her.

It's too late, though, because Ridge doesn't recognize her, and he opens my door so that we can move from Brennan's car to Ridge's right as she's walking by. She pauses in her tracks when our eyes meet.

Dammit.

I take Ridge's hand and slowly get out of the car. Tori looks like she's seen a ghost. But she doesn't run away like I wish she would. Instead, she walks the sacks of groceries she's carrying to the hood of her car and sets them down. Then she turns to me, hugging herself.

"Hi," she says. I can tell she wants to talk. And I just don't have it in me to be a complete dick to her.

I look at Ridge. "You go," I sign. "Two minutes."

Ridge glances at Tori and then at me. He nods and backs away, falling into step with Brennan as they head up to Ridge's apartment.

Tori looks good. She's always looked good. I find myself pulling at my ponytail and wiping a wisp of hair out of my face.

"Is that your boyfriend?" she asks.

I glance up at the top of the stairs. Ridge is walking into his apartment backward, looking down at us with concern. I give him a reassuring smile before he closes the door. I turn my attention back to Tori, folding my arms over my chest. "Yeah."

There's a knowing look in Tori's eye. "He's the guy from the balcony, right? The one you were writing lyrics for?"

I suddenly become protective of everything going on in my life, and I don't want to reveal anything to Tori. I don't even know why I'm out here right now. She just seemed like she really wanted me to stop and talk to her. Maybe so she can move past everything that happened between us.

I look behind her, at Hunter's car. There are FOR SALE signs posted in the side and back windows.

"Hunter is selling his car?"

Tori looks over her shoulder at it. "Yeah. We think it has water damage or something. It's been smelling weird for a while now."

I cover my mouth with my hand, ensuring she doesn't see my smile breaking through. When I'm certain I can hold it in, I move my hand and grip the strap of my purse. "That's too bad. I know he loves that car."

Tori's phone rings, and she glances down at it, then answers it, turning away from me a little. Almost as if she doesn't want me to be privy to her conversation.

"What?" she whispers. The way she answers the phone makes it seem like she's irritated with whoever is on the other line. She glances up at her apartment and says, "I still have another load of groceries to bring up. Give me a sec."

She ends the call and slides her phone into her pocket. She walks over to the hood of the car and starts grabbing the sacks of groceries. She stands in front of me, two sacks in each hand, arms down at her sides. "So, um . . ." She pauses and inhales a sharp breath, exhaling it just as quickly. "You wanna grab coffee sometime? I'd really like to catch up. Hear all about the new boyfriend."

I stare at her a moment, wondering why she would think I'm okay with that. I realize I was also a Tori at a very short point during mine and Ridge's friendship, but as mad as I am at Hunter and as mad as Maggie must have been at Ridge, there are few betrayals on earth that hurt worse than the betrayal of your very best friend. She's the person I shared my life with. A home with. All my secrets with. And the entire time we lived together, she was betraying me on a daily basis.

I don't want coffee with her. I don't even want to be outside chatting with her, acting like she didn't break my heart with ten times the strength that Hunter ever could.

I shake my head. "I don't think coffee is a good idea." I choose to walk around the back of her car so that I don't have to get even closer to her. Before I head for the stairs, I look at her. "You really hurt me, Tori. More than Hunter ever could have. But I still think you deserve better than a man who doesn't even bother to come down and help you carry up groceries."

I walk away and run up the stairs, away from her, away from that smelly car, and away from the sad reality that she still hasn't found happiness yet. I wonder if she ever will.

I walk inside the apartment, and Brennan is on the couch with his guitar. He nods his head toward Ridge's room. When I open the door to Ridge's bedroom, he's lying across the bed on his stomach, hugging a pillow. I walk over to him, but he's asleep. I know he's had a long twenty-four hours, so I don't bother waking him. I let him rest.

Brennan is at the table now, playing the song he and Ridge just wrote. I walk to the kitchen and pour myself a glass of wine. There's only enough left for one glass. Bridgette and I really tore through their stash. Ridge is probably going to start keeping the wine in a Windex bottle.

"Sydney?"

I turn toward Brennan, and he's hugging his guitar, his chin resting on it. "I'm really hungry. Do you think you can make me a grilled cheese?"

I laugh as soon as the question comes out of his mouth. But then I realize he's serious. "You're asking me to make you a sandwich?"

"It's been a long day, and I don't know how to cook. Ridge always cooks for me when I'm over here."

"Oh my God. How old are you? Twelve?"

"Transpose those numbers and you've got your answer."

I roll my eyes and open the refrigerator to take out the cheese. "I can't believe I'm making you a sandwich. I feel like I'm disappointing every female who has ever fought for our equality."

"It only counts against feminism when you make your man a sandwich. It doesn't count if it's just a friend."

"Well, we won't even be friends if you think you can ask me to cook for you every time you visit your brother."

Brennan smiles and turns back toward his guitar. He starts strumming it to a tune I haven't heard from him before. Then he starts to sing.

Cheddar, swiss, provolone. That is where I feel at home.

Slap that cheese on some bread. I like it more than getting head.

Grilled cheese,

Grilled cheese,

Grilled cheese from Sydney.

Blake. Not Australia.

I'm laughing at his impressive improv abilities, even though it was a terrible song. He's obviously just as talented as Ridge is. He just suppresses it for some reason.

He sets his guitar on the table and walks over to the bar. He grabs a paper towel and places it in front of him. I guess that's the extent of his sandwich prep.

"Do you even have trouble writing lyrics? Or do you pretend you can't write because of your guilt?"

"What would I have to feel guilty for?" Brennan asks, taking his seat at the bar.

"Just a hunch, but I think you hate that you were born with the ability to hear, and Ridge wasn't. So you pretend you need him more than you actually do. Because you love him." I flip the grilled cheese over. Brennan doesn't respond right away, so I know I have him pegged.

"Does Ridge think that, too?"

I face him full-on. "I don't think so. I think he loves writing lyrics for you. I'm not telling you to stop pretending you don't know how to write lyrics as well as he can. I'm just saying I understand why you do it."

Brennan smiles, relieved. "You're smart, Sydney. You really should consider doing more with your life than just making sandwiches for hungry men."

I laugh and pick up his sandwich with the spatula. I drop it on the paper towel in front of him. "You're right. I quit."

He takes a bite, right as the front door opens. Bridgette walks in holding a sack, wearing her Hooters uniform and a scowl. She sees us in the kitchen and nods, then walks to her room and slams the door. "Did she just nod her head at you?" Brennan asks. "That was an oddly nice gesture that didn't include a middle finger. Does she not hate you anymore?"

"Nah. We're practically best friends now." I start to clean the kitchen, but Bridgette yells my name from her bathroom. Brennan raises an eyebrow, like he's worried for me. I walk toward her bathroom and can hear a lot of commotion. When I open the door, she grabs my wrist and pulls me inside and then slams the door shut. She turns toward the counter and begins dumping out the contents of her sack into the sink.

My eyes go wide when I see five unopened boxes of pregnancy tests. Bridgette starts frantically ripping into one and hands me another. "Hurry," she says. "I have to get this over with before I freak out!" She pulls a stick out of the box and then grabs another one to open.

"I think one is enough to indicate if you're pregnant."

She shakes her head. "I have to be sure I'm not pregnant or I won't sleep until I have twelve periods."

I have two of the tests open, and she rips the last one open, then grabs a mouthwash cup from next to the sink and rinses it out. She pulls down her shorts and sits on the toilet.

"Did you even read the instructions? Are you supposed to pee in an unsanitized cup?"

She ignores me and begins peeing in the cup. When she's finished, she sets it on the counter. "Dip them!" she says.

I stare at her cup of pee and shake my head. "I don't want to."

She flushes the toilet and pulls her shorts up, then shoves me out of the way. She dips all five sticks into the cup at once and holds them there. Then she pulls them out and lays them all on a towel.

This is all happening so fast, I'm not sure I've had time to process the thought that we're about to find out if Bridgette is going to be a mother. Or whether Warren is going to be a father.

"Do either of you even want kids?" I ask.

Bridgette shakes her head adamantly. "Not even a little bit. If I'm pregnant, you can have it."

I don't want it. My idea of hell is having a child composed of pieces of Warren and Bridgette.

"Bridgette!" Warren yells, right before the front door slams shut. Bridgette cringes. The bathroom door swings open, and I suddenly don't feel like I should be in here anymore. "You can't text me something like that in the middle of my study group and then ignore me when I call you back!"

Warren . . . in *study* group? I laugh, but my laughter causes both of them to turn their glares on me. "Sorry. I just can't picture Warren in a study group."

He rolls his eyes. "It's a mandatory group project." He turns his attention back on Bridgette. "Why do you think you're pregnant? You're on the pill."

"Pickles," she says, as if that's a good explanation. "I

stole three pickles off my customers' plates tonight, and I hate pickles. But all I can think about are pickles!" She turns back toward the pregnancy tests and picks one up, but it hasn't been long enough yet.

"*Pickles?*" Warren says, flabbergasted. "Jesus Christ. I thought this was serious. So you craved a fucking pickle."

Warren is stuck on pickles, but I'm still stuck on the idea of Warren in a study group. "When do you graduate?" I ask him.

"Two months."

"Good," Bridgette says. "Because if I'm pregnant, you need to get a real job so you can raise this child."

"You aren't pregnant, Bridgette," Warren says, rolling his eyes. "You craved a pickle. You're so dramatic."

This entire conversation is making me want to ensure Ridge and I use double the protection from now on. I take my birth control religiously, but there's been a time or two that we haven't used a condom. Never again, though.

Bridgette picks up one of the pregnancy tests and presses her hand against her forehead. "Oh, fuck." She turns and tosses the stick toward Warren. It hits him in the cheek and then he fumbles as he tries to catch it.

"Is it positive?" I ask.

Bridgette nods, running her hands down her face. "There's a line! Shit, shit, shit, there's a really long, visible line! Fuck!"

I look at one of the boxes. "A line just means it's working. It doesn't mean you're pregnant."

Warren is holding the stick between two fingers when he drops it back on the towel. "That has your pee on it."

Bridgette rolls her eyes. "No shit, Sherlock. It's a pregnancy test."

"You *threw* it at me. There's pee on my face." He takes a hand towel and wets it under the faucet.

"You aren't pregnant," I reassure her. "It's not a plus sign."

She picks up another one of the tests and studies it, leaning against the counter. "You think?" She picks up one of the boxes and reads it, then sighs with relief. She pours the cup of urine out in the sink.

"Why didn't you pour that in the toilet?" Warren asks with a grossed-out look on his face. This, coming from the guy who ate a bar of cheese after Bridgette tried to wash herself with it.

"I don't know," Bridgette says, looking at the sink. She turns the water on to rinse it out. "I'm distressed. I wasn't thinking."

Warren slips in front of me and wraps his arms around Bridgette, bringing her head to his level. He brushes her hair back gently. "I'm not going to get you pregnant, Bridgette. After our first scare, I wrap my Jimmy Choo up hella tight every time."

I was on my way out of the bathroom to give them privacy, but I freeze when I hear Warren refer to his penis as a Jimmy Choo.

I turn back around. "Jimmy Choo?"

Warren looks at me through the reflection in the mirror. "Yeah, that's his name. Ridge doesn't nickname his penis after cool things?"

"Cool things?" I say. "Jimmy Choos are designer shoes."

"No," Warren says. "A Jimmy Choo is a rare Cuban cigar. Right, Bridgette?" he says, looking at her. "You're the one who named him."

Bridgette tries to keep a straight face, but she sputters laughter. She brushes past me and runs into the living room, but Warren is right on her heels. "You said Jimmy Choos were huge cigars!" They end up on the couch, Warren on top of her. They're both laughing, and it's the first time I've ever really seen them affectionate.

It's disturbing that a pregnancy scare is what brings out the best in them as a couple.

Warren kisses her on the cheek and then says, "We should go celebrate with breakfast tomorrow." He sits up and looks at me and Brennan. "All of us. Breakfast is on me."

Bridgette pushes Warren away from her and stands up. "I will if I wake up on time."

Warren follows her out of the living room and into their bedroom. "Girl, you aren't even sleeping tonight."

Their door closes.

I look at Brennan. He looks away from their door, toward me.

We both just shake our heads.

"I'm heading home," he says, standing up to pack his guitar. He grabs his keys and walks toward the door.

"Thanks for the sandwich, Sydney. Sorry I'm a brat. It's Ridge's fault for spoiling me for so long."

"That's actually good to know. If Ridge is the one who spoiled you, then I'm not going to have to break up with him for expecting me to make him sandwiches."

Brennan laughs. "Please don't break up with him. I think you might be the first thing that's ever made Ridge's life easier."

He closes the door behind him, and I can't help but smile at his parting words. He didn't have to say that, but the fact that he did makes me think Brennan and Ridge are more alike than I initially thought. Both thoughtful.

After Brennan leaves, I lock the front door. I hear a thumping sound behind me, so I spin around and listen for a few seconds to see where it's coming from.

Warren and Bridgette's bedroom.

Oh. *Gross.* Gross, gross, gross.

I rush to Ridge's bedroom and close the door, then crawl into bed with him. I wasn't planning on staying here tonight. I still have homework I haven't finished this weekend, and really do need to have some alone time in order to get it all done. Ridge is way too distracting.

"Syd," Ridge says, rolling toward me. His eyes are closed, and I think he might even still be asleep. "Don't . . . be scared . . . the chicken." He signs the last word.

He's talking and signing in his sleep. I grin at his nonsensical words. Did he talk in his sleep before he started verbalizing? Or is that something new?

I kiss him on the cheek and fold his arm over me as I snuggle against him. I wait to see if he speaks again, but he doesn't. He just sleeps.

• • •

I was awake by seven, but Ridge was still asleep. He woke up sometime in the middle of the night and took off his jeans and shoes, but then went right back to sleep.

I was making a pot of coffee when Warren walked out of his bedroom and told me to stop. "I'm treating you to breakfast, remember?" Then he went to wake up Ridge, but Ridge told him he needed two more hours of sleep.

"Let's let him sleep," I said. "Let me go change out of my pajamas and we can go."

Warren told me no, that the place we're going to eat actually requires pajamas.

I have no idea where we're going, but Bridgette wanted to sleep in, so now it's just me and Warren, going to breakfast in our pajamas to celebrate Bridgette's negative pregnancy test. *Without* Bridgette.

Nope. Not weird at all.

"Did this restaurant just open?" I ask Warren. "Is that why I've never heard of it?" He told me earlier it was called Fastbreak Breakfast, but it doesn't sound familiar.

"We're not going to a restaurant."

I glare at him from the passenger seat, just as he pulls into the parking lot of a hotel and drives around to the side of the building. "Wait here," he says, hopping out of the car. He takes his keys with him.

I sit and watch him as he stands next to the side entrance to the hotel. I start to text Ridge to ask him what the hell I've just gotten myself into, but before I can type out the text, a businessman walks out of the side door and doesn't even notice as Warren grabs the door handle and holds the door open. He waves me out of the car, so I get out and follow him inside, shaking my head. It's finally registered why he told me to wear pajamas. Because he wants it to look like we're guests here.

"Are you kidding me, Warren? We're sneaking into a free continental breakfast?"

He smiles. "Oh, it's not just any free breakfast, Sydney. They have Texas-shaped waffles here."

I can't believe this is his idea of treating people to breakfast. "This is stealing," I whisper, just as we walk into the breakfast area. He reaches for a plate and hands it to me, then grabs his own.

"Maybe so. But it doesn't count against your track record because I'm the one who brought you here."

We make our plates and take a seat at an area by the window that's not visible to the front desk. For the first ten minutes, Warren talks about school, since I was so intrigued by the idea of him actually sitting in a study group. He's majoring in management, which is something else that intrigues me. Baffles me, even. I can't imagine him in a position where he's in charge of other people, but I guess he does manage Sounds of Cedar pretty well.

I don't think I give Warren enough credit. He has a job, he goes to school full-time, he manages a successful local band, and he manages to keep Bridgette somewhat happy. I guess it's just his addiction to porn and his inability to clean up after himself that led me to assume he's got a lot of growing up to do.

When we're finished eating, Warren grabs a tray and piles muffins and juices on it, then brings it back to the table. "For Ridge and Bridgette," he says, covering the muffins with a napkin.

"How often do you come here? You seem to be experienced in the art of breakfast theft."

"Not very often. I have a few hotels around town that I frequent, but I try to mix it up every now and then. Don't want the desk clerks becoming suspicious."

I laugh, sipping the last of my orange juice.

"Ridge has never been on board. You know how he is, always trying to do the right thing. Maggie came with me a few times, though. She liked the thrill of possibly getting caught. She's actually why I call it Fastbreak Breakfast. We had to make a break for it once because a clerk walked around writing down room numbers and checking them to last names."

I look down when he says Maggie's name, not wanting to hear how good of friends he is with her. Not that I care if Warren and Maggie are friends. I just don't want to hear about it. Especially this early in the morning.

He notices my reaction, because he leans forward and

folds his arms over the table. He tilts his head in thought. "Our friendship with her really bothers you, huh?"

I shake my head. "Not as much as you probably think. What bothers me is how much Ridge stresses about it."

"Yeah, well, imagine how much Maggie stresses about it."

I roll my eyes. I know how much Maggie probably stresses about it. But just because she stresses more than I do doesn't mean I'm not allowed to stress. "I already told Ridge it's just going to take me a little time to get used to it."

Warren laughs under his breath. "Well, hurry up and get used to it, because I already told you once that he'll never leave her."

I remember that night very clearly. I don't need Warren to point it out again. It was when Ridge and I were hugging in the hallway. Warren walked inside the apartment and didn't like what he was seeing, because Ridge was dating Maggie at the time. Ridge didn't know Warren was in the apartment, but before Warren walked to his room, he made sure I was aware of his thoughts on our predicament. Warren's exact words were, *I'm only going to say this once, and I need you to listen. He will never leave her, Sydney.*

I lean back in my seat, growing defensive like I always do when Warren talks about Ridge's and my relationship. He always seems to take it a step too far, even though I feel like I've been more than accommodating and understanding when it comes to Ridge's friendship with Maggie. "You did say that," I agree. "But you were wrong, because they did break up."

Warren stands up and begins gathering trash from the

table. He shrugs. "They broke up, sure. But I didn't tell you they'd never break up. I told you he'd never *leave* her. And he won't. So maybe instead of trying to convince yourself that you just need time to warm up to the idea of her always being a part of his life, you should remind yourself that you already knew that. Long before you agreed to start a relationship with him."

I stare at him, dumbfounded, as he walks the trash to the trash can. He comes back to the table and reclaims his seat. I forget what a casual asshole he can be to everyone. I recall his words again, only this time they mean something completely different.

He will never leave her, Sydney.

This whole time, I thought Warren was saying Ridge would never break up with her, when all along, Warren just meant that Maggie would always be a part of Ridge's life.

"You know the one thing that could make this entire situation a little easier?" Warren asks.

I shake my head, unsure about anything anymore. He looks at me pointedly. "You."

What?

"Me? How could I make it easier? If you haven't noticed, I've worked really hard to try and have the patience of a freaking saint."

He nods in agreement. "I'm not talking about your patience," he says, leaning forward. "You have been patient. But what you *haven't* been is apologetic. There's a girl you seriously wronged, who is a huge part of Ridge's life. And even though she claims not to blame you, you probably still owe her an apology. Apologies shouldn't happen because of the response of the person who was wronged. Apologies should happen because of the wrong." He slaps his hands on the table like the conversation is over, and he stands up, grabbing the tray of food he made for Ridge and Bridgette.

My stomach turns at the thought of being face-to-face with Maggie after everything that has happened. And even though I don't take any responsibility for all the resentment she and Ridge have been building up toward each other over the years, I do take responsibility for the fact that I was a Tori for a hot minute and never once reached out to her to apologize.

"Come on," Warren says, pulling me up and out of my stupor. "There are worse things in life than having a boyfriend with a heart the size of an elephant's."

• • •

I'm completely silent on the ride home. Warren doesn't even try to get me to talk. When we get back to Ridge's apartment, Ridge is still asleep. I write him a note and leave it beside him on the bed.

> *Didn't want to wake you because you deserve the sleep. I've got a lot of homework to catch up on today, so maybe I can come over tomorrow night after work.*
>
> *I love you.*
>
> *Sydney.*

I feel bad lying to him, because I'm not going home to do homework. I'm going home to change clothes.

This drive to San Antonio is long overdue.

Chapter Eighteen

Maggie

My mother was a dramatic woman. Everything revolved around her, even when it wasn't about her. She was the type of person who, when someone close to her would experience something bad in their lives, would somehow relate it to her own life so that their tragedy could be her tragedy, too. Imagine what having a daughter with cystic fibrosis was like for her. It was her moment to soak up the sympathy—to make everyone feel sorry for her and the way her child had turned out. My illness became more of a problem for her than it was for me.

But it didn't last long, because she took a temporary position with her company in Paris, France, when I was three. She left me with my grandparents because it was "too cold" for me there, and it would be "too difficult" learning to navigate a new country with a sick child in tow. My father was never a part of my life, so that wasn't an option. But my mother always promised she would one day take me to Paris to live with her.

My grandparents had my mother at a very late age, and my mother had me in her late thirties. It was getting to the point that my grandparents could hardly care for themselves, much less a child. But my mother's temporary position became permanent, and every year when she would come home to visit, she would promise me she'd take me back with her when the time was right. But her Christmas visits would always end on New Year's Day, with her leaving to go back to Paris without me.

Maybe she did have intentions of taking me back with her, but after spending two weeks with me at my grandparents' every year at Christmas, she would be reminded of what a huge responsibility I would be in her life. I used to think it was because she didn't love me, but I remember the year I turned nine, I figured out that my illness was what she didn't love about me. It wasn't me.

I got the idea that if I could just convince her that I could take care of myself and that I didn't need her help, she would take me with her and we could finally be together. In the weeks leading up to Christmas the year I turned nine, I was extremely cautious. I consumed all the vitamins I could get my hands on so that I wouldn't catch a cold from my classmates. I used my vest twice as much as I was required to. I made sure I got eight hours of sleep every night. And even though Austin saw its first snow in years that winter,

I refused to go outside to experience it because I was afraid I'd catch a cold and end up in the hospital during my mother's visit.

When she arrived the week before Christmas, I was very careful never to cough in front of her. I wouldn't take my medications in front of her. I did everything I could to appear like a vibrant, healthy child so that she'd have no choice but to see me as the child she'd always wished I was and that she would take me back to Paris with her. But that didn't happen because on Christmas morning, I overheard her and my grandmother having an argument. My grandmother was telling my mother that she wanted her to move back to the States. She said she was concerned about what would happen to me when they died of old age. *What will Maggie do when we're gone if you're not around to care for her? You need to come back to the States and develop a better relationship with her.*

I will never forget the words my mother said to her in response.

You're worried about things that may never happen, Mother. Maggie will more than likely succumb to her illness before either of you succumb to old age.

I was so shattered by her response to my grandmother that I ran back to my bedroom and refused to speak to her for the rest of her trip. In fact, that was the last time I ever spoke to her. She cut her trip short and left the day after Christmas.

She sort of faded out of my life after that. She called

my grandmother to check in every month or so, but she never came back for Christmas, because every year I told my grandmother I didn't want to see her. Then, when I was fourteen, my mother passed away. She was traveling from France to Brussels on a train for a business trip and suffered a massive heart attack. No one on the train even noticed she had died until three stations past her stop.

When I found out about her death, I went to my bedroom and cried. But I didn't cry because she'd died. I cried because as dramatic as she was, she never made a dramatic attempt at winning my forgiveness. I think it's because it was easier for her to live a life without me while I was mad at her than when I was missing her.

Two years after her passing, my grandmother died. That was the hardest thing I've ever endured. I still don't think I've fully absorbed her passing. She loved me more than anyone had ever loved me, so when she died, I felt the absolute loss of that love.

And now my grandfather—the last of the people who raised me—has been put in hospice due to recently declined health, coupled with a case of pneumonia he's too weak to fight. My grandfather will pass away any day now, and because of my cystic fibrosis and the nature of his illness, I am not allowed to see him and tell him goodbye. He'll likely die sometime this week, and just like my grandmother feared, they'll all be gone and I'll be all alone.

I guess my mother was wrong about me succumbing to my illness before them. I'll outlive them all.

I know my experience with my mother hinders all my other relationships. It's hard for me to fathom that someone else could love me despite my illness, when my own mother wasn't even able to do that.

Ridge did, though. He was in it with me for the long haul. But I guess that was the problem. Ridge and I wouldn't have stayed together as long as we did if it weren't for my illness. We were too different. So I guess whatever end of the spectrum people are on—whether they are too selfish to take care of me or too selfless to stop—I'm going to resent them. Because for whatever reason, I seem to have lost a piece of myself to this illness.

I wake up thinking about this illness. I spend my days thinking about it. I fall asleep thinking about it. I even have nightmares about it. As much as I claim that I am not my illness, somewhere along the way, it has consumed me.

There are days I'm able to break out of this web, but there are more days that I'm not. It's why I never wanted Ridge to move in with me. I can lie to myself and lie to him and say that it's because I wanted to be independent, but in reality, it's because I didn't want him to see the dark side of me. The side that gives up more than it fights. The side that resents more than it appreciates. The side that wants to face all of this with dignity, when really, I can hardly even accept it with disdain.

I'm sure everyone who fights to live on a daily basis has moments where they give up every now and again. But these aren't just moments for me. Lately, they've become my norm.

I wish I could go back to Tuesday. Tuesday was great. Tuesday, I woke up wanting to conquer the world. And by Tuesday night, I sort of had.

But then Wednesday morning happened, when I overreacted and made Jake leave. Friday happened, when I finally swallowed my pride, but then ended up in the hospital, drowning in my own humiliation. Then Friday night happened, when I just wanted to forget the ups and downs of the past few days, but our fight was a new low for the week.

And if Friday night was my low, Saturday morning was my rock bottom.

Or maybe today is. I don't know. I'd say they've been equal.

I can't even focus on school. I have two months left, and I sometimes think Ridge was right. I've worked so hard on my graduate degree in order to begin work on my doctorate, only to feel like I accomplished something. But maybe I should have put all my energy into something more worthwhile, like making friends and building an actual life for myself outside of school and my illness.

I've worked at proving myself to no one but myself. In the end, it's left me with nothing but a graduate degree that no one really cares about but me.

I wish there were a magic pill that could get me out of this funk. I'm sure if Warren had his way, that magic pill would come in the form of an apology. He texted me this morning to let me know he was sorry for the stunt he pulled when he told Ridge I was upset, but then he scolded me for posting that picture of Ridge in my bed and told me I should apologize.

I didn't respond to him, because I wasn't in the mood for Righteous Warren this morning. I swear, every time there's a wrinkle in a scenario, he pulls out his iron and tries to smooth everything, while burning us all in the process. He's like a Sour Patch Kid. Sour and then sweet. Or sweet and then sour. There's no in between with Warren. He's completely transparent, and sometimes that's not a good thing.

But I've never had to wonder what Warren is thinking, nor have I ever worried about hurting his feelings. He's impenetrable, but I think because he's impenetrable, he assumes everyone else is, too. As much as I can appreciate him, it's not enough for me to respond to his texts from this morning with anything other than Don't want to talk about it yet. Text you tomorrow.

I knew if I didn't let him know I was okay, he'd show up at my front door to make sure nothing happened to me. Which is precisely why I texted him.

But . . . I don't think it worked. Because my doorbell is ringing. There's only a small chance that it's Warren, though. My bet is that it's my landlord. Since I informed her a few months ago that I'd be moving back to Austin soon to start my doctorate, she's brought me a loaf of banana bread every Sunday. I think she does it to make sure I'm still living here and that I haven't destroyed the house, but whether it's out of kindness or nosiness, I don't really care. It's damn good banana bread.

I open the door and force a smile, but my smile falls flat. It's not banana bread.

It's Sydney.

I am so confused. I glance behind her and look to see if she's here with Ridge, but Ridge isn't behind her. Nor is his car in the driveway. I look at her.

"It's just me," she says.

Why would Sydney show up at my house alone? I look her up and down, taking in her casual jeans and T-shirt, her flip-flops, her thick blond hair that's pulled up into a ponytail. I don't know why she's here, but if any other girlfriend showed up at their boyfriend's ex-girlfriend's house, they wouldn't show up looking this casual, even if it were just to borrow a cup of sugar. Women like making other women jealous. They especially like making the women who have slept with the men they're in love with jealous. Most women would show up in their most flattering outfit with sculpted makeup and perfect hair.

Seeing Sydney at my front door is jarring enough for me to want to close it in her face, but seeing that her goal has nothing to do with making me envious of her is enough for me to step back and wave her inside.

There can only be one other reason she's here.

"Are you here about the Instagram post?" *She must be.* She's never been here before. In fact, we haven't spoken since the day I read all the messages between the two of them.

Sydney shakes her head as her eyes dart around the living room, taking in my home. She doesn't seem nervous, but she steps inside my house so cautiously that it makes her seem somewhat vulnerable. I wonder if Ridge knows she's here. It's not like him to allow his girlfriend to show up and fight his battles for him. And Sydney doesn't seem like the type who would fight his battles.

Which can only mean she's here to fight her own battle.

"Sorry to just show up like this," she says. "I would have texted you first, but I was worried you would tell me not to come."

She's right, but I don't admit that out loud. I watch her for a moment and then turn and walk to my kitchen. "You want something to drink?" I ask, looking back at her.

She nods. "Water would be nice."

I grab two bottles of water out of the refrigerator and motion her over to my dining room table. Something tells me this conversation is going to be more fitting for the table than a couch. We both take a seat across from each other. Sydney sets her phone and her keys beside her and opens the bottle of water. She takes a big swig and then puts the lid back on it, hugging the bottle to her as she leans forward on the table.

"What are you doing here?" I don't mean for my voice to sound so stiff, but this is all so weird.

She licks her lips to moisten them, which makes me think she is nervous. "I'm here to apologize to you," she says, matter-of-fact.

I narrow my eyes, trying to make sense of this. I spend

the night fighting with her boyfriend, then I post a picture on Instagram in a moment of selfish stupidity, yet she says she's here to apologize to me? There must be a catch.

"Apologize for what?"

She blows out a quick breath but holds eye contact with me. "For kissing Ridge when I knew he was dating you. I never apologized to you. It was shitty of me, and I'm sorry."

I shake my head, still confused why she drove all the way here for an apology I'm not even in need of. "I've never expected an apology from you, Sydney. You weren't the one in a relationship with me. Ridge was."

Sydney's mouth twitches a little, like she's relieved I'm not full of rage, but she knows the situation doesn't call for a smile of relief. She nods instead. "Even still. You didn't deserve what happened to you. I know what it feels like when someone you love betrays you. I once punched a girl in her face for sleeping with my boyfriend, and you didn't even yell at me for falling in love with yours."

I appreciate that she recognizes as much. "It was hard for me to figure out who to be angry at after reading all the messages," I admit. "You both seemed to try so hard to do the right thing. But from what Ridge told me about your last relationship, that experience was a lot different from what happened between you and Ridge. Your friend and boyfriend put your feelings last with their affair, but you and Ridge seemed to at least attempt to put my feelings first."

Sydney nods. "He cares about you," she says, her voice

barely above a whisper. "He worries a lot. Even still." She takes another sip from her water bottle.

Her words fill me with even more regret over what happened between Ridge and me this weekend. Because I know he worries. And I feel like it's my fault he still has to worry about me. Not only because I don't take care of myself in all the ways he would like, but because I put this on him to begin with. I allowed a relationship to start up with him, knowing if we didn't work out in the end, a part of him would always stay with me because that's just the type of human he is. I'm not in a situation where he can choose to walk away from me completely and feel okay with that choice. Which must affect Sydney somehow, knowing she'll never be rid of me until I make that final choice to cut my friendship off from Ridge completely. It's just impossible to cut me out of his life entirely when we'll still have a mutual friend.

I lean forward and fold my arms over the table, tugging at my shirtsleeve while I look down at it. "Is that why you're here?" I ask, looking up at her. "To tell me you want me out of the picture?"

I expect her to nod now that I've pegged the reason she drove all the way from Austin. She needed to clear her conscience before asking me politely to never speak to Ridge again. But she doesn't nod. She doesn't shake her head. She just stares at me as if she's trying to form an answer that won't offend me.

"Ridge will worry about you whether he's an active

part of your life or not. I'm here because I want to make sure you're okay. And if you aren't, I want to know what I can do to help get you there. Because if you're okay, Ridge won't worry as much. And then I won't have to worry about Ridge."

I don't know what to say to that. I'm not even sure if I should feel offended by it. She's here, not because she's worried about *me* but because she's worried about Ridge. Part of me wants to tell her to leave, but part of me is relieved she said that. Because if she pretended to be worried about me, I wouldn't believe her. She's a little like Warren in that respect—transparent to the point that it sometimes stings.

Sydney blows out a heavy breath and then says, "I've spent a lot of time trying to put myself in your shoes. Telling myself what I would do differently if I were you." She's not looking at me as she speaks. She's fidgeting with the label on her bottle of water, avoiding eye contact with me. "I tell myself that I would take better care of my health than you do. Or that I wouldn't make irresponsible choices, like leaving a hospital before I'm discharged. But those things are easy for me to say because I'm not actually in your shoes. I can't even fathom what you go through, Maggie. I don't know what it's like to have to take multiple medications every day, or to visit the doctor more than I visit my own parents. I don't have to worry about germs every time I step foot out my front door or every time someone touches me. I don't base my entire schedule around treatments I'm forced to give myself in order to simply take a breath. I don't have to base every life decision I make on the chance that I'll likely die sometime in the next decade. And I can't sit here and assume that if I were in your shoes, I wouldn't fault Ridge for caring too much about me. Because the only thing that ties him to me is his love. There are no other factors tying him to me, so I can see why you would grow to resent that about him. He tried to protect you, but you just wanted him to ignore your illness so that you could ignore it, too."

She finally looks up from her water bottle, and I swear there are tears in her eyes. "I know I don't know you very well at all," she says. "But I do know that Ridge would not be as upset as he is if there weren't a million qualities that he sees in you. I'm hoping one of those qualities is your ability to swallow your pride enough to realize that you should apologize to him for making him feel the way he felt after leaving your house Saturday. He deserves at least that much after how hard he's loved you, Maggie."

She swipes at a tear. I open my mouth to respond, but nothing comes out. I'm in shock, I think. I wasn't expecting her to be here because she wants me to contact Ridge.

"You may think you don't need him, and maybe that's true," she adds. "Maybe you don't. But Ridge needs you. He needs to know that you're taken care of and that you're safe, because if he doesn't at least have that reassurance, his worry and guilt are going to eat at him. And to answer your question from earlier . . . No. I don't want you out of the picture. This was your picture first. Yours and Warren's and Ridge's. But now that I'm a part of it, we all need to figure out how to fit in the frame."

I'm still at a loss for words. I take a sip of my water and then slowly screw the cap back on, staring down at it, avoiding Sydney's teary eyes. I'm trying to make sense of everything she just said without taking too much time before I respond. "That was a lot," I say. "I need a moment."

Sydney nods. We sit together in silence for a bit while I process everything. While I process her. I don't understand her. How can one person be this understanding? It would be so easy for her to be in Ridge's ear right now instead of mine, convincing him that I don't appreciate him and all that he's done for me. But instead, she's here. More than likely without his knowledge. She's not fighting to erase me from the picture—one I honestly no longer belong in. She's fighting to fit into a picture that already exists. To embrace its inhabitants. *To be included.*

"You're a better person than me," I finally say. "I can see now why he fell in love with you."

Sydney smiles a little. "He once fell in love with you, too, Maggie. I find it hard to believe he didn't have a million reasons for doing so."

I stare at her, wondering if that's actually true. I've always felt like my illness was the reason Ridge fell in love with me. I even said that to him once. My exact words were, *I think my illness is the thing you love the most about me.* I said it right here in the living room when we ended things for good.

But maybe that wasn't true. Maybe he loved me for me, and in doing so, he really did want the best for me because of me, and not because of his personality.

My God, my mother sure fucked me up. I guess that's expected, though. When you have a mother who can't love you, how are you supposed to believe anyone else could?

Sydney is right. Ridge deserves a lot more respect than what I've given him. He also deserves the girl sitting across from me right now, because this situation could have taken so many possible roads, but Sydney chose the high one. When a person takes the high road, it encourages those around them to do the same.

It might be a tight and awkward fit at first, but I'm glad she's now in our frame.

Chapter Nineteen

Ridge

I'm walking around my apartment on eggshells, afraid to open doors, afraid to eat food out of the refrigerator, afraid to go to sleep. It's Warren's turn to prank me, so I'm expecting it every hour and with everything I eat or drink. But it never comes. Which makes me even more paranoid.

Maybe not pranking me *is* the prank.

No, he's not that clever.

I wish I could stay over at Sydney's place tonight just to get rid of this paranoia, but she works at the library until close, so she won't even be home until after midnight. Then she has class at eight in the morning.

I haven't seen her since Saturday. Or Sunday, really, but I slept so hard I don't even remember her leaving for breakfast or writing me the note. But it's Tuesday now, and I'm going through Sydney withdrawals.

I'm finally caught up on work, though. And I've sent Brennan lyrics to a whole new song. Now I'm googling new ways to prank Warren because I feel like I need to stay a step ahead of him, but the best Google can come up with are the Post-it note pranks we refuse to stoop to. Everything else, we've tried.

I'm watching a video compilation on YouTube of roommates pranking each other when I feel my phone vibrate on my bed.

Sydney: I'm tired of restocking books. They really should have robots for this by now.

Ridge: But then you'd be out of a job.

Sydney: Unless I was an engineer. Then I could be in charge of the robot.

Ridge: Maybe you should switch your major.

Sydney: What are you doing right now?

Ridge: Googling ways to prank Warren. I'm out of ideas. You got any?

Sydney: You should fill a box with five kittens and put it in his bedroom. Because buying your friend one kitten is kind of sweet, but buying them five kittens is terrible.

Ridge: I'm not sure that would be funny for me because he'd probably keep all five of them and I'd end up having to pay five pet deposits.

Sydney: Yeah, that was a terrible prank idea.

Ridge: I see nothing has changed. I'm still the prank master.

Sydney: Says the guy who's experiencing a bad case of pranker's block.

Ridge: Touché. Hey, do you get a lunch break tonight?

Sydney: Just took it at six. :/

Ridge: Dammit. I guess I'll see you tomorrow afternoon. You want me to come to your place?

Sydney: Yes, please. I want you all to myself for the night.

Ridge: Then I am yours. I love you. See you tomorrow.

Sydney: Love you.

I close out our texts and open up the missed text from Bridgette I just received while I was saying goodbye to Sydney. Bridgette never texts me unless it's to tell me something in the apartment is broken. Not this time, though. Her text simply says, Someone is at the door, like she's too busy to get up and answer it. She never does answer the door, though. I wonder if that's because she doesn't really feel like this is her apartment.

I walk to my closet and grab a T-shirt, pulling it over my head as I make my way to the front door. I look through the peephole while my hand is turning the doorknob, but I stop turning it as soon as I recognize Maggie. She's standing in front of the door, hugging herself as the wind whips her hair around.

The next few seconds are a little bizarre for me. I watch her for a moment, wondering what she wants, but not wondering enough to open the door in a hurry. I turn around and face the living room, needing a second to focus on my next move. This is the first time she's shown up at my apartment as something other than my girlfriend. I've never opened the door for her and not immediately kissed her.

I've never opened the door for her without pulling her to my bedroom. I have no desire to do either of those things, nor do I feel a loss because it's no longer our routine. I just feel . . . different.

I turn and open the door, just as she gives up and walks toward the apartment stairs. She glances up at me and pauses her foot over the first step, then slowly turns around and faces me. Her expression is calm. She isn't looking at me like she can't stand me—like she was looking at me this past weekend. She lifts her hand and pushes her hair from her face, waiting for me to invite her in. There's an air of humility about her as she glances down at her feet for a few seconds. When our eyes meet again, I step back and hold the door open. She stares at her feet as she walks into the apartment.

I slide my phone out of my pocket as Maggie stands in the middle of the living room. I don't want this becoming anything it isn't, so I text Sydney.

Ridge: Maggie just showed up unannounced. Not sure what she's here for yet, but I wanted you to know.

I slide my phone back into my pocket and look up at Maggie. She motions to the refrigerator and asks if she can grab something to drink. It's odd, because she would never have asked before. She would have just grabbed a drink. I nod and say, "Of course."

She walks to the refrigerator and opens the door, but she just stares inside blankly for a moment. That's when I realize I don't have any Dr Pepper for her. I used to keep the refrigerator stocked with Dr Pepper for whenever she showed up, but it's been months since she's been here. I stopped buying Dr Pepper after we broke up. It was odd at first, not grabbing the usual twelve-pack I used to get every time I went grocery shopping, but I don't even think about it anymore. Now I just make sure I have water and tea.

She grabs two waters and hands me one of them. "Thank you," I say.

She points to the kitchen table and signs, "Do you have a minute?"

I nod, but am very aware my phone hasn't buzzed in my pocket. Either Sydney hasn't read my text yet, or she's upset that Maggie showed up here. I'm hoping it's the former. I'm sure it is. Sydney is the most reasonable person I've ever met. Even if it upset her that Maggie showed up here, she would still text me back.

We're both at the table now, me at the head of it and her in the chair to my right. She takes her jacket off and then folds her hands together in front of her, resting her elbows on the table. She's staring down at them, inhaling a calming breath. Her eyes swing in my direction when she begins to sign. "I would have come by sooner, but my grandfather died two days ago. Sunday night."

I immediately blow out a breath and grab her hand. I squeeze it, then pull her in for a hug. I feel like such an asshole right now. I knew he was sick. No matter how things were left between us Saturday morning, I should have checked in with her about her grandfather. He died two days ago, and I had no idea. Why wouldn't she at least tell Warren?

I pull back to ask her if she's okay, but she answers the question before I'm even able to ask it. "I'm okay," she signs. "You know it's been expected for a while now. My aunt flew in from Tennessee and helped with the arrangements today. We decided against a service."

Her eyes are red and a little puffy, like she's already cried enough about it. "That's not why I'm here, though. I was in Austin and wanted to stop by because . . ." She pauses to take a drink and to gather herself. It's a big jump going from the death of her grandfather to another subject entirely. She seems a little jarred, so I give her a minute. She wipes her mouth with her sleeve and then looks at me again. "I'm here because I have a lot to say, and I'd like the opportunity to get it all out before you interrupt me, okay? You know how hard it is for me to apologize."

She's here to *apologize*? Wow. This isn't what I was expecting, because she's right. It's very hard for her to apologize. It's one of the things that are so different about Maggie and Sydney; it's difficult getting used to. Sydney is quick to forgive and quick to ask for forgiveness, whereas with Maggie, everything needs a period of adjustment.

Like right now. She takes an entire minute to adjust to what she's about to say before she actually says it.

"You told me once that when you wore hearing aids, they were a constant reminder that you couldn't hear. And that when you didn't wear them, you didn't even think about it," she signs. "That's how I've always felt about my illness, Ridge. About doctors and hospitals and medications and my vest. It's all a constant reminder that I have this illness, but when I'm able to avoid those things, I don't even think about it. And it's nice, being able to have those moments of normalcy sometimes. And being with you in the beginning was part of my cherished moments of normalcy. We had just begun dating, and we couldn't get enough of each other. But the longer we were together, you started to notice that I would skip treatments or doctors' visits in favor of being with you."

She pauses a moment, like what she's trying to say is taking a huge amount of courage. And it is. So I wait patiently without interrupting like I promised her I would.

"After a while, you started to worry about me," she says. "You took over my schedule to make sure I was on time to every appointment. You texted me several times a day to tell me it was time for my treatments. I even caught you counting my pills once so you could be positive I was taking them like I was supposed to. And I know that every single one of those things was for my benefit, because you loved me. But I started lumping you in with all the things I wanted to avoid, like doctor's appointments and breathing treatments." She looks me in the eyes. "You became one of the constant reminders that I was living with this illness. And I didn't know how to deal with that."

A tear falls out of her eye, and she swipes it away with her sleeve.

"I know I sometimes didn't show it, but I did appreciate you. I do appreciate you. So much. It's just so confusing for me because I also resented you, but my resentment had everything to do with me and nothing at all to do with you. I know that everything you did for me is because you wanted the best for me. I know that you loved me. The things I said to you the other day came from a part of me that I'm not proud of. And . . ." Her lips are quivering, and tears are beginning to fall down her cheeks in pairs. "I'm sorry, Ridge. I really am. For everything."

I blow out a quick, shaky breath.

I need out of this chair.

I stand up and walk to the kitchen and grab her a napkin, then take it back to her. But I can't sit down. I wasn't expecting this, and I don't even know how to respond to her. Sometimes I don't say the right things to her, and it upsets her. She's already upset enough. I put my hands on the back of my neck and pace the living room a couple of times. I come to a pause when I feel my phone vibrate. I grab it.

Sydney: Thanks for letting me know. Be patient with her, Ridge. I'm sure it took a lot of courage for her to show up there.

I stare at Sydney's text and shake my head, wondering how in the hell she's more understanding of my own situation than even I am. I honestly don't know why she's majoring in music. Her real talent is psychology.

I slide the phone back into my pocket and look over at Maggie, who is still sitting at the table, dabbing at her tearful eyes. This had to be hard for her. Sydney is right. Being here and then saying everything she just said has to be taking a huge amount of courage.

I walk back to my seat, and I reach across the table and take her hand. I hold it between both of mine. "I'm sorry, too," I say, squeezing her hand so that she can feel the sincerity in that statement. "I should have been more of a boyfriend to you and less of a . . . dictator."

My word choice makes her laugh through her tears. She shakes her head. "You weren't a dictator," she signs. "Maybe more of a mild authoritarian."

I laugh with her. Which is something I never thought would happen again after leaving her house Saturday morning.

Maggie's head swings in the other direction, so I look up to see Bridgette. She's leaving for work, but pauses when she sees Maggie in our living room, sitting next to me at the table. She glances at Maggie for a moment, then at me. Her eyes narrow.

"Dick."

She marches to the front door, and I'm pretty sure she probably slams it when she leaves. I look back at Maggie, and she's staring at the door. "What was that all about?"

I shrug. "She's become oddly protective of Sydney now. It's been . . . interesting."

Maggie arches a brow. "Maybe you should text Sydney and let her know I'm here. Before Bridgette does."

I smile. "I already did."

Maggie nods knowingly. "Of course you did," she signs.

She's smiling now, and the tears are no longer invading her eyes. She takes another sip of water and then leans back in her chair. "So. Is Sydney the one?"

I don't respond for a moment, because it's odd. I don't want Maggie thinking she lacked anything, but it's simply different with Sydney. It's more. It's deeper and better, and I crave it like I've never craved anything, but how do I express that without being insensitive to what Maggie and I had? I nod slowly and sign, "She is definitely the last one."

Maggie nods, and a sadness enters her eyes. I hate it. But I can't do anything to change it. Things are how they're supposed to be now, even if Maggie might sometimes feel regret for that.

"I wish life came with a handbook," she says. "Seeing what you and Sydney have makes me realize what an idiot I am for pushing away a really great guy. I'm almost positive I ruined that chance for good."

I shift in my seat with those words. I don't even know what to say. Did she think coming here would open up an opportunity to get back together with me? If so, I've been treating this entire conversation as something it isn't. "Maggie. I'm not—*we're* not ever getting back together."

Maggie's eyes narrow, and she gives me one of the looks she used to give me when I was being an idiot. "I'm not talking about *you*, Ridge." She laughs. "I'm referring to my hot doctor–slash–skydiving instructor."

I tilt my head, feeling both relieved and embarrassed. "Oh. Well. That was awkward."

She starts to laugh again. She swings a finger back and forth between us. "You thought . . . When I said *great guy* . . . you immediately thought of yourself?" She's laughing even harder now. I'm trying not to crack a smile, but I can't help it. I love that she's laughing, and I love even more that she's talking about someone else.

This is good.

Maggie stands up. "Will Warren be here Saturday?" I nod and stand as well. "Yeah, he should be. Why?"

"I want us all to sit down together and talk. I feel like we need to map out a plan going forward."

"Yeah. Of course. I'd love it if we could do that. Do you mind if Sydney comes?"

Maggie puts on her jacket. "She already has it on her schedule," Maggie says, winking at me.

Okay, now I'm confused. "You've talked to Sydney?"

Maggie nods. "For some reason, she felt like she owed me an apology. And . . . I owed her one. We had a good chat." Maggie walks toward the door but pauses before opening it. "She's very . . . diplomatic."

I nod, but I'm still confused about when they had this chat. Or why I didn't know about it. "Yeah," I say. "She is definitely diplomatic."

Maggie opens the door. "Don't let Bridgette ruin her," she says. "See you Saturday."

"See you Saturday." I hold the door open for her. "And Maggie. I'm really sorry about your grandfather."

She smiles. "Thank you."

I watch as she walks down the stairs to her car. Once she pulls away, I don't close my door. I rush to my counter and grab my keys, then slip on my shoes.

I drive straight to the library.

• • •

I spot her in the back corner of the library. She's next to a cart, holding a marker in her hand, crossing things out on a list as she restocks the shelves from her library cart. Her back is to me, so I watch her for an entire minute as she works. The place is mostly empty, so I don't feel like anyone will notice that I'm staring at her. I just can't understand when or how she and Maggie would have had a conversation. Or why. I pull out my phone and I text her.

Ridge: You and Maggie had a conversation and you didn't tell me?

I watch her reaction as she reads the text. She freezes, staring down at the phone, and then she rubs her forehead. She leans against the library shelf and inhales a deep breath.

Sydney: Yes. I should have told you. I just wanted the two of you to have the chance to speak before I brought it up, but I drove to her house on Sunday. Not to start drama, I swear. I just had some things I needed to say to her. I'm sorry, Ridge.

I look back up at her, and everything about her is on edge now. She's worried, rubbing the back of her neck now, refusing to pull her eyes away from her phone until I text her back.

I hold up my phone and snap a picture of her, then text

it to her. It takes a moment for the picture to come through on her end, but as soon as it does, she spins around. Our eyes lock.

I shake my head, just barely, but not because I'm upset with her in any way, shape, or form. I shake my head in slight disbelief that this woman would take it upon herself to drive to my ex-girlfriend's house because she wanted to make things better between us.

I have never felt this amount of appreciation for anyone or anything in my entire life.

I begin to walk toward her. She pushes off the bookshelf when I get closer and stands, stiff, anticipating my next move. When I reach her, I don't say or sign a single word. I don't have to. She knows exactly what I'm thinking, because with Sydney, all she has to do is be near me for us to communicate. She looks up at me, and I look down at her, and as if we're in perfect sync, she takes two steps back and I take two steps forward, so that we're hidden between two walls of books.

I love you.

I don't say or sign those words. I only feel them, but she hears it.

I lift my hands and run my fingers down her cheeks. I try to touch her with the same softness that she uses to touch me. I drag my thumbs over her lips, admiring her mouth and every gentle word that comes out of it. I slide my hands down to her neck and press my thumbs against her throat. I can feel her rapid pulse beneath my fingertips.

I lower my forehead to hers, and I close my eyes. I just want to feel her heartbeat against my thumbs. I want to feel her breath against my lips. I take a moment and do these things while I silently thank her, our foreheads still pressed together.

I wish we weren't in public right now. I would thank her in so many more ways, and without using a single word.

I keep my hands on her throat and press myself against her to turn and position her against the bookshelves behind her. When her back meets the books, I keep her face tilted up toward mine, while drawing our mouths closer together, barely connecting mine to hers. I can feel her rapid breaths crashing against my lips, so I hold still and swallow a few of them before I slip my tongue inside her mouth and coax even more of those rapid breaths out of her. Her mouth is warmer and more inviting than it's ever been.

She brings her hands to my chest, slapping the paper and the marker against my shirt while she steadies herself. The paper falls to the floor. She tilts her head up to mine even more and opens her mouth a little wider, wanting more of our kiss. I curve my right hand around the back of her head as I close my mouth over hers and inhale.

I kiss her. I love her.

I love her. I kiss her.

I kiss her.

I am so very in love with her.

It's the hardest thing I've ever had to do when I pull away from her mouth. Her hands are clenched in fists around my shirt. Her eyes are still closed when I pull back, so I stare down at her for a moment, convinced that Karma might actually know what she's doing after all. Maybe there was a reason so many shitty things had to happen in my life. It wouldn't have been a balanced life if I'd had a beautiful childhood, only to grow up and share a life like the one I know I'm going to share with Sydney. I think my childhood was the balance I needed so that I could have her. She is so good and so perfect, maybe I was made to suffer first before earning a reward of this magnitude.

I slide my hands to hers, which are still clenching my shirt. The paper she was holding has long since fallen to the floor, but the marker is still in her fist. I pry it from her fingers and she opens her eyes, just as I slip my fingers beneath the collar of her shirt. I pull it down, exposing the skin over her heart. I pull the cap off the marker with my teeth and then press the marker to her chest. I write four letters directly over her heart.

MINE

I put the cap back on the marker, and then I kiss her one last time before I turn and walk away.

It's the most we've ever communicated and the least we've ever said.

Chapter Twenty

Sydney

I'm sitting in the passenger seat of Ridge's car, staring out the window. My right hand is touching my chest, lightly fingering the word he wrote over my heart Tuesday night. *MINE*. It's faded now because it's been four days since he wrote it, but luckily it was a permanent marker, and I've avoided scrubbing it off in the shower.

When he left the library Tuesday night, I immediately had to sit down. He had left me so breathless, I almost felt faint. He wasn't even there five minutes, and it was the most intense five minutes of my life. So much so, I convinced my coworker to stay for the rest of my shift, and then I drove straight to Ridge's apartment to finish what he'd started. Those five intense minutes in the library became two intense hours in his bed.

Since then, we've spent three of the last four nights together.

He told me all about his conversation with Maggie. I hate that her grandfather passed away just hours after I left her apartment on Sunday. But knowing she was dealing with all of that, yet still made the time to stop by Ridge's and apologize to him, made me appreciate her effort even more. And it really did make a huge difference in Ridge. It's like a heavy weight was lifted after their talk on Tuesday. The last four days with him have been the best four days I've spent with him since the day we met.

In the beginning of getting to know him, every conversation we had was encased in guilt because of Maggie. Then, after his and Maggie's fight last week, every conversation we had was laced with worry because of Maggie. But since Tuesday, every time we're alone, it finally feels like we're actually alone. Somehow, merging Maggie more into our lives seems to have removed her even more from our relationship. It shouldn't make sense, but it does. Putting more focus on their friendship than on the fact that she's his ex-girlfriend will be better for our relationship in the long run.

Hopefully, Bridgette will be able to realize that soon. Because right now, she's not happy. Warren and Bridgette are in the backseat. Ridge is driving. Bridgette hasn't said a single word on the way to Maggie's house, because she and Warren got into a fight right before we left. She demanded she come with him, but he told her he didn't want her there because she doesn't know how to be nice to Maggie. That pissed her off. They went to their room and fought while Ridge and I sat on the couch and waited.

Actually, we sat on the couch and made out, so we didn't really care how long their fight lasted. But it still hasn't ended because we're pulling into Maggie's driveway, and the only words Bridgette has spoken between Austin and this driveway are, "I have to pee." She says it as she gets out of the car and slams her door.

Bridgette isn't the most reasonable person. But I'm growing to really like her and even understand her. She wears her emotions on her sleeve. But she has a lot of emotions, so it's more like she wears her emotions on several long-sleeved shirts, layered on top of one another.

No one has to knock on the door, because Maggie opens it as we're walking up the driveway. Warren walks in first and gives her a hug. Bridgette passes right by her, but Ridge gives her a quick hug. I do, too, simply because I'd rather start this off with a good sentiment.

"Smells good," Ridge signs as he tosses his keys on the counter.

"Lasagna," Maggie says. "I'm reading this book where the characters make lasagna anytime they need to talk through something. Thought it was fitting for tonight." Maggie looks at me as she walks into her kitchen. "Do you like to read, Sydney?"

"Love to read," I say, taking off my cardigan. I set it over the back of one of the chairs. "I just don't have a lot of time. Which is sad, considering I work in a library."

Bridgette walks to the bathroom, and Warren tosses himself dramatically on the couch, facedown into a throw pillow. "Kill me now," he mutters.

"Trouble in paradise?" Maggie says.

Warren lifts his head and looks at her. "Paradise? When have Bridgette and I ever lived in paradise?"

"Trouble in Sheol?" Maggie corrects.

Warren sits up on the couch. "I don't even know what that means."

"It's another word for *hell.*"

"Oh," Warren says. "You know not to use big words around me."

"It's only five letters long."

I'm watching them converse, my attention going back and forth between them. I finally focus on Ridge, who is standing in front of me now. "You thirsty?" he asks.

I nod. He walks to the kitchen and opens a cabinet, then begins getting us both something to drink. It's odd, watching him move his way around the kitchen like it's his kitchen. It makes me realize that in a way, it used to be. There's no telling how much time he spent here at her house. I guess this is one of those fairly awkward moments I'm going to have to get used to. Ridge brings me a glass of water, and then he takes a seat on the couch next to Warren.

I walk into the kitchen.

"You need any help?" I ask Maggie.

She shakes her head and opens the refrigerator, placing a salad inside. "No, thanks. Everything is finished except the lasagna." She looks at Ridge and Warren. "You guys ready to sit at the table and do this before we eat?"

Warren slaps his jeans. "Ready," he says, hopping up.

The four of us make our way to the kitchen table just as Bridgette walks out of the bathroom. Maggie is at the head of the table. I'm sitting next to Ridge, and Warren is seated next to an empty chair, but Bridgette chooses to claim the chair at the opposite head of the table so that there's an empty seat between Warren and her. He shakes his head, ignoring her.

Maggie opens up a folder and then sits up straight and signs everything as she begins to speak. I like watching her sign. I don't know why, but I find it a little easier to follow her than Ridge or Warren. Maybe because her hands are more delicate, but it seems like she signs a little slower and—if this even makes sense—with more enunciation.

She looks at all of us. "Thank you for agreeing to this." She directs her attention at me. "And thank *you*," she says, without being specific. I nod, but really, it's Warren she should be thanking. He's the one who gave me the kick in the rear I needed to finally make a forward move with Maggie.

"I've made a couple of decisions that I want to talk about first, because they affect the next year of my life. And, subsequently, yours." She nods her head toward her hallway. We all look at the hallway, and for the first time, I notice moving boxes. "My internship is over, and so is my thesis, so I've decided to move back to Austin. My landlord informed me on Wednesday that she was able to rent the house to someone else, so I have to be out by the end of the month."

I take her pause as an opportunity to interrupt with a question. "Isn't your doctor here in San Antonio?"

Maggie shakes her head. "She has a satellite office here one day a week. But she's based out of Austin, so it'll actually be easier for me."

"Have you found an apartment yet?" Warren asks. "The end of the month is just a few days away."

Maggie nods again. "I have, but it won't be ready until April fifth. The tenants just moved out, and they have to carpet and repaint."

"Is it the same complex as last time?" Warren asks.

Maggie's eyes flicker from Warren to Ridge. There's something unspoken there, even though she's shaking her head, giving them an answer. "They didn't have anything available. This one is in North Austin."

Warren leans forward and gives her a look that I don't understand. Ridge sighs heavily. I feel lost.

"What?" I ask. "What's wrong with North Austin?"

Maggie looks at me. "It's pretty far from you guys. Ridge and I . . . back when I had my apartment in Austin . . . we both chose complexes that were close to the hospital and my doctor. It made things easier."

"Have you checked our complex?" Warren asks. "I know there are units available."

Bridgette makes a noise of protest. She clears her throat and then plops her purse down on the table. She pulls out a nail file, leans back in her chair, and starts filing her fingernails.

I look back at Maggie, and she's looking at me. She shakes her head and says, "No, but North Austin should be fine. I've been here in San Antonio for a year now, and everything has been fine."

"I wouldn't say *fine*," Warren says.

"You know what I mean, Warren. I haven't had an emergency to the point that I would have died without you guys here. I think I'll be fine if I'm only on the other side of town."

Ridge shakes his head. "You would have died in my bathroom if Sydney hadn't found you. Just because you've been lucky doesn't mean it's been a smart move."

"Agreed," Warren says. "You live north of San Antonio. We live in South Austin. It takes forty-five minutes from our driveway to yours. But if you move to North Austin, with traffic, it'll take more than an hour to get to you. You might be moving to the same city, but it's farther away from us."

Maggie sighs. She looks down and lowers her voice a little. "I can't afford anything else right now. The only apartments near the hospital with any availability are too expensive for me."

"Why don't you get a job?" Bridgette asks.

We all turn our attention toward Bridgette. I don't think anyone was expecting anything to come out of her mouth. She's holding the nail file against her thumbnail, staring at Maggie.

"It's hard to hold a job when you're in the hospital on a regular basis," Maggie says. "I had to apply for disability three years ago just to be able to pay my rent." She's being a little defensive, but I get it. Bridgette doesn't seem to sugarcoat her questions around Maggie at all. Or anyone, for that matter.

Bridgette shrugs and goes back to filing her nails.

"Like I asked earlier, have you even checked availability in our complex?" Warren asks.

Again, Maggie's attention is on me when this is brought up. I glance at Ridge, and he looks at me. We read each other without saying a word.

I nod, even though it seems absurd if I give it too much thought. But for whatever reason, it doesn't feel absurd. Having her in the same complex as Ridge and Warren would make things easier on all of them. And I truly don't believe Ridge or Maggie want to go down a road they've already traveled, so I surprisingly don't feel at all threatened by the thought of it. Maybe I'm being naïve, but I have to go with my gut. And my gut is telling me that she needs to be closer to them rather than farther away.

"I don't mind if you live in the same complex as Ridge, if that's what's stopping you," I say. "My ex-boyfriend moved into the complex with my ex–best friend after I moved in with Ridge and Warren last year. We can see right into their living room from Ridge's balcony. Believe me, nothing can feel weirder than that."

Maggie smiles appreciatively at me and then looks

toward Bridgette across the table. Ridge puts his arm on the back of my chair and then leans over, quickly kissing the side of my head. I love his silent thank-yous.

Bridgette looks up, directly at Maggie. She doesn't look happy. She turns her attention toward Warren and leans forward. "Shit, Warren, why don't you just move her into one of the spare bedrooms? We can be one big happy family."

Warren rolls his eyes. "Bridgette, stop."

"No. Think about it. I moved in and you started sleeping with me. Sydney moved in and Ridge started messing around with her. It's only fair that Maggie gets a turn."

I close my eyes and drop my head, shaking it. Why did Bridgette have to go there? I glance at Maggie, and she's shooting daggers at Bridgette.

"I think you forget that I've already been with them both, Bridgette. I actually don't need a turn, but thank you for being considerate."

"Oh, fuck off," Bridgette says.

And . . . this just went from bad to worse. I don't even think Ridge knows what just happened. As soon as that sentence comes out of Bridgette's mouth, Maggie calmly scoots her chair back and stands up. She walks to her bedroom and closes the door. They both just took this way, way too far. My head is in my hands now, and all I can say is, "Bridgette. Why?"

Bridgette looks at me like I've betrayed her. She waves a hand toward Maggie's bedroom. "How can you be okay with this? She's ungrateful and always has been, and now she's moving herself into our complex and twisting it to make it look like your idea!"

For a second, I entertain her thoughts. But only for a second. After two seconds, I stand up and make my way to Maggie's bedroom. I honestly think Bridgette has her pegged wrong. I don't see Ridge loving someone who is that ungrateful and manipulative. I just don't.

I push open Maggie's bedroom door, and she's sitting cross-legged on her bed, wiping away a tear. I sit down on the bed next to her. Maggie lifts her head, looking at me with eyes full of guilt.

"I'm sorry. That was tacky. But Bridgette is wrong. I'm not trying to take over either of your lives," she whispers. I can tell by her voice that she's on the verge of more tears. "If it were up to me, I'd be so far out from under their thumbs, it would take hours for them to drive to me. But I'm trying to be more cooperative, Sydney. I'm trying to be more respectful of their time."

That I believe. I think Maggie would much rather live in a place where she could get away with being lax. "I believe you. And I agree," I say. "We're here because Warren and Ridge are going to be your primary caregivers when you're sick. I think we need to leave Bridgette's feelings out of it. And mine. And honestly, even yours. This is about how we can make things easier on Warren and Ridge, and you living in the same complex as them will definitely make things easier on them."

Maggie nods. "I know. But I don't want to cause trouble between Warren and Bridgette. I think it should ultimately be Bridgette's and your decision, but I don't think she'll ever agree to it. I honestly don't blame her."

She's right. It should be something we all agree to. I turn my head toward the door and yell, "Bridgette!"

I hear a chair scoot across the floor, followed by dramatic stomps heading in the direction of Maggie's bedroom. Bridgette finally opens the door, but she leans against the door frame and folds her arms across her chest.

I pat the bed. "Come here, Bridgette."

"I'm fine right here."

I look at her like I would look at an ornery child. "Get your ass over here right now."

Bridgette stomps to the bed and throws herself across the foot of it. She's being just as dramatic as Warren was being when he threw himself on Maggie's couch earlier. Their intense similarities make me want to laugh. Bridgette stares at me and avoids eye contact with Maggie.

I lean back against the headboard and tilt my head as I look at her. "What are you feeling, Bridgette?"

She rolls her eyes and lifts up onto her elbow. "Well, Dr. Blake," she says sarcastically, "I feel like the ex-girlfriend of both of our boyfriends is about to move into the same apartment complex as us, and I don't like it."

"You think I do?" Maggie says.

Bridgette looks at her. There is absolutely no love between the two of them. At all.

"How long have you two known each other?" I ask.

"She moved in with Ridge and Warren a few months before you did," Maggie says, talking about her like she's not on the same bed. "And I tried being nice to her at first, but you know how that goes."

"I think the three of us just need to get drunk together," I suggest. It worked for Bridgette and me. Maybe it could work for Bridgette and Maggie.

Maggie looks at me like I've lost my mind. "That sounds like an absolute nightmare."

Bridgette nods in agreement. "Alcohol can't erase years of history between her and Warren."

Maggie laughs, addressing Bridgette directly now. "Do you really think there's a chance in hell I would ever be romantically interested in Warren again? That's absurd."

Bridgette rolls onto her back and looks up at the ceiling. "I'm not worried about you falling for him. I'm worried about him falling for you. You're really pretty, and Warren is shallow."

Maggie and I both look at each other. Then we both start laughing. I shake my head, completely taken aback by Bridgette's insecurity. "Do you not realize what a knockout you are? Warren could be as shallow as a desert and he'd still be head over heels for you."

"I don't really want to compliment you because you're mean to me," Maggie says to Bridgette. "But Sydney is right. Have you seen your ass? It looks like two Pringles hugging."

What the hell does that even mean? Maggie's comment makes Bridgette laugh, even though she tries to hide it.

"You work at Hooters, for Christ's sake," Maggie adds. "If I showed up at Hooters, they'd turn me away, thinking I was a twelve-year-old boy."

Bridgette turns her head toward Maggie. "Go on . . ." she says, urging us to continue with the compliments.

I roll my eyes and stretch my legs out, kicking her playfully in the thigh. "Warren loves you. Get over your weird insecurities. You're lucky you have a man who has a heart big enough to want to care for one of his best friends."

Maggie nods. "It's true. He's a good guy. A really shallow, somewhat conceited, extremely perverted good guy."

Bridgette groans and then sits up on the bed. She looks at me, and then she looks at Maggie. She doesn't say it's okay for Maggie to move into the same complex, but she also isn't protesting anymore, so I'll take this as a victory. She stands up and walks toward the door, but pauses in front of Maggie's floor-length mirror. She turns around and looks at herself over her shoulder, cupping her butt with both hands. "You really think it looks like two Pringles hugging?"

Maggie reaches behind her and grabs a pillow, then throws it at Bridgette. Bridgette pats her own ass and then leaves the bedroom.

Maggie falls onto her bed and groans into her mattress, then sits back up and looks at me, her head tilted to the side. "Thank you. I've never known how to deal with her. She terrifies me."

I nod. "Me too."

Bridgette and I may get along now, but I'm still scared to death of her wrath.

Maggie slides off the bed and walks back toward the living room. I follow her. Once we're all seated at the table, she pulls her folder in front of her. I look at Ridge, and he smiles at me. *I love you*, he mouths.

He says it all the time to me, so I don't know why it makes me blush this time.

"They have two available units," Warren says, sliding his phone toward Maggie. "One up, one down. The one downstairs is at the other end of the complex, but I think you should be downstairs."

Maggie looks at his phone. "It says it isn't available until the third. I can call in the morning and reserve it, then just get a hotel for a few days between apartments."

"That's a waste of money," Bridgette says. "It's only a few days. Just stay in my old bedroom. Or Brennan's. They're both empty." She's filing her nails again, but the words that just came out of her mouth are monumental. It's the closest she could come to an apology without actually saying to Maggie, *I was rude. I'm sorry.*

Ridge looks at me and squeezes my hand under the table, then texts me.

Ridge: I'll stay at your place while she's at ours, if it's okay.

I nod. I would probably have made him, even if he hadn't suggested it.

I don't even know that I could disagree with her staying

there for a few days at this point because everything going on with the people at this table has long since passed the definition of normal. Warren once said to me, *Welcome to the weirdest place you'll ever live.*

I get it now. I don't even live with them anymore, but that apartment and the rotating door attached to it defy every boundary ever put into place.

Warren scoots his chair back and stands up, then claims the empty chair next to Bridgette. He reaches over and grabs her nail file, then tosses it into the living room. He pulls her chair closer to his and kisses her.

And Bridgette actually lets him for a good five seconds. It's both adorable and highly uncomfortable.

Maggie rolls her eyes and then pushes her folder in front of Ridge. "I've made a list of compromises. There are things I still want to do that I'm going to need you to be okay with. And in return, I promise I'm going to take better care of myself. But you can't be bossy with me until you've given me a little time to adjust. I'm a hot mess, and it's going to take some time to improve that part of my personality."

Ridge looks over the list for a moment, but looks up at her and signs something I don't recognize. Maggie nods. "Yes. I'm going bungee jumping, and you can't tell me no. We're compromising."

Ridge sighs and then pushes the list back in front of Maggie. "Fine. But you're joining a support group."

Maggie laughs, but Ridge doesn't.

"That's not a compromise," Maggie says. "That's torture."

Ridge shrugs. "We're compromising," he says. "If you hate it, you can stop. But I think it'll be good for you. I don't think any of us truly knows what you're going through, and I think it'll be good for you to talk with people who do."

Maggie groans and drops her head on the table, hitting it three times against the wood. She scoots back from her chair and looks at me. "You're going with me," she says, walking toward the kitchen.

"To your support group?" I ask, confused. I don't know why I'm suddenly being tortured in this compromise.

"Nope," Maggie says. "Not to support group. CF support groups are only online. You're going bungee jumping with me."

Bungee jumping. *Hmm.* My boyfriend's ex-girlfriend wants me to jump off a bridge. Kind of ironic when you think about it. I look over at Ridge and grin. I've always wanted to bungee jump. He just shakes his head and smiles back at me, like he was just defeated.

"I've always wondered something," Bridgette says, looking across the room at Maggie. Warren is in the living room retrieving Bridgette's nail file. "Why don't you just get a lung transplant? Won't that cure the disease?"

I've wondered that, too, but haven't brought it up to Ridge yet.

"It's not that easy," Warren says, handing Bridgette the nail file. "Cystic fibrosis doesn't just affect the lungs, so new lungs won't cure someone of the disease completely."

"Also, I'm not in that predicament yet," Maggie says. "In order to get new lungs, you have to have a really grim prognosis, but without being too sick to receive a lung transplant. Luckily, I'm too healthy to be a candidate right now. It's a tricky position to be in. New lungs would be nice, but I don't really want to be in the position to be a candidate because it means my health would have to decline first. And a transplant could prolong someone's life by a few years, but it could also cut it short. Way short. Not something I'm hoping for anytime soon, to be honest."

"New advancements happen every day, though," Warren adds. "Which is why we're really only discussing the near future tonight, not a long-term plan. If we try to plan too far ahead, it might discourage other possibilities. Maggie doesn't want to hinder our lives, and we don't want to hinder hers, so right now, the best scenario is to just tackle things a few months at a time with the tools we have to tackle them."

Ridge nods, but then responds to Warren. "Sometimes I feel like your brain is on a power reserve. It's off most of the time, but the few times you do turn it on, it's at high power."

Warren smiles at him. "Why, thank you, Ridge."

Maggie laughs. "I'm not sure that was a compliment, Warren."

"Sure it was," Warren says.

I think it was both an insult and a compliment, which makes me laugh.

We spend the next half hour eating the lasagna Maggie prepared and working out more compromises. Bridgette doesn't say much, but she's also not rude at all, which is a huge improvement from when we walked through the front door.

After we tell Maggie goodnight, Ridge grabs my hand and leads me to the backseat of the car. He forces Warren to drive home since he drove here, which is fine with me because I really want to share the backseat with Ridge on the ride home.

He reaches across the seat and slides his fingers through mine as we're pulling out of Maggie's driveway. He pulls out his phone and texts me one-handed.

Ridge: You're like the Bridgette whisperer. I don't know how you do it.

Sydney: She's not that bad. I think she's always so defensive because no one has ever really made any effort to break through that defensiveness.

Ridge: Exactly. It says something that you made the effort.

Sydney: So did Warren.

Ridge: Only because he wanted to sleep with her. I don't think he ever expected to fall in love with her. That was a surprise to everyone. Especially him.

Sydney: You have unique friends. I like them.

Ridge: They're your friends now, too.

He squeezes my hand after I read his text. Then he reaches over and unbuckles my seat belt, pulling me closer to him. Once I'm in the middle of the backseat, he refastens the middle seat belt around me, pulling me against him. "Better," he says, wrapping his arm around me.

His thumb is grazing my shoulder, but his hand eventually makes its way down, just far enough so that he can trace the faded letters he wrote over my heart. He presses his mouth against my ear. "Mine," he says quietly.

I smile and place my hand over his heart. "Mine," I whisper.

Ridge presses his mouth to mine, and I smile through the whole kiss. I can't help it. When he pulls back, he leans against the door, pulling me even closer. I lift my legs onto the seat and curl them under me as I snuggle against him.

This feels right. Finally. It used to feel so wrong, but nothing about us feels wrong anymore. I owe a lot of that to Maggie's willingness to forgive and move forward and even accept me into her life after everything that happened.

So much has changed in the past year. The day I turned twenty-two, I thought it was going to be the worst year of my life. But little did I know, a boy on a balcony with his guitar would change all of that.

Now I'm here in his arms, unable and unwilling to wipe the smile off my face because his heart is mine.

MINE.

Chapter Twenty-one

Ridge

It's really hard to tell Warren everything he's doing wrong when my hands are full with the mattress we're carrying upstairs and his headphones on. I'd really hate to see him try to maneuver a boat or back up a trailer if he can't even walk forward up the damn stairs while pushing a mattress.

I also don't understand why we're even moving Maggie's mattress upstairs. Her apartment will be ready in four days, and there's a couch, plus Brennan's bed is empty. But I'm not arguing, because if she's going to be in my apartment, I'd rather her be in the farthest bedroom from mine just so this will feel less awkward, even though I'll be staying the night at Sydney's this week.

Warren stops three steps from the top to take a break. He leans his arm on the railing and pulls his headphones off. "This is the only thing we're moving, right? Everything else stays in the U-Haul?"

I nod and sign for him to pick up the mattress again. He rolls his eyes and readjusts his grip, pushing it toward me.

Maggie's new apartment is on the other side of the complex. Close to Sydney's old apartment, actually. Maggie has tried to back out several times and find somewhere else to stay because she's worried it'll be too much, living so close. But this will honestly be better for everyone. She gets sick so often, and for the past year I've had to spend a huge chunk of my nights in San Antonio. Even if she's only a few miles away, her being in another complex would require me or Warren to stay overnight when she's sick because she gets so weak, she can't even get out of bed.

With her being in the same complex, it'll make everything easier. I won't have to spend uncomfortable nights in the same apartment as her, but she'll be close enough that Warren or I can run over there and check on her every hour. I honestly think that's why Sydney was so agreeable to it. She's seen Maggie during the sicker times, and Sydney knows that when Maggie's down for the count, even a glass of water is impossible for her to get on her own. Not to mention administering her medications, making sure she's doing her breathing treatments while she's weak and recovering from an illness, and ensuring her sugar levels are good every few hours. If she weren't in the same complex, her care would require a car to get to her, and leaving her alone wouldn't be possible. But being in the same complex, it actually requires less of my time and less of my presence and, in the end, will make Maggie feel more independent. Which is what she wants.

We're leaving everything else in the U-Haul because one of Warren's coworkers also works part-time for the company that is renting it to us. They're allowing us to keep it for the week for just nineteen dollars a day, so it'll remain full of Maggie's stuff and parked in the parking lot until she moves into her place.

Maggie is still down at the U-Haul, gathering what she'll need to get her through the next four days. Sydney went to pick Bridgette up from work. Warren and I finally get the mattress into the bedroom and plop it flat on the floor. Warren is breathing heavily with his hands on his hips. He looks over at me. "Why aren't you out of breath?"

"We went up a flight of stairs. Once. And I work out."

"No, you don't."

"Yes, I do. In my room. Every day."

He glares at me like my admitting that I work out daily is some type of betrayal. He stares back down at the mattress. "Is this weird?"

I look down at Maggie's mattress, finally inside the same apartment as me. I used to hate that she would never agree to move in with me, and now she kind of is for a few days, and not a single part of me wants it to happen the way that I used to. That's weird for me. For all these years, I assumed Maggie and I would end up living in this apartment together and that we'd eventually be married. I never imagined my life taking the turn it did, but now I couldn't imagine it any differently.

So, yes. To answer Warren's question, it *is* weird, so I nod. But it's only weird because it all seems to be working out. I'm just waiting for the other shoe to drop. Whether that's Maggie's or Bridgette's or Warren's shoe, I don't know. But I highly doubt it'll be Sydney's. She's handled this better than anyone, and she has the most reasons not to.

"What if Sydney and Bridgette lived together and they decided to move in some dude who they had both dated in the past? Do you think we'd be cool with it?"

I shrug. "Guess it depends on the situation."

"No, it doesn't," Warren signs. "You'd be pissed. You'd hate it. You'd act like a whiny little bitch, just like I would, and then we'd all break up."

I don't want to think I'd be like that. "More reason to let them know how much we appreciate them."

Warren kicks at a leaf on Maggie's mattress and then bends to pick it up. "I let Bridgette know how much I appreciate her all night last night." He grins, and I take that as my cue to head back down to the U-Haul.

On my way down the stairs, I receive a text. I look at my phone and pause on the steps when I see that it's from Sydney. It's a group text with Warren and me.

Sydney: At the DQ drive-thru down the road. Anyone want a Blizzard?

Warren: Does a one-legged dog swim in a circle? I'll take a Reese's.

Ridge: M&M please.

I look down at the U-Haul in the parking lot and watch Maggie walk up the ramp and disappear inside of it. This is one of the weird moments we're going to have to learn to navigate. I need to remind Sydney that Maggie is here and she might want one. But it feels weird to remind Sydney to include her. It's probably not as weird as anything else that's happened in the last two weeks of us dating. And part of me struggles with what to say to Maggie and whether I should even offer her ice cream, knowing she isn't supposed to have a lot of sugar. But I don't want to be the one to bring up her health right now. I'm trying to keep my distance with the hope that she's stepping up and taking control on her own.

Right in the middle of my internal struggle, Maggie sends a text through to the group.

Maggie: I'll take a large Diet Dr Pepper. Thanks!

I didn't even realize Sydney had included her in the group text. But of course she had. Every time any of this starts to feel awkward, Sydney somehow alleviates that awkwardness before it's even able to fully set in.

I walk to the U-Haul, and Maggie is all the way inside of it, digging in her top dresser drawer. She's throwing stuff on top of the dresser, in search of something. She finds the shirt that she's looking for and stuffs it in a bag. She looks up and sees me standing at the opening of the U-Haul.

"Can you grab this suitcase and bring it up?"

I nod and she signs, "Thank you," then walks out of the U-Haul and heads toward the stairs to the apartment. I walk over to the dresser to grab the suitcase from on top of it, but I pause when I see a sheet of paper on the floor of the U-Haul. I bend to pick it up. I don't want to be invasive, so I set it on top of the dresser, but it's unfolded, and I can see that it's a list. At the top, it says, *Things I Want to Do*, but the title next to it is scratched out and written over. I pick it up, even though I probably shouldn't.

There are three out of the nine things on the list scratched out: *skydive*, *drive a race car*, and have a *one-night stand*.

I know she went skydiving, but when did she race a car? And when did she have a . . .

Never mind. Not my business.

I read the rest of the items on the list, remembering how she used to talk about some of these things to me. I always hated that she had so many things she was so adamant about doing, because I always felt like I had to be the voice of reason and it would put her in a bad mood.

I lean against the dresser, staring down at it. We planned on a trip to Europe once. It was right after I finished my second year in college, about four years ago. I was terrified for her to go because even being in such close quarters with strangers on an international flight for ten hours was enough to put her health at risk. Not to mention the change in oxygen levels and atmosphere and being in a touristy area and in a country with hospitals that aren't familiar with her medical history. I tried so hard to talk her out of it, but she got her way because I honestly couldn't blame her for wanting to see the world. And I didn't want to be that one thing that was holding her back.

But in the end, it wasn't me who held her back from actually going. It was a lung infection she contracted that landed her in the hospital for seventeen days. It was the sickest I'd ever seen her, and the entire time she was in the hospital, I couldn't help but feel nothing but relief that she hadn't come down with the illness in Europe.

After that, I wouldn't even entertain the idea of an international trip. Maybe I should have. I realize that now, after knowing how much she resented my caution. And honestly, I don't blame her. Her life is not my life, and even though my only goal was to give her life more length, all she's ever wanted was a life with more substance.

I can see movement out of the corner of my eye, so I turn and look up, just as Sydney makes her way up the ramp to the U-Haul with two Blizzards in her hands. She's wearing one of my Sounds of Cedar T-shirts, and it's hanging off her shoulder because it's too big for her. If I had my way, she'd wear one of my shirts every day for the rest of our lives. I love this effortless look on her.

She smiles and hands me one of the Blizzards. She pulls the spoon out of hers and licks ice cream from it, then closes her mouth over the spoon.

I grin. "I think I like yours better, and I don't even know what flavor you got."

She smiles and stands on her tiptoes, kissing me briefly on the lips. "Oreo," she says. She pokes at her ice cream with her spoon and nods her head toward the sheet of paper I'm still holding. "What's that?"

I look down at the list, wondering if it's my place to even share something like this with her since it isn't mine.

"Maggie's bucket list. It was on the floor." I set it down on the dresser and grab the suitcase. "Thank you for the ice cream." I kiss her on the cheek and make my way out of the U-Haul. When I turn around to see if she's following me, she isn't.

She's picking up the sheet of paper.

Chapter Twenty-two

Sydney

When I was eight years old, we went on a road trip to California. My father stopped at Carlsbad Caverns National Park just in time for the bat flight. I was scared to death and hated every second of it.

When I was eleven, we spent two weeks on a train tour of Europe. We saw the Eiffel Tower, we went to Rome, we visited London. I have the picture of my mother and me on my refrigerator that my father took of us in front of Big Ben.

I've been to Vegas once with Tori. We went for my twenty-first birthday and stayed one night because we couldn't afford more than that, and Hunter was upset that I was gone on my birthday.

I've done several things that are on Maggie's bucket list, and while I didn't take the trips for granted, I certainly don't think I appreciated them enough. I've never thought about writing a bucket list or what would even be on it if I did. I don't plan that far ahead.

That's just the thing, though. Neither does Maggie. But far ahead for her and far ahead for me have two completely different meanings.

I set my Blizzard on top of the dresser and stare at number seven on the list. *Bungee jump.*

I've never been bungee jumping. I can't say that it would have been a bucket list item for me, but the fact that it's a bucket list item for Maggie and she asked me to join her gives the entire sentiment a whole new meaning.

I fold the list and grab my ice cream, then make my way out of the U-Haul and up to Ridge's apartment. Ridge is in the kitchen with Warren. They're leaning against the counter, finishing their ice cream. Bridgette is probably taking a shower because she smelled like chicken wings. I walk to Maggie's bedroom, and she's kneeling in front of her suitcase, rifling through it. She looks up to see me standing in the doorway.

"Can I come in?"

She nods, so I walk in and sit on her mattress. I set my cup on the floor next to the mattress and unfold her list. "Found this," I say, holding it up for her to see. She's just a few feet away, so she reaches over and grabs it, then glances down at it. She makes a face like it's as useless as trash and then tosses it on the bed.

"I was a big dreamer." She gives her full attention back to her suitcase.

“This might make you think less of me,” I say, “but I’ve been to Paris, and I probably shouldn’t admit this, but the Eiffel Tower looks just like a really big transmission tower. It’s kind of underwhelming.”

Maggie laughs. “Yeah, you definitely shouldn’t admit that to anyone else.” She folds the top of her suitcase shut and then moves to the bed, lying down on her stomach. She grabs the list and pulls it in front of her. “I crossed off three of these in one day.”

I remember the day she went skydiving because it wasn’t that long ago. Which means . . . the one-night stand wasn’t that long ago, either. I’m curious about it, but I’m not sure we’re at a point where I want to ask about her sex life.

“Most of the other ones I wrote down are a little far-fetched. I get sick too easily and too often to travel internationally.”

I look at the Vegas one. “Why would you want to lose five grand instead of win five grand?”

She rolls onto her back and looks up at me. “If I had five grand to lose, it means I’d be rich. Being rich is an inadvertent item on my bucket list.”

I laugh. “Do you plan on doing anything else on the list other than bungee jump?”

She shakes her head. “It’s really hard for me to travel. I’ve tried it a couple of times and never made it very far. I have too much medical equipment. Too many medications to worry about. It’s really not all that fun for me, but I didn’t realize it when I wrote the list.”

I hate that for her. I almost want to alter a couple of these just so she can mark more of them out. "How far are you able to travel without it being an inconvenience?"

She shrugs. "Day trips are cool. And I could probably go somewhere for a couple of nights, but there's nowhere around here I haven't already been. Why?"

"One sec." I stand up and walk to the living room and grab a pen and spiral notebook off the table. I go back to Maggie's room, feeling Ridge and Warren watching me the whole time. I turn around and smile at them before walking back to Maggie's bed. I place her bucket list on the spiral notebook. "I think with a little modification, these are all doable."

Maggie lifts up onto her elbow, curious as to what I'm doing. "What kind of modification?"

I scroll down the list. I stop on Carlsbad Caverns. "What interests you about Carlsbad? The bats or the caves?"

"The caves," she says. "I've seen the bat flights here in Austin a dozen times."

"Okay," I say, drawing an open parenthesis next to Carlsbad Caverns on the list. "You could go to the Inner Space Cavern in Georgetown. Probably not nearly as cool as Carlsbad, but it's definitely a cave."

Maggie stares at the list for a moment. I'm not sure if she thinks I'm crossing a line by writing on her bucket list. I almost hand her back the list and apologize, but she leans over and points at the Eiffel Tower. "There's a mock Eiffel Tower in Paris, Texas."

I smile when she says that, because it means we're on the same page. I write *Eiffel tower in Paris, Texas* next to number nine.

I scroll the list again with the pen and then pause at number three. *See the Northern Lights.* "Have you ever heard of the Marfa Lights in West Texas?"

Maggie shakes her head.

"Doubt it's even remotely the same, but I've heard you can camp out there and watch them."

"Interesting," Maggie says. "Write it down." I write *Marfa Lights* in parentheses next to *Northern Lights.* She points to number four. *Eat spaghetti in Italy.* "Isn't there a town somewhere in Texas called Italy?"

"Yeah, but it's really small. Not even sure they'd have an Italian restaurant, but it's close to Corsicana, so you could get spaghetti to go and take it to a park in Italy."

Maggie laughs. "That sounds really pathetic, but definitely doable."

"What else?" I ask, scrolling the list. She's already apparently driven a race car and had a one-night stand, which we've successfully avoided discussing. The only thing left that we haven't modified is Vegas. I point to it with the pen. "There are casinos right outside of Paris, Texas. Technically, you could just go there after visiting the fake Eiffel Tower. And maybe you should"—I scratch out two of the zeros—"only lose fifty dollars instead of five grand."

"There are casinos in Oklahoma?" she asks.

"Huge ones."

Maggie pulls the list from me and looks it over. She smiles while she reads it, then pulls the notebook and pen from my hands. She places the list on top of the notebook. At the top of the list, it reads, *Things I Want to Do. Maybe One of These Days . . .*

Maggie scratches out part of the title so that the list reads, *Things I Want to Do. Maybe Now.*

Chapter Twenty-three

Maggie

I was scolded today.

It's the first time I've seen my doctor since she walked out of my hospital room—right before I bailed. The first half of my appointment today was spent apologizing to her and promising to take things more seriously from now on. The second half of my appointment was spent with different specialists. When you have cystic fibrosis, your team comes to you in one central location, as it's not safe to sit in the different waiting rooms for each specialist. It's one of the things I love about my doctor that I didn't get the full benefits of while living in San Antonio. I really do feel like my health will be easier to maintain now that I'm back in Austin. I just have to quit letting my frustration over this illness win out over my will. Which is hard, because I'm very easily frustrated.

I've been gone most of the day, but when I pull back up to the apartment, I'm surprised to see Ridge's car here. He's been staying at Sydney's the majority of the week. Today is Friday, and I was supposed to move tomorrow, but it's been pushed back to Sunday. I'm sure Ridge will be happy to have his own bed again.

Or not. I doubt he's all that upset about spending so much time at Sydney's.

When I open the living room door, they're both on the couch. Ridge is holding a book in front of him, his feet propped up on the coffee table. Sydney is leaning against him, looking at the words on the pages as he reads aloud.

Ridge is reading. Out loud.

I stare at them for a moment. He struggles with a word, and Sydney makes him look at her as she sounds it out for him. She's helping him pronounce the words out loud. It's such an intimate moment, I want to be anywhere else when I close the door and gain Sydney's attention. She looks up and then sits up straight, putting a little distance between herself and Ridge. I notice. So does he, because he stops reading and follows Sydney's gaze until he sees me.

"Hey." I smile and set my purse on the bar.

"Hi," Sydney says. "How was the appointment?"

I shrug. "Overall, it was good. But I spent most of it being scolded." I grab a water out of the refrigerator and then head toward the bedroom I'm staying in. "I deserved it, though." I walk to my room and close the door. I fall down onto the bed because it's the only thing in here. There isn't even a dresser or a TV or a chair. Just me and a bed, and a living room I feel slightly uncomfortable in.

Not because Ridge is in there with Sydney. I honestly don't mind seeing them together. The only thing that bothers me about it is that seeing them together reminds me of Jake, and I feel a sting of jealousy that it's not me and Jake cuddled together on a couch somewhere. I feel like Ridge and Sydney fit together in a way that's similar to how Jake and I fit together. Or *could have* fit together.

It's interesting to me, looking back, just how wrong Ridge and I were for each other. And it isn't at all because anything is necessarily wrong with us as individuals. We just didn't bring out the best sides of each other. Not like Sydney does with him. I mean, he's sitting on a couch, reading to her. And he's doing it because it's his way of perfecting his speaking voice. That's not a side of him I ever brought out. Or even encouraged. We had conversations in the past about why he didn't verbalize, but he always just shrugged it off and said he didn't like doing it. I never asked for a deeper explanation than that.

I remember the day I was in the hospital and found all the messages between him and Sydney. I didn't read them all in that moment because I honestly didn't want to. I was hurt and a little blindsided. But once I made it home, I read every word. More than once. And the conversation that hurt me the most was when Ridge explained to Sydney where the band Sounds of Cedar got its name.

The reason it hurt so much is because I realized, in all

the years we'd been dating, I'd never once asked Ridge where the band name came from. And because of that, I'd never known exactly how much he'd done for Brennan when they were younger.

There was a lot I read that I once wished I'd never read between the two of them. Between all the iMessages and Facebook messages, I sat there for hours reading. But reading all of it also made something very clear to me: There was so much more to Ridge than I was aware of. There were things he shared with Sydney over a short period of knowing her that he never once shared with me over a six-year stretch. And that wasn't because Ridge was hiding anything from me about himself or his past, or lying in any way. There were just things about both of us we never dug deep enough to figure out. It occurred to me that maybe we didn't share those things because they were sacred to us. And you only share the really sacred stuff with the people who reach you on that deep of a level.

I didn't reach Ridge on the level that Sydney did. And Ridge didn't reach me.

I ultimately decided to end our relationship because of their connection. Not because they had formed it . . . but because Ridge and I never had.

People are supposed to bring out the best in each other. I didn't bring out the best in Ridge. He didn't bring out the best in me. But seeing Sydney on the couch with him just now, helping him . . . She brings out the best in him.

I noticed how she pulled away from him a little when

she realized I was in the room with them. It bothers me that she felt she needed to do that. I want her to know that their physical affection is not something they should feel obligated to hide on my account. I actually, in a weird way, like seeing how much they like each other. It gives me even more reassurance that I made the right choice by not allowing Ridge to use my illness as a reason to stay with me.

I stand up and make my way back to the living room. The only thing that's going to alleviate the awkwardness when we're all in a room together is to force us all to be in a room together even more. Me hiding in my bedroom isn't going to get us anywhere.

Sadly, Ridge is no longer on the couch with Sydney when I walk back into the living room. She's in the kitchen, rummaging through a cabinet. Ridge is no longer in the room.

I walk to the bar and take a seat, watching Sydney. "What are you guys doing tomorrow?" I ask her.

She spins around and her hand is over her heart. "You scared me." She laughs and closes the cabinet. "I think we all planned to help you move tomorrow, so the day is open now that you aren't moving until Sunday."

"What do you mean *we all*? Is Warren off tomorrow, too?"

She nods. "Bridgette, too. Although I don't think she was actually going to help with the move."

I laugh. "I would have been shocked if she did."

"True. Why are you asking?" Sydney says. "Do you have something in mind?"

I shrug. "Nothing specific. I just thought . . . I don't know. Maybe it would be good for all of us if we spent more time together. Now that . . . well . . ."

Sydney nods, like she's been thinking the same thing. "Now that the dynamics have changed and it's hella awkward?"

"Yep. That."

Sydney laughs and then leans forward on the counter in thought. "Maybe we could do the cave thing. In Georgetown."

"I was thinking more along the lines of lunch," I admit. "I don't expect you guys to spend your entire Saturday with me."

"The caves sound really fun, though."

I tilt my head, watching her for a sign that she's just saying that to be polite. Sometimes she seems too nice and too accommodating, to the point that it makes me suspicious. But I also get nothing but an authentic vibe from her. Maybe some people just don't stoop to the same levels of jealousy that others do. As if Sydney can sense the suspicion in my expression, she continues speaking.

"Remember the night of Warren's birthday party?"

I nod. "You mean the night I thought your bra was cute and stupidly wanted Ridge to see it?"

Sydney cringes a little. "That's the night," she confirms. She looks down at her hands, clasped together on the counter in front of her. "I had a lot of fun with you that night, Maggie. I really did. At the time, I thought there was a chance we'd end up becoming friends, and it excited me because I really needed a friend after what Tori did to me. But then I kind of ruined that opportunity when I broke girl code and kissed your boyfriend." She looks up at me. "I've always hated that I ruined what I really do think could have been a good friendship between us. And now, months later, here we are again. And for whatever reason, you're extending an olive branch. So, yes, lunch tomorrow sounds good. But I also really want to see the caves, so if you can find it in yourself to extend an entire olive *tree*, then I think it'll be fun."

She looks nervous as she waits for my answer. I don't make her wait long, because I don't want her to feel nervous. Or awkward or guilty or anything else this girl doesn't deserve to feel. I smile at her. "You didn't ruin anything by breaking girl code, Sydney."

My words make her smile. "Bet you don't bring guys around me ever again, though. And I would completely understand."

"I'm done with guys," I say with a laugh. "Especially after what I did to the last one."

Sydney's eyebrow rises in curiosity, and I suddenly realize I spoke more than I should have. I don't want to talk about Jake, but based on the look she's giving me right now, she wants details.

"Is this your one-night stand?"

I nod. I was honestly surprised she didn't ask me about it when she was modifying my bucket list the other day. "Yeah. His name is Jake. I freaked out on him."

"Why?"

"He cooked me breakfast."

Sydney shoots me a look of mock horror. "Oh, how *dare* he," she says.

I laugh at her sarcasm and then cover my face with my hands. "I know. I *know*, Sydney. And I tried to rectify it a couple of days later but then ended up in the hospital and found out he has a kid, and I don't know . . . it just felt stupid of me to try and pursue him at that point."

"Why? Because you hate kids?"

"No. No, not at all. I was in my hospital room, and I could hear him outside talking to his son on the phone, and it all just felt so real in that moment. Like not only would this guy—who is really awesome and smart and funny—be entering my life, but so would his kid, who sounded like a great kid, and I just . . . I got scared."

"Of what?"

I sigh. That's a good question, because even I'm confused as to why I kept pushing him away. "I think my fears flipped on me somewhere along the way. I told myself that I didn't want to break his heart or become his burden. But in all honesty, I'm more scared that he'll break mine. It hit me when I realized how much I liked him that maybe most people aren't as committed as Ridge and aren't willing to put up with what a relationship with me could entail.

I became terrified that he would end up being the one to walk away, so I did it first. Maybe I didn't want things with him to end badly. I don't know. I question my choice every single day."

Sydney regards me silently for a moment. "If you had the chance, knowing Ridge's and your relationship came to an end, would you take back the six years you spent with him?"

I don't even need a second to answer her. I shake my head. "No. Of course not."

Sydney lifts her shoulder in a knowing shrug. "If things ended badly between you and this Jake guy, I doubt you would take back the time you spent with him, either. We shouldn't revolve our lives around their possible endings. We should revolve our lives around the experiences that *lead* to the endings."

It's quiet for a while.

Her words stick with me. Cling to me. Absorb into my skin.

She's right. And while it's been my goal to try to live life without focusing on the ending, that's exactly what I keep reverting to. Especially when it comes to Jake. I don't know why I've been telling myself that I can't do both—experience my life to the fullest *and* allow myself to experience another relationship. It's not like I can only have one and not the other.

"Maybe you should give him another chance," Sydney suggests.

I let my head fall back with a sigh. "This poor guy," I say. "I'm gonna give him whiplash with as much as I've gone back and forth with him."

Sydney laughs. "Well, make sure you only go forth with him from now on, and not back."

I take a deep breath and then stand up. "Okay. I'm going to call him."

Sydney smiles, and I try to ignore my nerves as I walk back to my bedroom. I pull out my phone and open up my contacts. My hand begins to shake as I select his contact. I lean against my bedroom door and close my eyes after I press his number and put the phone on speaker.

It rings twice and then is immediately pushed through to voice mail.

He just pushed me through to voice mail.

It's a crushing blow, but one I probably deserve. I wait for his voice.

"Hi, you've reached Dr. Jacob Griffin. Please leave a detailed message and I'll return your call as soon as I'm available."

I wait for the beep. And then I stutter my way through. "Hey, Jake. It's Maggie. Carson. Um . . . call me if you can. Or if you want, rather. If not, I understand. I just . . . yeah. Okay. Bye."

As soon as I hang up, I groan and then fall onto my mattress. I can't believe he pushed me through to voice mail. But then again, I can. And now the only thing he has that could change his mind is a nervous, embarrassing voice mail he's probably listening to right now.

I wallow in self-pity for a few moments, but then I push myself off the bed and walk to the living room. Sydney is still at the bar, but Ridge is now back in the room. He's showing her something on his phone, but Sydney gives her attention to me as soon as I walk out of my bedroom. I wave off her curiosity.

"He pushed me through to voice mail."

She makes a face. "Oh. Maybe he's busy?"

I shake my head and fall down onto the sofa, staring up at the ceiling. "Or maybe he realizes what a psycho I am for kicking him out of my house before he even finished cooking the bacon."

"Yeah, that could be a possibility as well," Sydney says.

I throw my arm over my face and try to come up with all the reasons why Jake isn't worthy of this much regret.

I come up with nothing. He is absolutely worthy of my regret.

• • •

It's been two hours. I've showered, put on my pajamas, and looked at my phone five thousand times. Ridge left to go pick up dinner for everyone. Bridgette and Warren are here now and are actually sitting on the couch with me. Warren is in the middle, and Bridgette is on the other side of Warren. I'm playing Toy Blast on my phone, but not because I'm interested in the game. I'm just obsessed with staring at my phone screen now. Waiting. Hoping.

"*Lesbian Libidos*?" Warren asks.

"Not even close," Bridgette says.

I glance over at him, wondering why the hell he keeps spouting off weird titles that sound like porn. He's scrolling through a list on his phone.

"*Babes in Bali*?"

Bridgette actually laughs at that one. "If I got to go to Bali to film a porn, I wouldn't be working at Hooters."

Warren turns to her. "Wait," he says. "How long have you worked at Hooters? Is it a Hooters-related porn?"

Okay, now I'm staring at both of them. *What in the hell are they talking about?*

Sydney is at the kitchen table doing homework. Apparently, she senses my confusion, because she offers up an explanation. "Bridgette kissed a girl in a porn film, and she refuses to tell Warren the name of it so that he can watch it. It's become his life's mission."

Wow. "That explains so much," I say.

Warren looks at me. "How many porn movies do you think are filmed every year?"

I shrug. "I wouldn't even know how to make a guess."

"A fucking lot. That's how many."

I nod and then give my complete focus back to Toy Blast. I don't even want to think about how much porn Warren feels forced to watch.

There's a quick knock at the front door before it swings

open. Brennan walks in, and I immediately jump up, excited to see him. I don't think I've seen him since Warren's birthday party.

"Maggie?" He immediately wraps his arms around me and hugs me, then puts his hands on my shoulders, holding me at arm's length. "What are you doing here?"

I wave my hand toward Bridgette's old bedroom. "I'm staying a few days until my apartment is ready."

He shakes his head. "Apartment? Where? *Here*?" His confusion is genuine. It surprises me Ridge hasn't mentioned it to him. He glances over at the table and sees Sydney. He releases my shoulders and takes a step back, eyeing me. Then he looks around the room. "Where's Ridge?"

"He went to grab dinner," Warren says. "Tacos. Nom nom."

I walk back to the couch to reclaim my seat and immediately check my phone for missed calls, even though the ringer is on. Nothing. I look back up at Brennan, who is scratching his head in confusion. He's literally scratching his head. It makes me laugh.

"You're moving into the same complex as Ridge?" he asks. Then he looks at Sydney. "And you're okay with that?" He looks back at me. "What is happening?"

I look at Sydney, and she's fighting a smile. "Welcome to maturity, Brennan," Sydney says.

"*Breasts of Burden?*" Warren asks Bridgette. We all look at him. He shrugs innocently. "Hey, I'm not the mature one. Don't look at me."

Ridge walks through the door with tacos, and Brennan immediately forgets about the odd arrangement that just threw him for a loop, and Warren is off the couch with a one-track mind that has nothing to do with porn movies.

Tacos can alleviate pretty much any issue. I'm convinced of that now.

I'm making my plate when my phone starts to ring. "Oh my God," I whisper.

Sydney is standing next to me. "Oh my God," she says.

I rush to the living room. Jake's name is flashing across the screen. I look at Sydney, wide-eyed. "It's him."

"Answer it!" she yells.

I look down at the phone.

"Who is it?" Bridgette asks.

"A guy Maggie likes. She didn't think he'd call back."

I look at Bridgette, and she's looking at me expectantly now. "Well, answer it," she says, waving at my phone, annoyed with me.

"Maggie, answer it!" Sydney says. I love how she sounds just as nervous as I am.

I swallow my nerves, clear my throat, and then slide my finger across the screen.

I walk toward the bedroom, slip inside, and close the door. "Hello?" It doesn't matter that I cleared my throat before I said that. My voice still shakes with my nerves.

"Hi."

I let my head fall back against the bedroom door when I hear his voice. I feel it in every part of me.

"Sorry I put you through to voice mail earlier," he says. "I was in a meeting. Forgot to silence my phone."

His admission makes me smile. At least it wasn't because he was annoyed that I'd called.

"It's okay," I say. "How have you been?"

He sighs. "Good. I'm good. You?"

"Also good. I moved to Austin a few days ago, so I've been busy."

"You moved?" he asks, not expecting that response from me. "That's . . . unfortunate."

I walk over to my bed and sit down. "Not really. I have a rule against dating anyone in the same zip code, so it's a good thing. Keeps things from becoming overwhelming."

He laughs. "Maggie, I'm too busy to be overwhelming, even if we lived on the same street."

"I don't think you can help but be a little overwhelming, Jake. We've had sex. You're hardly *under*whelming."

I expect him to laugh, but he doesn't. His voice is quiet when he says, "I'm glad you called."

"Me too." I lie back on my bed, pressing a hand to my stomach. I haven't been this nervous talking to a guy . . . ever. I don't know how to process all the things his voice does to my stomach, so I just press my hand against it as if that will somehow calm the storm brewing inside me.

"I can't talk long," he says. "I'm still at work. But I want to say something before I go."

I blow out a quiet breath, preparing for the impact of his rejection. "Okay," I whisper.

He sighs heavily. "I feel like you don't know what you want. You agree to go out with me, but you tell me on our date you don't want to see me for a second time. But then we have an entire night of incredible sex. Then you kick me out the next morning before I'm even finished cooking breakfast. A few days later, you show up at my office, then you shoot me down the same day at the hospital. Now you're leaving me a voice mail. I'm not asking for anything other than a little consistency. Even if that consistency is agreeing to never speak again. I just . . . I need consistency."

I close my eyes, nodding to myself. He's right. He's so right, I'm surprised he even called me back. "I can respect that. And I can give you that."

He doesn't say anything for a moment. I like the quiet. It's almost as if I can feel him more in the quiet. Almost half a minute goes by without either of us saying a word. "I've wanted to call you every day."

Those words make me frown more than smile because I know exactly what he's been feeling, and I don't feel good for making him feel that way. "I've wanted to apologize to you every day," I admit.

"You don't need to apologize for anything," he says. "You're a woman who was certain you didn't want a relationship with anyone. But then you met me and we had such a great night together that your feelings confused you. I like that I was the guy who put a wrinkle in your plan."

I laugh. "You have a really unique way of looking at my extreme indecisiveness. I like it."

"I figured you would. Listen, I have to go," he says. "Want me to call you tonight?"

"Actually . . . are you busy tomorrow?"

"I have a lecture at the hospital I have to attend tomorrow. From eight to ten. But I'm free after that."

"You're free the whole day?"

"The whole day," he says.

I don't know that I've ever asked a guy on a date before. This might be a first. "I'm going with some friends to Georgetown tomorrow. To Inner Space Cavern. You can come if you want. Or we could just do something after if you think going to look at caves with people you've never met before is a little weird."

"Won't be weird if you're there. I can be in Austin by noon at the latest."

I'm smiling like an idiot. "Okay. I'll text you the address."

"Okay," he says. I can almost hear the smile in his voice, too. "See you tomorrow, Five Hundred."

I stare at the phone after he ends the call, fingering my smile. How does he fill me so full of feels, even over the phone?

They all look at me as I get to the living room, and Sydney pauses midchew. After I grab two tacos out of the sack in the kitchen, I say, "We might have to take two cars tomorrow so we'll all fit."

It's all I say, but when I look over at Sydney, she's smiling.

So is Bridgette, but her smile is a little more sinister. "This should be fun. A shiny new toy for Warren to break in."

I look at Warren. Then back at Bridgette. Jake is going to spend the day with these two tomorrow. The entire day.

What was I thinking?

Chapter Twenty-four

Ridge

It's been a good week. *Finally.* I've stayed at Sydney's the last few nights, and honestly . . . I don't want to leave. I love sleeping next to her. I love waking up next to her. I love doing absolutely nothing with her. But I also know that this is a very new relationship that already seems to be moving at warp speed, so the last thing we need to do is live together.

Tomorrow night will be the last night I stay here before going back to my own apartment. I'm bummed because I'd much rather be here with Syd than in an apartment with Warren and Bridgette. But that's what's going to happen because I'm not speeding this relationship up even faster. Once we move in together, we'll live together forever. I want to wait until Sydney has experienced life on her own before making that kind of commitment.

I finish brushing my teeth, and then head to the living room. Sydney is on the couch with her computer in her lap. She sees me walk into the room, and she makes room for me on the couch next to her. Like a fluid dance, I sit and she moves and then we're effortlessly situated in what's become our standard positions on the couch this week. Me in a half-seated, half-lying pose against the arm of the couch while she lies with her back against my chest and my arm wrapped around her.

We can't communicate this way very well since we aren't facing each other, so we usually chat on messenger. Her with her laptop, me using my phone. It feels natural, though. And I like it in the evenings when we spend time together like this because she wears headphones and listens to music on her laptop while we chat. I like it when she listens to music. I like watching her feet sway with the music. I like feeling her voice against my chest when she sings along to some of the lyrics. She's singing right now as she scrolls through iTunes on her computer. She has the newest Sounds of Cedar album pulled up. They released it as an indie album a couple of weeks after Sydney moved in with us, so none of the stuff she helped me write is on the album she's browsing. The songs I wrote with Sydney haven't officially been released yet.

That's not to say none of the songs on the album she's browsing were inspired by her. She just doesn't know that. I watch as she opens her messenger app and types me a message.

Sydney: Can I ask you a question?

Ridge: Didn't I tell you once to never propose a question by asking if you can propose a question?

Sydney: I just called you a dickhead out loud.

I laugh.

Sydney: The song called "Blind." Did you write that about Maggie?

I look away from my phone and down at her. She tilts her head and looks back at me, her eyes full of genuine curiosity. I nod and look back down at my phone, not really wanting to discuss the songs I wrote about Maggie.

Ridge: Yes.

Sydney: Did it make her mad?

Ridge: I don't think so. Why?

Sydney: The lyrics. Specifically the part you wrote that says, "A hundred reasons for the pain and only one on my mind. When did looking out for you make me go blind?"

Sydney: I just feel like if she listened to that, she would have understood what you meant by it and it might have hurt her feelings.

Sometimes I think Sydney understands my lyrics better than I do.

Ridge: If Maggie took those lyrics literally, she never made it seem that way. I write very honestly. You know that. But I don't think Maggie knows that. She didn't think everything I wrote was really how I felt. Even though it is, in some form or another.

Sydney: Is that going to be an issue going forward with us? Because I'll be dissecting every single word of every lyric. Just so you know.

I laugh at her comment.

Ridge: That's the beauty of lyrics. They can be interpreted many different ways. I could write a song and you might not even know it was inspired by you.

She shakes her head.

Sydney: I would know.

I smile. Because she's wrong.

Ridge: Play the third song on that album called "For a Little While."

Sydney presses play on the song and then sends me a message.

Sydney: I know this song by heart.

Ridge: And you think you know what it's about?

Sydney: Yes. It's about you wanting to escape for a little while with Maggie. Like maybe it's a song about her illness and how you wish you could get her away from it all.

Ridge: You're wrong. This song was inspired by you.

She pauses and then tilts her head, looking up at me. She looks confused, and rightfully so. This song was released shortly after she moved in with me, which probably made her think none of these songs were related to her in any way. Her fingers start tapping at her keyboard as she writes a response.

Sydney: How is this song about me? You would have had to have written it before I even moved in with you. They were already cutting this album when I moved in.

Ridge: Technically, the song isn't about you. It was just inspired by you. The song is more about me, and how sometimes being outside on that balcony, playing music for the girl across the courtyard, was my escape. It was the little bit of time I got every day where I didn't feel so stressed. Or worried. I didn't know you. You didn't know me. But we were both helping each other escape our worlds for a little while every night. That's what the song is about.

Sydney immediately stops the song and restarts it from the beginning. She pulls up the lyrics on Google and reads along as the song plays.

"For a Little While"

I don't know what you want but you do
If you told me I would make it true
Oh, for a little while
Oh, for a little while

Something changes when the sunlight shines
Shadows fall out of my worried mind
Things go right and then I feel just fine
You and me will be just one tonight
Oh, for a little while
Oh, for a little while

You know for a little while
Oh, for a little while

For a little while I feel okay
For a little while I float away

For a little while I can stay
For a little while I'm on my way

For a little while I'll be all right
For a little while I'll be outside
For a little while I'll be okay

I'll be okay
For a little while
For a little while
For a little while

When the song ends, she closes out the lyrics and lifts a hand to her eye, presumably to wipe away a tear. I stroke her hair with my fingers while she types.

Sydney: Why have you never told me this song is about us?

I inhale a breath and release it, pulling my hand from her hair so I can respond to her.

Ridge: It's the first song that was inspired by you while I was still with Maggie. It was innocent between us because we had never even spoken at the time, but the sentiment still made me feel guilty. This song was my truth and I think I tried to hide it, even from myself.

Sydney: I can understand that. In a way, the song kind of makes me sad for you. Like you were living a life you needed a break from.

Ridge: Almost everyone needs a break from their real life

every now and then. I was content with my life before I met you. You know that.

Sydney: Are you still content with your life?

Ridge: No. I was content before I met you. But now I'm deliriously happy with my life.

I lean forward and press a kiss into Sydney's hair. She leans back and gives me access to her lips, but from an upside-down angle. I kiss her, and she laughs against my mouth before lifting her head and returning her attention to her keyboard.

Sydney: My father used to say, "A life of mediocrity is a waste of a life." I used to hate that he would say that because he only said it to prove a point to me about how he didn't think I should become a music teacher. But I think I get it now. I'll be content with becoming a music teacher. But he wanted me to be passionate about my career. I always thought that was enough—to just be content. But now I'm scared it's not.

Ridge: Are you thinking about changing your major?

Sydney nods, but she doesn't type her response.

Ridge: To what?

Sydney: I've been thinking lately about going into psychology. Or counseling of some form. I'm just so far into my degree that I would practically have to start over.

Ridge: People's passions change. It happens. I think if you really see yourself in a different line of work other than being a music teacher, it's better it happens now than ten years into the future. And . . . for what it's worth . . . I think you would be an amazing psychologist. You're good with music, no doubt. But you're incredible with people. You could even combine the two majors and do music therapy.

Sydney: Thank you. But I don't know. Starting over just seems so daunting, especially because I'll need to get my master's degree. Which means I'll be struggling financially for another five years. Which will become your issue, too, if we ever move in together. I won't have much money to contribute to the bills. It's just a lot to think about. If I stick with my current major, I'll be done in less than a year.

Ridge: We don't need much to get by. I think it's more important that you do what your heart is telling you to. As long as you're doing what you really want, I'll do whatever I need in order to help you see it through to the end. Whether that's next year with a teaching degree or ten years and a doctorate from now.

Sydney: I'm adding that to my Things Ridge Says folder. In case I have to refer back to it in the future. Because if I change majors, I'm going to be really broke. So broke, I won't even be able to buy new clothes. I'll be wearing this same shirt five years from now.

Ridge: Even if your clothes are faded, they'll always look new on you.

I feel her laugh.

Sydney: Oh, that's a good line. You should put that in a song.

Ridge: I will. I promise.

She slides her laptop off her lap and flips over, climbing up me. She kisses me. "Do you want some ice cream? I want dessert."

I shake my head. "I'll just take a bite of yours."

She kisses me again and then stands and walks to the kitchen. I readjust myself on the couch and open up a text to Warren.

Ridge: What time are we leaving tomorrow?

Warren: I dunno. Let me open up a group text and ask Maggie.

Warren: Maggot, what time are we leaving for the caves tomorrow?

Maggie: Call me that again and I'll use all the hot water tonight. I don't know. It'll be after lunch. Jake can't be here until noon.

Ridge: Are we doing lunch on the way or should we eat before?

Maggie: Let's eat on the way. I'll feel bad if he gets here and hasn't eaten.

Warren: Okay. Lunch. Be hungry. Got it. Ridge, you and Syd meeting us here or do we need to pick you up?

Ridge: We can meet you guys there.

Maggie: Can I ask a favor? And this is mostly of Warren.

Warren: I'M GOING TO BE NICE TO HIM! STOP WORRYING, MAGGIE!

Maggie: I know you'll be nice. I don't worry about that. I worry about you being completely inappropriate.

Warren: Oh. Well, yeah. You should definitely worry about that.

I laugh and set my phone down because Sydney is walking back to the couch with a spoonful of ice cream in her mouth, and I don't want to think about anything else right now. As if she can see my thoughts, she grins a little, pulling the spoon out of her mouth.

"You want a bite?"

I nod.

She doesn't sit next to me on the couch to share it with me. She straddles me, holding the bowl of ice cream between us as she adjusts her legs on either side of me. She scoops a small spoon of the ice cream and gives me a bite. I swallow it, and then she dips her head and kisses me. Her mouth tastes like vanilla. Her tongue is cold as it slides against mine.

I pull her closer, but the bowl of ice cream between us is hindering me. I grab the bowl and set it aside on the table next to her and then pull her to me. I kiss her as I slowly lower her to the couch.

She's about to melt, just like her bowl of ice cream.

Chapter Twenty-five

Maggie

Last night I dreamt Jake showed up with a date. A tall redhead with a French accent and black Louboutin heels.

Who goes to explore caves in high heels?

Or . . . better yet . . . *who shows up for a date with a date?* I was covered in sweat when I woke up, but I'm not sure if it was because Jake showed up in my dream with a date or because Warren and Bridgette shared one body with two heads. Both aspects of my dream were equally disturbing.

I don't know if it's my dream that has me so shaken, or if it's the fact that I've yet to have a conversation with Jake about the dynamics of our group, but I'm standing at the bathroom sink trying to brush my teeth, and my hand is visibly shaking.

I want to be able to talk to Jake before he meets everyone, but he'll be here in half an hour, and I can't very well call him minutes before he arrives and say, *Oh, by the way, you're about to hang out with my ex-boyfriend today.* Both *my ex-boyfriends, actually. It'll be fun!*

I should have canceled.

I almost did when I woke up after the nightmare I had last night. I had an excuse all typed out in a text to him about why I needed to cancel, but I was too scared to send it. He'd see right through it. I've been unreliable one too many times with him, and pushing him away again would probably be the last contact he'd have with me. Besides, in our conversation last night, he said he wants consistency. I don't want our consistency to be me pushing him away. I want it to be me following through with him. I just have to get him alone somehow before he meets Warren or Ridge. He deserves to know what he's getting into before he walks into this apartment.

If I could get him from the front door to my bedroom without him meeting anyone, it would give us a few minutes alone to reacquaint ourselves without standing in the danger zone that is the communal living room of this apartment.

That's what I'll do. I'll somehow drag him to my room before introductions.

As soon as I finish brushing my teeth, I dry my mouth with a hand towel and stare at my reflection. Other than the absolute fear in my eyes, I look like I usually do. I return my toothbrush to my toiletry bag, just as Bridgette swings open the bathroom door that leads to their room. She pauses when she sees me. I pause when I see her.

It's always been awkward between us, but we've never had to share a bathroom before, so the fact that she's in her barely there underwear takes awkward to a whole new level. For me, anyway. She doesn't seem bothered that I'm seeing her nearly nude, because she walks straight to the toilet and pulls down her panties to pee.

She's just as uninhibited as Warren.

"So," Bridgette says, unrolling toilet paper into her hand, "does this guy realize what he's getting into?"

"What do you mean?"

She waves a hand in a circle. "You know. This whole group he's about to spend the day with. Does he know the history?"

I close my eyes for a second, breathing in steadily. "Not yet," I say, exhaling.

Bridgette does something she rarely does. She grins.

No . . . she *smiles.* A huge, excited smile that reveals all her perfect white teeth. She should smile more often. She has a great smile, although it's appearing at an odd moment.

"Why do you look so happy?" I ask with caution.

"It's just been so long since I've been this excited about something."

I look away from her without responding and glance back at my own reflection. I look pale. I can't tell if it's because I'm nervous or if my blood sugar levels are off. Sometimes it's hard to tell the difference between low blood sugar, high blood sugar, or the onset of a panic attack.

I leave the bathroom and walk to the kitchen. My purse

is on the counter, so I dig through it until I find my glucose monitor kit. I lean against the counter while I check my blood sugar. As soon as I insert the test strip into the monitor, the front door begins to open.

Ridge and Sydney walk into the apartment, hand in hand. Sydney greets me, and Ridge nods, then signs to Sydney that he's going to shower. On his way to his bedroom, though, he does a double take when he sees the testing kit in my hands. His forehead naturally creases with worry.

"I'm fine," I sign. "Just wanted to check it before we leave to be safe."

Relief floods his expression. "How long before we leave?"

I shrug. "No rush. Jake isn't even here yet."

He nods and heads to his bedroom. Sydney sets her purse on the bar next to mine and opens a cabinet, grabbing a bag of tortilla chips.

My glucose levels are in the normal range. I sigh, relieved, then put the kit back in my purse. I grab my phone and open up my texts with Jake. We had a quick conversation this morning. I sent him the address to our apartment, and half an hour later he responded with a text that said, Conference over. On my way.

That was almost an hour ago. Which means he'll be knocking on the door any minute now.

"You okay?" Sydney asks.

I look up from my phone. She's leaning against the

counter, staring at me with concern as she munches on chips. "You look a little nervous," she adds.

Is it that obvious? "I do?"

She nods softly, as if she's trying not to offend me with her observation.

I wasn't even this nervous when I woke up this morning from my nightmare. But as the hours progress, so does my regret. I wring my hands together as I glance toward Ridge's and Warren's bedroom doors to make sure they're closed. I look back at Sydney once I'm positive she's the only one in my vicinity. "I've picked up my phone to cancel at least three times this morning, but I was never able to hit send on the texts. I just know there's no way he could possibly enjoy today. I don't even know why I invited him. I was so flustered when he called back yesterday that I didn't think any of this through."

Sydney tilts her head and smiles at me reassuringly. "It'll be fine, Maggie. He obviously likes you, or he wouldn't have agreed to drive all the way here and spend time with people he doesn't even know."

"That's the problem," I say. "He *does* like me. But he likes a version of me that's confident and independent and has one-night stands. He hasn't hung out with the insecure version of me who is living on a mattress on the floor of the spare bedroom of my ex-boyfriend's apartment."

Sydney dismisses my comment with a flippant wave of her hand. "For one more day. You're moving out tomorrow, and you'll be independent and in your own place again."

I shrug. "Even still. It doesn't change the fact that I've been an emotional toddler for most of the past couple of weeks." I let my head fall back, and I groan. "I've been so hot and cold with him. He probably only agreed to today because he's hoping I'll impress him enough so that he can forget about all the times I was *un*impressive."

Sydney sets down the bag of chips. She rolls her eyes and walks up to me, placing her hands on my shoulders. She backs me up against a barstool, keeping her hands on my shoulders as she forces me to sit. "Do you know what I did for the first two weeks of living here?"

I shake my head.

"I cried every day. I cried because my life was shit, and I cried because I got fired from the library for having an emotional breakdown and throwing books at the wall. And, sure, I got better for a while. But a few months later, when I moved out and got my own place, I cried every day for weeks again."

I raise an eyebrow. "Why are you telling me this?"

"Because," she says, releasing my shoulders and standing up straight. "I was all over the place with my emotions for months on end. But every time I saw you, you were the epitome of strength. Even the day you found out about me and Ridge, I was so intimidated by your resolve. And . . . maybe even a little impressed. But you seem to be forgetting about all of that, and instead, you're focusing on a few bad days you've had." She reaches down and grabs my hands, looking at me with an expression full of sincerity. "No one is the best version of themselves all the time, Maggie. But what creates the difference between confidence and insecurity are the moments in our past that we choose to obsess over. You're obsessing over your shittiest moments when you should be obsessing over the better ones."

I haven't been around her a whole lot, but when I am around her, she impresses me more and more with how right she always is. I put a lot of weight on that as I cycle through a couple of breaths. I begin to nod. I've definitely had some unpleasant moments. So has she. So has Ridge. So have Warren and Bridgette. And . . . even though he seems perfect . . . Jake has had moments in his past when he hasn't been perfect. And I'm sure if I knew about his imperfect moments, I wouldn't hold them against him for a second. Which means he probably doesn't hold my indecisiveness against me like I've been worried he might. Otherwise, he wouldn't be knocking on the door right now.

Oh, God. He's knocking.

"Oh, God," I say out loud.

Sydney glances at the door and then back at me. "You want me to answer it?"

I shake my head. "No. I'll do it."

She waits for me to stand, but I don't. I just stare at the door, unmoving.

"Maggie."

"I know. I just . . . I don't think I'm ready for introductions yet. Can you . . ."

She nods, pulling me out of my chair. "I'll disappear," she agrees. "You answer the door."

Sydney gives me a quick shove toward the door as she rushes off toward Ridge's bedroom. Jake knocks again, and I'm scared if I don't open the door right away, Warren will walk out of his bedroom to answer the door. Or worse . . . Bridgette.

That thought swings me into action. I open the front door, and Jake is here, standing right in front of me. He's taller than I remember. Cuter. I suck in a breath at the sight of him, but I don't give myself time to give him a once-over. I grab his hand and pull him inside the apartment and across the living room. I don't release his hand until we're safely alone in my bedroom. I turn and shut the door behind us, leaning my forehead against it. I blow out a breath, still facing the door. I'm slightly more at ease now that we're out of the danger zone, but still nervous as hell as I slowly turn and face him.

He's standing a couple of feet in front of me, looking down at me like he's trying not to laugh.

God, he's cute. He's wearing jeans and a navy-blue graphic T-shirt with an anatomically correct heart on the front of it. *Funny.* I stare at the shirt for a moment, admiring how good he looks in it. Then I look him in the eye and stand up a little straighter. I clear my throat.

"Hi," I say.

He tilts his head a bit, curiosity clouding his expression. He's probably wondering why I rushed him into this room like there were zombies chasing us. “Hello, Maggie.” I can see all the questions he isn’t asking as he narrows his eyes, lifting a brow.

“Sorry. I just wanted a minute alone with you before introductions.”

He smiles, and I just want to sink to the floor. Not because his smile melts me, but because I’m so embarrassed about the conversation I’m about to have with him. I’m embarrassed by the condition of this bedroom. I’m embarrassed that he’s a doctor who seems to have all his shit together, whereas my life is currently akin to a broke college coed’s, living in a sparse dorm room.

Jake’s hands slide into his back pockets and he glances around the room—at the mattress on the floor. He looks back at me. “Is this your bedroom?”

“Just until tomorrow. All my stuff is in a U-Haul downstairs. I’m moving to another unit in the complex.”

He laughs a little, like he’s relieved to know I own more than just a pathetic mattress pushed against the wall of an empty room. He’s a few feet away from me, but I still have to look up at him. I suck in a shaky breath after I respond to him. He notices.

“You seem nervous,” he says.

“I am,” I admit.

He smiles at my honesty. “Me too.”

“Why?” I blurt out.

He shrugs. “Same reasons you are, I assume.”

I know for a fact we aren’t nervous for the same reasons.

"Please," I say, rolling my eyes with a laugh. "You're a cardiologist raising a half-grown child. I'm just a college student with roommates, sleeping on a mattress on the floor of an empty room. I can assure you we are not nervous for the same reasons."

Jake stares at me a moment, contemplating my words. "Are you saying you feel inferior to me?"

I nod. "Just a little," I lie. Because I feel a *lot* inferior to him.

He releases a quick laugh, but he doesn't respond. He just takes a step away from me and looks around the room again, turning his back to me. His focus falls on my mattress for a moment. He looks back at me over his shoulder and then half turns, reaching out his hand.

I look down at his hand, beckoning for mine. I slide my hand into his, admiring the strength behind his grip as he closes his fingers around mine. He pulls me with him, walking toward the mattress.

He sits down, scooting to the middle of the mattress, resting his back against the wall. He still has a grip on my hand, so he pulls on it, urging me to follow suit. As soon as I begin to kneel, he pulls one of my legs over his lap so that I'm straddling him.

Not what I was expecting.

We're almost eye to eye, but I haven't relaxed yet, so I'm slightly taller than him in this position. He leans his head back against the wall, looking up at me.

"There," he says, smiling gently. "Now, you're in

a position of control. It should make you a little less nervous."

He rests his hands on my waist. I feel some of the tension leave my shoulders when I realize what he just did. I smile as I'm reminded how patient and kind he is. He returns my smile, and I suddenly feel like melting to the floor again, but not out of embarrassment. This time I want to melt because he's so damn perfect, and it's making me blush.

Also, I can't help but be relieved that he didn't show up with a high-heeled French redhead. I exhale. "Thank you. This helps."

He breaks eye contact and finds my hands, threading his fingers through them. "You're welcome."

Now that I've relaxed a little, I lower my legs until our thighs are flush together. We're eye to eye now, and I feel stupid for how nervous I've been. I forgot how everything about him is so calming. He's been a calming presence since the moment we met and I was scared to death to skydive until he sat down next to me to fill out my paperwork. His presence is like a sedative, flowing through my veins, taming my thoughts and my worries. In a matter of minutes, the fear in my eyes has been subdued, and now I'm forcing myself not to grin. He makes me feel somewhat giddy, but I don't want him to know that.

"How was your lecture this morning?" I ask, hoping to direct the subject toward him.

Jake laughs a little. "Justice told me I shouldn't go into

doctor mode when I'm around you. He says I'm boring when I talk about medical stuff."

That couldn't be further from the truth. "Our medical talk was the highlight of our date for me. It's the first time anyone has ever been that interested in the details of my thesis."

Jake narrows his eyes. "Really?"

I nod. "Yes, really. You probably shouldn't take dating advice from an eleven-year-old."

Jake laughs at that. "Yeah, you're probably right." He brings my hands to his chest and places them there, moving his own hands to the tops of my thighs. "We had a speaker who is about to have a new study published in the *Journal of Medical Science*. He presented about communication signals between the brain and the heart and what happens when those signals are severed."

Yeah, Justice is definitely wrong. I absolutely want to hear this. "And?"

Jake leans his head back against the wall again, relaxing a little. He lifts one of my hands off his chest and brings it up between us. "In ancient times, humans believed the heart was at the center of all thought process and that the brain and heart didn't communicate at all." He touches my wrist with two gentle fingers. "They believed this because when you feel an attraction to someone, your brain doesn't respond in a noticeable way that would suddenly make you aware of that attraction. But the rest of the body does." Jake begins to move his fingers in a delicate circle over my wrist.

I swallow heavily, hoping he doesn't notice what it's doing to my pulse.

"The heart is what makes a person most aware of physical attraction. It increases in speed. It begins to beat harder against the walls of the chest. It creates an erratic pulse whenever you're around the person you're attracted to."

It's quiet as he presses his fingers firmly against my wrist, waiting several seconds before he begins to speak. He grins a little, and I know it's because my pulse has changed so much since we started this particular conversation.

"It doesn't feel like that attraction is being manifested in the brain," he says, pressing his other hand right over my heart. "It feels like it's developing right here. Right behind the walls of your chest, in the very core of the organ that goes haywire."

Jesus Christ. He pulls his hand from my chest and releases my wrist. He lowers his hands to my waist, gripping gently.

"We're aware the heart doesn't retain or produce actual emotion. The heart is simply a messenger, receiving signals directly from the brain that let the heart know when an attraction is present. The heart and the brain are in sync because they are both vital and they work as a team. When the heart begins to die, a flurry of signals is sent from the brain, which ultimately causes the demise of the heart. And in turn, lack of oxygen from the heart is ultimately what causes the demise of the brain. One organ cannot survive without the other." He grins. "Or so we thought. In today's lecture, we learned that a new study proves that if communication between the heart and brain is severed in the minutes before death, an animal lives up to three times as long as those whose heart-brain connection is still left intact. Which, if proven correct, means that when the chemical connection is severed between the two organs, one doesn't immediately know when the other begins to die because they're unable to communicate. Therefore . . . if the heart begins to die and the brain is unaware, it gives doctors more time to save the heart before the brain begins to shut down. And vice versa."

I could honestly listen to him talk like this all day. "Are you saying that the heart and the brain might actually be detrimental to one another?"

He nods once. "Yep. It's almost as if they communicate *too* well. The study suggested that if we can make one organ temporarily oblivious to the failing of the other organ, we may be able to save them both."

"Wow," I say. "That's . . . fascinating."

Jake smiles. "It is. I thought about it the entire drive over. Essentially, if we could figure out how to sever some of the communication between the heart and brain in *non*-life-or-death situations, we could likely make it so that attraction wouldn't manifest physically in a person."

I shake my head. "But . . . why would a person not want to feel the full extent of an attraction?"

"Because," he says, matter-of-fact, "that way when a doctor develops an intense attraction to a girl he meets while skydiving, his mind won't be completely distracted for every minute of the two weeks that follow, and he might actually be able to focus on his job instead of thoughts of her."

His words make me blush so heavily, I immediately lean forward and lower my head to his shoulder so that he can't see my reaction. He laughs at my response, running a hand up my back and into my hair. He presses a quick kiss to the side of my head.

I eventually pull back and look at him. Everything he just said makes me want to lower my head again, but this time I want to lower it so that my mouth is positioned right against his. I refrain, though. Somehow.

He inhales and loses some of the smile in his eyes, trading it for a more serious expression. His hands slide up and then back down my arms. "I came back to the hospital to see you Saturday, but you were already gone," he admits.

I close my eyes briefly. I wondered if he showed back up.

I don't want to admit to him that I left before I should have. But I don't want to lie to him, or even omit the truth. "I left Friday night. Before they discharged me." I look him in the eyes, needing to explain myself before he passes judgment. "I know you're a doctor and you're going to tell me it was a stupid move, but I already know that. I just couldn't take being there for another second."

He stares back at me for a quiet moment, but he doesn't look angry or annoyed. He just shakes his head softly. "I get it. I have patients who practically live in hospitals, and I know how draining it is, both emotionally and physically.

Sometimes I want to look the other way and tell them to run because I know how much they don't want to be there."

I have no immediate reply to that because it's not a reaction I'm used to. I love that he didn't scold me just now. But I'm sure he sees patients with all different levels of frustration, so it would make sense that he'd be more empathetic than disapproving.

Jake lifts a hand to my hair and twists his fingers in a few strands of it. He stares at my hair as it slides through his fingers. When our eyes meet again, I can tell he's about to kiss me. His eyes drop briefly to my mouth. But I can't allow that until I explain to him the real reason for most of my nerves today.

"I need to tell you something," I say. I'm hesitant to bring it up, but he's here, and he's about to meet everyone, and he needs to know what he's getting into. He looks back at me patiently as I continue. "This is Ridge's apartment. My ex-boyfriend that I told you about on our date?"

Jake gives no hint of a response in his expression, so I continue, glancing away from him and down at our hands. I lace our fingers together. "Ridge and his girlfriend, Sydney, are going with us today. So are Warren and Bridgette, who are the other two roommates here. You'll meet them all in a little while. I just . . . It's why I wanted you to come to my room before meeting them, so if our history is brought up today, you won't be caught off guard." I make eye contact with him again, releasing a pent-up breath. "Does that bother you?"

Jake doesn't answer right away. I don't blame him, so I give him a moment to process everything I just said. It's a weird situation that I probably shouldn't have put him in.

"Does it bother *you*?" he asks, squeezing my hands.

I shake my head. "We're friends now. I really like Sydney. I feel like all of us are exactly where we need to be, but after I invited you here, I became paranoid that maybe I shouldn't have. I don't want it to be awkward."

Jake lifts a hand, sliding it against my cheek. His fingers graze the back of my head as he looks at me intently. "If it doesn't bother you, then it doesn't bother me," he says with finality.

His quick acceptance makes me smile with relief, even though I fail to tell him that it is *very* awkward for me.

Sydney is wrong. Some people are the best versions of themselves all the time.

That thought fills me with immediate guilt, because there's so much more to the situation than what I just admitted to Jake. He has no idea that Warren and Ridge are basically the only family I have. But I don't want to put too much on him at once. Not until we know for sure that this thing between us might actually go somewhere beyond today. I honestly don't know that I want it to until he has a clear idea of who I am, but I have no idea where to start. He spent one of my better days with me, but he hasn't gotten to know all of me yet. He knows I'm spontaneous and indecisive, but what else does he actually know?

"I'm fickle," I blurt out. "And sometimes I can be selfish." I know I should shut up, but the blunt honesty feels warranted. He needs to know exactly what he's dealing with. I don't want to experience another relationship with someone I'm not completely up front and open with. "I have a rebellious streak that I'm really trying to work on. I sometimes spend entire days binge-watching Netflix in my underwear. I've lived alone most of my adult life, so I eat ice cream out of the tub and drink straight out of the milk carton. I've never wanted children of my own. I kind of want a cat, but I'm too scared of the responsibility. I love show tunes and Hallmark Christmas movies, and I absolutely hate Austin traffic. And I know none of that really matters because we aren't even dating, but I feel like you should know all those things about me up front." When I'm finished, I bite my bottom lip nervously, waiting for him to either laugh at me or run. I'd completely understand either reaction.

He reacts in a completely different way than what I expect. He sighs and tilts his head a little, pulling our hands to his chest. His thumbs brush back and forth over mine.

"I internalize everything negative that happens at work," he says. "I need solitude on the really bad days. Sometimes even from Justice. And . . . I'm messy. I haven't done dishes in four days or laundry in two weeks. Most doctors are organized, and their houses are spotless, but mine is chaotic most of the time. And I probably shouldn't admit this because I'm a cardiologist, but I love fried food. I've watched every episode of *Grey's Anatomy*, although I'll deny it if you ever repeat that. And . . . I've only been with two women, so I don't even know that I'm all that impressive in bed."

The fact that he just admitted all that makes me feel like I might get a little emotional, but luckily, the last part of his admission makes me laugh. "You're impressive, Jake. Trust me."

He arches a brow. "Am I?"

I nod, feeling the heat rise to my cheeks just thinking about it.

"Can you be more specific?" he teases. "What was your favorite part?"

I think back on our night together, and honestly, all of it was great. But if I had to narrow it down to a favorite moment, I know exactly which one it is. "The second time. When you kept your eyes open and watched me while we . . ." My voice trails off. I can't even finish that sentence. Jake stares at me very seriously for a moment. His hands cover mine completely. "That was my favorite part, too."

I duck my head a little, breaking eye contact with him. Not because I'm nervous anymore, but because I'm trying to prevent myself from kissing him.

He reaches out and slides his hand to the nape of my neck, pulling my gaze back to his. His other hand slides around to my lower back, pulling me closer. "There were a lot of parts I liked about that night." He smiles as he inches his mouth closer to mine. "I liked undressing you as we stood next to your bed," he whispers, right before he presses his lips to mine.

I close my eyes, completely weakened by his kiss, but he pulls back.

"And I liked it when I lowered you to the bed." His lips lightly feather mine, and I feel him shift as he leans forward and lowers me to the mattress. I'm no longer in the position of control, but I don't mind it. My eyes feel heavy when I open them, looking up at him while he hovers over me. "And I really liked it the next morning when I woke up and you were wrapped around me so tight, it took me ten minutes to sneak out of the bed without waking you."

I open my mouth slightly, preparing a response, but he doesn't allow it. He dips his head and kisses me. As soon as his lips close over mine, I'm reminded of everything I felt the first time he kissed me. I don't know how I was able to deny him even once, much less twice.

Sometimes I'm impressed by my own strength, because right now, there's no way I could choose anything else over this kiss. I don't even care if we leave this room today, because his tongue has found mine and my hands are sliding through his hair, and *why can't I be in my own apartment already?* I'm conscious of every noise I want to make right now.

Luckily, he stops it before more parts of us get involved in this make-out session than simply our mouths. He kisses me softly, twice, before pressing his cheek to mine and releasing a heavy sigh into my hair.

I sigh right along with him, realizing that we're going to have to leave this room at some point. "I guess I should introduce you to my roommates now."

His gaze scrolls my face for a moment. "Yeah. I guess so."

I swallow, feeling the nerves start to build as I think about him meeting everyone. Specifically Warren. "Can you promise me something?"

Jake nods.

"Don't judge me too harshly based on a couple of my roommates. Warren's sole purpose today will be to embarrass me as much as he possibly can."

Jake's mouth breaks out into a devilish grin. "Oh, I can't wait to meet him now."

I roll my eyes and push against his chest. Jake rolls off me and onto his back. I stand up and straighten out my shirt, but he remains on the bed, staring up at me with an unusual expression.

"What?" I ask, wondering why he looks so . . . satiated.

He stares for a moment longer, then shakes his head and pushes off the mattress. He stands up, pressing a quick kiss to my forehead. "You're so fucking pretty," he mutters, almost in passing, as he grabs my hand and walks me toward my bedroom door.

That one comment completely eviscerates every hesitant, nervous feeling that remained from before he arrived. If he weren't pulling me out of the bedroom right now to go and meet everyone, I would make him wait so that I could find a pen and add another line to my bucket list. It would only be two words.

Jake. Griffin.

It wouldn't say, *Make love to Jake Griffin* or *Marry Jake Griffin.*

The entire tenth item on my bucket list would simply be his name, almost as if I could somehow accomplish him as a whole.

Item number ten to accomplish:

Jake Griffin.

Chapter Twenty-six

Jake

When people ask me why I became a doctor, which is quite a common question, I give them the quintessential answer: I want to save lives. I want to make a difference. I like helping people.

It's all bullshit.

I became a doctor because I love adrenaline.

Of course, the other answers are true as well. But the main reason is adrenaline. I love being the difference in a life-or-death situation. I love the rush I get when my skills are put to the test against a rapidly failing organ. I love the satisfaction I get when I win.

I was born competitive.

But there's a difference between being competitive and being in competition with someone else. I'm not competitive against other doctors or other people. I'm only competitive against myself. I'm in a constant battle to improve my own skill set in everything I do, whether that's in the operating room, jumping out of an airplane, or being the absolute best father I can be to Justice. I'm always on a quest to be a better me tomorrow than I was yesterday. It's never been about competing with anyone other than myself.

Until this moment. Because in this particular moment, I find myself hoping Ridge doesn't measure up to me. I haven't even met him yet, but I've never been in a situation where I'm about to meet the ex-boyfriend of the girl I'm interested in. It's not something I was prepared to do today. *Or ever.* When I started dating Chrissy in high school, I was her first legitimate boyfriend. I was her first kiss. Her first date. Her first everything. And considering we spent more than ten years together after that, I've never had to deal with feeling competitive with another man.

I'm not sure I like it.

When Maggie mentioned Ridge for the first time on our date, she talked about how he'd met someone else while he was dating her, which was ultimately what led to their breakup. I don't know the guy, but that was an automatic strike against him in my book. She also mentioned he writes music for a band, which is another strike against him. Not that being in a band is a bad thing, but it's hard to compete with a musician, even when you're a doctor.

What little she did say about Ridge gave me the impression that she doesn't regret the demise of their relationship. But it's still slightly uncomfortable knowing this is his apartment. Maggie is his ex. I'm about to spend the day with his friends. I can't imagine many guys being okay with their ex bringing along a new guy, so unless he's some kind of saint, I probably have good reason to suddenly be on edge. I don't like that I'm experiencing jealousy over a girl for the first time, and I haven't even met the guy who is the cause of my irrational jealousy.

But that's about to change because we're walking out of Maggie's bedroom now, specifically for introductions. I open the door and step aside so that Maggie can walk out of her bedroom first. She looks up at me as she passes, and she smiles with a hint of calm appreciation in her eyes, despite her own nervousness.

It's the same look she gave me when I was helping her with her skydiving paperwork the first day we met. She was a ball of nervous energy—enough for me to have felt it from all the way across the room. But as soon as I sat down next to her, she somehow smiled at me with an appreciative look in her eyes that made me feel as though I were in the process of jumping out of that plane with her. She says a lot without saying anything. I've never met anyone else whose expressions hold entire conversations.

Right now, her expression is saying, *This is awkward, I know. But it'll be fine.*

She leaves her bedroom door open and walks ahead of me across the living room. There's a guy standing in the kitchen with his back to us. I can't tell from this view, but it looks like he may be on his phone. There's a blond girl standing near the bar, slipping into a pair of shoes. She glances up as soon as she hears us exiting Maggie's bedroom. Her whole face lights up when she sees me next to Maggie.

Maggie waves her hand toward her. "Jake, this is Sydney."

Sydney continues twisting her shoe into the carpet to get it on her foot. Once she does, she walks over to me, half hopping as she extends her hand. "It's so good to meet you," she says, pulling on the other shoe.

I return her handshake. "You too."

Maggie mentioned Sydney's name to me earlier, and that she's Ridge's current girlfriend. I'm not sure how this scenario played out, but Maggie and Sydney seem to get along, which says a lot about them as individuals. And there's something about Sydney that feels genuine. I like her almost immediately.

I can't say the same for the guy behind her in the kitchen with his back still to us. He's obviously completely uninterested in introductions. I can only assume this is Ridge, but before I can put too much thought into what his reaction means and how this is definitely a competitive move on his part, two people walk out of one of the other rooms.

Based on Maggie's passing, almost agitated look as she turns to face them, I can only assume the guy walking toward me is Warren. The gleam in his eyes screams *mischief*, and Maggie did mention Warren's sole purpose today is to embarrass her.

He's holding his arms out as he makes his way over to

me. He pulls me in for a hug. I reluctantly hug him back. I'm not sure I've been greeted with a hug from another guy in years. In my occupation, it's handshakes and professional introductions and inquiries about which golf course you prefer to frequent on Sundays.

It isn't bear hugs and pats on the cheeks. This guy is *actually patting my cheeks.*

"Wow," he says. "You are really good-looking." He glances at Maggie. "Good job, Maggot. He looks like Captain America."

I laugh and back up a step, not sure if embarrassing Maggie is his sole intention. I think he wants to embarrass both of us.

"Warren, this is Jake," Maggie says, already appearing exhausted with him.

Warren salutes me. "Good to meet you, Jake."

With as much enthusiasm as Warren is showing, the other guy is still showing none. He continues to ignore the situation, completely uninterested that I'm here. Maybe this is why Maggie warned me. Because I'm not exactly welcome by everyone.

I give my full attention back to Warren. "Good to meet you, too."

Warren points at the brunette standing next to him. "This is my girlfriend, Bridgette."

She doesn't say anything to me. She just nods and walks to the refrigerator.

Warren points at Ridge. "Did you meet Ridge already?"

I shake my head. "Not yet." I'm not sure I *want* to meet Ridge at this point. He obviously has no interest in meeting me.

Warren closes the distance between himself and the kitchen and taps Ridge on the shoulder. When Ridge turns, Warren begins to sign at the same time he says, "Jake is here." Ridge spins around fully and finally makes eye contact with me.

I always teach Justice not to make assumptions about people. Yet here I am . . . being an assumptive asshole. Ridge isn't bothered that I'm here. He didn't *know* I was here.

He walks around the bar, closing the distance between us. "Hi," he says, shaking my hand. "Ridge Lawson." His voice is a clear indicator that he wasn't intentionally ignoring me and that I am, in fact, an assumptive asshole.

I return his handshake with relief. "Jake Griffin."

I don't know if Maggie intentionally left out that Ridge is deaf, or if his deafness is their norm and she just didn't think to mention it. Either way, I'm relieved by it, because five seconds ago I was ready to call it a day when I assumed I was intruding, but now his genuine welcome is as comforting as Sydney's.

I no longer harbor the competitive, jealous feelings I was attempting to suppress on the way out of Maggie's bedroom. I don't know the history between these people beyond what Maggie has shared, which isn't much, but there doesn't seem to be any ill will between any of them.

Although I still haven't spoken to Warren's girlfriend. Maybe she's just shy.

The next few seconds are a flurry of activity. Ridge is putting on his shoes, Sydney is pulling on a jacket, Warren walks over to the girl who just shut the fridge . . . *Bridgette* . . . and tries to kiss her, but she pushes him away.

I glance over at Maggie, and she smiles at me. "Let me grab my sweater." She walks back to her bedroom. I look around at the apartment and notice there are several doors leading to other rooms. Maggie mentioned how she and Ridge know each other, but I still don't know the connection between everyone else.

"Are you all roommates?" I ask, looking around at the four of them. "Is that how you all know each other?"

Bridgette is in the middle of sipping from a bottle of water, but she perks up at my question, just as Maggie reappears from her bedroom with a sweater. "Oh, I'll happily explain how we all know each other," Bridgette says, screwing the cap on her water bottle.

Maggie says her name in what appears to be an attempt to stop Bridgette from speaking, but Bridgette ignores her.

"Warren and Ridge have been best friends for years," Bridgette explains, pointing between Warren and Ridge with the water bottle. She then points it in Maggie's direction. "Warren used to date Maggie, but they didn't last very long before Ridge swooped in and claimed her."

Wait. *Both* of these guys used to date Maggie?

"Maggie and Ridge dated for six years, but that ended when Sydney moved in last year. Now *Sydney* is dating Ridge, but she doesn't actually live here with us anymore. Maggie does, though. Until her new apartment is ready, which is here in the same complex as both of her ex-boyfriends." Bridgette looks at me. "And no, none of this is weird. At all. Especially right now as we all pretend we're best friends and we spend the whole day doing best-friend stuff together. *Yay.*"

Bridgette says the last word of that sentence with absolutely zero enthusiasm.

I guess I had her pegged wrong, too. She isn't shy at all.

The next ten seconds are quiet. Quieter than any ten seconds have ever been. I glance at Maggie, and she has a look of horror on her face. Sydney glares at Bridgette, silently scolding her. Bridgette looks at Sydney and shrugs like she did nothing wrong.

Then my phone rings.

The interruption is an immediate excuse for everyone to scatter. Everyone but Maggie, who is watching me, waiting for my next move.

I pull my phone out of my pocket, knowing by the distinct ring that it's Chrissy. She never calls unless it's important. Long gone are the days when we called each other just to chat. I swipe my finger across the screen and then pull the phone to my ear as I point toward Maggie's bedroom, letting her know I'm heading in there to take the call in private. I close the door partially as I walk into the room.

"Hey."

"Hey," Chrissy says, breathless. I can tell she's rushing, probably pulling on her scrubs. "Got called in. Can I drop Justice off with you?"

I close my eyes. He's almost twelve. We leave him alone on occasion, but not when I'm more than a block away. "I'm in Austin." I squeeze the back of my neck. "It'll take me an hour to get back."

"Austin?" she says. "Oh. Okay. I would send him to Cody's house for the day, but he woke up in the middle of the night with a stomach bug. Should I call my mom?"

I glance at Maggie's bedroom door. "No. No, I'm on my way. I'll pick him up and take him over to my place for the night."

Chrissy thanks me and ends the call. I stare down at the phone, wondering how Maggie will take this. I sort of wish she'd heard the entire conversation so she doesn't think I'm making up an excuse to get out of today after Bridgette's spiel.

I slide the phone into my pocket and walk toward Maggie's door. When I open it, she glances at me from the kitchen, where she's talking with Sydney.

"Can we chat?" I point back toward her room to indicate I'd like to do it in private. She nods and then shares a quick glance with Sydney before walking back to her room. She closes the door once we're both inside.

"I'm sorry," she says. "Bridgette made it all seem so weird, but I swear—"

I hold up my hand, interrupting her. "Maggie, it's fine. I know you wouldn't have invited me here if you were still hung up on someone else."

She looks relieved by my comment.

"My timing couldn't be shittier," I say. "But Chrissy, my ex-wife, just called. Justice is sick, and she got called in to work. I have to head back home."

There isn't a single shred of doubt in Maggie's expression. Only concern. "Is he okay?"

"Yeah, it's just a stomach bug."

She nods, but I can tell she's somewhat disappointed that I'm leaving. So am I, though. I pull her to me to give her a hug goodbye. She molds to my chest, making it difficult to want to release her.

"Downfall of two doctors sharing a child," I say. "You're on call even on the weekends you aren't on call."

She pulls back and looks up at me. I slide my hands to her cheeks and bend down to give her a kiss. I can't help but notice that our physical interaction is way ahead of our relationship. We aren't even dating, but the way I hug her and kiss her and respond to her would indicate otherwise. It's why I make sure our kiss goodbye is nothing more than a peck. The last thing I want to do is overwhelm her again. "Have fun today."

She smiles. "I will. I hope Justice feels better soon."

"Thank you. And send me some pictures of the caves. I'll call you tonight after you're back if it's not too late."

"I would like that," she says. "Want me to walk you out?"

"I would like that."

• • •

One would think that a man who regularly slices through people's chests wouldn't be bothered by a little vomit.

Not the case with me.

I'm convinced Justice has vomited more today than he did the first five years of his life. Or maybe it just seems that way because he's older and bigger and produces more vomit, but fuck, there was so much vomit. I couldn't be happier that it's over. For now. There can't possibly be anything left in the poor kid to even puke up.

When I'm finished scrubbing the bathroom, showering, and checking on Justice, I finally settle into the couch to catch up on my conversation with Maggie. They returned from the caves a little over an hour ago, and she sent me a few pictures. I told her I'd FaceTime with her as soon as I got Justice to bed.

She answers almost immediately. The smile on her face disappoints me, but only because I'm not seeing it in person.

"How is Justice?"

I love that she asks this before we even say hello.

"Asleep. And empty. I think he's expelled everything he's eaten since January."

She makes a face. "Poor kid."

She's lying on her bed, her hair spread out over the pillow. She's holding the phone above her. It's the same view I had of her earlier today as I was hovering over her, preparing to kiss her. I force the thought out of my head before she sees through me. "Was the trip as fun as your pictures made it seem?"

She nods. "It was. Well, mostly." She pushes the hair away from her forehead to reveal a small bandage near her temple. "Warren thought it would be a good idea to hide from us and then scare us. I turned really fast, and me and Bridgette butted heads." She laughs, smoothing her hair back in place. "Warren felt so bad, he bought us all dinner. I mean, it was Taco Bell, but still. Warren never pays for anything ever."

I smile. I like that she seems to have had fun. Happiness looks really good on her. "You ready for the big move tomorrow?"

She nods, rolling onto her side as she lowers the phone. "I'm ready to have my own bathroom again."

"I'd offer to come help, but Chrissy is on call until Monday. I should probably keep Justice at my place until he's feeling better so there isn't a lot of back-and-forth."

"We have plenty of help. I don't have a whole lot to move, anyway. But I'll FaceTime you tomorrow night and show you my new place after we're finished."

"I'd like it better if I could see it in person."

She grins. "When's your next day off?"

"I have an early day on Wednesday. I could drive to

you . . . We could order takeout. Can't spend the night this time, but I could stay a few hours."

"That sounds good. I'll cook for you," she says.

"Do you know how long it's been since I've had a home-cooked meal?"

She smiles again and then follows her smile up with a sigh. I open my mouth to tell her how pretty she looks, but I'm interrupted when Justice walks into the room. "Hey, buddy," I say, looking up from my phone. "You feeling okay?"

Justice nods but doesn't look at me. He walks to the kitchen and opens the refrigerator.

"I'll let you go," Maggie whispers, pulling my attention back to my phone.

I smile appreciatively at her. "Call me tomorrow when you're all settled."

"I will. Goodnight."

I stare at her a moment, not quite ready to end my conversation with her. But I also don't want to be on the phone with her while Justice is in the room. "Goodnight, Maggie," I whisper. She waves and then ends the call. I toss my phone on the couch and then walk into the kitchen with Justice.

He's standing with the refrigerator door open, and he's opening a slice of American cheese. He takes a bite out of it, leaving the slice dangling from his mouth while he grabs the deli meat. He pulls out a slice of ham and shoves it in his mouth, along with the rest of the slice of cheese.

"It would be easier if you just let me make you a sandwich," I offer.

Justice grabs the bag of ham and closes the fridge. "I can't wait that long. I feel like I might die of starvation." He grabs a bag of chips and sits down at the bar with the ham in front of him. He opens the bag of chips and puts a few in his mouth. "Who were you talking to?"

"I take it you're feeling better."

"If you count starving to death as feeling better. Who were you talking to?" he repeats.

"Maggie."

"The same girl you went to see in the hospital?"

This is why I didn't want to be on the phone with her while he was in the room. He doesn't shy away from anything. And I'm a big believer in being honest with him, so I nod. "Same one."

"Why was she in the hospital?"

"She has cystic fibrosis."

"That sounds serious."

"It is. You should research it."

Justice rolls his eyes because he knows I'm being serious. Every time he asks a question that I tell him to research, I always follow up with him the next day to make sure he did. Then I correct him on anything he learned that was inaccurate. That's the downside of Google. There's a lot of information, but you have to know how to weed through the bullshit. I think that's really why I always have him research answers to a lot of his questions—so that he can learn how to properly navigate the bullshit.

"Is Maggie your girlfriend?"

I shake my head. "Nope."

"But you've had sex with her?"

The combination of my eleven-year-old asking if I've had sex with someone while chewing on a mouthful of ham is both odd and entertaining. "*What?*"

"You mentioned something about not being able to spend the night with her again. Which means you've spent the night with her before. Which probably means you've had sex with her because Cody says that's what adults do when they spend the night with each other."

"Cody is eleven. He isn't always right."

"So that's a no?"

I feel guilty because I'm currently wishing Justice were still in bed sick. "Can we put this conversation on pause until you're about fourteen?"

Justice rolls his eyes. "You say you like that I'm a curious kid, but then you never want to feed my curiosity."

"I like that you're curious. I like feeding your curiosity. But sometimes you're too hungry." I open the refrigerator and grab him a water. "Drink this. You haven't had enough liquid today."

Justice grabs the water from me. "Fine. But on my fourteenth birthday, be prepared to revisit this conversation."

I laugh. *God, I love this kid.* But at this rate, I'm not sure

I'll make it until he's fourteen. His curiosity is going to kill the cat. I'm the cat.

"You want me to make you something else to eat?"

Justice nods and closes the deli meat. "I'll take some cinnamon toast. Can we watch *Signs*?"

I want to tell him no because the idea of watching one of his favorite movies for the twentieth time sounds excruciating. But I know before long, the last thing he'll want to do is watch movies with his dad. As a father, I've learned to take what I can get while I can get it, because none of the phases a child goes through last forever. Eventually, the things you once found repetitive and irritating become the very things you'd give anything to repeat.

"Yeah, we can watch *Signs*. Get it started while I make your toast."

Chapter Twenty-seven

Sydney

I scan the radio stations in search of a song I can sing to. I'm in the mood to sing. My windows are down, the weather is gorgeous, and it occurred to me on my way home from work that I haven't been in the mood to sing at the top of my lungs in my car in a long time. I don't know if it's because of the trajectory my life took over the past year, or if it's college, or a combination of both. But something shifted this past week. It's as if my life were a roller coaster, speeding through dark tunnels and spinning through loops with my entire body being jerked left to right and front to back and then . . . *whoosh.* The emotional roller coaster is coming to a smooth, slow, comforting part of the ride where I can just release a breath and know that I'm safe and everything inside of me is beginning to settle.

That's what this feels like. My life is finally beginning to feel settled.

After helping move Maggie in on Sunday, we were all exhausted. We sprawled out on her living room furniture, me and Ridge on one couch, Maggie and Bridgette on the other, and Warren on the floor. We all watched the season finale of *The Bachelor*—a show none of us has seen a single episode of all season, but we couldn't find the remote, and no one felt like changing the channel. Warren got really into it and started arguing with the TV when he felt the guy picked the girl Warren would have bet against if Warren had money.

When it was over, Ridge and I walked back to his apartment and crashed for the night. I was too exhausted to drive home, and we were both too exhausted to even shower. We walked straight to the bed and fell on top of it. We must have fallen asleep right away without even removing our clothes, because I woke up in the middle of the night to him slipping off my shoes and pulling the covers over me.

It's been three days since then, and it's all just felt so right. So good. It's strange how I don't even have my shit together yet, being a college student living paycheck to paycheck. But I feel like I would be happy with my life if it stayed this way forever. It goes to show that a person really doesn't need much if they're surrounded by the right people. Loved by the right people.

If I could bottle up the love I have for my life today, I would. It's a love worth saving.

I pull into my complex and grab my phone to check it as I exit my car. There's still no text from Ridge. He told me he'd text when he finished up with work today, but it's after seven, and I haven't heard from him.

Sydney: You coming over tonight?

Ridge: Do you want me to?

Sydney: I always want you to.

I insert my key into the lock and open my apartment door. I'm staring down at my phone as I walk inside, waiting for Ridge to text me back, when someone grabs me from behind. I scream, but realize almost immediately that it's Ridge, just by the feel of his arms wrapped around me. I spin in his arms, and he's smiling down at me.

"I'm glad you didn't say no, because I'm already here."

I laugh. My heartbeat is erratic. I wasn't expecting anyone to be here, but I couldn't be happier to see him right now. He kisses me, and it somehow makes this day even better.

I can't even stand myself right now. I don't recall ever being this in love with my life before today, and I don't know how to get used to this new version of myself. I got so used to being so full of gloom for so long, it's like I'm discovering a part of me that didn't exist before this month.

Or maybe it always existed . . . I just never had anyone who could pull out the best parts of me like Ridge does.

I stand on my tiptoes and kiss him. His hands cradle my cheeks, and he kisses me back, walking me until my back meets the counter. We kiss for a good minute before I recognize that my entire apartment smells like a restaurant. I pull away from him and turn around to find dinner prepared on the stove. When I look back at Ridge, he's smiling at me. "Surprise. I cooked."

"What's the special occasion?"

"There doesn't need to be a special occasion for me to want to make you happy. I'll be treating you like this for the rest of your life."

I like the sound of that.

Ridge leans in and plants quick kisses down my neck before pulling away and walking to the stove. "It'll be ready in five minutes if you want to change."

I smile on my way to my bedroom. He knows me too well. He knows that no matter what time of day it is, as soon as I walk through the door, I like to be comfortable. That means getting rid of my bra the minute I get home. It means getting out of my jeans and pulling on a pair of pajama pants and one of his T-shirts. It means pulling my hair up in a knot and having absolutely zero care about anything but being as comfortable as I can possibly be.

I love that he loves that about me.

When I walk back into the kitchen, he's setting the table. He made baked chicken and vegetables with a side of risotto. I honestly don't know that my kitchen has ever experienced this kind of meal before. I rarely cook full meals because it's just me. Sometimes Ridge and me. But it's rare that we go all out and do something as drastic as use the oven. Microwave, sure. Stovetop, maybe. But the oven means a serious meal, and we haven't had much time for that. I sign and tell him it looks delicious, and then proceed to eat half of it without stopping. It tastes even better than it looks.

"Seriously, Ridge. It's delicious."

"Thank you."

"I can't cook like this."

"Yes, you can. It just tastes better to you because you didn't make it. That's how cooking works."

I laugh. Hopefully that's true. "How was work today?"

He shrugs. "Played catch-up. But Brennan texted and said he needs me to play a show with him because they're short a guitarist next weekend."

"Where at?"

"Dallas. You want to come? Make a weekend of it?"

I nod. Watching Ridge onstage is my favorite thing. "Absolutely. Will Sadie be there?"

Ridge gives me a look to let me know he doesn't know who I'm talking about.

"Sadie the singer," I clarify. "The girl who started opening for Brennan. I think he likes her."

"Oh yeah. I'm sure she will be." He grins. "That should be interesting."

From what I've learned about Brennan, he doesn't get crushes on girls very often, which makes me invested in seeing how this turns out. I hope I get to meet her.

That thought leads me to my next thought. I can't visit Dallas without stopping to see my parents. "Since we'll be in Dallas . . . do you want to have dinner with my parents?"

Ridge answers immediately. "I would love to meet your parents, Sydney."

I don't know why, but that sentence makes my heart melt a little. I smile and take a drink.

"Have you told your parents about me?" he asks.

"I told my mother I have a boyfriend. She asked me twenty questions."

He grins. "Only twenty?"

"Maybe twenty-five."

"What did you say? How did you describe me?"

"I said you're very talented. And very cute. And good at pranks. And good in bed."

Ridge laughs. "I'm sure you did." He leans back in his chair, casually bumping my knee with his. He's staring at his plate, scooting around the rest of his risotto. "Did you tell them I'm deaf?"

I didn't tell them, but for no other reason than it just didn't come up, and I honestly didn't think about it. "Should I have?"

Ridge shrugs. "Might be worth mentioning. I don't like to catch people off guard if I can avoid it. I like for them to have a heads-up."

"You didn't give me a heads-up."

"It was different with you."

"How?"

He tilts his head and contemplates his answer. Then he

picks up his phone, which means he wants to explain something that he feels he can get across better in text than if he were to verbalize.

Ridge: In most cases, I like to warn people before we meet. It makes for less of an uncomfortable moment when they find out. I didn't warn you because it felt like . . . I don't know. It was just different with you.

Sydney: A good different?

Ridge: The best kind of different there can possibly be. My whole life I've been the deaf guy. It comes first with every person I ever meet. Being deaf and how a person will react to that is my first thought in every new conversation I have. It's most likely the first thought of the person I'm having the conversation with. It defines how they treat me, how they react to me, and how I react to them. But with you, I sometimes forget that part of myself. With you, I forget the one thing that defines me to everyone else. With you . . . I'm just me.

I'm glad he texted all that, because it's one more thing he's said to me that I want to keep track of and remember forever.

"My parents are going to love you just as much as I do."

Ridge smiles for a moment, but the smile is fleeting. He tries to hide it as he reaches for his drink, but I saw the split-second conflict in his eyes. It makes me wonder if he's only agreeing to meet them to appease me. What if he isn't ready to take that step? It's not like we've been dating long at all.

"You okay?" I sign.

He nods, reaching for my hand. He rests his on top of mine on the table, brushing his thumb across it. "I'm good," he says. "It's just that sometimes you make me wish I had better parents. Parents who could meet you and know you're perfect for me. Parents who could love you."

His words make my heart ache for him. "You have Brennan. He loves that you're happy."

"Yeah," he says, smiling. "And Warren."

"And Bridgette."

Ridge makes a face. "Oddly enough."

"Right? I really like her," I say with a laugh. "If someone would have told me six months ago that me and Bridgette would eventually be good friends, I would have bet my life savings against it. It's only five hundred dollars, but still."

Ridge laughs. "If you would have told me six months ago that me and you would be dating and spending an entire day helping Maggie move into my complex, I would have bet your life savings against it, too."

"Life is strange, isn't it?"

Ridge nods. "Beautifully strange."

I smile at him, and we finish eating in comfortable silence. I clear the table and load the dishes into the dishwasher. Ridge hooks his phone up to the Bluetooth on my stereo and turns on one of my Spotify playlists.

This is how I know he truly loves me. He does things that don't have an impact on him at all, like making sure there's always music playing, even though he can't hear it. He knows I like it, so he does it to make me happy. It reminds me of the first time he did this. We were in his car, driving home from the club, and he turned on his car radio for me.

It's the small things people do for others that define the largest parts of them.

Ridge folds his arms over the bar and leans forward, smiling at me. "I got you a present."

I grin as I turn on the dishwasher. "You did?"

He reaches out for my hand. "It's in your bedroom."

I have no idea what it is, but I grab his hand with both of mine and pull him to the bedroom because I'm excited. He pulls me back so he can walk through the door first. He lets go of my hands so he can sign what he's speaking. "We were writing a song together once when you mentioned how you wish you had one of these."

He pushes open the door and walks to my bed, then pulls a huge box out from beneath it. It's an electric keyboard, complete with a stand and a stool. I recognize the brand immediately. It's the same one I use in my music classes, so I know exactly how much he spent on this gift, and I immediately want to tell him I can't accept it. But at the same time, I'm so excited about it, I rush over to it and run my hand over the box.

I throw my arms around him and kiss him all over his face. "Thank you, thank you, thank you!"

He laughs, knowing how happy he just made me. "Is it the right one?"

I nod. "It's perfect."

I had a piano growing up at my parents' house, but it's too big to travel with. I grew up playing it, which started my love for music. I've slowly been integrating other instruments, but the piano is where my heart is. Ridge sets the keyboard up against the wall. I sit down and start playing a song, and Ridge sits down on the bed. He watches my hands with the same appreciation as someone who would be able to hear what they're creating.

When I finish playing the song, I run my hand appreciatively over the keys. I can't believe he remembered one comment I made a long time ago about wishing I had a piano like the ones we use at school. "Why did you get me this?"

"Because. You're good at songwriting, Syd. Really good. You deserve an instrument that can help you create music."

I crinkle up my nose at him because he knows I'm weird with compliments. Just like he is, I guess. I crawl onto the bed with him and wrap my arms around him, looking him in the eyes. "Thank you."

He brushes my hair back, sliding his hand to the side of my head. "You're welcome."

I'm inspired. By him, by his gift, by the feeling I had on my way home, when the windows were down and the music was blaring. "Let's write a song right now. I got an idea on the way home from work." I lean over to the nightstand and grab the pad of paper and pens. We both sit up against my headboard, but the guitar he leaves here is against the wall. He doesn't retrieve it, and instead, we decide to start with lyrics first.

On the way home, I had the thought that I wanted things

to feel this way forever. I wanted to bottle up his love and save it forever. As soon as I had that thought, I knew I wanted to write a song that revolved around that feeling. At the top of the page, I write the potential title, "Love Worth Saving." I write the first few lines of lyrics as they come to me.

Got a little money
Enough to get us by
Our house ain't pretty, honey
But baby, it keeps us dry

Our friends ain't rich or famous
But we pretend on the weekend

I tap the page as I move my fingers across the lyrics to give Ridge an idea of the pacing of the song. He pats his hand on his knee in time with mine and then reaches for the pen and writes, "Chorus," then follows that up with a few lines of his own.

Even if our clothes are fading
They'll always look new on you
Even when the times are changing
Nothing's gonna change my view on you
You know we got a love worth saving

As soon as I see the lines, *Even if our clothes are fading, they'll always look new on you*, I smile. Last week we were having a conversation about my possibly changing degree paths. I still don't know what I want to do, but he is supportive of whatever I decide, even if it means we'll struggle financially a little longer. He said those words to me, that clothes would look new on me, even if they're faded, and I told him he better put it in a song. It's almost as if he's been waiting for this moment and already had those lyrics prepared. It's incredible how seamlessly we work together. Writing music is such a solitary thing, much like how I assume writing a book would be. But when we're together, it just works. It's like we're better together than we are alone.

He's tapping through the beat of the chorus, but I'm still stuck on the lyrics he wrote. I draw a heart next to them to let him know I love them. Then I pause for a moment until I can come up with the next few lines of lyrics.

Don't need no gold or diamonds
Got the glow right in your eyes
If it's your love you're selling
You know I'm gon' keep on buyin'
We can make something outta nothing
Just keep that feel-good coming

Ridge hops off the bed and grabs his guitar. I decide to use the record feature on the keyboard, so I move over to the bench and he sits on the bed. He spends the next fifteen minutes working out the song on his guitar, and I use what he's creating on the guitar to match it with the piano.

He adds a few more lyrics and another chorus, and within an hour, the song is mostly worked out. We just need to give it to Brennan for a rough recording this week to see how it sounds. This was one of the easier ones we've written together. I record us playing through it again and then hit play on the keyboard so I can listen to it. It's more upbeat than most of the songs we write together.

I love writing with two instruments. The options to add more variations using the keyboard makes the song sound more polished than ones we've sent Brennan in the past just using Ridge's guitar. I'm so excited about the song and the gift Ridge gave me that it makes me want to dance as it's playing back.

Ridge sets his guitar aside and watches me dance around the room as the song plays. I laugh every time our eyes meet because I'm in such a good mood. At one point, when I glance at him, he's not smiling. I pause, wondering what just changed in him.

He signs, "I wish I could dance with you."

"You can. You have."

He shakes his head. "Not to a slow song where I just stand there. I mean like this." He waves his hand toward me. "To a faster rhythm."

My chest tightens with his words. I step toward him and grab his hand, pulling him up. "Ridge Lawson, you can do anything you want."

I wrap one hand around his neck, and he places his hands on my waist. I start tapping my other hand against his chest along with the beat of the song. I move left to right to the rhythm, and he starts to follow my lead. I sing the lyrics so he can watch my mouth and know where we are in the song. When the song ends, I reach over and hit play again so we can keep going.

Ridge starts to fall in line with the rhythm, and I laugh when it finally happens. He laughs, too, as he starts to take over and keep up with a beat he can't even hear. He leads me around the room as I sing and tap against him. At the end of the final chorus, he spins me and then pulls me against his chest as we both come to a slow stop.

He holds me there, staring down at me as I look up at him. We're both smiling. Looking in his eyes, I can see the complete appreciation he has for me like I've never seen before. Like I just gave him something he thought he would never experience.

For me, it was a simple dance—something I do all the time and take for granted. For him, it was a breakthrough. Something he's never done before that he believed he couldn't do.

How he's probably feeling right now is how he makes me feel every time he turns on the stereo for me. It's the little things like these that create the biggest moments between us.

He takes my face in his hands, preparing to say something to me. But instead of speaking or signing, he just drags in a speechless breath as he stares silently at me. He lowers his mouth to mine, kissing me gently on the lips. Then he meets my eyes, conveying more with one look than he's ever conveyed through any other form of our communication.

"Sydney," he says quietly. "Everything we've gone through to get here. Right here. It was all worth it."

There isn't a thing I could signs or words I could say that could top the meaning in what he just spoke to me.

I reach over and hit play on our song again. He grins as I clasp my hands behind his neck. He presses his forehead to mine, and we dance.

Chapter Twenty-eight

Ridge

I wanted to send Brennan a rough cut of the song Sydney and I wrote tonight, but I needed my laptop to do it. Which is why we just showed up at my apartment and placed ourselves in this horrible predicament.

Us, standing at the door.

Warren's ass, staring back at us from the couch.

It's so . . . *pale.*

Sydney spins around as soon as we walk through the apartment door. She's covering her eyes, even though she's not facing the direction of Warren's ass anymore. She's shaking her head like she wishes she could unsee what she just saw. I wish that, too.

I think Bridgette might be yelling now. Thank God I can't hear it. All I see is Warren covering her up with the throw blanket from the back of the couch. *Mental note to wash that blanket tomorrow.*

Warren covers his junk with a throw pillow. *Wash the pillow, too.*

"Knock much?" he signs.

"Lock doors much?" I sign back. I grab Sydney's hand and pull her to my bedroom. When we're safe from Warren's nudity, she finally opens her eyes.

"I'm never sitting on that couch again," she says, walking to my dresser. She kicks off her flip-flops. I point to the restroom, and she nods. Right before I walk away, she says, "I'm gonna borrow sunblock."

I'm in the bathroom with the door shut before I realize what she said didn't make sense. Or at least I didn't read her lips right. Sunblock? It's nighttime. She doesn't need sunblock. What did she say if she didn't say sunblock?

Some *socks.*

She's gonna borrow some socks.

Shit! The ring!

I swing open the bathroom door, but it's too late. The sock drawer is open. The box is in her hands. The box is open, and she's looking down at the engagement ring with a hand covering her mouth.

Chapter Twenty-nine

Maggie

My old landlord texted me this morning and said she had some of my mail, so I decided to drive to San Antonio to meet up with Jake rather than have him drive to Austin. I texted him after I picked up my mail to let him know he didn't have to come to me for dinner. He responded almost immediately with his address. That text was followed by another that read, Key under the rock next to the grill on the back patio. I'll be there in a couple of hours.

That was seven hours ago.

He's texted several times since then, apologizing profusely. He got called into an emergency surgery. I keep reassuring him that it's fine. I even offered to come back another time, but he made me swear I wouldn't leave before he got home.

So . . . in an attempt to make hanging out for seven

hours in the home of a guy I'm not officially dating a little less strange, I've kept myself busy. I think I underestimated Jake's honesty when he said he was a messy person. Because . . . even after a trip to the store for cleaning supplies and hours of straight work . . . this place still isn't spotless. I've done four loads of laundry, two loads of dishes, made his bed for what I'm sure is the first time ever, scrubbed both bathrooms, and now I'm prepping dinner.

I came to his house prepared to stay the night. I'm not sure if that's something he'll ask me to do, but just in case, I brought my medications, an extra set of clothes, and my respiratory vest. The thought of using it in front of him is embarrassing, but the thought of avoiding my responsibilities and ending up sick again would be even more embarrassing.

I do get the feeling he'll want me to stay the night. Our texts started getting flirty a couple of hours ago. The last text I sent him was a picture of my hand touching his sparkling clean kitchen sink, and he responded with, That is the sexiest fucking picture I've ever seen.

I'm layering the cheese on the pizza when I hear his key in the front door. When he opens it, I get this tiny little quiver inside my stomach. It's so dumb, but I like him so much. It helps that he's fun to look at. He's wearing a pair of faded jeans and a light blue shirt with a black tie. And a smile. He tries to take in his kitchen as he walks closer to me, but his eyes keep falling back to mine. I can tell by the way he's looking at me that he's been waiting for this moment all day.

"Do you wear scrubs at work?"

He tosses his keys on the counter. "Yes. Most days, but I keep them at work. Sterilization purposes." He begins to undo his tie while he stares at me. "You should move in with me."

I laugh at his deadpan humor. "No, thank you. I have no plans to be your maid." I face the counter again and finish putting the toppings on the pizza.

Jake walks up behind me and wraps his arms around me. I lean into him, missing the way he feels and smells. He lowers his mouth to my ear. "If you were my maid, I could pay you in orgasms."

"After today, I think I'm already due one or two."

He laughs against my neck. "Considering the pristine condition of my kitchen, I owe you quite a few."

I toss the chopped onion onto the the pizza and wash my hands. He's still behind me, his arms around me. "Are you spending the night?" He sounds hopeful.

I don't want to seem desperate, so I fail to admit my change of clothes is already in his bedroom in my backpack. "We'll play it by ear," I tease.

I feel him shake his head, and then he spins me so that I'm facing him. "No, I say we go ahead and call it now. Stay the night."

"Okay." *I'm way too easy.* I move around him and slide the pizza onto the oven rack.

"How long does that take to cook?"

I close the oven door and turn around and face him. "About as long as it would take you to pay back one of the orgasms you owe me."

Finally, he kisses me. Then he lifts me, carries me to his bedroom, and lays me on his perfectly made bed. He looks around for a moment when he realizes I also cleaned his bedroom. Then he leaves me lying on his bed while he walks to his bathroom. When he sees his spotless bathroom, he then walks toward his laundry room.

He eventually makes it back to the bed, where he crawls on top of me. "Maggie Carson."

That's all he says. Just my name, with a smile. And then he disappears from my line of sight as he makes his way down my body, to the button on my jeans.

He thanks me, and when he's done, we still have five minutes to spare before the pizza's ready.

Chapter Thirty

Sydney

"It's not what you think," Ridge says.

I lift my gaze and drop my hand from my mouth. "I think it's an engagement ring. Is it not?"

Ridge shakes his head as he walks over to me and says, "No. *Yes.* I mean . . . it is, but it isn't. It is an engagement ring . . . but . . . it isn't yours."

He's treading very carefully, so it takes me a moment to realize why there's nothing but a cautious, regretful look in his eyes. I look back down at the ring that isn't meant for me. "Oh," I say. "I didn't know you ever proposed to her."

He shakes his head, almost adamantly. "I didn't."

The poor guy looks terrified of my potential reaction. What he can't see is how fucking *relieved* I am. We haven't even been officially dating for a whole month yet. If he had already bought me a ring with the intention of proposing,

I probably would have cried, but not from feelings of joy. I'm pretty sure, based on how I'm feeling right now, I would have been scared. Which is weird. I love Ridge more than I could ever love anyone, and I would love to be his wife. I would love to be married to him. But I want to enjoy the stages of our relationship for as long as we can.

I would love to be his fiancée, but I love being his girlfriend just as much. I want more of the boyfriend/girlfriend thing before we move it to the next level.

I laugh, clutching my chest. My heart is beating so fast. "My God, Ridge. I thought you were about to propose to me." I sit on the bed, still clutching the box. "I love you, but . . . too soon."

All the tension in his neck and jaw eases with my response. "Oh, thank God," he says, running a hand down his face. But then he tries to quickly recover. "Not that I don't want to propose to you. Just . . . yeah. Someday."

He sits down next to me on the bed, and I bump him with my shoulder as I grin at him. "Maybe someday."

He smiles back. "Maybe someday."

I look back down at the ring and run my finger over it. It looks like an antique. "It's a beautiful ring."

He picks up his phone and begins texting me. I pull out my phone to read it.

Ridge: It belonged to Maggie's grandmother. Her grandfather gave it to me while she and I were dating, but I never got around to asking her. I've been meaning to give it back to her since our breakup, but the timing was always weird. She doesn't know I have it.

Sydney: You keep it in your sock drawer. That's the most obvious place for a ring to be hidden. She's more than likely seen this.

Ridge: It's been in my closet for three years. I just moved it to the sock drawer two weeks ago to remind myself to give it to her.

Sydney: You've had it for three years and never proposed? What was stopping you?

Ridge shrugs and then says, "It never felt right."

I want to smile, but I don't. It's just that hearing him say it never felt right makes me feel good. Should it? Who knows? I'm honestly tired of second-guessing my reactions to every little thing I feel. From now on, I just want to feel. Unabashedly. Without guilt. And right now, I feel relieved. Relieved that the ring isn't for me, but also relieved that he never gave it to Maggie.

"I'll give it back to her tomorrow." He reaches for it, but I pull it away from him.

"No," I say. "I think you should wait."

"Wait? Why?"

I text him my lengthy response because it's too much to try to sign for me and too much for him to try to understand.

Sydney: I think this ring would mean a lot to Maggie. And I know it's still new between them, but I think Jake means a lot to her, too. Maybe you should wait and see how things go with the two of them. If they fall in love, I think you should give the ring to Jake. Not Maggie.

Ridge smiles after he reads my text. Then he looks at me appreciatively. “Okay.”

I hand him the ring, and he walks it back to the drawer. He slides his hands into his pockets. “What do you want to do for the rest of the night?”

I shrug. “Seeing Warren’s ass got me out of the mood for round two.”

Ridge laughs and drops down on the bed next to me. “We could go watch a movie.”

“Nope,” I say, shaking my head immediately. “Not sitting on that couch ever again.”

“No, I mean at a theater.”

“But . . . how would that be fun for you? There aren’t any captions.”

“Then take your earplugs and we’ll deaf-watch it together.”

I stand up, eager and ready. A date. I may not be in the mood for sex right now, thanks to Warren, but I am so in the mood for a date with my boyfriend of less than a month, whom I love with all my soul, but do not want an engagement ring from quite yet.

Chapter Thirty-one

Jake

When I woke up this morning, I made her breakfast. Bacon, eggs, biscuits. The works. And just as I had hoped, the outcome was the complete opposite from when I made her breakfast at her place, after the first night we spent together. She walked over to me, wearing nothing but a bra and the shirt I came home from work in yesterday. Unbuttoned. I couldn't stop staring at her; I almost burned the eggs.

She kissed me on my cheek and then made herself something to drink. I was already running late, but I didn't care. I wanted to eat breakfast with her, so I stayed another half hour. When I started to leave for work, she was getting dressed. The thought of not seeing her again for another week or two was not a thought I wanted to entertain.

"Stay," I said, pulling her to me before I walked out the door.

She smiled up at me. "Why? So I can clean the kitchen you just destroyed while cooking for me?"

I'm still so embarrassed she cleaned my house yesterday. Appreciative, yes. But it was in the worst condition it's ever been in. I've worked so much over the last couple of weeks, all I can do is crash when I get home. And Justice was sick, so his chores weren't getting done. I'm a messy person, but I've never been as messy as what she walked into yesterday.

"Stay and be lazy. Watch Netflix. I have chocolate in the pantry."

She grinned. "What kind of chocolate?"

"Reese's. Maybe some Twix."

Her nose scrunched up. "Sounds tempting, but I need to watch my sugar."

"There's sugar-free chocolate, too."

"Ugh," she said, letting her head fall back in defeat. "I can't say no to that. Or you. What time will you be back?"

"I don't know. I'll try to move around some afternoon appointments."

"Okay. But I'm taking your advice and not cleaning." She gave me a peck on the lips and then dropped down onto the couch. "I'm staying right here. All day."

"Good." I leaned over her and gave her a kiss. A good kiss. No, a *great* kiss. One that stayed with me all day. One I can't wait to get back home to repeat.

I was able to move around my last three appointments today. It's the second time in two weeks I've done this. It's out of the norm for me, so my nurse, Vicky, knew something was up. When I was on my way out the door, she said, "Have fun on your date."

I paused and turned around to look at her. She shot me a knowing look and walked back down the hallway.

I didn't think I was being transparent, but it's hard to hide this kind of euphoria. I'm not sure I've ever known this side of a relationship. With Chrissy, we became parents so early on in our relationship. Before that, we were just kids. Between medical school and raising Justice, we never really took the time to just enjoy each other.

I like it.

I'm really enjoying Maggie's company. I hate the idea that she'll probably leave tonight or in the morning, but I've also vowed not to beg her to stay like I did this morning. Weak moment. I need to remember this is the same girl who freaked out on me twice already. I'm new at getting back into the dating game and don't want to scare her away again.

• • •

Yeah, that promise I made to myself earlier lasted three hours.

We just got back from dinner, and she's shoving her things into her backpack.

"Leave in the morning," I say.

She laughs and shakes her head. "Jake, I can't. There has to be some rule that says you can't stay two nights in a row with someone you aren't even officially dating."

"Then let's make it official. Be my girlfriend. Spend the night."

She looks at me funny.

"Oh, was that not a hint that you wanted to make it official?"

"No, I only said that because it's a concern. I don't want to smother you."

I brush her hair out of her face. "I wouldn't mind that."

She drops her forehead against my chest and groans, then takes a step away from me. "We have responsibilities. I have three weeks left of school. You have to work tomorrow. We can't just pretend this is how it's going to be. Some blissful, romantic whirlwind of a relationship."

"Who's pretending?"

She raises an eyebrow like maybe I'm about to freak her out again. I can see her guard going up. I wrap my hand around her wrist and pull her back to me. "You know what?"

"What?"

"I am not your ex."

"I'm very much aware of that," she says.

"But just because I haven't been around for most of your past doesn't mean I'm not aware of our present. And all the things that might or might not happen in the future. Stop pretending we need to be more responsible than we are just because you're scared of where this whirlwind takes us."

"That was deep."

"I'm trying to be shallow. I don't want you to think about responsibilities or illnesses or what the rules of relationships should be tonight. I want you to drop your bag, kiss me, and stop worrying so much." I press my forehead to hers. "Live in the moment, Maggie."

Her eyes are closed, but I can see the smile spread across her face as she drops her backpack to the floor. "You are so good for me, Jake Griffin. But also kind of bad." She kisses my chin and then lifts up and kisses me on the mouth. Her arms find the hem of my shirt, and she slips her hands beneath it and slides them up my back.

I help her out of her shirt and then walk her to the bedroom. Counting our one-night stand, this is our fifth time to have sex. I wonder when I'll stop counting.

We spend the next half hour living in the moment. Me on top, then her, then me again. When the moment is over, I roll onto my back to catch my breath. She lays her head on my chest and moves with my breaths.

God, I could get used to this. I run my fingers through her hair, wondering if we made it official. I don't think she objected, but she also didn't agree.

"Maggie?"

She lifts her head and rests her chin on my chest, looking up at me. "Yes?"

"Are we official?"

She nods. "After that round? *Very* official."

I smile, but my smile is smacked right off my face when I hear the front door open.

"Dad?"

"Shit!" I roll off the bed and grab my jeans.

Maggie stands up and grabs hers. "What do I do?" she whispers. "Do you want me to hide somewhere?"

I rush to my closet door. "Yeah, hide in here."

She makes her way to my closet without question. I can't help but laugh. I grab her wrist right as she reaches the door. "I was kidding, Maggie." I try to stifle my laughter, but *she was really about to hide in the closet*. "He already knows about you. Get dressed and come meet him."

She stares at me a moment, then slaps me in the chest. "Ass."

I'm still laughing as I grab my shirt from the floor. "Dad?" Justice calls out.

"Coming!" I say.

When I'm dressed, I give Maggie a quick kiss and then leave her to finish dressing in the bedroom. Justice is standing in the kitchen with his friend Cody.

"What's up?" I say, as casually as possible.

Justice turns around. "Not much, Dad. What's up with *you*?"

I pause. He knows something. He's smirking.

His friend Cody holds up Maggie's shirt. "Whose shirt is this?"

They both start laughing. I grab the shirt and walk it back to my bedroom. I open the door and toss Maggie her shirt, then wait for her to put it on. "Thanks," she says. "I was worried they would see it."

I fail to tell her they did. She pulls it on and follows me out of the bedroom. When we walk into the kitchen,

Cody's jaw drops when he sees Maggie. He nudges Justice with his elbow.

"Dude," Cody says to Justice. "Your new stepmom is hot."

Justice rolls his eyes. "Not awkward at all."

Maggie just laughs. *Thank God.*

I introduce them. "Maggie, this is my son, Justice." Justice waves at her. "And his best friend, Cody."

Maggie smiles at them. "Hi. I'm . . . *not* anyone's stepmom."

"Even better," Cody says. I glare at him, and he wipes the smirk off his face.

The microwave dings, and Justice pulls a bag of popcorn out of it. "Mom got called in. She told me to call first and make sure it was okay that I came over."

"And why didn't you call first?"

Justice smiles and says, "Because then you'd know I was coming." Justice looks at Maggie. "Do you know who M. Night Shyamalan is?"

"The director? Of course."

Justice shoots me a look of approval, and then looks back at Maggie. "What's your favorite movie of his?"

She makes her way over to the bar and takes a seat. She seems comfortable. I'm glad. I didn't want this to be weird, but I also wasn't planning on introducing them so soon. But hiding her would have been even weirder.

"Hard to say," she says. "*Signs*, obviously, but *The Sixth Sense* will always hold a special place in my heart."

"What's your stance on *The Happening*?" Justice asks.

"I've never seen it."

Cody opens the bag of popcorn and says, "Well, Maggie, *who is not a stepmom*, tonight is your lucky night."

Justice pours the popcorn into two bowls and hands one to Maggie. She pops a piece in her mouth as Justice and Cody make their way to the living room.

I blow out a breath, although I'm not sure why. They're eleven years old. Not sure why all of that just made me nervous.

"I like him," she says.

"I told you he was great."

She stands up and puts a piece of popcorn in my mouth. "I might even like him more than I like you." She walks past me, spinning to face me as she goes. "Nobody puts Maggie in a closet."

I laugh. "Clever." She walks away, into the living room. I follow her, because that's what boyfriends do, right?

Justice and Cody have taken the main sofa directly in front of the TV. Maggie and I sit on the love seat. She leans against me, positioning herself lengthwise so she can see the TV better. She props her feet up on the arm of the couch.

Justice starts the movie, and I'm not even disappointed that I've seen it four times. I'm just happy this is how the night has ended up.

Tomorrow, that thought might scare me, knowing what I'm getting my heart into with this girl.

But right now, I just want to live in the moment.

Chapter Thirty-two

Three months later

Sydney

I've been trying to get Bridgette to warm up to Maggie since Maggie moved into their complex several months ago. As it stands, Bridgette is still pretty cold.

She's sitting on Maggie's bed while I help Maggie pick out an outfit for tonight, so we're making progress. She hasn't been over here since Maggie moved in, other than one time when Maggie had to stay a few nights in the hospital for an illness. Bridgette came to get some clothes for her, but only because Warren made her.

"I think the black shirt would look better with these," Maggie says. "I'm gonna try it on." She grabs the shirt I brought over and takes it to her bathroom, closing the door behind her. I look at Bridgette. She's on her back, staring up at the ceiling, yawning. I pull out my phone and text her because I don't want Maggie hearing our conversation.

Sydney: You're making this uncomfortable.

Bridgette reads the text and then looks at me, holding up a frustrated hand.

Bridgette: What?! I'm just being me.

Sydney: Yeah, no offense, but that's the issue. Sometimes people have to make an effort NOT to be themselves in order to make situations around them a little more tolerable. You haven't said a word to her. Make an effort. Ask her questions.

Bridgette: I AM making an effort. I'm here. Besides, I don't have any questions for her. What would I even say? I don't know how to do fake.

Sydney: Ask her about her graduation. Ask her about when we went bungee jumping. Ask her how she and Jake are doing. Lots of potential conversation starters if you just try.

Maggie walks out of the bathroom just as Bridgette drops her phone onto the bed and rolls her eyes.

"I like that shirt on you," I say to Maggie. She's turning back and forth in the mirror.

I look at Bridgette and make a face. Bridgette sits up dramatically, slapping her palms against the bed. She clears her throat.

"So . . . *Maggie*. How are . . . you and *Jake* doing? Well? I hope?" She forces a smile but sounds like a stiff robot.

Maybe this was a bad idea. I glance over at Maggie, and she's just standing there, staring at Bridgette with her head tilted.

I glance back at Bridgette and shake my head. "Wow. You really don't know how to talk to people."

Bridgette throws her hands up and says, "I *told* you!"

Maggie looks at me. "Did you make her ask me that?"

I shrug. "I'm just trying to teach her how to interact with humans in a normal way."

Looking back at Bridgette, Maggie says, "It doesn't suit you."

"See?" Bridgette falls back on the bed. "I should just be me. I'm good at being me."

"Fine. I'm sorry I tried." I give my attention back to Maggie. "But how *are* you and Jake doing?"

Bridgette sits up on the bed again and throws a hand out toward me. "Why does it sound so normal when *you* say it?"

Maggie and I both laugh. She looks in the mirror and fingers her hair. "We're good," she says, smiling into the mirror. "It's all been so easy with him. He's just . . . simple. He likes to have fun, doesn't take anything too seriously. Until he needs to."

"But is he good in bed?" Bridgette asks.

I see a pattern here. The only conversations that come naturally to Bridgette always have to do with sex. *Does Ridge moan during sex? Is Jake good in bed?*

"He's *very* good," Maggie says without hesitation.

"Who is better?" Bridgette asks her. "Ridge or Jake? Or *Warren*? Wow, you've slept with all three of our boyfriends."

I slap a hand to my forehead. She's a lost cause.

Luckily, Maggie just laughs it off. "Yeah, Bridgette, let's just not do the whole conversation thing, okay?"

Bridgette pouts. "But I actually want to know the answer to this question. I bet it was Warren."

Maggie looks at me and scrunches up her nose while shaking her head. *It wasn't*, she mouths.

Bridgette mutters something about wanting a snack, so she heads to the kitchen. I hand Maggie a purple button-up shirt. "Try this one on. I think you'll like it better than the black one."

"What's it even matter? Jake is on call all weekend, so he won't be there." Maggie goes back to the bathroom just as Bridgette walks back into the bedroom, crunching on chips. She looks at herself in the mirror, turning so she can see her ass. She holds up a Pringle and positions it so that it covers her butt in the mirror.

"What are you *doing*?" I ask her, just as Maggie comes out in the purple shirt. "Definitely that shirt. It's perfect."

"Maggie," Bridgette says, still looking at herself in the mirror. "When you said my ass looked like two Pringles hugging, was that a compliment?"

Maggie laughs. "Have you *seen* your ass? Of course it was."

"I don't see it." Bridgette pulls another Pringle out of the can and holds both chips back to back so that they're curved away from each other. "This is not attractive."

Maggie walks over and grabs the two Pringles, turning them inward. "Like this."

Bridgette stares at the chips and nods, like it finally clicks. "Oh. Yeah, it kind of *does* look like that."

• • •

Ridge and Warren have been at the venue helping the band set up for the show, so Maggie and I rode with Bridgette. Ridge isn't playing tonight, though. He said sometimes he just likes being a spectator.

Maggie has a smile on her face as we get out of the car, but I can tell it's strained. She pauses as she looks up at the building. "I wish Jake could have made it," she says quietly.

I grab her hand. "He can come to the next one. Just try to have fun."

I'm anxious to get inside, so I pull her after me and text Ridge to let him know we're at the back door. A moment later, the door opens and Ridge walks out. He's followed by Warren. I feel bad because Ridge is giving me a hug, and Warren is giving Bridgette a hug, and Maggie is just standing there, awkward and alone.

It won't last long, though.

Just when the door slams shut, it's pushed open from the inside. Jake walks out.

It's been hell keeping it from her, but he really wanted to surprise her. He was able to switch his on-call weekends, but he didn't want her to know. He's planning on staying with her until Monday morning.

As soon as she realizes he's actually here and she's not seeing things, she lights up all over and runs at him. She jumps on him and wraps herself around him like a spider monkey, her feet locked around his back, her wrists locked behind his neck. He's holding her with little effort, and it makes me envious that I can't jump on Ridge like that. I mean, I guess I could. But I'm not as tiny as Maggie. We'd need to plan it. We'd need a spotter. And a mattress for when we fell.

They're so in love. It's so adorable.

Ridge leans into my ear and says, "You look beautiful." His comment gets him a kiss. *We're so adorable.*

Warren opens the back door and holds it for everyone as we all shuffle inside. I feel my phone vibrate, so I look back at Ridge and he indicates he just texted me something.

Ridge: I gave Jake the ring.

Sydney: You did? Did it freak him out? Or did he seem appreciative?

Ridge: He thanked me like five times and kept staring at it on the drive over. I doubt he waits long.

That makes me smile. I know marriage wasn't an item on Maggie's bucket list, but I think she's at a point in her life where she wants to add more to the list. And Jake isn't going anywhere. I can see that just by the way they look at each other.

The room is packed when we get out to the floor. Luckily, one of the crew members saved an area up front for us. *Perks of writing music for the band.*

Jake and Maggie stand next to us. He's standing behind her with his arms wrapped around her. When Brennan and the band walk onstage, Maggie separates herself from him and starts clapping and jumping. I have no idea how long it's been since she's seen them play, but she's genuinely stoked to hear them. It makes me think about everyone's dynamic and how she's been a part of these people's lives since right after they started the band. I'm sure Brennan and everyone onstage mean more to her than I ever realized.

It makes me appreciate what we had to go through to get here even more. Had we all not figured out a way to co-exist, she would have had to give up huge pieces of her life. I never would have felt right about that.

I look over at Warren and Bridgette, and even she's smiling and clapping as Brennan introduces the band to the audience. Warren has his hands cupped around his mouth as he yells for the band. Then he drops his arm and wraps it around Bridgette's waist. She looks up at him and he smiles down at her, then gives her a quick kiss. It's so odd to see them in moments like this, but when I do get glimpses of it, it's beautiful. They love each other, even if they do it differently from everyone else.

That's the beauty of love, isn't it? It comes in so many different forms, shapes, sizes, textures. And it's ever changing. Like the love Ridge held for Maggie. It's still there . . . It's just a different form. And that's what I love the most about him. He never stopped loving her. He never stopped caring for her. And now that she's one of my closest friends, I can't help but love that for her, because she deserves it. She deserved his love then as his girlfriend, and she deserves his love now as one of his best friends.

Ridge moves closer behind me and wraps his arms around me, lifting one hand to my chest. He rests his palm at the base of my throat and presses his head to the side of mine. He wants to hear the concert through me, so I start singing along to the music. And I don't realize it until halfway through the song, but I'm crying.

I don't even know why.

I just love him so much. And I love being here with him. And I love his friends.

I just . . . *love.*

Chapter Thirty-three

Ridge

She knows every word to every song. I'm not sure when she learned all the songs that were written before I met her, but it makes me wonder if she learned them for me. For these moments when we're watching the band onstage, so she can sing them to me.

When the song ends and she starts clapping, I notice tears are falling down her cheeks. I wipe one of them away and then lean in and kiss her briefly before walking away. She tries to grasp at my shirt, but I disappear into the crowd before making my way onstage. Brennan told me to come up after the first song to perform the one I wrote for her, but I didn't tell Sydney I wrote a new song for her.

When I get up on the stage, I can feel the excitement of the room, even though I can't hear it. The looks on their faces, the people in the front few rows jumping up and down, the heat from the lights, the smile on Sydney's face when I finally find her in the crowd. I lean in to the microphone and sign while I tell her out loud why I wrote the song.

"Sydney." *She's grinning so wide right now, it makes me smile.* "I wrote a happy song for you this time. Because . . . well . . . you make me happy. No matter what happens or where we go . . . we're in it together. And that makes me so fucking happy."

She laughs and wipes at a tear, then signs, "You make me happy, too."

I take the guitar Brennan hands me and wait for his cue. Then I close my eyes and start playing the chords, repeating the lyrics quietly in my head while Brennan uses his voice to sing them out loud.

Well, maybe we can be
Somewhere where the land and the water meet
Somewhere where the worry just can't be
Only got enough room for you and me

Well, maybe the sun will rise
And peek through the pulled-down bamboo blinds
Shine across your slept-on perfect hair
And we won't care
No, we won't care

Cuz we got everything, everything we need right here
The world can try to make it all disappear

But let me tell you something that I happen to know
It's gonna feel like this wherever we go
Wherever we go

Well, what if all we saw
Was the rain dancing off the roof as it falls
Swaying in the leaves at the top of the tree
Water washing sand right from our feet

Well, what if all we knew
Was right from wrong with no point of view
The day can go off the tracks, up in the air
And we won't care
No, we won't care

Cuz we got everything, everything we need right here
The world can try and make it all disappear
But let me tell you something that I happen to know
It's gonna feel like this wherever we go
Wherever we go

You know we'll be here for a while
I think we better do it with a little style
So we make the most of every day like it's faded away
We'll be all right

Cuz we got everything, everything we need right here
The world can try and make it all disappear

But let me tell you something that I happen to know
It's gonna feel like this wherever we go
Wherever we go

When the song is over, I hand the guitar to Brennan and make my way back down to the floor. I find Warren and Bridgette. I see Maggie and Jake. I spin around, but there's no Sydney. I look at Maggie and sign, "Where did she go?"

Maggie points to the stage.

I spin around and look at where I was just performing. *Why is Sydney onstage?*

Brennan is saying something to her as she takes a seat on the barstool. He looks out at the crowd and says something into the microphone, then signs it for me. "This is Sydney Blake. She's one of our songwriters, and this is her first time onstage. Give her a round of applause."

She looks nervous, but I don't think she's as nervous as I am for her. I had no idea she was doing this.

Brennan starts to play, and I move closer to the stage to see which chords he's playing . . . which song. And I realize almost immediately that it's "Maybe Someday"—our song. I look at Sydney, just as the lyrics are about to start, but there's no microphone in front of her.

That's when she starts to sign the words.

Holy shit. She's signing the song for me.

Fuck. How am I supposed to just stand here and not get emotional?

I shake my head when she makes eye contact with me.

I'm in complete disbelief as I watch her sign the lyrics to a song she's completely rewritten into a new song.

"Maybe ~~Someday~~ Now"

I am right in front of you, here to stay
Breathe a little easier every day
Now that I'm yours, and you are mine
You ask me what I'll want someday
It's the same as yesterday
All I want . . . is you

With you I'm at my best
Someday has been laid to rest
I am ready to make that a vow
Maybe tomorrow
Maybe now

When you speak, I listen close
Hear all the words you say in prose
We're only silent when we kiss

I smell my perfume in your bed
Thoughts of you invade my head
Truths were written, now they're said

With you I'm at my best
Someday has been laid to rest

I am ready to make that a vow
Maybe tomorrow
Maybe now

You hear my heartbeat every night
Life with you, it feels so right
We are endless, like our song
Only good can come this way
Nights with you turn into day
Forever yours, forever mine

With you I'm at my best
Someday has been laid to rest
I am ready to make that a vow
Maybe tomorrow
Or maybe now

I don't remember when the song ended or when she walked off the stage or when she appeared right in front of me. I just know that in one moment, I was watching her onstage, and the next moment, I was kissing her. I can feel the music to the next song playing, and I'm still kissing her. My hands are in her hair when I finally pull back and press my forehead to hers. "I love you," I whisper.

I do. I love her so damn much.

• • •

I'm not even sure what other songs were played after that. I couldn't focus on anything other than Sydney. After the show, everyone met with the band backstage to figure out where we were going for dinner. While they chatted, Sydney and I stayed out in the hallway and made out. We're at dinner now, and it's torture keeping my hands off of her.

Brennan and the guys needed to get on the road, so it's Syd and me, Maggie and Jake, and Warren and Bridgette. I'm not sure why we even got a communal table, because none of us couples are paying attention to each other.

Well . . . we weren't. But Warren has turned his attention on Sydney now.

"Settle something for us," he says, referring to Bridgette and him.

"What's up?" Sydney says.

"So . . . in the song you rewrote . . . you mentioned vows. Was that a hint that you want to get married?"

Sydney laughs and then looks at me. She looks back at Warren and shakes her head. "We talked about how we weren't ready a few months ago. When I was rewriting the song, I realized maybe I am. I mean . . ." She looks at me. "Did you take it that way? I wasn't saying I expect a proposal. I just meant whenever you're ready . . . *I'm* ready."

Yeah, I'm ready. But I don't tell her that. She deserves a more thought-out proposal.

"Hold up," Warren says before I can even respond. "Slow down. Bridgette and I have been together the longest. We should get married first."

"No," Bridgette says. "I think Jake and Maggie should get married first. She has less time."

I was hoping I misread her lips, but she just made Sydney spew out her drink, so I guess I understood what Bridgette said just fine. Bridgette is lucky that Maggie is laughing at her right now, rather than choking her.

"*What?*" Bridgette says innocently. "It's true." She looks at Maggie. "I'm not trying to be mean. But seriously, you should try to do as much as you can as fast as you can. It makes sense. Add marriage to your bucket list and get it over with."

Maggie's cheeks are a shade darker than they were before all the attention was on her. Bridgette doesn't seem to care that she's embarrassing her. Or maybe she just doesn't notice.

"We aren't getting married," Maggie says. "We've only known each other for a few months. Statistically speaking, the less time you date someone before you marry them, the greater your chances of it ending in divorce."

Warren leans forward, holding up a finger in thought. It always makes me nervous when he tries to impart wisdom on other people. "Maybe so," he says. "But wouldn't adding marriage to your bucket list be worth the risk? You and Jake can date like this forever and you'll never know what it's like to get married. Or you can risk it and possibly experience marriage *and* divorce before you die."

Jake cocks an eyebrow and glances at Maggie. "Sounds like a win-win to me."

Maggie's eyes widen. Jake smiles at her while he takes

a sip of his drink. And then he says, "It makes sense if you think about it. At the risk of sounding like a medical professional, your life expectancy isn't as long as mine. So . . . I'm ready when you're ready."

Maggie stares at him blankly. We all do, actually. I don't think anyone was expecting him to *agree* with Warren.

"I hope that wasn't a proposal," Maggie says to Jake. "It didn't even come with an *I love you.* Or an engagement ring."

Jake stares back at Maggie for a moment. Then he reaches his hand out across the table. "Give me your keys, Ridge."

I don't even hesitate. I give him my keys, and Maggie watches him in bewilderment as he leaves the restaurant. "What is he doing?" she says. "Is it something I said?"

Warren is shaking his head. "Fucker is gonna beat me to it."

"To what?" Maggie says.

She seems confused, so none of us gives her any hints that we know what's happening. When Jake walks back into the restaurant, he approaches the table with purpose. He's holding the ring I gave him earlier, but before he opens the box, he stands at the head of the table and looks at Maggie. Warren signs everything he says.

"Maggie . . . I know it's only been a few months. But it's been the best few months of my life. From the moment I first saw you, I have been absolutely consumed by you. I wish I had this speech and this moment planned out, but we both like spontaneous." He gets down on one knee and opens the box. None of us can tell what Maggie's thinking. This could go one of two ways, and I'm not so sure it's going to go the way Jake wants it to.

He opens the box. "This ring belonged to your grandmother. And I wish more than anything that I could have known her, because I would have thanked her for raising such an amazing, independent, perfect woman. And the perfect woman for me. Whether you marry me or not, this ring is yours." He pulls it out and lifts her hand, then slips the ring onto her trembling finger. "But I would really love it if you would take the biggest risk you've ever taken and marry me, despite knowing very little about me or if we're even compatible for a lifetime or—"

Maggie interrupts him by nodding her head and kissing him.

Holy shit. He did it.

Sydney is crying. Even Bridgette wipes away a tear.

Warren stands up, grabbing his wine glass to make a toast. "Congratulations, you two," he says toward Maggie and Jake, even though they're still kissing and not paying attention to him. "But this also kind of sucks because tonight was supposed to be my night."

To everyone's shock, Warren pulls a box out of his pocket. He opens it and turns toward Bridgette. "Bridgette, I wanted to propose tonight. I still do, even though I'm irritated that Jake did it first. So, before Sydney and Ridge steal the rest of my thunder, will you please marry me?"

Bridgette is looking at him like he's crazy. Because he is.

"You didn't get down on one knee," she says.

"Oh." Warren drops to his knee. "Will you marry me? Is that better?"

Bridgette nods. "Yes."

"Yes what?" Warren says. "Yes, that's better? Or yes, you'll marry me?"

She shrugs. "Both, I guess."

Holy shit.

What in the hell is happening tonight?

We sat down to dinner as three couples who were dating. Now four of the six of us are engaged. I look at Sydney, and she looks radiant . . . smiling as always as she watches everyone else. Jake and Maggie and Sydney are all clapping for Warren and Bridgette.

Warren pulls away from Bridgette and looks over at Jake and Maggie. "Congrats. You might have been engaged longer than us, but we're getting married first."

Maggie laughs. "You go right ahead, Mr. Competitive."

"Or . . ." Warren says, turning to look at me. "Maybe we should just do this right now. Ridge, ask Sydney to marry you. Then let's all go to Vegas."

I laugh. If there's anything in our relationship I want to be taken more seriously than anything else, it's the moment I ask Sydney to marry me. I have it all planned out already. I'm writing a song for it. I'm going to perform it onstage at one of Brennan's concerts. Sydney deserves more than a spontaneous proposal.

"Oh, come on," Warren says. "What are you waiting for? You gonna write her a love song and play it onstage like you've already done twice before?"

That fucker. "I mean . . . that was the plan," I sign, defeated.

"Well, it's predictable. And lame. But six best friends getting married all at once is memorable and fucking *epic.* Let's all go to Vegas and *do* this shit!"

Bridgette is looking at me with her hands beneath her chin, mouthing, *Please, please, please, please.*

My heart is beating twice as fast as it was two minutes ago. I turn to look at Sydney—to gauge her response—and she smiles. "Just say when," she signs.

"When," I say. I blurt it out faster than I would have been able to sign it.

Sydney's mouth is on mine, and we're both laughing. And . . . *I think we just got engaged.*

Holy shit.

"I'll buy you a ring tomorrow. Whatever you want."

She shakes her head. "I don't want a ring. Let's get tattoos."

"In Vegas," Warren says, pulling out his phone. "I'll look up flights."

"I'm already on it," Jake says, looking down at his phone. "We have to keep Maggie's health in mind, so I'd like to get the shortest flight. And as soon as we land, I want to set her up an appointment with a colleague of mine as a precaution. Then after that we can do the whole wedding thing."

That's something I would have never entertained—going to Vegas with Maggie. I would have been adamantly against it. He really is better for her than I was. He's throwing caution to the wind . . . while somehow still being cautious. My eyes move from Jake to Maggie. She's staring at her ring with tears in her eyes. When she catches me staring, she just smiles and mouths, *Thank you.* Because she knows how Jake got the ring. I smile back at her, glad that I'm here to see this moment. I've always wanted the best for her, and now that she's found it, I couldn't be happier.

I honestly couldn't.

This . . . right now. Everyone I love is exactly where they belong. My crazy best friend with the only girl on the planet I would say is perfect for him. My amazing, incredible ex-girlfriend about to experience life with a guy who is a better balance for her than I could have ever been.

And Sydney. The girl on the balcony I tried so hard not to fall in love with.

The girl I fell in love with anyway.

The girl I am confident I will *stay* madly in love with far beyond my last breath.

I take her hand and bring it to my mouth, kissing her ring finger, which won't be bare for long. "We're getting married," I say.

She nods, smiling up at me. "This better not be one of Warren's and your pranks."

I laugh. I laugh hard. And then I pull her to me and

whisper in her ear, "My love for you is forever off-limits to our pranks. Tomorrow, you'll be my wife."

I wrap my arms around her and bury my face in her hair. Maybe Warren was right. Maybe predictable isn't always preferable. Because I can't imagine this happening any other way than it did. I saw three people I love most in my life get everything they deserve and more.

As for me and Sydney . . . our *maybe someday* just became our *absolutely forever.*

Epilogue

Sydney

Dear Baby Lawson,

You're due in twenty-seven days. I can't begin to tell you how excited your daddy and I are to meet you.

Everyone *is so excited to meet you. Your uncle Warren has been trying out nicknames for you since we found out I was pregnant. So far, he's called you Bean, Tomato, Sausage Patty, and, most recently, Silly Putty. I hope none of the nicknames stick; I've hated them all so far. But I've got your back. I'll make sure whatever he calls you, it'll be something that won't be too embarrassing.*

Your aunt Bridgette is even more excited to meet you than Warren is. He's hoping for a niece, but she's hoping you're a boy, so they've got a five-hundred-dollar wager going. Bridgette says she wants a nephew because she gets along better with boys than girls, but I'd beg to differ. She gets along great with anyone who has the patience to truly get to know her.

I'm just excited things have gone well with the pregnancy so far, and that you're healthy and growing like you should. Hopefully you'll look like your father and have his talent.

Your father listens to you a lot. You'll learn as you grow up that your father can't necessarily hear things in a traditional way, but he's the best listener I've ever met. He sleeps with his hand on my stomach every night, wanting to feel you move around and kick and roll over. I don't think I've seen him this excited since we got married in Vegas four years ago and he went to his first Cirque du Soleil show.

He was so entranced by everything going on—the lights, the movement, the vibrations, the vibe. We ended up seeing every Cirque show they offered that weekend, and we've been back to two new ones since then. I'm sure it will be something he takes you to experience with him as soon as you're old enough to appreciate it. We go back to Vegas every year to celebrate our anniversary, and I don't think we'll stop once you're born. We're just going to take you with us and celebrate our anniversary with an extra person we love in attendance.

I think some people assume a quick Vegas wedding might be a little tacky, but it was honestly the best weekend of our lives. I don't regret it for a single second. Your father and I exchanged vows with each other alongside your aunt Maggie and uncle Jake, and your aunt Bridgette and uncle Warren. I know they aren't your legitimate aunts and uncles, but I can promise you they'll be there for you in a heartbeat, just like your uncle Brennan, for the rest of your life.

You're going to go through a lot of friends in your lifetime, but when you find the loyal ones, hold on to them. There's something magical about being able to choose the people you keep in your life. No matter how lonely you may feel at times, because all of us do at points in our lives, you're never alone when you surround yourself with the right people.

I sometimes want to tell you all about how I met your father and how I met his friends, but these aren't things I've ever asked my own parents about themselves, so would you even want to know? I still have twenty-seven days before I get to meet you, so maybe I'll write down everything I can about the times your father and I had together before you came along. Maybe that's something you'll want to know someday. It's definitely an interesting story, but probably not one I want to share in my first letter to you.

What I will tell you is that everything about our relationship is unusual, from the way we met right down to the wedding. We didn't plan the wedding—it just sort of happened, which is why we got married in Vegas on a whim.

We decided to do it because it was just one of those perfect moments spent with our friends, when we all decided we were with our forever partners, and we were all so happy, we wanted to celebrate that happiness with each other. After a quick conversation about it, we all decided to head to Vegas and get married.

It was a triple wedding. Your uncle Warren and aunt Bridgette argued the entire way there over whether we'd get married by an Elvis impersonator. But I'm sure you'll come to realize that when the two of them argue, it's always in fun. Your father and I didn't care whether Elvis married us or not, and neither did Maggie or Jake. Bridgette was adamant she didn't want to get married by a singer whose music she didn't know, but Warren wanted to have the most typical, cheesy Vegas wedding he could.

They finally came to a compromise, and Warren agreed not to get married by an Elvis impersonator if Bridgette would share the name of a movie he'd been searching for for over two years.

Needless to say, after their agreement, we did not get married by an Elvis impersonator. Instead, we got married in a twenty-four-hour chapel, and I don't even remember the name of who married us. All I remember is that it was somehow the most nontraditional triple wedding I never dreamed of, but that I wouldn't have wanted any other way. To share that day with our friends was a dream, but to be able to sign my vows to your father while he spoke his back to me was magical. And the three days we all spent in Vegas after the wedding were three of the best days of my life. I'm positive those days will be easily overshadowed on the day we get to meet you, but knowing there are multiple days in my life I'd give anything to relive again is a testament that I am certainly where I need to be and with who I need to be with.

The journey here wasn't always easy, though. I was at a lonely point in my life when I met your father and his friends, and the road was bumpy, but I learned so many lessons along the way.

Many of them I learned through the patience and love your father has for others. I know as you grow up, you'll see exactly what I mean. He's unlike any other man I've ever met, and I am so glad I get to love him. I'm even luckier that I ended up being someone he wants to love in return for the rest of his life.

You and I are very lucky to be loved by a man with a heart like his. I can honestly say I've never met another person like him. And even though we don't know you yet, your father and I are very lucky to be blessed with raising you together. We can't wait to meet you. We can't wait to hold you. We can't wait for you to cry and laugh and walk and talk and sing.

But just be warned. The people in your life love to play pranks on each other, but I'm getting really good at it, and I'm more than willing to teach you all my tricks, as long as you don't share them with your father.

I don't know who you'll be yet, or what we're even going to name you, but I already love you so much more than I thought one heart was capable of. Whether you're a girl or a boy, or someday decide to identify as neither, we are more than ready to support you and love you. Unconditionally. Forever.

Love,
Your mother, Sydney Lawson

Acknowledgements

I miss them already! This series holds a huge place in my heart, and I'm not sure I would feel that way if it weren't for you. The readers. Especially those of you who followed along as I was writing this on Wattpad. Your excitement, anger, and joy over the characters is what prompted me to write this and (finally) finish it.

When *Maybe Someday* ended, I felt as though Ridge and Sydney's story was over. But I always had Maggie in the back of my mind, knowing her story didn't get tied up with a pretty pink bow. I felt I owed it to her to dive back into the lives of these characters and figure out how they were going to fit everyone in the same frame. I hope you guys enjoyed exploring that as much as I enjoyed writing it.

And now for the thank-yous.

This book was written in real time, uploaded chapter by chapter, so I wanted to preserve the feel of that and not send it through heavy rounds of rewrites and editing. Murphy Rae and Marion Archer, thank you for the quick turnarounds and the insightful comments. Murphy is always a little bit meaner than Marion, but that's what sisters are for.

CoHorts, as always, you complete me.

To the members of the Maybe Now discussion group. I'm sorry I had to leave the group in order to finish the project, but your passion fueled me all the way to the end. I want to thank each and every one of you for your help. And, of course, the admins of the group: Tasara Vega, Laurie Darter, Anjanette Guerrero, Paula Vaughn, and Jaci Chaney. Your messages gave me life.

Thank you to Sean Fallon for being Griffin's Stephanie. If you don't know what that means, Sean, just know that it's the highest compliment I can give you.

And last but certainly not least, I want to thank Griffin Peterson. It doesn't matter if it's the middle of the night or first thing in the morning or if I need something yesterday, you are always on top of it with the best attitude. Collaborating with you on this series and combining book tours with concerts has been one of the best experiences of my life. I appreciate your talent, but even more, I appreciate you as a human. #GriffinIsLegit